MW01199984

Alice Chen's
REALITY
CHECK

KARA LOO &
JENNIFER YOUNG

QUIRK BOOKS
PHILADELPHIA

For Max and Eric, with love

Copyright © 2025 by Kara Loo and Jennifer Young

Library of Congress Cataloging-in-Publication Data
[TK]
[TK]
[TK]
[TK]
[TK]
[TK]
[TK]

ISBN: 978-1-68369-477-9

Printed in the United States of America

Typeset in Sabon LT Pro

Designed by Andie Reid
Cover illustration by Jacqueline Li
Production management by Mandy Sampson

Quirk Books
215 Church Street
Philadelphia, PA 19106
quirkbooks.com

10 9 8 7 6 5 4 3 2 1

*"Abandon all hope,
ye who enter here."*
—Dante Alighieri, *Inferno*, Canto III

*"Hell was the journey,
but it brought me heaven"*
—Taylor Swift, "invisible string"

Chapter One

Hell Is Having to Make a Phone Call

The heat in my classroom has gone out.

It's not the first time. In fact, it happens so often that I'm beginning to suspect the district is secretly turning off our heat to cut costs. Or the universe just hates me. Normally, I prepare for the cold by layering my fleece jacket under a puffer vest and counting on my natural performance anxiety to ratchet up my body heat. But today, right as I was heading out the door, my mom called to ask about a hospital bill, and I left all my warm layers on the kitchen counter while frantically reassuring my mom that everything was totally and completely fine.

So here I am, hours later, making do in my frigid classroom with only my anxiety and a lukewarm cup of coffee to power me through six hours of hyping up eighth graders like a Peloton instructor with a passion for algebra.

"Ms. Chen, it's *freezing*. Can we start a trash-can fire?" a student asks.

The class clamors in agreement. I'm so cold that I briefly consider it.

"Don't worry, we'll warm up with some hot quadratic equations," I say, flourishing a stack of tests at him.

He groans but takes a paper before passing the rest back.

"It's Friday and we just finished a module, so you know what that means!" I say with my trademark over-the-top enthusiasm.

"Test day!" the whole class shouts back with the same way-too-dialed-up energy.

"You know the drill. Bring the tests up front when you're done." I spot a hand shoot up from the middle row. "And yes, Michael, you may go to the bathroom first."

Michael leaps up from his desk and Naruto-runs out of the classroom to gales of laughter.

I settle back in my chair as the sounds of pencils scratching and paper rustling fill the room. I have about ten minutes before Inez, our resident genius who skipped two grades, turns in her test early. Just enough time to get answers for my mom. Hopefully.

I log in and out of various health apps, trying to find out which doctor billed us for what. The specialist consultation and the labs from a month ago were paid off already with the last of my mom's savings and my latest paycheck. The only outstanding bill we should have is the hospital visit from a week ago, but I thought we'd already talked to someone about a payment plan.

When I can't take it anymore, I text Chase. Not because he's my fiancé of three years who I can count on for anything. To be honest, there isn't much I can count on him for. He's great, don't get me wrong, but I once caught the guy trying to microwave a Hydro Flask full of clam chowder. What he's good at, though, is encouragement, and I need that right now.

ALICE

i'm dying in 2-factor
authentication hell

save me

CHASE

u got this babe

His next text is a grainy image of a cat hanging from a tree, meowing "Hang in there!" in sparkly Comic Sans. It's the kind of thing his grandmother forwards to him every week—and, by transitive property, the kind of thing Chase texts to me when I'm feeling low. It's not exactly the virtual shoulder I wanted to lean on, but it helps.

> **CHASE**
>
> guess what
>
> i've got super amazing LIFE CHANGING news!!! 😍🙌👀⚖️☀️🎴

The last time Chase told me he had "life-changing" news, he came home with a giant bottle of truffle parmesan oil with Guy Fieri's face on it. He'd won the bottle in a raffle at work.

> **ALICE**
>
> i could use some good news. You're not at Costco are you?
>
> if so, can you get me a hot dog

> **CHASE**
>
> i'll explain everything when i see you tonight
>
> you're gonna be BLOWN AWAY 😱💨

By sixth period, I realize I'm going to have to call the hospital. Their billing department closes at 3 p.m. on Fridays because of course they do, which leaves me a very narrow window. I survey the class and start compiling a to-do list in my head:

- Buy groceries
- Cook dinner for mom
- Grade tests
- Email admin about heating (again)
- Sleep (6 hours hopefully)

I mentally add "call the hospital." Hopefully, I'll have enough time on the drive over to the supermarket to make it past the automated phone tree and reach a real human being.

I'm halfway through reviewing my to-do list again—and cutting down the amount of sleep I get to have—when my first student turns in their test. A flurry of tests come in after that, which means everyone either aced it or gave up early.

A hand shoots up.

"Ms. Chen, can we do Rapid Fire Friday?"

It's Theresa Ramirez, one of my star students who could give Inez a run for her money. Theresa lives for extra credit, which I deeply relate to.

Rapid Fire Friday is a game I invented back in September after a lesson plan fell through. I bring it back whenever it's too late to start a new assignment but too early to let the kids roam free in the halls. The game goes like this: One student volunteers to sit on the hot seat, aka my chair. Whoever's on the hot seat has to answer rapid-fire questions posed by the rest of the class. To ask a question, you have to solve a math problem. And if you're on the hot seat or if you ask a good question, you get extra credit—dispensed at my discretion, of course.

It originally started out as a way to kill time, but we ended up learning a lot about each other. We discovered that Kit Ahmad composes music, and Adrien Wooley can do ballet, and Hailee Tanaka likes Oreos dipped in sriracha sauce.

"Sure, who's in the hot seat today?" I ask.

"You are, Ms. Chen!" Theresa's best friend, Adrienne, pipes up. "You said the point of Rapid Fire was to get to know everyone in the classroom, and you're someone in the classroom."

"I think you're setting me up," I say skeptically.

"Aw, come on, Ms. Chen! It'll be fun!"

"We promise we won't roast you, Ms. Chen!"

"Okay, fine," I say. I give them a stern look. "But remember the rules: First person to answer the math problem on the board gets to ask a question. No hurtful, mean, or embarrassing topics. And as always, I have veto power." I jot a pretty simple quadratic equation on the whiteboard.

My students start solving the problem with way more focus than they showed during their exam. Of course, Theresa is the first to get the answer right.

"Can you tell us about your fiancé?" she asks immediately.

I knew it. They *were* setting me up. I hesitate. I feel like I shouldn't talk about my love life in class, but it's not like they don't know Chase exists. I usually don't wear my engagement ring to school—both because I'm paranoid about losing it and to avoid tipping my hand about my personal life—but I slipped up and forgot to take it off before I left my apartment last week. Liam from third period spotted it, and the news that I actually had a life outside school spread like wildfire.

In the spirit of playing along I take a deep breath and answer. "His name is Chase. We met in college. He works in finance, and his favorite food is French fries."

I put the next equation on the board, making this one twice as hard. I figure half the class will give up, but when I look back, every single student is furiously scribbling. Oh no.

Ravi raises his hand first.

"The square root of twenty?"

I didn't even know Ravi knew what a square root was. He's spent the whole year zoning out and doodling robots in his math notebook. But I guess he just needed the right motivation.

"That's right," I say. "Good work, Ravi. What's your question?"

"Are you in love with your fiancé?" Ravi asks.

The class goes absolutely bananas, and I can feel myself blushing.

"Yes," I say. "That's why we're engaged."

The class groans. I can tell that's not what they wanted to hear. I put another problem on the board that's so hard, I know I won't have to answer any more questions. I've just barely started teaching imaginary numbers. There's no chance they'll get it, except—Theresa raises her hand and answers correctly.

"Why do you love him?" Theresa asks. "Like, how do you know it's *really* love?"

This is getting way too deep for Rapid Fire Friday. But from the way the kids are watching me, I know I can't back out now. I might have veto power, but there's no reason I can't handle a simple question like this. I should know the answer.

"He's thoughtful," I begin. "He always remembers my birthday and Valentine's Day. He cheers me up and takes me on adventures we'll enjoy. And he always makes me smile."

Nailed it.

"He sounds perfect," Theresa sighs. One of my students makes an exaggerated gagging noise.

"He kind of is," I say, laughing. Everything else about my life is a dumpster fire right now, but at least one thing is going right. At least I have Chase.

The bell rings, rescuing me from any more probing questions. Once the classroom's empty, I rush to pack my bag. My fingers are stiff from the cold, and I fumble with my keys as I lock up.

I hustle to my trusty old Honda Civic, cutting across the parking lot as I call the hospital. In my car, I set the phone on speaker and head to Pacific Market, the Asian supermarket in my mom's neighborhood. Jazzy hold music starts to play, the same staticky bop that I've long since memorized, and I try to decide what to cook.

Right after my mom's diagnosis, I put about seventeen cancer cookbooks on hold. I was determined to cook nutritious, nausea-friendly meals for my mom while she was recovering. Before she got sick, I never really made food for her. She's an amazing cook, but I can barely steam rice to her satisfaction—though I'm not sure if that's a product of my incompetence or her sky-high standards. I can never devein shrimp or stir-fry bok choy properly, so my cooking is like nails on a poorly fried chalkboard to her—mixed metaphor aside, you know what I'm saying. But now that her job is to rest and recover, she's been grudgingly letting me cook for her with only a minimal amount of judgment.

I'm halfway through making my grocery list—and mapping out the most efficient path through Pacific Market to get everything in under ten minutes—when the music abruptly cuts off. A woman's voice speaks, all crisp and formal.

"Grace Hospital, billing department."

I unmute and run through the spiel I know by heart. "Hi, I'm Alice Chen, calling on behalf of Florentina Chen. And, yes, I know her patient account number." I rattle off the twelve-string alphanumeric code from memory with her birth date and invoice number for good measure. "My mother received a bill this morning and was surprised by the amount. We're on the payment program currently, so I'm a bit concerned that there's been a mistake."

"Let me take a look at your account, honey." I hear the clackety-clack of keys as the lady on the line types. Finally, she sighs and says, "I'm sorry, Ms. Chen. The amount listed *is* part of the plan, and your first payment is due in the next two weeks and then every month after that. Do you want to know the total amount due?"

I don't *want* to know anything, but she rattles off a number that's twice as much as my rent. I can make this month's payment if I hit pause on paying back my student loans, but the month after that? I have no idea.

"Check or card, honey?" the lady asks, and the cold stiffness in my fingers has now crept all over me, spreading down my legs and up my back. I shiver as she continues, "If you use card, I have to tell you there is a three percent—"

"I'll, um, pay online." I hear myself cut her off. "Thank you." I hang up, my mind reeling. How am I going to pay this new bill next month? Where am I going to get the money? I can take on more shifts at the private tutoring center I work at for extra cash, but there's only so many hours in the day. Maybe I can sell my eggs. I wonder if I could get away with selling goop in a jar on eBay if I said it was Henry Cavill's spit.

I'm snapped out of my spiral by a honk behind me. I curse and focus on the road. I'll take it day by day. Payment by payment. I can make the numbers work. I have to.

Ten minutes later, I'm in the grocery store with a basket in hand. As I pass by the snack aisle, I remember the little paper cylinder of haw flakes my mom used to buy me when I was a kid. I always wanted to savor the fruity, coin-shaped candies, but I couldn't seem to make a roll last beyond the car ride home. Part of me wants to take a detour down the aisle and throw some snacks into my basket—haw flakes, lychee jelly cups, sachima cakes, sesame egg rolls, and wasabi peas. But it's a luxury I can't indulge in.

Instead, I veer away, picking up fresh noodles and tofu and Chinese broccoli neatly swathed in plastic wrap over white Styrofoam trays. My mom claims that dark leafy greens can cure any illness, and the aunties in her Bible study agree, so it's my daughterly duty to make sure she gets her fill.

In my list of priorities, getting my mom healthy is at the top. Figuring out how to pay for it all is a distant second.

After checking out, I park down the street from my mom's place and do a weird sidewalk dance as I juggle the groceries, my coffee thermos, and my purse. I create another list of steps as I go:

- Prep the veggies (bok choy, mushrooms)
- Get stock going
- Make garlic paste

I'm jogging up the stairs to my mom's apartment when two things strike me at once.

There's the shrill alarm blaring, the sound growing louder and louder as I go up.

And there's the gray haze I can see billowing out of a cracked window.

Mrs. Stewart from down the hall pokes her head out the door and shouts something, but all I can hear is that alarm. I drop everything and sprint up the steps.

"Mom!"

The heavy smell of something burning hits me as I wrench open the door. All I can see is a thick wall of smoke and the faintest outline of furniture, nothing else.

I should call for help.

But there's no time, and it's just me here.

I run in. The smoke is everywhere, stinging my eyes.

"Mom!" I scream. That's a mistake. I immediately start coughing.

I duck my head low and cover my face with my jacket, my mind frantically dredging up the fire safety and first aid classes I took to become a teacher.

It's a good thing I know my childhood home by heart. I grope my way to the kitchen, where I can smell burnt rice and oil. Flames are leaping up from the stove, and on the floor, beside a cutting board and scattered vegetables, is my mom. She's lying still, too still.

My heart plummets. My legs feel like lead, and I drop to my knees as I feel the moment spinning out of my control. I can't move, can't breathe, can't think.

Then I hear her cough. I jolt back into what's happening, like I've just grabbed a live wire. I crawl to her side.

I take hold of my mom and manage to get her out, lifting her with a strength I didn't know I had. I leave her with a crowd of neighbors, all older aunties and uncles, then dash down the hall, grab the fire extinguisher, and blast everything in the kitchen with foam.

When I'm done, I dial the hospital. I don't know if I'm crying from relief or stress as I take my mother's hand, and she weakly squeezes my fingers back.

Chapter Two

Hell Is a Hospital Waiting Room

Several hours and a lifetime later, I'm in the waiting room at the hospital, sitting scrunched up in one of the chairs, trying to answer emails on my phone. But my brain is having a hey-day, ricocheting from worst-case scenario to worst-case scenario. If I'd stopped to talk to another teacher after class or taken too long at the grocery store, I wouldn't have made it in time. This was a close call. Too close.

And how are we going to foot the bill for the ambulance and this hospital visit? What if my mom had suffered a concussion or something worse than a mild case of smoke inhalation? Would I need to take time off work? Could I even get a sub in?

When I nearly send an email to a student's parent instead of my co-teacher, I slide the phone back into my pocket. I can't afford to make more mistakes, not now.

I slump back in my chair, my gaze snagging on a stack of fashion and sports magazines on the side table. I pick up *Glam Gossip* from the top of the pile and start thumbing past the paparazzi shots of celebrities in sweats, balancing bags of Dunkin' Donuts, and glossy images of other celebrities strutting on the red carpet. There's a short interview of a TV-star-turned-influencer debuting a new skincare line, followed by a two-page spread of a glamorous-looking blond actress. The bold headline shouts: "Dawn Taylor 'Makes It Work' After Devastating Setback!" I skim the article to see if any of Dawn's strategies would work for me. Turns out, I can easily make a comeback with the right spiritual guide, truckloads of acai-infused water, and a million-dollar PR team.

"There's the hero of the hour!" It's Chase, striding down the hallway with my fleece and a latte in hand. He looks sheepish. "Sorry I'm late. I left my phone in the bathroom, and I didn't see your calls until after work. But I brought fuel!"

"I'm really glad you're here," I say. I stand, dropping the magazine next to me, and sink into his arms. He wraps the fleece around my shoulders, and for the first time all day, I feel almost warm.

"Don't lie. I know you're just happy to see the coffee," he teases, handing me the cup. I smile at him, even though the idea of spending six dollars on a cup of coffee hurts my head. I resist the urge to remind him that there's free coffee in the hospital. The gesture is very sweet, but I've seen Chase's credit card bills, and I know how much is left before they max out. He may not have student loans to pay, or family to support, or really any responsibilities whatsoever, but he does need to start being more fiscally smart. For someone in finance, he's shockingly bad at money. My best friend swears he was a personality hire.

But today was a terrible, no good, very bad day, and my life planner app is always sending me notifications about gratitude. I focus on the warmth of the latte as I take a sip.

"Thank you," I say, and I mean it.

"Of course," he says, grinning. Then he sobers. "How's your mom doing?"

"I haven't gotten the full report, but I think she's going to be okay. So far it seems like it's only smoke inhalation. We got lucky," I explain, using the doctor's exact platitude to get the words out. "They want to monitor her for twenty-four hours, and since they're putting her in an overnight room, they said I should hang out here."

"That's great, babe," he says, running his hands up and down my arms. "What about you? Are you okay?"

I'm not, and I haven't been since I opened my mom's door, but I nod anyway. "Don't worry, an EMT already checked me out."

"I bet he did. Have you *seen* you?" Chase says, winking at me. He fans himself.

I can't help but laugh because Chase is the looker of the two of us. I often catch baristas trying to get his number at our coffee shops, or heads turning on the sidewalk just to catch a second glimpse of Chase with his sandy-blond hair, vivid green eyes, and "I'm made of boyfriend material" demeanor. Mrs. Tabitha, the social studies teacher in the classroom next to mine, once called him my "trophy boyfriend."

"Seriously?" I say with a smile. "I look like garbage right now." I've been stress-sweating, and I smell like a Korean BBQ gone wrong. I feel like I've aged ten years in the last few hours.

"Well, you're the sexiest garbage I've ever seen."

"Gross," I say, grimacing. Chase leans in to kiss me, but I don't feel like kissing him in front of everyone in the waiting room, so I pull back and deflect. "Hey, tell me something good. What was your life-changing news?"

"Oh yeah!" His face lights up. "I know you've been worried about your student loans and your mom's bills and stuff, but I've got it all figured out."

"Uh-huh?"

"We're going to become millionaires!" he crows. His arms drop from my shoulders to gesture widely. He's probably imagining he's holding one of those huge novelty checks.

"And how do we do that?" I'm praying he hasn't used his credit card to buy a million lottery tickets.

"We're gonna go on . . . reality TV!"

Right. I almost wish he'd bought lottery tickets. I take another sip of my latte, but it's lukewarm and all the foam's gone.

"Look, I know it sounds crazy," he says. "But hear me out. FlixCast is putting out this new show where they 'put couples to the test.' It's like *The Amazing Race*, but for relationships. And it's on a tropical island."

"So it's nothing like *The Amazing Race*."

"You got me there," he laughs. "I know I'm not doing a very good job explaining, but it's a fantastic opportunity. Just check this out." He searches "dawn taylor dating show what is it" on his phone and opens the first result.

Dawn Taylor to Play Host and Executive Producer on New Reality TV Show
Dawn Tay's Inferno: Love Is Hell

Get a first look at the new reality TV show that puts true love under fire.

BY MAXINE DEAN, GLAMGOSSIP.COM

Hollywood, CA. After walking out of her last project and retreating from the public eye for the last three years to "underline focus intensely on herself," Dawn Taylor, 48, the sassy and dynamic celebrity best known for her lead role in the sitcom *Cocktails & Confessions* and her salacious, modern-day "Dear Abby" style talk show *Drama Trauma*, is ready to take on the world of reality TV as the host of her latest project, *Dawn Tay's Inferno: Love Is Hell*.

Love Is Hell is a competition-based reality show where loving couples compete in a series of challenges designed to test their commitment to each other. Inspired by the epic poem the *Inferno* by Dante, which describes a journey through the nine circles of Hell, each episode is themed around common human failings such as anger, gluttony, and greed, forcing couples to navigate obstacles that range from smolderingly sexy to deeply emotional, all aimed at uncovering how well each person truly understands their partner.

Dawn Tay's Inferno: Love Is Hell is set to premiere in the spring as a ten-day special event, with new episodes airing daily and only hours after filming concludes, thanks to new proprietary editing technology touted by Get Real Productions executive producer Peter Dixon.

This marks Taylor's first foray back into the spotlight after controversy surrounded her departure from what would have been her film debut in *Beauty and the Beaker*, a rom-com about a supermodel who falls for a scientist in postapocalyptic LA. Taylor took heat on the set for demanding a private security team of "hotties only," ultimately walking off the set and quitting the project. Cast members and the director cited her as a precipitating factor when production subsequently shut down and executives shelved the entire film.

[You have reached the maximum number of free articles for this month. Gain unlimited access to Glam Gossip—and a free tote—when you sign up now!]

486 COMMENTS

GLAMFAM12: wasn't dawn cancelled lol

SECRETSXSECRETS: She was being STALKED. She could have been murdered dead!! She quit to save her life

GLAMFAM12: IIRC her fans sent her bougie cookies not a bomb

RIDEORGOSSIP77: creepy that they knew how to get to her imo

RYANW: ok but I too would like a hotties only team of bodyguards

SECRETSXSECRETS: THAT IS FAKE NEWS SHE NEVER ASKED FOR THE HOTTIES

LOAD MORE COMMENTS

Chase bounces on his heels as I skim through the controversial comments section. "The winning couple gets a cash prize of a million dollars," he says excitedly.

I love his enthusiasm, even if he's being completely delusional right now. I humor him. "I do like the sound of a million bucks. So how would we win exactly?"

"With our powers combined," Chase says, wrapping an arm around me and squeezing. "I'll handle the physical stuff, and you'll handle the mental stuff. We've got brains and brawns! We're a dream team. The dynamic duo. The three musketeers minus one!"

"You know our odds of getting on a reality show are very slim, right?" I say gently.

"Normally, they would be," Chase says, "but my old lacrosse buddy works for the studio. He hit me up this morning. He said they're looking for more diversity in the cast, and he thought we'd be a good fit since, you know."

"Since I'm Asian," I say.

"Oh yeah, maybe that's what he meant," Chase says. "I thought it was because you're a math teacher. They probably don't get a lot of those on reality TV."

Maybe it's the roller coaster of a day I've had, or the adrenaline from literally saving my mom's life, but I feel distinctly untethered from reality. Could this really happen? Could Chase and I actually go on a reality show and win?

There's no way. But then again, I'm an expert at winning. Not at life, clearly—just look at my bank account. But reality TV isn't real life. Plus, I've got a competitive streak a mile wide, and I'm killer at strategy. Put me in any kind of competition, and I'll crush it. Board game night, team-bonding laser tag, academic quiz bowls, you name it.

I can't believe I'm considering this. I've never thought about going on a TV show. What if I completely embarrass myself? What if I say something weird, or have a nip slip? What if they have to pixelate my boob on the top streaming platform in America, and my mom sees it?

Competing on a reality TV show is so far outside my comfort zone.

But my comfort zone doesn't have a million dollars.

"Let's discuss it," I say finally.

"Way ahead of you. Already applied," says Chase. "Bryan said that the applications were coming in fast and furious, but he'd make sure we were at the top of the talent pool. All you have to do is sign the waiver. We'll have to submit an audition tape too, but that's just a formality."

Chase texts me a link and when I open it, I'm met with a solid wall of text that goes on for over a hundred pages.

"What is all of this?"

"No idea. Pro tip: You don't have to read it. You just have to sign it," Chase says.

I scan the first few pages. It seems fairly standard: I grant permission to use my image and my voice in perpetuity, for promotional purposes, and so forth. But there are a few lines that jump out to me. "'I release Get Real Productions from any and all liability for any injury, dismemberment, death, or trauma, emotional or physical, that may occur," I read out loud. "I don't like the sound of dismemberment. Or death."

"Don't worry," Chase says. "That's all regular waiver stuff. It's reality TV. Nothing bad's actually gonna happen."

I think of the news article I'd scrolled past about a contestant on *Nepo House* getting airlifted out of Joshua Tree because he was vomiting so hard he ruptured his esophagus.

"Chase," I say, pinching the bridge of my nose. "I can't sign this. You didn't even ask me if I wanted to apply for this show."

"But I'm asking now," Chase says.

"That's not—" I begin, and a door swings open.

A nurse looks around, clipboard in hand. "Ms. Chen?" he calls. "Your mom's settled in her room now. You can come back and see her."

The nurse brings us to my mom's room, and there she is in the bed, connected to an oxygen tank and vitals monitors. But she's awake and alert, and that's enough for me. I don't know if I want to rush to her side or cry at the door. Luckily, Chase knows what to do. He puts a hand on the small of my back and walks us both forward.

"Mrs. Chen, so good to see you," Chase says. "Maybe a little too young to take up smoking, yeah?"

My mom smiles indulgently at him, patting his hand. "You're so funny, Chase."

"Tell that to Alice," he says, and they laugh like I didn't pull my mom out of a burning apartment earlier this evening.

"He's funny, Alice," my mom says. "When's the wedding?"

"*Mom,*" I choke. "We haven't talked about it."

"Alice is still recovering from my proposal," Chase puts in.

There were a lot of dark nights when my mom first found out she had cancer, when we weren't sure how things were going to go. We fought a lot, both of us stressed and afraid. During one of our fights, I found out that my mom was terrified that I wasn't married yet.

"What if something happens to me, and I leave you here all alone?" my mom had asked, tears in her eyes.

"I have Chase," I told her.

"He hasn't even proposed, and it's been three years," my mom said, sniffling.

"We're not ready," I said. "And it's not like he's the only person in my life. I have friends, you know." I didn't point out the obvious, which is that my mom is divorced, but that doesn't mean she's tragically all alone in the world. I mean, she has me. But that was too low of a blow.

I'd broken down later and told Chase all about our fight, and the next week he proposed. And I said yes, because it made sense.

The ring had been gorgeous, a large diamond set among a dazzling array of other tiny diamonds. I made him return it and get me a much more modest ring for a fraction of the price. We only got store credit on the return, so now whenever we have to buy something, I just hope that Macy's carries it.

My mother was never a big fan of Chase. He wasn't a doctor or a lawyer or an engineer—hell, he barely graduated from college—and worst of all, he wasn't Chinese. My mother said I was a different person around him. But I thought that was probably a good thing. Chase made me cooler, more relaxed, more confident. My mom would say *complacent*.

But I guess she changed her tune after she found out about the cancer, because she cried actual tears of joy when she found out we were engaged.

"Don't tell me Alice still wants to do the ceremony at the courthouse," my mom says, still holding Chase's hand.

"I know you want a big wedding, Mrs. Chen. Don't worry, I've got your back on this," Chase says with a wink.

"We'll talk about it later," I say firmly. "Mom, why were you trying to cook tonight? You know you're supposed to be resting. The doctor said you shouldn't push yourself too hard."

I can tell by the scrunch of her nose that my mom doesn't appreciate my tone. She hates being told what to do.

She waves her hand as if sweeping my words away. "You had a long day. I wanted to cook for you."

But I don't need home-cooked meals. I need my mother. I need her alive. I can't bring myself to say that, though. It'd be like turning down a hug from her. Food has always been her love language, for better and for worse.

I kneel so that I'm eye to eye with her, and switch to Chinese. "Mama, you have to take care of yourself. That's your job now. I can take care of everything else," I promise, even though I can barely take care of myself some days.

Speaking of which, we never had dinner, and my mom can't afford to be skipping meals. "I'm going to get dinner for you, okay?"

Because she's stubborn as hell, I can tell my mom's about to object and say she doesn't need anything. But instead, she starts coughing. I offer her a sip of water, but she flaps her hand at us, motioning for us to go.

"I'm going to rest now," my mom announces, like she's making a royal proclamation. At the door, I look back, and she's already falling asleep. She looks so small in her bed, her wispy gray hair falling over her face. Her wrinkled hands are curled into her blanket, and her mouth is pinched, like she's about to fight someone over the price of eggs. Despite her nagging and her smiles earlier, she looks more fragile than ever. My chest squeezes at the sight, and I close the door before the feeling overwhelms me.

There are egregiously high prices posted outside the hospital cafeteria, so instead of going in, I steer Chase past it, toward the vending machines.

"Vending machine dinner?" he asks.

"Vending machine dinner," I confirm.

"Just like in the dorms. Good times," Chase says. He genuinely means it, and I love him for that. "What are you feeling? Oreos or ramen?"

I scan the machine for something nourishing for my mom. In addition to borrowing all those cookbooks, I joined a Reddit group when my mother first got diagnosed. There's a whole subsection devoted to the ideal diet for battling cancer—fresh vegetables, expensive mushrooms, the works. Some people swear by a brand of olive oil from Italy that costs over three hundred dollars a bottle. But right now, I'm balking at a five-dollar granola bar. Frustrated, I knock my fist softly against the glass.

To hell with it. I'm getting her something from the hospital cafeteria. Something filling and nutritious, no matter the cost. And in that moment, I decide.

"Chase?" I say as I bring up the waiver on my phone.

"Yeah, babe? You want some of these Oreos? They've got *Star Wars* flavor."

"I'm in," I say, showing him the waiver. I skip to the end and sign it, right then and there. "But if we do this, we'd better win."

[FILE #B045 AUDITION TRANSCRIPT:
CHASE DE LANCEY AND ALICE CHEN]

INTERVIEWER: Tell us a bit about yourselves. How did you meet?

CHASE DE LANCEY: Alice and I met in college during our senior year. She was a math major—

ALICE CHEN: With a minor in public health, thank you very much—

CHASE DE LANCEY: And I was majoring in communications. I kept seeing her at the Campus Grind, the café near the university library, and she was always so busy studying.

ALICE CHEN: Look, not all of us are brilliant auditory learners.

CHASE DE LANCEY: She would take up a whole table and cover it in textbooks. You ever see the movie *A Beautiful Mind*? It was like that. I thought she was cute, so I asked if I could get her a coffee, which didn't go so well.

ALICE CHEN: I thought he was just a very hardworking barista. I had no idea he was asking me out!

CHASE DE LANCEY: So anyway, I took her order, hopped behind the bar and—

ALICE: And made me the absolute *worst* cup of coffee that I've ever had. And then the manager came over and kicked him out.

CHASE DE LANCEY: But not before I left my number on her receipt.

ALICE CHEN: The whole thing was so funny that I ended up texting him just to find out what his whole deal was.

INTERVIEWER: Can you tell us more about your relationship? Chase, what do you love about Alice?

CHASE DE LANCEY: Alice is cool. She's fun to hang out with, and she has an answer for everything. And she's got, like, survival skills. Did you know if you don't empty the little lint trap in the dryer, it catches on fire?

INTERVIEWER: And Alice, what do you love about Chase?

ALICE CHEN: Chase . . . well, he's just impossible not to like. He collects friends like those katamari balls. Every time we go somewhere, he makes a new friend. And I'm a natural worrier, so it's nice to be around someone who's so confident and positive. Even when things are going wrong, he's there with a joke to lighten the mood.

CHASE DE LANCEY: And I'm great in bed.

ALICE CHEN: *Chase!*

[Alice buries her face in her hands.]

INTERVIEWER: What makes the two of you think you can beat the competition?

CHASE DE LANCEY: We're amazing together. Alice just gets me.

ALICE CHEN: Our relationship is solid. A perfect equation.

INTERVIEWER: And what makes the two of you think you're a good fit for this show?

CHASE DE LANCEY: Oh, that's easy. We're winners.

Chapter Three

Hell Is a Best Friend Who Wants the Tea

My best friend Cindy Kuo may be just shy of five feet tall, but she's got a tall personality. And the full force of that personality is being directed at my front door as she rings the doorbell over and over again. It's been a scant twenty minutes since I texted her asking if she could apartment-sit for me, and she's already here on my doorstep.

"Alice Chen, you bitch!" she says, spilling into my foyer when I open the door. She kicks off her shoes and tosses her scarf and coat on the nearest chair.

"Come on in," I say to the empty hallway, closing the door. She throws herself on the couch and sets a cardboard tray of three boba drinks on the table. I grab the taro one. She has the decency to wait for me to take a sip before she starts in on me.

"You cannot just ask me to water your succulents while Chase *waters your succulents* on *reality TV*! I *demand* compensation!"

"I'll Venmo you," I say. I take another sip, and oh, man, this hits the spot.

Cindy takes up her own drink—jasmine, half sweet, full ice, with extra honey boba, of course—and levels the stabby end of the straw at me. "I don't want money. I want gossip! Details! Tell me *everything*!"

"It's not that interesting," I protest.

"I thought I taught you better, Alice," she says, a perfect parody of my mom. "Let's start with the obvious question. Are you going to be naked on live TV?"

"No."

"Is *Chase* going to be naked on live TV?"

"God, I hope not!" I laugh.

"What are you packing? What are you wearing? When exactly do you leave?"

"I haven't packed yet, but I'm making a list," I say. "I'm tackling things one at a time. Like my plant babies. Can you take care of them for me?"

"I don't know, can I?" Cindy asks and stabs her straw into her drink viciously.

"Okay, fine. I'm going on a show called *Dawn Tay's Inferno*. It's a reality TV competition that tests the strength of a couple's relationship. Chase and I will be a team, and we will be competing against other couples."

"I get the picture. I think Tara wants to watch it?" Cindy whips out her phone, and I just know that she's texting her girlfriend about the show. Still typing, she says, "And what brain transplant did you have to make you sign up for this?"

"The prize is one million dollars."

She nods and looks skeptically back up at me. "Yup, okay, everything makes sense now."

"I have a fifteen-step plan for preparing and winning," I say, holding up a yellow legal pad. "Cindy, I need the money. And I'm good at winning. I can do this." My gaze goes to my trophy wall, which, okay, maybe it's a little childish to still have all of my trophies and medals from high school and college on display, but I worked hard for those.

"Wow." Cindy shakes her head. "Way to flex on me." She eyes a small medal for second place. "I'm surprised you didn't toss that one. You hate losing. Who was that guy you were always competing with in high school? The one you loved complaining about?"

I know exactly who she means. I glare at her. "We don't speak of him in this household."

"Still sore about that, huh?" Cindy snickers.

That's an understatement. Even though it's been years, I haven't forgotten my old high school nemesis and greatest academic rival. I still remember the first time we met, the memories vivid and almost too sharp. It was one month into my freshman year of high school, the day I made my debut as a member of Eastridge's Quiz Bowl team at our first competition.

As the only freshman who'd made the cut, I was the most junior member of the team, and I had everything to prove. I'd started the morning in a bad mood, but that was nothing new. Back then, a feeling of wrongness hovered over me like my own personal rain cloud.

"You come home so late! Why even come back at all?"

"You're right. If I didn't come home, I wouldn't have to listen to you complaining all the time!"

I was haunted by the jagged shards of overheard arguments and the suffocatingly quiet dinners that followed. When I closed my eyes, I could see my dad's car pulling out of the driveway for the last time, the rear lights casting an eerie glow on the garage door in the night.

But none of that mattered in Quiz Bowl.

No one was expecting much from me or from our team that day. Eastridge didn't have a reputation for winning. Our school usually had trouble even fielding a full team at all.

To make matters worse, we were up against Charles Exeter Prep, one of the most expensive and exclusive boys' prep schools in the state—the kind where the guys all wore tailored suits and shiny shoes and carried briefcases instead of backpacks.

No one even glanced our way as we took our places.

The Quiz Bowl moderator was already at the podium in the center. He looked like someone's poor uncle, dressed in an ill-fitting suit and a crumpled tie. After introducing both of our teams to the audience—a handful of dedicated parents, two teachers, and Cindy, who had stopped by before SAT tutoring—he jumped into the questions.

"Okay," the moderator began, "let's start off with something easy.

What is the chemical symbol for ordinary table salt?"

I slammed my hand on my buzzer before anyone else could even twitch.

"NaCl," I said, adrenaline rushing through me. The Exeter Prep boys looked startled. They probably expected our team to just give up and wave the white flag of surrender, but here I was, putting up a fight. Even their captain was eyeing me with a narrowed look. The competition had only just begun, but I was loving every second.

"Slay, queen!" Cindy called from the stands. She'd produced little pom-poms out of her backpack and was cheering like this was the homecoming game. I should've known that even if she could only show up for a few minutes, she'd show up big.

"Next category is classic literature," the moderator said. "In *The Great Gatsby*, what does the color green symbolize?"

My hand smashed the buzzer, but the Exeter Prep captain beat me to it.

"Hope," he said, looking right at me. He was challenging me.

I scowled back. I had to be faster. Better.

"What is mitosis?"

I buzzed in before the moderator even finished the question.

"The process of cell division," I said, my words tumbling out in a rush.

"Correct again!"

As a freshman, I wasn't eligible to be captain, but question after question, it was my hand that hit the buzzer first, and my answers that lit up the scoreboard. The only person who posed a threat to me was the captain of the opposing team, and with every question it felt more and more like a duel between just the two of us.

As I competed, the feeling of wrongness that had been plaguing me dropped away. There wasn't much I had control over back then—not my family, not the way I could hear my mother crying in the bathroom, or the fact that we were moving out of our house and into an apartment—but I could control the outcome of this match, and I was going to win. All those long hours of studying would be worth it.

At the break, the Exeter Prep captain approached me. I was reviewing my flash cards and snacking on haw flakes in an isolated corner of the gym with my back against the wall, my fingers idly tearing the paper tube to shreds.

The captain loomed over me, a scarecrow of a teen boy, with a thin frame and broad shoulders. His hair was black, cut short and even, perfectly neat except for an errant strand that I'd seen him brush away from his dark brown eyes throughout the competition. He had high cheekbones and a pretty face, which was a weird thought to have, and I shoved it away immediately.

"Hey, I'm Daniel," he said with a friendly smile, sticking out his hand.

I stared at him suspiciously, ignoring his hand. "Daniel Cho. I already know who you are."

"Oh. Uh. Cool," he said. "And you're Alice Chen, right?"

"I'm the competition," I said. I brushed my hair back from my shoulder, hoping the gesture looked cool and flippant.

"I know," he said, dropping to a crouch next to me. "I don't think you've gotten a single answer wrong yet."

"That's right. In fact, I think that might be the most correct thing you've said today," I said. "Despite being the team captain and the two-time winner of the Regional Science Olympiad."

I knew I was being rude, and I didn't care. I'd always been competitive, but during those early days, right after my dad left, I couldn't shake the feeling that nothing I did would ever be good enough. I had this gnawing need to prove myself, and you could see that need written on my face and hear it in my words. In short, I was insufferable.

Daniel didn't seem offended, though. He simply said, "You know about me, huh?"

I rolled my eyes. "Of course. I'd never go into battle unprepared."

He laughed. "You get that this is just Quiz Bowl, right?"

"Just Quiz Bowl. *Just* Quiz Bowl?" I repeated.

"Yeah, just Quiz Bowl," he said with a laugh. "We're competing for a title and a plastic trophy. The stakes couldn't be lower."

I was on my feet before I even knew what I was doing. I leveled my best, most venomous glare at him.

"Maybe the stakes are low for *you*," I said, jabbing a finger in his face. "But they aren't for me. Even though this isn't the finals, or even the semifinals, or even the quarterfinals, it might as well be for my team. Exeter Prep has won the Quiz Bowl championship every year for the past ten years. And *you*, Daniel Cho, were the top contributor to that success last year, and now you're the first sophomore to be team captain in Quiz Bowl history. You might be comfortable resting on your laurels and acting like this is just another day in your perfect and completely unremarkable life, but I am here to win."

My heart was racing by the end of that speech. Daniel was blinking at me, taken aback by my outburst. He'd clearly come over to my little corner planning to distract with friendly overtures, but I'd seen through his trap. He wasn't my friend. He was my competition and my enemy, and I'd just told him as much.

I expected Daniel to storm off or report me to a teacher or *something*. But he just nodded thoughtfully and said, "When your friend yelled 'slay, queen,' I don't think she was telling you to literally slay me. We're not gladiators in the arena trying to decapitate each other."

"I know that," I said, annoyed.

"You sure don't act like it, Slayer," he shot back.

"Slayer?"

"It suits you. I mean, just look at the way you dominated the first round," he said. He raised his eyebrows, and I felt the last of my rage and adrenaline drain out of me.

"You're right. I did basically destroy you," I said.

"So you agree. Slayer's the perfect nickname for you." He grinned. "I'm calling you that from now on."

"You don't even know me!" I protested.

He tilted his head at me as the bell rang, signaling the end of the break. "You know, Slayer, something tells me that's going to change."

That had been the start of three years competing against Daniel Cho and being at each other's throats in every kind of competition you could imagine, from Mock Trial and academic triathlons to spelling bees and charity bake sales. We were perfectly matched in every way, always vying for the top spot. When he went away to college during my senior year, I'd celebrated. But I came to realize that competing without him just wasn't as fun.

That doesn't mean I don't hold a grudge though. We were rivals, not best friends.

"Anyway," Cindy says, interrupting my thoughts, "about this show. It's reality TV, not an academic quiz bowl."

"Oh, my sweet summer child," I say. "Any and every challenge can be broken down, analyzed, and solved for. And you know me. I have a plan."

"Of course you do. Well, let's see it," Cindy says, holding out her hand. "I bet it's color-coded."

"All the best plans are," I say. I show her the legal pad. "I'm starting with the source material. Since the show is themed around Dante's *Inferno*, I've reread the poem to study up on the circles of hell, and I've created the skeleton of a rubric."

"A rubric," Cindy repeats. "Of what?"

"Ultimately, it should cover what's essential for the winners in these types of competitions."

"God, you're such a nerd," Cindy says. "Hate to break it to you, but rereading a poem by a dead white guy and taking lots of notes is not enough to win a reality show."

"I know," I say. "That's where you come in. You're a reality TV expert. You can tell me which episodes I need to watch to flesh out my rubric."

Cindy breaks into a huge smile. "Oh, honey. Tara and I can do *way* better than a watch list. If you're really going on this show, then we're putting you through reality TV boot camp."

"Sign me up," I say.

"Ohmygod, this is my dream," Cindy says, already texting Tara. "What are you doing this weekend? Never mind. Clear your calendar. We're going to be marathoning *Operation: Bikini* at my place." Cindy looks up from her phone, a frown crossing her face. "Hang on. You got me all excited about rotting on the couch. I wasn't done interrogating you."

"I told you everything. What else is there?"

"Well, what about you and Chase? This show tests your relationship with him, not your ability to solve for x."

"I'm not worried about that," I say. "Our relationship is rock solid. We make sense together. We've solved for all the variables. Now we're just a perfectly balanced equation."

"Very romantic," Cindy says drily.

"Romance plus compatible interests plus aligned life goals equals a perfect relationship," I say, only half joking. "We make a good team."

Cindy takes a long, noisy slurp of her boba, clearly still skeptical. I know what she's thinking, but she's wrong. I've dated Chase for three years. I've got him all figured out. That's why I like him—he's safe and he's predictable.

Finally, Cindy says, "Okay. Any other juicy details I should know about?"

I shake my head. "Not really. They sent along a packing list and a meeting point. We'll be staying on some mystery island for a couple weeks during filming."

"You'd better take so many photos," Cindy says, perking up. "Let me live vicariously through you. I haven't gone on vacation in years."

"I can't," I say. "They're going to take our phones away."

"Right, I guess that's standard," Cindy says. "So let me get this straight. You're going to be shooting on a remote island, with no phone, surrounded by people you don't know, doing who-knows-what in front of the whole world on television?"

"Pretty much."

Cindy mulls this over. "And this was Chase's idea?"

I give her a look that says *of course* this was Chase's idea.

"Who are you and what did you do to my sweet, hyper-logical, risk-averse Alice?"

I bury my face in my hands. "She's still here, and she needs money, and she also needs someone to water her plants. You know I killed my last three Haworthias. I'm proud of this one!"

"Girl, your plants are safer with me than you," Cindy says.

She's right about that. I tend to overwater my plants. I worry that they're not getting enough water and end up literally drowning them with my anxiety.

Sometimes I think Cindy knows me better than I know myself. After all, we grew up in the same town, living in the same tight-knit community of Chinese families. She adopted me on the first day of fourth grade, when I was too shy to talk to anyone.

When my dad left the summer before my freshman year of high school, she refused to let me wallow in self-pity, instead dragging me out to the library every day to borrow stacks of manga. She stuck with me through the worst of it, when I was prickly and sullen and wanted everyone to leave me alone. And when the other teens in youth group started whispering about my family, she was the one who marched to the front of the room and gave them all a lecture that was so stern, they ended up crying.

Right up until college, we did everything together. We went to Chinese school together, snuck out of school to get fro-yo together, and read all the same fantasy books together. And after college, we picked up right where we left off. Neither of us was quite the same, but I liked who we became. On paper, we don't make sense at all. And I kind of love that.

"Is this a bad idea?" I ask Cindy. "Be honest."

"I think," Cindy says slowly, "it's not bad. It's ridiculous and it's ambitious and it's different. And I think if anyone can win a reality show through sheer bloody-minded competitiveness and determination, it's you."

"Thanks, Cindy," I say. "Have I mentioned I love you?"

"I love you too, you weird little nerd," she says, and taps her boba cup against mine. "Just be careful out there. And yes, I will water your succulents."

STORY NOTES FOR EDITORS: SEASON 1 TV SPOT "DAWN TAY'S INFERNO: LOVE IS HELL"

Executive Producer(s): Dawn Taylor, Peter Dixon

DAWN TAYLOR, VOICEOVER: Get ready for the newest reality show to hit the beach! Can love survive a journey through HELL?

[B-roll footage: Contestants in bikinis splash in the water.]

[Dawn Taylor, barefoot and walking across a sandy beach, straight to camera.]

DAWN TAYLOR: Babes, it's Dawn Taylor calling, and you better pick up. Here on this sexy, sexy tropical island, I'll be putting ten couples to the ultimate test. If their love can survive my inferno, one couple will win *one million dollars!*

[Footage: Chase De Lancey and Alice Chen on yacht in talking head interview.]

CHASE DE LANCEY: We're in love, and we're ready to prove it to the world!

DAWN TAYLOR, VOICEOVER: But to secure the bag, they'll have to pass through all my circles of hell: lust, treachery, anger . . . and some other ones.

[B-roll footage: A couple kisses passionately.]

[B-roll footage: A woman runs from the competition in tears.]

[B-roll footage: Multiple people vomiting.]

DAWN TAYLOR, VOICEOVER: Welcome to . . . *Dawn Tay's Inferno!*

Chapter Four

Hell Is Your Past Coming Back to Bite You in the Ass

It's hard to believe that just last week, I was going about my normal, everyday life: teaching my last class of the school year, signing yearbooks, and wrapping farewell gifts to hand out during the eighth-grade graduation ceremony. Now here I am, on a luxury yacht, speeding toward paradise, about to be on reality TV for the first time in my life.

They took my phone away when I stepped on the yacht, but not before I sent a text to my mother promising that I would drink water, and then another text reminding her where I'd left a Post-it note of emergency contacts. She'll be fine, I remind myself. She's in between treatment rounds, so she shouldn't be too worn out. Plus, she has friends checking on her, and Auntie Yee from church is bringing home-cooked meals to her every day. I told my mom I was going to a teachers' conference in Arizona and wouldn't have time to check in. It might be wishful thinking, but I'm hoping my mom just never finds out about this. I don't think she even knows what reality TV is.

Without my phone, I'm forced to admire my surroundings. I squint against the sun and fight the urge to beg the PA to let me send one last text. I'm already antsy without a phone, which is kind of sad, given that it's only been like forty minutes. My hand keeps going to my empty pocket to check for messages or alerts.

Chase lounges beside me, his tanned shoulder pressing warmly against mine. He's handsome as always, but there's something about being in this setting, with the sun catching the gold in his enviably wavy hair, that makes him extra jaw-droppingly hot. He's got a jawline that could cut butter and a body destined for 4K resolution.

The water around us is the kind of deep and fathomless blue that you see in cruise ship commercials. Everything about this moment screams romance. If a Hollywood filmmaker was going to direct the story of my life, this would've been the scene where Chase drops down on one knee and proposes, rather than where he actually proposed—in the middle of Arby's. *This* place, however, is the perfect setup.

Well, except for all the people congregated in front of us. At the very front of the crowd is our producer, Leah, standing beside the camera-man and a sound tech. They're all laser-focused on me, waiting for me to deliver the soundbite they want.

"Alice, just say what you feel," Leah advises.

I nod, even though there's no way I'm doing that. If I said what I felt, I'd be talking about the mosquito bite that's already starting to swell up on my left arm or the slight nausea I feel from the rolling waves buoy-ing up the yacht. And that's not fair to Leah, who, judging by the way she's raking her manicured hands through her mass of red curls, has decided that I'm either going to be her greatest success or her greatest failure. My money's on the latter. At this point, Leah's made no fewer than seventeen corrections to my posture, my stance, my tone, and, bafflingly, my vibe.

"We're in love. And we're ready to prove it to the world," I say brightly, my forced smile making my cheeks hurt.

"Again, but this time, hold Chase's hand," Leah says, her green eyes projecting earnestness even as I notice her mouth thin. She's clutching a snakeskin notebook and aggressively clicking the pen sandwiched between the pages.

I take Chase's hand, and he winks at me. Unlike me, he's a natural at all of this. Anything that would check a D&D character's charisma stat, he's going to nail. That's what drew me to him in the first place.

(That, and the free coffee.) He's got enough confidence to bend reality, and it made me want to hang around him, as if that confidence could rub off on me. At the very least, I get the halo effect of his good luck and charm.

But that's not enough to allow me to coast like him. I have to work to get what I want. I mentally review my checklist.

Day 1 goals:

- Analyze competition for weaknesses
- Seek out tactical advantages in challenges
- Avoid drama
- Befriend our producer

And in the short term, as a sub-bullet to befriending our producer, I add:

- Nail soundbite to Leah's satisfaction

I can do this. I talk in front of people—okay, tweens—all the time. I breathe in and imagine I'm standing at the front of my classroom, about to explain quadratic equations.

"We're in love, and we're ready to prove it to the whole wide world!" I say. In a burst of enthusiasm, I hold up our linked hands for the cameraman to capture.

The sound tech nearly falls over from the sudden screech from the mic. The cameraman chokes on his laughter and starts pounding his chest. Leah clicks her pen so hard that it leaps out of her hand and skitters across the deck. She doesn't seem to notice, and I resist the urge to go crawling after it. Hey, good pens are hard to come by. I've got a whole collection of bank pens I swipe from the counter every time I have to make a withdrawal. I figure Bank of America can take the loss.

Leah sighs. "No, not like that. Look, Alice, honey. You're trying too hard. That tone might work with your preschoolers—"

"I teach middle schoolers—" I interrupt, but Leah barrels on.

"But that doesn't work here. We need you to sound genuine. Like you're really, truly in love. I can tell you're nervous, but I'm just here to get the right footage to tell your story. I'm on your team, and I want you two to look good! Just . . ." Leah scans me up and down, and clearly finds me wanting. "Just fake it 'til you make it, okay?"

"Fake being genuine," I say skeptically.

"Yes, exactly!" Leah claps her hands together. "You're smart. You get it. You're a Harvard genius!"

I didn't actually go to Harvard. I went to a state school—and still managed to rack up a mountain of student debt—but Leah doesn't give me a chance to correct her.

"Just let your passion come through naturally, but make sure you're really enunciating for the mic, okay? Now, from the top."

Relax, but with more passion. Play it up but do it naturally. No problem.

I don't consider myself a shy person. If this were my high school Speech and Debate club, I'd be killing it right now. But instead of discussing facts or arguing a position, we're talking about my (ugh) feelings. Not something I've had a lot of practice in. My mom's way of showing affection was almost always food-related, like packing a homemade lunch for me every morning—even if it meant waking up early after staying late at the accounting firm. It was practical, heartfelt, and nourishing, with no physical contact or verbal communication required.

I'm nowhere near as bad as my mom. I've read those pastel Instagram infographics about emotional connection and self-care. I know how to talk about my feelings. But I still feel a little bit like I'm oversharing, exposing my soft underbelly. And doing it in front of a giant camera? That's a lot to ask.

Head in the game. I just need to center myself. People love centering themselves. I take a deep breath and scrutinize the sparkling, crystal-clear water all around me.

Despite everything, I can appreciate the beauty. It's a view I never could've afforded if a production company weren't paying for all this. Looking around, I can almost see price tags hovering over everything. The boat we're on? Probably $15,000 just to charter it for the day. The extravagant papaya and pineapple fruit platter that's been laid out has to be at least five hundred dollars. The drink being poured for the cast is actual champagne, and not the cheap stuff. That can't be less than seventy-five dollars per bottle. My stomach feels sick as the numbers keep going up, up, up.

I glance down at my feet—five-dollar sandals from the clearance section. If we were playing a game of "what doesn't belong?," the answer would be immediately obvious: Alice Chen. My entire outfit adds up to less than one of those bottles of Veuve Clicquot.

I've always been good with numbers. It isn't always a gift.

"You've got this," Chase says, breaking through my thoughts. "Don't get too in your own head, okay?"

He affectionately taps my forehead, and I resist the urge to swat his hand away. He says, "Hey, you know I'm right. Nothing good happens in there when you've got that look on your face."

Chase never overthinks things, and as far as I can tell, it's only served him well. He's like a charmed golden retriever, making friends out of strangers at bar trivia night and getting chosen first for every pickup game of basketball.

Before I can do anything but scowl, Chase jostles my shoulder.

"Hey, there's the island!" he exclaims, pointing.

I twist around to see and catch my first glimpse of paradise.

The beach is picture-perfect, as if every palm tree has been freshly planted and the sparkling white sand has been precisely arranged and swept—which, considering the army of PAs and crew members on hand, is definitely a possibility. Plush white couches, looking both opulent and ridiculously out of place, are arranged on the beach. Beautiful arrangements of tropical flowers are set against palm fronds, creating a green oasis on the beach.

It's all gorgeous, but there's something that makes me feel uneasy about the scene. It looks too perfect, if that's possible.

When I was sixteen, my mom had to go to an accounting conference in Las Vegas and she brought me along. It was the first time I'd gone on anything resembling a vacation. I couldn't get enough of the all-you-can-eat buffets, and we even went to see a Cirque de Soleil show.

While my mom attended the conference session on tax credits, I wandered through the lobbies of all the fanciest hotels. They were filled with fake rocks and manicured trees, like they'd tried to take the best parts of nature and recreate it, but instead of capturing its wild beauty, they'd killed it. Looking at this beach, I'm struck with that feeling again. The wrongness of it all.

I shouldn't be thinking about that. I turn back to Chase. His smile is so genuine and encouraging. I focus on him.

Paradise. Chase. Love.

I try to render my words just as real, just as tangible as my mom's lunch box of chicken stir-fry.

"We're in love," I say, putting weight into each word, "and we're ready to prove it to the whole world." I squeeze Chase's hand this time, and he squeezes back.

"Okay, I like the intensity, but you need to dial it back just a smidge. We're going for light and fun. Easy-breezy." Leah squints at me. "You know what? This isn't working," she says, gesturing to all of me.

This is it. The moment they realize I don't belong among all this glitz and glamour, and they kick me—and by extension, Chase—off the show. My stomach sinks. I came on this show for a reason. How will I pay for my mom's treatment without the prize money?

I'm ready to put on my best teacher voice and convince her with bullet points about why I should be here when Leah claps her hands. "I've got it. You need a new look. You can't be easy-breezy when you're in that straitjacket!"

I look down at the navy-blue cardigan I'm wearing. It's literally the most expensive thing I own, and I think it looks cute. It makes me look like I'm someone who summers in the Hamptons. Someone with a personal chef. Someone who doesn't know what the federal minimum wage is. But I'm realizing now that with Chase in his swim trunks, we look like we're filming two entirely different scenes. He's beach Ken, and I'm courtroom Barbie.

I can swing a wardrobe change. I reach for my carry-on, but before I can open it, Leah snatches it out of my hands and starts rummaging through it.

"Let's take a look at what we're working with," Leah says. "Ah, I see the problem. Oversize Hawaiian shirt. Black tank top. Cream turtleneck. Didn't you bring anything bright and sexy? Who goes to a tropical island with a *one-piece Speedo?*"

Leah holds up my old forest-green swimsuit between two fingers.

"I thought this was a competition," I say defensively. I'm starting to regret not taking Cindy's advice to buy a cute two-piece from Target. Instead, I'd stuck with my tried-and-true Speedo for better hydrodynamics. I figured that comfortable and practical clothes would give me a competitive edge. But I'm realizing now that I probably should've prioritized fashion a little more. In my defense, I didn't have the funds to splurge on a new wardrobe anyway.

"Oh, it is."

"And I'm not a bikini person," I say. Bikinis are cute, but they aren't practical. You constantly have to keep everything in place. How can you possibly swim your fastest under those conditions? It doesn't help that my mom definitely doesn't approve of showing cleavage. The one time I wore a borrowed bikini at the public pool, I kept looking over my shoulder like my mom was going to leap out of the bushes and throw a beach towel over my anatomy.

Leah unceremoniously tosses my swimsuit overboard. "You are now."

"Hey!" I shout, rushing over to the railing. I make it in time to see my swimsuit—$7.50 from Ross—disappearing beneath the waves. In that moment, looking at Leah's perfect face, I want to toss *her* into the ocean.

But Chase pulls me close to him.

"Yeah, I guess that one was getting a little old, huh?" He laughs, smoothing over the moment.

"Exactly. Time for a trip to the wardrobe department," Leah says. She takes my hand, like we're girlfriends going shopping, and I will my anger to dissolve.

Leah's just doing her job. She's here to manufacture drama, but she's also the only one on the production crew looking out for us. I need her as an ally. I know how cutthroat these competitions are. Cindy and Tara had made sure of it when they put me through Reality TV 101, which included not just reality shows, but also nonfiction books, podcasts, and tell-all articles. And yes, I did take notes. So I know that when it comes to winning, having your producer in your corner is pretty up there. And to ensure that, I have to play the game.

A few moments later, I'm in a bathroom strewn with boxes of clothing, being crammed into a bikini.

"Come on out," Leah prompts.

"Ready, babe?" Chase asks.

I don't know if I'll ever be ready. I feel naked, and not in a fun way. How long can I possibly stay in this bathroom? I imagine days going by while I survive on slices of pineapple speared onto bamboo cocktail picks.

My fingers twist around the empty place on my ring finger that usually holds my engagement ring. I took it off for the boat ride, worried that it might fall into the ocean or something. But now I feel even more naked without it.

"You can do this," Chase calls. "Remember, you graduated with honors! You're the reigning champion of the California Math League's annual alumni competition. Your high school voted you Most Likely to Succeed. You can pull off a bikini!"

"I don't think any of those skills are really transferring here," I mutter.

Still, it's enough to put things in perspective. Emboldened, I take a deep breath and step out. Leah and Chase both cock their heads in the same direction as they take in my new look.

"Better," Leah says, but she still sounds a bit doubtful. She rakes her fingers through her curls again.

"Lookin' good, babe," Chase says, flashing me a thumbs up. "I don't think I've ever seen you in, uh, neon yellow before."

"My mother's going to have a heart attack if she sees me on TV wearing this," I say. I really, really hope she doesn't find out about this. "I'm never going to hear the end of it."

"Not if we win the money," Chase reminds me. "A million dollars would make any mom proud."

Well. When he puts it that way.

My mind flashes back to two months ago, the day I'd decided to go on this show. In my nightmares, I can still smell the smoke and feel the hopelessness of seeing my tough, stubborn mother on the floor.

I hadn't been there when she needed me, and what's worse, she'd been trying to take care of *me*. Even though I'm twenty-five years old, she still doesn't think I can take care of myself. I have to prove that I can take care of not just myself, but both of us.

If I won a million dollars, I'd be able to take time off work and be with my mother through the rest of her cancer treatments. I could pamper her, the way she deserves. We could order DoorDash every day. I could download Caviar or one of the more expensive apps. Heck, we could eat *actual* caviar. Or even better, organic maitake mushrooms smothered in that three-hundred-dollar olive oil.

I'll do whatever it takes to win. For that to happen, I need Leah on our side, pulling for us over every other couple here.

I straighten my shoulders. "Let's do this."

"That's what I like to hear." Leah breaks into a smile, waving to the cameraman and the sound tech. "From the top!"

I take my seat next to Chase and draw in as deep a breath as I can manage without spilling out of the top of the bandeau, and say, "We're in love, and—"

Leah cuts me off. "Actually, wait, new idea. Alice, you sit there looking hot and sexy and Chase, dear, why don't we hear it from you?"

"You've got it, boss," Chase says cheerfully. He pulls me in close and says, "We're in love, and we're ready to prove it to the whole world." He punctuates this with a kiss.

The kiss, like all of Chase's kisses, fills me with a warm, fizzy feeling, like drinking prosecco straight from the bottle on a warm summer evening. I lean into it, trying to enjoy the moment, but I'm conscious of the camera in my face. Finally, Leah calls cut and Chase breaks it off.

"There it is," Leah says briskly. "And just in time. We're here."

The beach is even more perfect up close. It looks like every brochure advertising tropical getaways for the low, low price of your entire life savings.

"Everyone, circle up!" a voice calls, cutting through all the noise and chatter. Up to this point, the production crew has kept all the contestants separate from one another. But now, Leah leads us over to a growing group of couples.

The man who called us together is standing in front with a headset over one ear. Even though he's wearing casual clothes—chino shorts and a white linen button-down—he seems to radiate authority. His salt-and-pepper hair marks him as older than the other crew members, and while everyone else seems to be scurrying around trying to accomplish two or three things at once, he carries himself with a more languid ease.

Leah's attention is locked on him. He's a handsome older guy, a bit like George Clooney if you squint, but Leah seems unimpressed. She observes, "Looks like he's had his yearly Botox. His forehead's barely moving."

The man claps to get everyone's attention. "Welcome, everyone! What a beautiful group we've got here. The casting department really outdid themselves."

The contestants all cheer, and Chase and I join in, the thrum of excitement infectious.

"I'm Peter Dixon, one of the executive producers here on the show. Normally, I'd be in some cushy office in LA, but this show is my baby, so you're going to be seeing a lot of me. Between us, this is going to be big. *Huge.* Think of whatever show is your favorite, and double it, and then double it again. That's what this show is going to be, thanks to all of you. Now, in just a few moments, the cameras will start rolling, and your journey through hell will begin."

Laughter ripples through the crowd. I catch a few couples eyeing each other nervously.

Peter Dixon grins. "Maybe that wasn't the best choice of words. This is why I'm not the host. You'll be meeting her very soon."

A few people glance around, like *the* Dawn Taylor is going to emerge from the waves, ocean water cascading down her age-defying, swim-suit-model body.

"But first," says Peter Dixon, "to get to our tropical island, we're asking you to trust your partner and take a leap of faith off this boat together!"

Producers and production assistants swarm in, escorting contestants to the bow of the boat. Chase and I are brought to the highest point of the bow, and I realize the crew is waiting to see what we'll do. I reach out for Chase.

But he's already gone.

"*Awesooooooome!*" he shouts, doing a backflip over the edge of the boat. It's a twenty-foot drop, and the water is so clear that I can see the jagged rocks that line the bottom of the bay.

I can't move. My brain starts calculating the speed at which I would fall, the force with which I'd hit the water, the amount of impact need-ed to cause a concussion that would take me out of the show.

Chase calls something to me from the water, but I can't tell what he's saying. Everything sounds fuzzy and far away. All I can hear is the boom of my heartbeat—until I feel a hand, solid and warm, on my shoulder.

"*Slayer?*"

That nickname.

That voice.

Suddenly I'm sixteen again, in the auditorium of the community center where all the league competitions for our local high schools were held, staring down my nemesis: the only person who could match my arguments in Model UN *and* my SAT score. The one who always had a clever comeback no matter what insult I threw at him, and who'd witnessed my greatest victories and my most humiliating losses.

He can't be here at this place, at this time. There's no way.

"*Daniel?*" I whisper. I turn to look, praying I'm wrong. And there he is, with those sharp, curious brown eyes, his dark eyebrows tilted with amusement, and his full lips quirked into a smile. The mole dotting the space between his eye and his temple. I keep looking for something, anything, to prove that I'm hallucinating, that I'm dreaming, but he's really here. "Daniel Cho?"

His smile widens as he steps closer.

"I thought that might be you. I didn't recognize you at first. In that." His gaze briefly darts down to my bikini and then quickly snaps back up to my face. "What are you doing here?"

I open my mouth, but to my horror, I can't find anything to say. But I've never been speechless in front of Daniel. I *can't* be speechless in front of Daniel. I need to escape. And there's one way out.

I jump off the boat.

The weightlessness is a relief, all my fear coalescing into the triumph of actually following through, and I hit the water, sliding underneath the waves. Underwater, it's beautifully blue and quiet, almost blissful, then I start floating upward, and everything seems to speed up again. When I break through the surface, I gasp for air, desperately combing my hair out of my face and frantically adjusting my bikini top, which has ridden up.

"Knew you could do it, babe!" Chase says, surfacing next to me.

"You left me!" I shout, splashing him. I hope it looks playful, but honestly, I'm pissed, and I'm shaken by my encounter with my old high school rival. "We were supposed to do it as a couple," I say, just loud enough to be heard over the water. Around us, other couples are making their way to shore, their shouts and laughter mingling with the sound of the ocean.

"Okay, okay." Chase holds up his hands in surrender as he treads water. "Point taken. Let's get out of this water, huh?"

Swimming far, far away from here as quickly as possible seems like a great idea. We paddle to the shore. Chase tries to wait for me, but he can't resist swimming faster and catching up to the others. By the time I'm able to stand up in the surf, I find myself arriving at the beach with the one person I was trying to avoid.

"You beat me to the beach," says my living nightmare personified. "I'd expect nothing less from you, Slayer. It's been what, seven and a half years since I kicked your ass at Regional Quiz Bowl Finals?"

"I remember that somewhat differently," I huff. He's talking like no time has passed, and without meaning to, I fall back into old habits. "And it figures that you'd remember one of the few times you came out on top. Remember the state spelling bee? Mock Trial? The interschool performing arts bake sale?" I wave three fingers in his face.

He puts his hand over mine, curling my fingers down. "You're over-counting, Slayer. Bake sales aren't a competition."

I stare him. People don't usually interrupt me when I'm in the middle of making excellent points, but of course Daniel isn't just anyone.

His fingers are warm against mine as his hand lingers. We've shaken hands before, at the end of a match, but this feels different. More electric. All my senses are focused on this point of contact, and I really don't need this right now.

This has to be a calculated move, a tactic designed to throw me off my game. I hate that I'm clearly the only one reeling from our surprise reunion. Daniel's strength has always been his adaptability, and that obviously hasn't changed over the years. I, on the other hand, thrive on planning and strategizing—but I've never been good at rolling with the punches. Every single one of my bullet points has flown out of my head.

Regrouping, I shake his hand off. "All a competition requires is something quantifiable. And by every single metric, I decimated you. Number of cupcakes baked? Amount of money raised? Flyers designed, printed, and posted? Take your pick."

"The real winner was the Hillsborough School District's performing arts program," he says with a smirk.

"For which I raised over two thousand dollars," I shoot back.

"Your cupcakes might've been a bit overpriced if you asked your customers."

"They were made with artisanal and fair-trade chocolate, *Midas*, and they got the job done, unlike your cookies-and-cream fudge disaster."

He cocks an eyebrow. "Still haven't forgotten that old nickname, huh?"

"Not any more than you've forgotten 'Slayer,'" I say.

We've been sparring like no time has passed, but it's been years since we last saw each other. I find myself really looking at him, taking in all the little ways he's grown up since high school. He'd always been athletic, but I've never seen him like this—tanned, muscular, and glistening, his black hair casually swept back. I bet the hair and makeup team loves him.

"What?" he says.

"Huh?"

"You're staring." He ruffles his hand through his hair. "Is there something on my head?"

"It's your hair," I deflect. "It's different." It's hot. Daniel's hot. *Oh no, Daniel's hot.*

He chuckles. "Couldn't keep the bowl cut forever. Nice of you to notice."

"I wasn't—I didn't say—" I stammer.

"All right, cut!" Leah says, and I startle. I whip around, suddenly realizing that not only has an audience gathered, but at least three cameras are trained on me and Daniel. "Finally! Something we can use, Alice. Love the banter. That's going into the sizzle reel."

"Nice," Chase says. "Sizzle." He slips an arm around me as Leah rattles off more directions to some of the crew about the footage.

"Hey! There you are, Danny!"

An outrageously attractive woman who's defying several laws of gravity with her bikini leaps into Daniel's arms.

"Danny?" I repeat. "You always hated when people called you that."

"Oh, but the way I say it, it's just *so* cute," the new woman says as Daniel sets her down on the sand. She must be Daniel's partner.

Daniel gives a half shrug. "It's better than *Midas*."

"Okay, *Danny*," I say, grinning.

"Who's this?" Daniel's girlfriend asks, tucking herself into his side. With her sun-kissed tan and the balayage highlights in her long wavy hair, she and Daniel fit like two pieces of a sexy beach puzzle.

"Selena, this is Slayer—"

"I go by Alice actually," I interrupt. "And this is Chase."

"So, Danny, you and Alice know each other?" Chase asks, pointing at Daniel. "This gives us a leg up on the competition! We've got to lock this in now. How about a secret alliance?" Chase shoots finger guns at Daniel and Selena.

Daniel opens his mouth, but Selena squeals, "Yes! Yes, secret alliance! I love it, I love it so much."

Chase grins. "Awesome! Final four, baby. Locking it in!"

Selena and Chase high-five, and I can see one of the cameras pointed at them, capturing this moment in real time.

Daniel raises his hand up for me to do the same, but I stare it down. Daniel lifts an eyebrow, and I raise an eyebrow back. Obliviously, Chase slaps Daniel's hand for me.

"Never leave a bro hanging!" Chase says, and I try to calm the rising panic I feel at being in a "secret alliance" with my nemesis. I still can't believe he's here.

The voice of one of the producers cuts through the gentle roar of the surf and gets everyone's attention.

"Everyone, Dawn Taylor's on her way. Get your mic packs checked, and we'll be filming the first scene to kick off the competition in ten minutes."

Several more producers have arrived off the yacht and are now ushering us to the couches in the sand and taking drink orders. Chase and I sink into a plush loveseat while techs and makeup artists surround us to get the scene camera-ready.

A few minutes later, the production assistant comes around with a tray full of colorful, tropical drinks, offering them to each of the contestants. When she reaches us, Chase grabs his trademark whiskey sour. I scan the tray for the water I requested.

"This is for you," the PA prompts me, pointing to a hurricane glass with a pineapple wedge in it.

I shake my head. "I asked for water."

"Sorry about that," she says, frowning. "They must've missed your order. Do you mind just taking this one?"

She's already pushing the drink into my hand. I really don't want to cause trouble, but I have to say it. "I wasn't really planning on drinking alcohol. Is there somewhere I can go to just grab a water bottle? You don't have to get it for me." I incline my head toward the row of off-white canvas tents that have been set up down the beach. Surely one contains water.

"No, the cast can't leave their marks right now. Filming's about to start. But don't worry. I'll tell someone to come around with water bottles," the PA promises. She practically dumps the glass into my hand and moves on to the next couple.

Chase takes a sip of my drink and grins. "Try it, babe, it's like a little tropical party in a glass."

I sigh and look at the drink in my hands. The glass is cool against my fingers, and I'm so far beyond dehydrated, it's not even funny.

But there are three very good reasons why I shouldn't drink it.

One: Anytime I drink more than a half glass of wine, I flush bright red. Not the best camera look.

Two: I'm a complete lightweight. Chase could easily drink two or three of these and still be perfectly normal. One drink and I'm tipsy. Two, and I'm practically falling over.

Three: I talk. More than I should. More than I usually do. All of the thoughts that normally crash around in my head are suddenly allowed to escape. And if there's one thing I've learned, it's that people usually prefer that I keep these thoughts bottled up.

But it's *so* hot, and surely one sip won't hurt.

I take that sip, and oh, wow. It's delicious, fruity and light with hints of guava and pomegranate, and it's the perfect relief as we all bake under the sweltering heat of the tropical sun. I take another sip, a bigger one. It can't be *too* alcoholic if it tastes like this, right? It must be mostly fruit juice.

"Here we go," Chase says, clinking his glass against mine and gesturing to Peter Dixon, who is striding to the center of the group.

"Now that we're all refreshed and the drinks are flowing, it's time we met our amazing, talented host Dawn Taylor. And when she comes out here, I'm going to need all of you to scream like it's 2023 and you just got tickets to the Eras tour. Ready? Three . . . two . . . one . . . Here she is, ladies and gentlemen, Dawn Taylor!"

Everyone goes wild as Dawn Taylor emerges from one of the production tents and joins Peter Dixon.

Everything about her defies reality—blond hair styled in an artfully loose braid, every strand perfectly in place despite the heat and the humidity, a shimmery white pencil skirt and hot-pink blazer without a single wrinkle, and not a single bead of sweat marring her perfect smoky-eye makeup.

I can't even imagine how hard her hair and makeup team must be working to keep her in such pristine condition.

"Aw, you guuuuuys. You're making me blush." Dawn Taylor flips her braid and winks. "Now you all know who I am, and if you don't, then you'd better get off my island!" She laughs, and we all laugh with her. "Babes, I'm Dawn Taylor, and I'm here to put you through hell."

She's talking straight at the cameras now, but everything about her posture, the way she moves, and the tone of her voice feels like she's talking to a girlfriend at brunch.

"What's at stake? One. Million. Dollars. If you lovebirds survive the flames of my inferno and stay together, you'll win a cash prize, an all-expenses-paid vacation to the Bahamas, and a sponsorship by Mega Glam Cosmetics. If you flame out or break up, you'll be sent into exile in the wastelands. And babes, there's no catering there. Are you all ready to play?"

On cue, we all cheer and clap. Chase lets out a whoop.

"You've already passed the first test: your leap of faith into the ocean!" Dawn Taylor pivots to face another camera. "But before we can truly begin our descent into hell, our daring couples must escape 'Limbo.' And to do that, they'll need to *limbo*!" Dawn Taylor does a shimmy. "And they won't just have to limbo. They'll have to limbo while tied together in a three-legged race. It's the ultimate test of teamwork, communication, and *flexibility*."

A *three-legged race?* My stomach drops. I glance at Chase, but he's clapping along with everyone else.

Dawn Taylor winks at the camera. "Babes, try not to die."

"Okay, cut!" Peter Dixon shouts. "Thank you, Dawn Taylor. Let's take five and get the couples tied up."

I turn to Chase. "If we're going to be running, I need some water first."

"Yeah, go for it. I'll save our spot," Chase says, then takes another swig of his whiskey sour.

I get up, scanning the beach for somewhere I can get water. I spot the sound tech who was recording us earlier, crouching behind the cameras and gulping from a plastic water bottle. The sound tech is wearing the all-black uniform of the technical crew and has their hair short in a sleek undercut. Right now, with this heat, I wish my hair was that short, too. I run up to them, concentrating hard on not stumbling on the sand.

"I'm so sorry, but can I ask you something? Where did you get that?"

The sound tech jumps. "Whoa! Yeah, I'm not supposed to talk to you."

"Sorry, I don't want to get you in trouble. I'm just really dehydrated, and if I have another one of those mixed drinks, I don't think I'm going to be able to walk straight, much less do a three-legged limbo."

The sound tech hesitates. "You can't get it from a PA? I'm not really supposed to—"

"I asked, but they're busy and we're about to start," I say. "Please? There's over a hundred people on this set. I know the production company must have brought in enough water for all of us. I'm just asking you to tell me where it is."

The sound tech glances around quickly. "They keep the water for the crew over there." The sound tech nods toward the palm trees, where equipment and a cooler are pushed together on a tarp. "The producers really push the drinks on the contestants, so if you have a water bottle, don't keep it on you. Pour the water into your cup."

Pouring alcohol into people stranded on a hot beach with no water sounds like, I don't know, an OSHA violation. I know the PA did promise to bring water around later, but later could be hours from now.

"It's a recipe for disaster," I say out loud.

The sound tech adjusts their headphones and scowls. "That's kind of the point. You must be new here, huh?"

"Aren't we all new here?" I say, gesturing at the contestants in the distance.

"No, I mean, new to being on reality TV," the sound tech clarifies. They pause to listen to their headset. "You should get back. Take this." The sound tech produces a second water bottle from their backpack and tosses it to me. I down it quickly.

Thank God. I feel alive again. I say, "Thank you. You're a lifesaver.

Seriously. I'm Alice."

"I know." When I look surprised, the sound tech just shrugs and taps the headphones they're wearing. "It's kind of my job to be listening in on all of you all day."

"Oh, right. Of course." I think back to everything I said today. From trying to get out of wearing a bikini to yelling at Chase and being surprised by Daniel. "I guess you know me pretty well then," I say, laughing uncomfortably.

"Mhm. Get out of here," the sound tech says, shooing me away.

"Wait, can I get your name?" I say. They're right. I'm new to all this, and even though I may have taken a crash course from Cindy and Tara on the ins and outs of being on set, it's nothing like experiencing the real thing. It wouldn't hurt to make a friend, or at least know people's names.

"I'm Lex," the sound tech says.

"Thank you, Lex," I say. I must still be feeling a bit out of it because I sketch a goofy little bow, like I'm a court jester. Lex laughs at that.

I turn back to the beach, and as I walk away I stumble and fall in the soft, white sand. I need to clear my head if I'm going to win this race. I thought I only had to focus on beating my competitors, but I'm realizing that the competition itself is just the tip of the iceberg. I want to win; I have to win. But I know it isn't going to be easy.

As I pick myself back up, I glimpse someone in a blue baseball cap standing stock-still in the shadows of the palm trees. Everyone on the beach is busy—the crew are setting up the shots, and the couples are lining up together. Even Dawn Taylor is doing yoga off to the side. But among all this activity, one person isn't moving.

I squint, trying to make out this person's face, but it's hard to see anything from this distance. I shake my head and tear my gaze away when Lex calls after me, "Have fun in hell!"

Let's Get Real: Reality TV Gossip at Its Finest
Love Is Hell . . . Worth it or nah?

If you're like me, you're cautiously optimistic about this summer's newest reality TV show. But who will be watching? The cast's identities have been under wraps until today, so I'm going to break it down for you:

Couple #1: Ava (product manager) and Noah (engineer)
All work and no play for these Forbes 30 Under 30 powerhouses. They're all about ice baths and 5 a.m. wake-up calls to hit the ground running.

Couple #2: Mikayla and Trevor (relationship influencers)
If you don't know #Trekayla or #boyfriendgoals, are you even on IG? Catch us swooning over Trevor's latest date night inspos every week.

Couple #3: Daniel (lawyer) and Selena (model)
Selena is already semifamous and most likely just doing this to boost her modeling career, but she should be entertaining to watch. Checking the archives, these two just hard-launched their relationship right before coming on the show.

Couple #4: Brittany (waitress) and Jaxon (works on a farm)
Just a small-town couple living in a lonely world. Their social media consists mostly of cows and baby sheep, which I'm not mad about.

Couple #5: Kendall and Tarun (food influencers)
Their favorite word is umami. If you ever wanted to see 10,000 images of uber-fancy food on tiny plates, check out their feeds.

Couple #6: Firefly and Bacon (occupation unknown)
Burning Man may be 38 days, 18 hours, and 25 seconds away, but these two bring the playa with them year-round. If you like badasses who can weld as well as they meld, this is the couple for you.

Couple #7: Chase (finance consultant) and Alice (math teacher)
Not much on the social media front. He's into intramural lacrosse, surfing, and eating sausages (#SausageFest, #itsnotwhatyouthinkhorndogs). She likes math, presumably.

Couple #8: Zya and Dominic (lifestyle influencers)
Zya and Dominic show how you can dominate life and love on their YouTube channel. Subscribe to get tips on leveling up in leading the pack, assuming you're alpha enough to do it.

Couple #9: Naiah (tarot reader) and Sage (occupation unknown)
They're all about good vibes and knowing way too much about astrology. Naiah is into tarot and sells scented candles and healing stones.

Couple #10: Bella (social media manager) and Blake (fitness coach)
I strongly suspect Bella and Blake live at the gym. The two are fitness influencers, but it seems like there's trouble brewing in paradise for them. Check out these comments from Bella on Blake's latest post:

[Alt Text: Image of a glass of champagne next to a beer with Bella's and Blake's hands clasped together.]

BLAKEWITHTHEABS off to the tropics with **@bellabae** to win a million dollars! wish us luck! :shamrock:
LOVEYDOVEY69 ur so hot :flame:
    BELLABAE thirsty much? wud u say this to my face? Tacky!
XOXOGLAMOURGIRL kiss for luck! :smooch:
    BELLABAE get out of his comments! he's taken!

Chapter Five
Hell Is a Three-Legged Limbo Race

Chase is chatting with our producer Leah when I rejoin them on the sofa. Leah holds up a bundle of bright-purple Velcro straps. "Let's get you two tied up."

Leah takes my leg and snuggles it up next to Chase's leg, binding us together from our ankles to our knees. I'm a foot shorter than Chase, so I can already tell this is going to throw us both off as we try to stand up.

Leah looks at my face. "You're red. Give me a sec." She roots around in her bag for a moment before producing face powder. She fluffs a pouf in my face a few times and then tilts her head as she checks her work. "A little better," she says under her breath.

"I can hear you," I tell her.

"I mean, you look great! Why don't you two head to the starting line? Try to get used to moving together."

"Sure. Chase, why don't we—" I begin, but Chase starts walking away without so much as a glance at me, and I'm dragged along like a Chihuahua attached to a Great Dane. And sure enough, within a few steps, the two of us crash into the sand. I go down face-first.

Damn it. Before coming here, I'd prepped for the physical challenges: I'd upped my cardio, practiced sprinting to my classroom on school days, and taken the stairs up to my mom's apartment instead of the rickety elevator. But now it's clear I've made a crucial mistake. The challenges aren't just about me, they're about *us*. Chase and I may work well together in our daily lives, but out here, in this totally different world of reality TV, Chase and I aren't in sync at all.

Plus, I'm super drunk.

"We need a real plan," I say to Chase, spitting sand out of my mouth. I eye the beach and try to marshal my fuzzy brain into working order. "A real, actual working plan. With steps. And action items. And . . ."

"Aw, babe, you're tipsy!" Chase says, patting my shoulder. "I say, let's not overthink it. We just need to, y'know," Chase gestures a walking motion with his hands.

Of course, that's the exact moment Daniel and Selena drop down next to us in one smooth motion.

"You guys good?" Daniel asks.

"Very," I say. "Extremely. Super. And I'm completely sober."

Daniel looks at me, a little concerned. "Sober? Slayer, did you—"

"I'm fine!" I insist quickly. "May the best couple win."

"Secret alliance!" Selena cheers, pumping her fist before she and Daniel take a graceful leap toward the starting line.

"Okay, let's just coordinate our moves, and—" I don't get to finish because Chase stands up, leaving me flailing after him. I loop my arms around his waist, hanging on for dear life as he lopes along toward the starting line. We're the last couple to take our places.

I glance around at the competition. Every couple here has their own distinct style. I can almost imagine the casting department picking out the country-cute couple rocking cowboy hats and boots paired with their rustic plaid swimsuits, then putting them next to a boho-chic couple sporting flowing blond hair with flowers woven in. The woman is wearing crochet bikini top and artfully faded jean shorts, while the guy wears a yellow tank top with an image of a sunrise on it and a fringed vest. Selena gives us a conspiratorial wink.

"Final four," she mouths.

"Secret alliance," Chase mouths back with a fist pump. They beam at each other.

Chase has formed a secret alliance with my high school nemesis and his girlfriend. It really hits home how completely I've lost control of this situation.

But it's not too late to get things back on track. I summon up my list of goals. Right, I have to assess my competition. The show didn't release any information about who we'd be competing against until today, so I didn't get the chance to study up on them beforehand. Instead, a cram session will have to do.

I survey the people beside me. Selena and Daniel are known quantities. The couple on our other side looks like they just came straight out of bottle service at a Vegas nightclub. The guy is wearing distressed jeans and a muscle tee, and his partner is wearing a tight swim coverup that somehow manages to make her look less covered up. But while this choice of outfit probably thrilled the producers, I can tell she'll have trouble running in that skirt. She's tiny, and her boyfriend is massive and absolutely ripped. They're even more mismatched in size than Chase and me.

Also, this guy seems totally distracted. I catch him blatantly ogling the other women on the beach until his partner notices and grabs his arm, pulling him into a deep—and distinctly slobbery—kiss to get his attention.

Behind them, I can see another couple who's all business. They're both decked out in blazers, which seems hilariously out of place on the beach. The woman has her black hair slicked back in a sharp, short ponytail. Beneath her blazer, she's wearing a white shirt covered with the words "Rise and Grind." Instead of suit pants, though, she has on black bikini bottoms. Her partner matches her. He's wearing a hawklike expression, his sharp eyes narrowed and his dark, perfectly groomed eyebrows furrowed in concentration. He adjusts his glasses as he scrutinizes the course like he's trying to pick it apart.

"Make room for the winners," an obnoxiously loud voice calls out. Mr. Rise and Grind is shoved to the side by a redhead wearing a muscle tank with frat letters plastered across the front. As he barrels past, I clock the barbed-wire tattoo circling his bicep.

"The hell?" Mr. Rise and Grind snaps.

"What? Sorry, I don't speak loser," the guy says.

"Dominic, you're so bad," his partner says, playfully swatting his arm. She's a sporty-looking woman in army-fatigue joggers and a black sports bra. Her long brown hair is pulled back into messy pigtails, and she's got earrings in that look like daggers. The two of them are in matching camo trucker hats.

"We're not here to make friends, Zya," he tells her. "We're here to win!"

She rolls her eyes. "Please, these other girls are going to be too busy worrying about messing up their makeup to be any match for me."

I already sort of hate this couple. They're competitive, which I can respect, but also obnoxious as hell. I make a note to steer clear of them.

I can't really scope out the rest of my competitors without making it obvious what I'm doing, so I turn my focus to the obstacle course before us, which is laid out on the sand next to the waterline. There are limbo poles speared into the sand about thirty feet apart, three in total before a finish line. The poles get progressively closer to the ground, each one more difficult to limbo under than the last.

I'm still studying the course when one of the production assistants signals us to quiet down. Dawn Taylor saunters over to face the cameras.

"Babes, it's time to *limbo* your way out of Limbo!" Dawn Taylor says, doing a little shimmy. "The first couple to make it through the obstacle course will win a luxury date in our Paradise Cabana. The losers get to spend some quality time on the beach. And whoever comes in dead last? Well, you'll be dead to us—and eliminated from the competition."

One of the cameramen runs parallel to the line of contestants, getting one last shot of us lined up. I concentrate on looking determined while Chase strikes a pose, flexing his muscles like an old-timey strongman.

Dawn Taylor raises her hands. "Love is hell. Can you take the heat?

We're about to find out! Your journey begins *now*!" We start to launch ourselves forward.

"Everyone, hold your places!" Peter Dixon calls from the sidelines. "Dawn, DT, love it, no notes. But let's get a few more takes with some other catchphrases. Freya, take this." Peter Dixon waves over the PA who was handing out drinks earlier, a timid-looking woman with black hair in two braids, and has her run a piece of paper over to Dawn Taylor.

A flash of annoyance crosses Dawn Taylor's gorgeous features, but once she's facing the camera, she flashes a brilliant smile and fires off a dozen phrases.

"Get ready to catch hell!"

"There's gonna be hell to pay!"

"Let's raise hell!"

Is this really funny or am I just drunk? Maybe it's a little of both. I put my hand over my mouth and try to quiet my laughter, but I catch Lex the sound tech looking over at me. Clearly, they can tell I'm laughing, thanks to the mic pack I was outfitted with earlier.

Meanwhile, Dawn Taylor is still going. How long is this list?

"We're about to have one hell of a time!"

"Ready, set, hell!"

At that last one, she turns to Peter Dixon. "I think we got it. Let's move this along."

"But you're just getting to the good stuff," Peter Dixon says.

"Pete, honey, I love you but if I don't get a glass of mango iced tea right this second, I'm not going to be able to say another word today," Dawn Taylor says, pouting.

Peter Dixon chuckles. "Fine, you win. Can someone get DT here a drink?" One of the crew breaks from the pack, scurrying away toward the tents.

"Thanks a mil," Dawn Taylor says. She flounces her way off to the side, toward a colorful beach chair with a matching umbrella. I don't know how she's managing to walk in heels on the sand. Sorcery, maybe. Or Pilates.

"So, should we start?" I ask.

"Oh, yeah. Um, please go," the quiet PA—Freya, my mind supplies after a beat—says.

Ripples of confusion move through the line of contestants.

"Did she say go?"

"Are we starting?"

"Go, go, go!"

And we're off. The part of me that's attached to Chase is already running. Chase is two feet from the starting line before he seems to remember that we're Velcroed together.

"Chase! Too fast!" I shout.

"Sorry, babe, got too excited," Chase says, flashing me his best golden retriever grin.

Chase all but scoops me up. This time, I keep my arm wrapped around his waist. It works for a couple steps, but Chase is too tall and I'm too short, and our strides are hilariously mismatched.

New strategy: I'm going to cling to Chase with everything I've got and let his momentum carry us through this.

Ahead of us, several couples have already made it to the first obstacle. Selena and Daniel bound up with an annoying amount of confidence, and Selena even manages to do a cute little shimmy as she ducks below the pole. The Rise-and-Grinders pause, but only long enough to figure out that they can make it if they stagger their turns underneath the pole—then they, too, are racing to the next set.

How is everyone making this look easy? The way things are going, Chase and I won't even make it out of Limbo. And then our failure is going to be broadcast on television to millions of people—to all my friends, to my co-teacher, to Coach Raza and his husband, who I *know* are tuning in because they watch every reality show under the sun. Hopefully not to my mom, who exclusively watches tai chi videos on YouTube and K-dramas. The worst part is that Daniel, my high school nemesis, is here to see it all live and in person.

Like hell am I going to go out without a fight. I channel every last bit of spite I have into moving my aching legs. The gap between us and the next couple shrinks, and we reach the limbo pole just behind them.

It's the couple who look like they just left the club. The bodybuilder is too huge to easily make it under the limbo pole, and his bulging bicep nearly knocks over the pole. And his partner has to drop to her knees to shimmy under the pole, thanks to the skintight cover-up.

Chase barrels toward the pole. I yell, "Wait! Let me go first—" But it's too late. Chase rams me into the pole.

"Ow!"

"Oops, watch out!" Chase says, maneuvering to give me space. He scoops me up again, and we're off, definitely worse for wear. At least we're neck-and-neck with our closest competition now.

The bodybuilder glances over at us as we sprint by.

"Blake, are you kidding me?" his partner screeches. "You're checking that chick out *now*? Right in front of me?"

"Bella, baby, I wasn't! I was just seeing where they were!" Blake protests, pointing at me.

Bella whips her head around to glare at me. In a flash, I remember Bella's jealousy, Blake's wandering eye. I give Blake an almost cartoonishly suggestive wink.

Bella's voice rises an octave. "What the hell? Did you hook up with that girl? She's not even your type!"

This is our chance. I urge Chase onward, and we edge around them, running up to the second limbo pole. At this point, I think I've got the hang of it. In our best moment of coordination yet, my weight helps pull Chase under the pole, and we clear it without too much struggle.

Bella and Blake, on the other hand, are too busy arguing to see where they're going, and they run smack into the second pole. Blake scrambles to get up, but his tight jeans are keeping him from lunging wide enough to stand. I can hear Bella's furious shrieks as Chase and I make it past the third limbo pole, then half limp, half run to the end.

"We did it!" Chase shouts as we cross the finish line. Once I've undone the Velcro around our legs, he twirls me around. "Babe, we're still in the game!"

I laugh along with him, buoyed by our close finish. We've survived to fight another day. But my moment of elation fizzles out when Dawn Taylor announces, "And the winners are . . . Daniel and Selena!"

She triumphantly raises Selena's and Daniel's hands, beaming. A cameraman pans around them as Selena shimmies and Daniel does a Superman pose.

Everyone cheers, with Chase cheering the loudest. He lets out an enthusiastic whoop before mouthing *secret alliance* at me. But through the applause, I can tell that other people's smiles are strained, almost angry. We all came to win, and Selena and Daniel just pulled ahead of the pack.

"Congratulations, you've won a date in the sexy cabana," Dawn Taylor says, doing a sensual body roll. She follows that up with, "As for all of you losers, you get to rough it on the beach for your date. But before that, we must bid farewell to Blake and Bella. I'm afraid that the two of you fell victim to Limbo. It's time for you to get the hell out of here."

Bella and Blake link hands. I feel a rush of gratitude for this trainwreck of a couple, and even for my neon bikini. I bet that's why Blake looked at me. The beacon-bright yellow color is as good as a signal flare.

"Say your goodbyes," Dawn Taylor says solemnly. "Your flame in hell is about to be extinguished."

Two PAs start to bring over a pair of torches, but Peter Dixon waves them off.

"Freya, Anton, we don't need those," Peter Dixon calls out. "DT, love this direction, but hell is literally *on fire*. Why are you putting out their torches?"

"It's *symbolic*," Dawn says sweetly.

"I think we should skip it."

"*Pete*, we agreed to this months ago."

"It's coming off a little derivative. Too *Survivor*."

"That's a good thing. Our whole pitch is *Survivor* in relationship hell, remember?"

"I hear you, DT. But you know what they'll say online."

By the looks going around, I can tell we're all starting to feel the weird vibe between Peter Dixon and Dawn Taylor. I think they can tell, too, because in a flash, Dawn Taylor flips her scowl to a charming smile.

"I guess torches are a bit passé," she says. She turns on her heel to face Bella and Blake again. "Bella and Blake, say your goodbyes. Your journey through hell ends here."

On cue, Bella's face crumples and a single tear tracks down her cheek. Blake goes in for a side hug, and she shrugs him off, clearly still pissed. The other contestants crowd around them.

"I'm so sorry you're leaving. I'm gonna miss you so much!" the girl in the cowboy hat cries, throwing her arms around Bella.

As Bella pulls away, her eyes fall on me.

"You *bitch*!" Bella sobs. "You distracted my man with your *feminine wiles*!"

"Hang on," I protest. "I didn't *wile* anyone—"

Bella lunges for me, but the cowgirl catches her, holding her back. "Sweetie, don't do this. No man is worth embarrassing yourself on TV for."

"But she—" Bella struggles for a moment, and then sags, her head hanging. "Ugh. You're right."

Cindy's warnings about getting the villain edit ring in my head. I have to make things good with Bella now, before the narrative takes hold. I say, "Bella, I'm sorry about the wink. It was just a joke. A stupid one."

Bella looks at me, her face glistening with tears. "I forgive you. It's not your fault that you're super hot."

There has to be some kind of sexy alchemy at play because no one's ever called me "super hot" before. I have got to get in front of a mirror and find out what I look like in this bikini. I'm fully aware that my attractiveness level is "model in an Old Navy ad campaign" at best. In a Jane Austen novel, I'd be called "tolerable," and that suits me just fine.

Before I can respond to this mind-boggling statement from Bella, Leah swoops in. "I think we've got enough footage here. Let's debrief, kiddos."

As she takes me and Chase away, the smell of food hits me, and my mouth immediately starts watering. The other contestants are heading for the catering tent, where a sumptuous buffet has been laid out—and is that a whole roast pig sizzling over an open fire? My stomach rumbles, and I realize that I haven't eaten anything since before we jumped off the boat.

"Dinner?" I ask hopefully.

"Later. When you're done with your interview," Leah says firmly.

Leah leads us over to a dusty rose–colored love seat in the shade and gestures for us to sit. There are already glasses of champagne on the table beside us.

I think longingly of the water bottle I chugged and abandoned hours ago and pour myself onto the love seat next to Chase.

Lex is there, and I drunkenly wave to them before remembering that I'm not supposed to talk to the crew. They ignore me, like the professional they are.

The cameraman focuses on me as Leah checks her notes.

"So, Alice, do you feel lucky to be staying?"

"Yes! So lucky."

"Okay, try that again, but I need you to repeat my question in your answer. That will help give context to the viewers. For example, 'Do you feel lucky to be staying?' 'I feel lucky to be staying.'"

"Got it," I say. "I feel really lucky that we're still in. If Bella and Blake hadn't totally melted down, we'd have been in big trouble. Like mega, Godzilla-sized trouble."

I fling out my arms, gesturing widely to make my point. Chase snorts, and then I giggle, and soon the two of us are laughing so hard it hurts. Leah folds her arms and glares at us.

"Sorry," I say, my laughter subsiding. "Did that answer your question?"

"Yes, but not in any way that's helpful. It's fine." Leah jots something down. "Chase, what did you think of Bella going after Alice?"

"That was wild," Chase says, his eyes wide. "Bella was so mad. But I knew my girl Alice would stay calm. She's always cool as a cucumber."

"That's me," I say, feeling the giggles start to bubble up in me again. "A cucumber."

Leah rubs the bridge of her nose. "Uh-huh. Alice, can you say something nice about Blake and Bella? We need the viewers at home to know that there are no hard feelings. Something like, 'Bella and Blake are total sweethearts. I'm so sad to see them go.'"

"Yeah." It feels like she's slipping me the answers to a pop quiz. "I'm so sad to see Bella and Blake going home. They're total sweethearts. I feel so bad. But also relieved that they're going home and not us."

"Usable," Leah mutters to herself. "Okay, we're done. Go get dinner."

Relieved, I get to my feet. Blood rushes to my head, and I waver before catching myself. I really need some food in me.

I rush to catch up with Chase, who's already making a beeline for the catering tent. We pass by the winners' cabana, and I crane my neck to see if I can get a glimpse of Daniel. When I do, I wish I hadn't.

Daniel and Selena are snuggled up together in a white hammock with a fluffy blanket across their laps. The PAs must've worked hard to set this all up, because it's the picture of a romantic getaway: Strings of tropical flowers dangle from the cabana ceiling and candles cast a soft, warm glow. Selena is resting her head on Daniel's chest. His arm is tucked around her, and I can see his muscles gleaming in the candlelight.

There's a tattoo that circles Daniel's bicep, a series of thick dashes. He definitely didn't have *that* when we were in high school.

Daniel was cute back then. I would've rather died than admit it, but it's the truth. He had this dorky haircut and his uniform was always too big for his frame, but the way he grinned when his team pulled into the lead—it was like there was a magnetic field around him, pulling my gaze in. But seeing him now, I'm struck by how he's both the same infuriating team captain I knew from so many years ago and someone completely different. His cocky attitude has mellowed out into an easy, understated confidence, and he's handsome in this comfortable, effortless way. He looks like he'd be right at home on a page of Instagram thirst traps or strolling down the cereal aisle at the grocery store.

In the cabana there's also a couple of crew members, a cameraperson, and Peter Dixon himself. As we pass by, I can hear Selena brightly saying her soundbites and nailing every one of them.

"One thing's for sure. We're in for one hell of a ride!" Selena chirps for the camera.

"Perfect," Peter Dixon says. "Mark that take. Use it in all the promo spots. That delivery was, mwah, chef's kiss."

Selena beams. "Let me know if there's anything else I can do. We all want this show to be a hit, Mr. Dixon."

"With your help, it will be," he says. "Seth, I think we're done here. Enjoy your night, folks."

While Selena and Daniel hang back to chat with their producer, Seth, Peter Dixon and another producer start walking toward the catering tent—and toward us. I speed up, hoping to avoid any small talk, but Chase waves to them.

"Bryan, Mr. Peter Dixon, hi!" Chase calls. The producer named Bryan gives Chase one of those upward nods that bros do when they see each other in the wild. He must be Chase's lacrosse friend who got us onto this show.

"Chase and Alice, was it?" Peter Dixon asks, offering Chase a handshake. He reaches for my hand next, but I'm still a bit unsteady on my feet. Instead of shaking his hand, I end up patting his arm. "What'd you think about your first day on the island?"

"It sucks," I blurt out.

"Shit, what happened?" Peter Dixon asks, looking genuinely concerned. "Who do I have to fire?"

He's joking, I think. "No one! Everything's been great. I just mean, we almost lost," I rush to explain.

"*Almost* is the key word there," Peter Dixon says. "You're not out yet, so you still have a fighting chance. And hey, I've got a good feeling about you two. I'm rooting for you."

"Damn right," Chase says, slinging an arm around me. "We're taking this all the way to the top, baby!"

"Hell yeah," Bryan says, high-fiving Chase.

Peter Dixon holds up his phone. "Duty calls. You all have a good night now," he says and veers away from the path to the catering tent.

Once Peter Dixon's gone, Bryan brings Chase in for a one-armed hug, clapping his back. In this light, he looks a bit like Chase, if Chase had close-cropped brown hair, a PGA Tour baseball cap, and a trust fund.

"Good to see you, man," he says. "I'm glad you both made it on the show. Saved my ass, actually. This new kid Anton thinks he's some kind of hotshot, but he's the worst PA ever. Managed to erase half the database of talent we had lined up, and it turns out, it wasn't in the cloud. Took weeks to sort that out."

"Happy to help," Chase says. "Anything for a lax bro."

"Thanks for thinking of us," I say.

"Of course." Bryan jerks a thumb toward Peter Dixon's back. "Anyway, I gotta go. Dawn Taylor wants me to tail him, make sure he gets where he needs to go. Peter Dixon's a great guy, real Hollywood trailblazer, but he'd lose his Stanley mug if it weren't in his hand. See you around."

"How do you know him again?" I ask after Bryan gives Chase a goodbye that consists of three more fist bumps than is strictly necessary. "You said you were on the lacrosse team together?"

"Yeah, in college. We go way back. We met in freshman year and took a few lectures together. I lost touch with him after he moved out to

Hollywood, but he reached out that day when, you know . . ."

"When my mom's apartment nearly went up in flames," I say.

"Yep. Why do you ask?"

"No reason. Just curious."

Before, I'd assumed that Chase's lacrosse buddy had tapped us for the show as a favor to Chase. But after the conversation we just had, I'm starting to wonder if we're actually the ones doing him a favor. After all, it shouldn't be hard to recruit for a show like this, even if you're in a pinch and didn't back up a few files. Maybe Bryan wanted to bring someone he knew into the cast, for whatever reason.

I don't bother speculating about any of this aloud. Chase is so trusting, there's no way he would be willing to question Bryan's motivations. But I was raised by a woman who would clip out newspaper articles about homicide cases and leave them on my desk for me to read. You don't survive in America as an Asian immigrant without a healthy dose of paranoia, and my mother never let me forget it.

As Cindy pointed out so many months ago, I'm on a remote island with no cell service, surrounded by perfect strangers. The only person I truly have on my side is Chase, and that isn't exactly reassuring.

I'm taking one step after another, my feet sinking into the soft sand, and I have to focus to avoid stumbling. I reach out to steady myself on Chase's shoulder, but he's no longer matching my pace and is rapidly leaving me behind.

I don't know if it's the alcohol or the deep exhaustion settling into my bones, but for a second, I'm struck with the feeling that I am completely and utterly alone.

[INTERVIEW FOOTAGE: SOLO TALKING HEAD— DANIEL CHO, ALICE CHEN]

DANIEL CHO: Seeing Alice here was certainly a surprise.

[Cut to Alice on the beach, squinting into the sun]

ALICE CHEN: Are you kidding me? What are the odds that he would be here? Am I cursed?

[Cut to Daniel, leaning against a palm tree]

DANIEL CHO: Were we close? I wouldn't say that, but we were friendly, in a competitive way. We went to different schools, but we were always crossing paths at academic events.

[Cut to Alice, scowling and wiping sweat off her forehead]

ALICE CHEN: He was the literal bane of my existence.

[Cut to Daniel with a smile on his face]

DANIEL CHO: We haven't seen each other since high school. I'm excited to catch up with her.

[Cut to Alice, glaring at someone off camera]

ALICE CHEN: All I know is he better stay out of my way.

Chapter Six

Hell Is Sitting at the Popular Table

I make a beeline for the buffet, determined to get my strength up and shake off the weird mood that just descended on me. I could cry when I see a spread that looks like it came straight out of *Food Network Magazine*. The roast pig is surrounded by chafing pans filled with tender-looking brisket and fall-off-the-bone spareribs, an array of grilled vegetables and tropical salads, and bowls of fresh salsa. Sprays of hibiscus frame the table, and my god, it's all so beautiful. Cindy likes to say I'm food-motivated, like one of those orange cats who do anything for treats, and she's not wrong.

Everyone else has gotten their food already, but there's enough left over for me to feast. I pile my plate full of barbecue pork, coleslaw, roasted pineapple skewers, and papaya salad. Right behind me, Chase has plopped a giant rack of ribs on his plate.

He shoots me a thumbs-up. "This is the life. We should go on reality TV all the time."

"Uh-huh. Where should we sit?" I ask, scanning the beach. I know there are ten couples competing in total, and three picnic tables outside the catering tent. Daniel and Selena are eating in their cabana, so that means there should be three couples at each table. But the other contestants seem to have ignored this perfectly logical breakdown, because four couples have crowded onto one picnic table, with two couples at each of the other two. I'm about to suggest we head to the closest table with room when Chase points at the already-crowded table.

"Over there! That looks like the place to *be*," he says and breaks into a trot, his plate of ribs held high like he's a waiter. I cast a longing glance at the emptier tables, but he's right. It's in our best interests to befriend the other contestants—and maybe pump them for information—and the easiest way to do that is to eat with them.

"Hey, party people! Make some room," he says with his most charming smile.

For a split second, the other contestants look up at him, clearly trying to assess him. I'm struck by how gorgeous everyone is. Duh, this is reality TV, and we all have producers ensuring we look better than our best. But it's one thing to know that, and another thing to be faced with four hot couples right in front of me. Part of me, the part that still feels like a nerdy kid with off-brand shoes and Rite-Aid makeup, expects these supernaturally beautiful humans to laugh and pelt us with their pineapple skewers.

But I should've remembered that this is Chase doing the asking.

"Of course!" The closest woman slides over to make room for us, and her partner gives Chase a welcoming clap on the back. I recognize him from the beach—he's still wearing his cowboy hat and boots.

"We were just introducing ourselves," he says.

"Perfect timing," Chase says. "I'm Chase, and this is my girl Alice. She's a math teacher." He says that last part proudly, and I give a little wave.

"We're big fans of teachers. I always say they're doing the Lord's work. I'm Jaxon and this is my girlfriend, Brittany," the guy says. Jaxon is tall, tanned, and seriously built. His blond hair is cut short, and his eyes are blue enough to rival the crystal-clear water we're surrounded by.

"Hey, y'all," Brittany says with a matching Southern drawl. "We're just so excited to be here. We've never left Alabama before this trip if you can believe it! I don't know if it's just that they haven't fed us all day or this is really the best barbecue pork in the world, but it is delicious!" Brittany is rocking a red flannel shirt tied over her bikini top and jean cutoffs, and she's got her brown hair pulled back into two pigtails.

"This food is a cut above what I was expecting, but it's no Michelin-starred establishment," the guy next to me says as I take a seat. He's wearing stylish dark-rimmed glasses, and he's now wearing a loose, patterned button-down and dark-blue Bermuda shorts. I glimpse metallic red highlights in his wavy black hair.

The woman on his other side snorts out a laugh. "Tarun, the cameras aren't rolling. Rein it in. I'm Kendall, by the way." Kendall has her jet-black hair cut short and slicked back. She looks impossibly cool, with a dazzling constellation of piercings – I'd say sixteen in total. Dangling from her ears are two smiling avocadoes. Her shirt has loopy writing that says *Live to Eat*. On closer inspection, the pattern on Tarun's shirt is actually colorful pieces of sushi.

Kendall notices me staring and waves a hand at their shirts. "Our producer Seth told us to really play it up," she explains. "They don't exactly go in for nuance on reality TV. I'm sure when they show us on screen, there's going to be a caption that says 'Foodies Forever' or something."

Chase chuckles. "I wonder what we're supposed to be?" he says, glancing back at me.

Brains and Brawn? Math Teacher and Hot Fiancé? Hopefully not anything too bad.

"I'm not sure I want to know," I say.

"I told Bryan we'd better be Ava and Noah, Power Couple, Forbes 30 Under 30, Successful Adventurepreneurs," the woman across from me says. She's still wearing her Rise and Grind T-shirt from earlier, but she's draped her blazer over the back of her chair.

Her boyfriend—or husband or partner in business and life—Noah is tall, with gelled dark-brown hair, a white collared shirt, and black business-suit pants. He takes Ava's hand. "I don't think all of that will fit in the subtitle, darling, but if anyone can negotiate for more screen space, I'm sure it's you."

There are two other people at the table, but we don't get around to hearing their introductions because they're locked in a sloppy make-out session. They're both wearing black clothes covered with more zippers, spikes, and clasps than one would expect. They have coordinated knee-high black combat boots with spiked toes, and matching elbow-length gloves with the fingertips cut off. The woman's hair is dyed bright green, and her partner has black hair with matching green highlights. They look like they're ready either for a Mad Max–style fight to the death or to repair a bunch of postapocalyptic tanks.

"They've been like that since we got here," Ava says dismissively. "I don't even think they managed to eat yet."

"What, sucking face doesn't count as getting your daily essential nutrients?" Kendall cracks.

"Too bad they didn't take first place," Brittany says. "They'd be puttin' that cabana to work."

I think of Daniel and Selena in the cabana, putting it to work. Nope, no thank you. Not thinking about that. It's so weird, seeing Daniel with someone. I don't think he ever dated anyone seriously in high school. He always seemed, well, like me. Laser-focused on our studies and nothing else. But I'm with Chase now, so I guess we've both changed.

This day has been a lot. Jet-setting around the world, jumping off a boat, falling on my face in the sand on national television, and seeing Daniel Cho again after almost eight years of total no contact—it's enough to make my head spin.

After dinner, I want nothing more than a blisteringly hot shower and a comfy bed to collapse in, but Leah has other plans for us.

"Last event for the evening before we get you to the villa," Leah says as we follow the crew. "We need some photos of the happy couples."

It's just before sunset, and the ocean is shimmering with the fading sunlight. Gone are the luxurious couches and wicker side tables from earlier. They've been replaced with beach towels placed at regular intervals down the beach, with tiki torches flickering at each end of the row.

"This is your beach time," Leah explains. "The light won't last forever, so we'll get a few promo shots of everyone lounging around, and
then we can call it."

Oh right, our punishment for losing Limbo is an evening date on
the beach. It's not much of a punishment, but compared to Daniel and
Selena's flower-lined cabana, it's definitely a step down.

I sink down next to Chase on the beach towel. My bikini, which has
made it into my Top Ten Most Hated Outfits of All Time, immediately
rides up as I sit, and I struggle to discreetly pick out my wedgie as the
wind picks up, causing goose bumps to erupt along my arms.

"Can I go get my sweatshirt?" I ask Leah.

"Sorry, Alice, no time. We're already losing the light. Besides, you're
not going to pop on screen with a sweatshirt. You'll just look like a
sack of potatoes next to, well." She gestures at Chase, who's all abs.
"Don't worry, we'll keep this short. No filming, just photos."

Between standing up to adjust my bikini and the uneven sand, when
I finally try to settle back down, I end up stumbling right into Chase's
lap.

"Whoa, there," he says, setting me right. "Slow down. The race is
over, babe."

He goes to put his arm around me, but I pull back.

"About that," I say, remembering how today's competition went. I
should be relieved that we made it, but all I can feel is the sharp edge
of near failure. "Chase, if we're going to win, we've got to get better at
working together. What happened at Limbo can't happen again."

"I thought we did great!" He gazes at me, puzzled.

"We can do better," I say firmly.

"Oh, you're overthinking it. We're fine."

I can tell Chase believes what he's saying. In his world, everything
is just that simple. I'm overthinking, and everything is fine. I want to
push back, but a camera flashes at us, and I remember where we are. I
snap my mouth shut.

Chase fills the silence. "We've got this. I'm good at arm-wrestling, you're good at math. We've got this on lock. It's like destiny is sending us million dollars. We're gonna put your mom in the fanciest hospital on the planet!"

"That's not exactly how hospitals work—"

"We can travel the world! We can go to that hotel where your room is sticking out of the side of a cliff!"

"I think that was a fake AI-generated photo—"

"We could get a waterbed and fill it with Jell-O!"

"Why would we—"

Before any of my concerns can make it into Chase's head, one of the producers claps his hands—Seth, I think.

"And that's a wrap, everyone!" he calls.

Chase pops up to follow the crowd off the beach. It takes me two tries to get my footing in the sand. It's only then that the steady red light of a film camera catches my eye. I swear Leah said they were only taking photos, not filming, but there's no mistaking the eerie glow in the darkness. I shudder. I'm not sure if it's the long day, the stress of being on camera, or the alcohol, but I don't feel right. I feel disoriented and unsettled. And it doesn't help to realize that a live camera has been pointed at us the whole time.

....

I follow the crowd, and soon we're cresting over a sand dune and getting our first glimpse of the villa.

"Welcome to Villa Paradiso!" Leah says.

In beachy tones of off-white and cream, the villa stands four stories tall, with impressive fire pits, floor-to-ceiling windows showing off both the ocean view in front and the flourishing jungle toward the back, and a huge crystal-blue pool stretching out in front of it. It's chic and modern and expensive. It looks like a summer home belonging to an A-list celebrity.

Brittany squeals. "We get to stay *here*?"

"Not bad at all," Noah says approvingly.

"Oh, party's *on* tonight," Jaxon says, sweeping Brittany off her feet and throwing her over his shoulder. She giggles as he carries her straight to the bar by the pool.

"There's no way I can drink any more," I whisper to Chase, but immediately, I realize I'm talking to myself—Chase is already sprinting after Jaxon.

"Shots! Shots! Shots!" he shouts.

Selena follows Chase, joining his chant and pulling Daniel with her. I join them at the bar, where an obliging bartender has set out a rainbow of shots for us.

"Trevor, wait, camera eats first!" says a woman with red hair cascading in waves down her back. She raises a Polaroid camera and is about to snap a photo of the shots. Trevor drapes an arm around her shoulder.

"Good catch, Mikayla," he says, kissing her temple.

Whoever they are, this couple looks like they stepped straight out of a sponsored ad post from Instagram. They're a matched set, with Trevor in his pressed chambray shirt and Mikayla in a flirty denim sundress. Her makeup is dewy, with what I'm guessing are fake freckles dusting her cheeks, and her red hair is pulled back with a set of hair clips that I've seen advertised on TikTok.

Before Mikayla can take her photo, Dominic—still in his fratty muscle tank—blows past her, grabs one of the shots, and downs it.

"Hey, do you mind, dude?" Trevor snaps. "We're making content here."

"You snooze, you lose," Dominic says, passing a shot to Zya.

"Ugh. I can't stand girls who live for the 'gram," Zya says, giving Mikayla a pitying look. "It's *so* pathetic."

I can feel the fury radiating off of Mikayla. A cameraperson elbows past me to capture the moment. I edge away from the unfolding drama and bump into Chase, who hands me a pink shot glass.

We're joined by Selena and Daniel, and soon I find myself toasting with the two of them. I'm still not sure drinking is a good idea, but when Daniel eyes me after he downs his shot, I know what I have to do. I can't back down now.

I keep eye contact with him as I tip the shot into my mouth. The alcohol goes down smooth and tastes like strawberries and summer. I don't break my gaze even after I plant the glass down on the bar with an audible clink and lick the last of the shot from the corner of my lip.

Daniel swallows and looks away.

Ha. I win.

"Hey, anyone up for the hot tub?" Selena asks, her hand in the air.

Daniel slings an arm around her waist. "Sure."

"I'm in," Chase says. "Come on, Alice!"

The four of us head over. A few other couples drift into our orbit as we slide into the hot tub part of the huge pool. The glow of the lights in the water throws ripples of ethereal blue across us. My sore muscles welcome the relief of the hot water, and I sink farther in.

"Okay, I seriously had to get away from those two," Mikayla says, slipping in next to me. She nods over at Dominic and Zya.

"They seem to be looking for trouble," Daniel observes. Dominic and Zya are arguing with the green-haired Mad Max couple now.

"My advice? Don't give those clowns the time of day," Selena says. "In my experience, it's not worth engaging with people like that."

"I know," Mikayla sighs. "But they're seriously pissing me off. I would kill for access to a meditation app right about now."

"Girl, same," Selena says sympathetically.

Mikayla peers at her. "Wait, sorry to derail, but haven't I seen you before on TV?" Mikayla asks. "You're Selena Rivera, right? You totally rocked it in *Hottie Havana*. I still remember that episode when you saved Rayleighanne's life by doing the Heimlich maneuver while blindfolded on a suspension bridge. And weren't you on *Bikini World*, too?"

"No, but I was on *Operation: Bikini*," Selena says with a camera-ready smile and a shrug that's clearly meant to be self-effacing but looks adorable. Cindy and Tara's reality TV crash course had included *Operation: Bikini*, but we'd skipped the season with Selena in it. Too bad, maybe I would have more intel on her if I had.

"Wow. I didn't know we had a professional in the cast," Brittany says. "I bet your brain doesn't turn to cotton fuzz when the cameras are rolling, like me."

"I wish experience in front of a camera gave me and Trev more of a leg up," Mikayla says. "But social content just isn't the same."

"Oh!" Selena snaps her fingers. "I know where I've seen you and Trevor before! You're Trekayla! I love you guys. Hashtag couple goals, hashtag dream boyfriend, hashtag dream girl, right?"

Trevor beams at her. "Hey, thanks for being a fan."

"They've got, like, over a hundred thousand followers on Insta," Selena says to the rest of us. "They've really made it. They're living the dream."

"That's the idea," Trevor says. "And if this show goes well, we can keep on living it."

Mikayla pipes up. "I was nervous about working with Dawn Taylor since all of that drama three years ago, but she's been great so far. Total girlboss. And can you believe Peter Dixon's on this? I didn't even realize this was one of his projects when we applied!"

"What's the deal with him?" I ask. I'd read about Dawn Taylor's somewhat contentious career online during my research, but I didn't really look at Peter Dixon's background since I didn't think we'd be seeing much of him. From the little I've seen so far, he seems all right. He's affable in a way that puts me in mind of how the president would behave in a kindergarten classroom. It's obvious that he and Dawn Taylor don't see eye-to-eye, but given her history, maybe that's not unusual.

"People outside the industry might not know," Mikayla says conspiratorially, "but Peter's the secret sauce behind the success of Get Real Productions. He's never produced a flop before, so this show is guaranteed to blow up—"

"More shots!" Trevor interrupts with a yell. One of the PAs is coming around with a floating tray of shot glasses.

"To winning! And a million dollars!" he cheers, and everyone takes a glass, lifts it, and shoots it. This one tastes more like paint thinner than summer, and I resolve to cut myself off.

Chase pumps his fist. "Hell yeah, they broke out the Grey Goose!"

After that, the party really gets going. The power couple, Ava and Noah, head to bed early. So do the obnoxious camo couple and the goth-meets-steampunk couple who were making out at dinner—though I have a feeling they're going to be doing anything but sleep. Everyone else, though, isn't ready to turn in quite yet. I'd love to go to bed, too, but I know I need to bond with the other contestants.

As usual, Chase is the life of the party, handing out fist bumps and doing showy backflips into the pool. Selena matches him flip for flip.

I keep an eye on them, just to make sure Chase doesn't give himself a concussion, and settle down off to the side, perching on one of the fake rocks that has been artfully sculpted into the pool to simulate a waterfall.

I wonder whose job it was to sculpt a fake rock. Did they study real rocks to get the texture just right? Or did they use a real rock to make a mold, and there's an identical rock somewhere out in the world, living a free-range rock life? Does that make this rock some kind of rock clone?

"You look thoughtful," a voice says, cutting through the dull roar of the party.

I look up to see Daniel offering me a drink.

"I really don't need any more alcohol," I tell him.

He laughs. "I know, Slayer. This is just herbal tea."

I take a suspicious sip, but if Daniel is anything, it's honest. It occurs to me that maybe I misread his look earlier when we were taking shots. Instead of a challenge, maybe it was a look of concern. No, that's ridiculous. Daniel would never be concerned about me.

"Thanks," I say through gritted teeth.

A smirk. "Did that hurt, Slayer?"

"Yes, actually," I say. "As much as it hurts being in a 'secret alliance' with you."

Daniel looks out at the party, where Selena is doing a keg stand while Chase holds her ankles, and chuckles.

"What?" I demand.

"Our partners seem to be getting along a lot better than we do, and we're the ones who've known each other for—well, for far too long."

"That's the problem," I say. "If I had just met you, I probably wouldn't have anything against you."

"Nah," Daniel says, leaning back against the clone rocks with me. "Something tells me that no matter how we met, you'd find a reason to see me as the competition. I've just never been sure *why*. Oh, don't give me that look. You're glaring like I just asked to cheat off your homework."

"I am not glaring," I say, glaring. "And may I remind you, back when we met, you were literally my competition. And you still are. Right now." I yawn. "Besides, you shouldn't be taking advantage of my current state to pump me for information."

"That's not—" Daniel shakes his head. "You're right, Slayer. You need sleep."

"I can just sleep here. Anywhere can be a bed if you're sleepy enough," I murmur, sliding down onto my precious fake rocks.

"Hey, come on. If you pass out here, production will have a field day. Go to bed. "

"Make me!" I say, pointing a wavering finger at him.

"Uh-huh. Where's your boyfriend?"

We squint toward the bar, just in time to see Chase toss Selena into the pool and jump in after her.

"He's too wet to help," I tell Daniel. My eyelids are so heavy, and I can feel myself starting to drift off. I mutter, "Good night. I'm turning into a pumpkin now."

"Alice . . ." Daniel lets out an aggravated sigh. My eyes are already closed when he sweeps me up in his arms.

"No, I don't want to go," I grumble. "Leave me with my rocks!"

He's warm and solid, and the fabric of his linen shirt feels so nice against my cheek. I

should be balking at being this close to Daniel, at letting my sworn nemesis give me a helping hand. But all I feel is calm. It's like I'm floating, and it's so easy to let go and relax into his hold. As Daniel heads up the stairs, my face presses into the crook of his neck, and I catch the scent of sunscreen mingled with his cologne, a fragrance that must have pine or cedar or some other sexy tree essence in it.

Who knew my greatest rival could smell so good? is the last coherent thought I have before finally giving in to sleep.

PRODUCTION NOTES

LEAH'S COUPLES:

~~Blake and Bella~~ - *OUT on Limbo*

Alice and Chase - *Alice is a total lightweight, get her drunk. Chase acts without thinking and gets along with everyone. B.D. says he'll never leave a bro hanging. USE THIS*

Brittany and Jaxon - *Southern charm, rural cowboy themed branding. Been together forever, but on totally different pages*

SETH'S COUPLES:

Tarun and Kendall - *Wannabe food critics. Will they starve without a 5-star restaurant on the island? Give them something under-seasoned to eat?*

Naiah and Sage - *Crystals and tarot, just started dating two weeks ago. Remind them that Mercury is in retrograde*

Mikayla and Trevor - *Insta couple #Trekayla. Trevor looks like he does the heavy lifting in the relationship. Can he carry Mikayla or will her dead weight drag him down? *A.B. *L.K. *B.D.*

Zya and Dominic - *Alpha Male meets Pick Me Girl. Just point him at a target and watch the fireworks go off. Easy to hate, villain edit*

BRYAN'S COUPLES:

Ava and Noah - *Will self-destruct without email access after 24 hours. Super intense *L.G. *S.V.*

Bacon and Firefly - *#VanLife for the aesthetic and because no one will rent to them. Credit score is in the tank. Will do anything for a sponsorship*

Selena and Daniel - *Hottest interracial couple here, good for promo shots. Been together one month. Selena likes to party *S.H. *F.J.*

Chapter Seven

Hell Is an Unscheduled Hangover

When I wake up the next morning, the first thing I notice is the beam of sunlight shining directly in my eyes.

This never happens to me, because I have thick blackout curtains hanging in my bedroom. I block the sun with my hand and squint as the fog of sleep starts to lift and reality floods in.

My blackout curtains have failed me because there are no curtains.

There's no cozy familiar bed or worn gray comforter that Chase steals over the course of the night. There's no cramped apartment, filled with math textbooks and stacks of exams for me to grade. There's no faint lavender scent from the essential-oil diffuser Tara bought for me for my birthday or even the smell of burning bacon because Chase tried to cook it in the toaster—again.

Instead, I'm curled up next to Chase, who's snoring away on a military-style cot in the living room of a tropical villa. A villa that would, in other circumstances, be the perfect summer getaway, with its soaring four-story-high ceilings, elegant marble tiling, and designer furniture. Sunlight streams in through the tall windows, which offer a breathtaking view of the ocean.

But it's hard to really appreciate the view, given the situation all around us. The room is crammed full of suitcases and duffel bags. Sandy clothes are strewn everywhere, and half a dozen people are passed out on cots.

It looks like Ava and Noah had the right idea. I vaguely remember a producer saying that the bedrooms were first come, first serve—and the couples who turned in early must've snagged them. The rest of us have been relegated to living it up dormitory-style in this beachside mosh pit.

The previous day comes rushing back to me. I groan and flop back onto my cot, wishing I could erase my memories of last night. My head pounds, and my whole body feels slow and heavy. I feel like I'm one of those characters in *Naruto* who has to wear training weights that they can't take off until they're fighting a worthy opponent. (Thanks to my eighth graders, I know too much about *Naruto*.)

Brittany is on the cot next to me. When she pops up with a stretch and a yawn, still sporting the same red plaid shirt from yesterday tied at her midriff, she looks like a Folgers coffee commercial come to life.

"Good morning," Brittany says cheerfully. "Where'd they go?" she asks, gesturing at the empty bedroom across from us.

"Ava and Noah," Brittany clarifies. I'm about to say I have no idea where they are when I hear a thudding noise. We look out the window and spot Ava jumping rope while Noah punches a punching bag in a makeshift gym on the patio.

"Guess they never stop rising and grinding," I say, and Brittany laughs.

When Brittany leaves to do her makeup, I'm left alone with my thoughts. Unbidden, my mind dredges up the memory of Daniel, hands in his pockets, talking to me by the pool. I can't believe he's here.

And, oh god, he saw me drunk last night.

My face burns with embarrassment. What was I talking about? Did I say all that stuff about rocks *out loud*?

I rub my eyes. It's fine. Everything is totally, completely fine. I don't care what Daniel thinks about me.

And, besides, this isn't even the first time he's seen me drunk. The first time was junior year of high school, during Quiz Bowl Regional Finals. I'd convinced Cindy to join Quiz Bowl so that we'd have enough people to field a team. I promised her I'd do all the studying, and all she had to do was show up. She did it for me, but she also did it for the free overnight hotel stay paid for by the school.

As luck would have it, the brackets had shaken out such that we were facing off against Daniel's school in the Regional Final—which meant both teams were staying at the same hotel in Sacramento the night before the competition.

That night, I had everything all planned out. I was going to go through my stack of flash cards, then I'd take the vitamin C tablets my mom made me pack every time I traveled, brush my teeth, and go to sleep at 10 p.m. sharp. But Cindy had other plans.

"We're having a party!" she exclaimed, bursting into the room waving a handle of vodka in one hand and a canvas tote of cups and bottles of juice in the other.

I glared at her. "We are definitely *not* having a party! And where'd you get that vodka?"

"Alice, I know this competition is a big deal for you, but we're staying overnight at a hotel with no parents within a hundred-mile radius. And you've already studied your ass off. Like, I'm genuinely worried your ass is not there anymore."

"Hey! Rude."

"Look," Cindy said, putting the vodka and juice down. "You've done everything you can. It's time to let go. It won't hurt to have a little fun."

"Counterpoint," I said. "Studying *is* fun."

Cindy rolled her eyes. "Well, I already told everyone, so it's too late—" A knock sounded, and Cindy gestured at the door. "I think that's them."

"Fine," I grumbled. "Have your party. I'm going to the business center to study."

"Oh, come on, Alice—"

I opened the door, and our entire Quiz Bowl team poured into the room. By the time I finished gathering up all my flash cards, they'd already set up a big punch bowl on the mini fridge and a drinking game involving way too many red plastic cups.

"Don't stay up too late," I called over my shoulder to the team.

But as I power walked down the hallway, head bent and laser-focused on geology facts, I walked straight into someone. No, not just someone—Daniel Cho.

Note cards went flying. As they fluttered down around us, Daniel rubbed the spot on his chest where I'd collided with him.

"What are you doing lurking in our hallway?" I demanded. "Spying on us?"

"Yeah, I'm here to steal your top strategies for conquering flip cup," he said dryly. Now that I wasn't focused on my flash cards, I could see that a few of his Exeter Prep teammates were behind him. "No, Cindy invited us."

"*Cindy invited you?*" I managed to squeak out.

"Hey, guys!" Cindy leaned out of the hotel room and waved. "Over here!"

I turned back to glare daggers at her, and she mouthed *sorry* at me. I shook my head, crouching down to pick up my scattered flash cards.

Daniel knelt down next to me, reaching for a card. I snatched it away.

"Nice try," I snapped, "but these are proprietary."

He held his hands up. "Whoa there, Slayer. I just wanted to help."

"I don't need your help," I said, gathering the rest of the cards. Despite my warning, he'd managed to snag a few cards and handed them to me as I stood up.

"I take it you're not staying?" he asked.

"I need to study," I said. "Unlike *some people*, I plan on winning."

"Too bad," he said. "We could've hung out."

"Why? So you can sabotage me?" I narrowed my eyes at him.

"You got me. I was planning to steal your flash cards and draw butts on all of them." Daniel nodded at me. "Well, have fun studying. I'll see you tomorrow."

As I watched Daniel walk away, the unfairness of it struck me all at once. Why should Daniel Cho get to have a party in *my* room with *my* best friend? And if Daniel thought he didn't need to study tonight, then surely I didn't need to either. I was just as prepared as him. No, I was way more prepared. And I was going to prove it to him.

I returned to the room, where the party was already in full swing.

Daniel raised an eyebrow at me. "You're back."

"I figured I should keep an eye on you."

"I'm flattered."

"Don't be." I grabbed a cup and ladled out some punch.

Daniel followed suit. "To the Regional Quiz Bowl Finals," he said, raising his cup.

I tapped my cup against his and took a swig. It tasted of pineapple and was sweet, but not too sweet, with hints of spice. I didn't hate it, and sipping the drink meant that I didn't have to make small talk or play—and lose—a drinking game.

One of the Exeter Prep boys had brought a Nintendo Switch, and K-pop was playing through iPhone speakers. It was getting a bit warm in the hotel room, with everyone crammed together in there, but otherwise, this was nice. Maybe Cindy was right. I'd studied enough. I deserved this break.

"You throw a good party, Slayer," Daniel said as I downed the rest of the drink.

I made a face at him. "First of all, it's in my room, but it's not my party. Second of all, I never approved that nickname."

"I didn't realize I had to submit it to the committee," he said, smirking. I hated that smirk. It was like he was showing off his dimples on purpose.

"You know, not everyone is as charmed by you as you think," I said, feeling unusually candid.

"What about you?" he asked, pointedly. "You said 'not everyone.' But you didn't say '*I'm* not charmed.'"

"You know what I meant," I said, scowling. I turned to get more punch, nearly tripping over Cindy's sweater on the floor. I refilled my cup and was about to drink when Daniel covered my cup with his hand.

"Hang on, Slayer," he said. "You know this isn't just juice, right?"

"What do you mean?"

"I don't know how strong your friend made this punch, but I think you're more than buzzed already. And hey, if that's what you want, go for it. But I can't imagine you actually want to be hungover during Regional Finals."

"But I didn't put any vodka in it," I said, looking from the near-empty handle to the punch bowl.

"Slayer. The vodka is in the punch," he said gently.

I pressed a hand to my cheek. Oh shit. The hotel room wasn't getting warmer. I was. My cheeks were flushed from the alcohol. Daniel was right.

"I'm going to kill Cindy," I said, dragging my hands through my hair. "I need to—" I shook my head, trying to clear it.

"You need to drink water," he said. "No, wait. I can do better than water. Come on."

So I ended up at the business center after all. I lay on the ground, waiting for the hotel to stop spinning, while Daniel bought coconut water from the vending machine.

"Here," he said, handing me a bottle. "Electrolytes."

I sat up to drink and then flopped back down on the floor.

"Stop being so tall up there," I ordered.

He sat down next to me.

"Still too tall," I grumbled.

With a laugh, he lay down next to me, a respectable distance away. "Does this meet with your approval?" he asked.

I nodded, which made the room swirl even more violently. "Why are you doing this?" I asked. "You didn't have to tell me the punch was spiked. You could've let me drink my way to a humiliating loss tomorrow."

Daniel looked thoughtful. "I could tell you it was the honorable thing to do, but I don't think you'd believe me."

"No, I wouldn't."

"How about this? I'm a senior now, and this is the last time we'll face each other in competition. I'd hate to win under dubious circumstances. I want the record books to reflect that I beat you fair and square with no asterisk next to it explaining that my adversary had been compromised, even if it was by her own doing."

"Wow." I looked over at him. My mind caught on the first part of what he'd said. "The last time, huh?" We'd been locked in battle for the past three years.

He flipped to his side to face me. "What are you going to do without me?"

"What I already do. Win."

The next day, I powered through a mild headache to ace every question I managed to buzz in to. But thanks to the night before, the rest of my team couldn't keep up. The Exeter boys weren't in prime condition themselves, having partied right alongside my team, but it wasn't enough of an advantage.

I had to carry my team, which wasn't new, but I wasn't used to doing it while nursing a hangover. Exeter beat us by one measly point, and Daniel himself answered the question.

"Who was the fabled king who could turn any item into gold?"

Daniel hit the buzzer lightning-fast. "Midas!"

Afterward, Daniel offered me a handshake. "I'll miss you, Slayer."

I hated losing. But I hated letting Daniel have the last word even more. "No, you won't. Because the next time we meet, I'm going to win. Don't rest on your laurels, Daniel *Midas* Cho."

"A little late for giving me a nickname, isn't it?"

"It fits you." It really did. We'd both gone to the party, we'd both had the punch. But the price for me was defeat, while he walked away with the victory. He was the fabled king, with his team rallying behind him, and everything he touched turned to gold. But I'd known from the beginning, from the first day I'd joined the team and even before that, when I realized that it was just me and my mom against the world, that I could only ever count on myself.

I'm busy wallowing in regret when Leah sweeps in, looking fresh as a daisy.

"Rise and shine, lovebirds," she says. I jostle Chase to try to wake him.

"I'm up, I'm up!" he insists, eyes still closed.

"It usually takes him a minute," I tell Leah.

"Well, you don't have a minute. I brought you both breakfast," Leah says, flourishing two cups of bright-pink something. "Hangover smoothies!"

I regard my smoothie skeptically. "What's in it?"

"Some hair of the dog, but not too much," Leah says with a shrug. "We want you relaxed for the cameras, not wasted."

"Is there anything else to drink?" I ask, looking around. I should've nabbed more water last night while I had the chance.

"Not really. Oh, we do have these." Leah digs around in her large carry-all purse and pulls out two aluminum cans.

H2Whoa, the can reads. *Water with personality.*

Good enough. I grab the can, pop open the tab, and take a sip. There's a whisper of lemon with a metallic note, but it's blissfully non-alcoholic. I down the whole thing, then crack open the other one and hold it up to Chase's mouth.

"Drink," I tell him.

He takes a couple of swallows until he's able to sit upright. Then, to my surprise, he snaps his eyes open and makes grabby hands for the smoothie Leah's holding, then sucks that down as well. Finally, he grins. "All right! Let's do this!"

"That's the spirit," Leah says. She pours my smoothie into the pot of a nearby monstera plant. "Today, before the challenge, you both get to visit the wardrobe department. Trust me, you're going to have a *lot* of fun."

The wardrobe department is on the third floor of the villa, and I have to admit that Leah was right—it's significantly more impressive than the bathroom on the boat.

Chase and I are split up the moment we arrive. Leah disappears somewhere while a PA escorts Chase to a different room, and I'm left alone.

While I wait, I take the chance to explore. The room I'm in is lined with clothing racks laden with barely-there bikinis, breezy maxi dresses, floral-print casual wear, and so much more that I can't even begin to take in. Separate racks closer to the floor house footwear—flip-flops and sandals, high-top sneakers and sleek athletic shoes, and a fortune in Louboutin heels. I run my fingertips over the heels on one rack and estimate that I've touched over ten thousand dollars' worth of merchandise in ten seconds.

A blush-pink curtain divides the room, and behind it is a gold-trimmed mirror reflecting still more racks of clothing. When I turn to examine them, I'm met with heart-stoppingly beautiful gowns in an array of jewel tones. My fingers brush up against one of the ball gowns—a sparkling, dark-blue floor-length dress with a plunging neckline and an ombré of gold cascading through the skirt.

"Ah, a Tadashi Shoji," a smooth, deep voice says behind me.

I nearly jump as I yank my hand back. "I'm sorry, I—"

I trail off as I take in the extremely hot man in front of me. He looks like he's just stepped out of one of those cheesy, over-the-top Old Spice commercials, the kind where the camera zooms out and reveals that he's part centaur. His wavy dark hair is long and swept back. His shirt is unbuttoned, revealing a toned, muscular chest, and his jeans are entirely too tight for the fit to be practical.

"You've done nothing to apologize for," the man purrs in an Italian accent. Honestly, that's the only way to describe it. A purr. "In fact, you must try it on."

I'm allergic to cats, my brain supplies, unhelpfully. My brain adds, *but I love them anyway.* I open my mouth, but nothing comes out. He's beautiful to the point that he doesn't even look like he belongs on this plane of existence.

I don't think this moment can get any more surreal, and then, it does.

"Let me help you," he says, and his hand goes to my shoulder, where he begins to slip my tank top strap off.

"Wait," I say, backing up a step and colliding with the rack of expensive dresses. "What are you doing?"

He deftly reaches out a hand to steady me. "Apologies, I'm Matteo, the head of the wardrobe department," he explains. "You were told I'd be here to help you, yes?"

"Oh. Oh!" I relax a very small amount as my alarm is replaced with embarrassment. Of course. That's what's happening. The head of the wardrobe department is helping me . . . wardrobe.

"I will be dressing you for your next challenge," he says. "And so I must ask you to try on that gown. It is meant for you. Go ahead."

Matteo steps around the curtain, leaving me alone. I carefully take the gown off the hanger and lay it down on a deep-green velvet couch in the corner. I hurriedly strip out of my clothes and slip the gown over my head. It slides on so smoothly, it feels like I'm pouring silk over my body.

But when it comes to closing the back, I quickly realize it's impossible. The zipper is unreachable, even if I twist and stretch to try to grab it. I grunt with the effort and nearly fall over.

"Everything all right in there?" Matteo calls.

I'm being stupid. I should ask for help. He's here to help, right? This is his job and he's a professional. Better to ask for the help than to risk ripping this delicate gown.

"I can't quite get the zipper up," I admit.

"I thought that might be the case," Matteo says with a warm chuckle. "I shall assist you."

I hold the gown in place to keep myself covered, and he joins me behind the curtain. He places his hands on my waist and gently turns me around so he can tug the zipper up into place.

"There. A perfect fit. You are as gorgeous as I knew you'd be. You and this gown are a match made in heaven," he says. Is this what wardrobe department heads do? Make ordinary and extremely hungover people feel like Paris Fashion Week icons for a day?

"Thanks" is all I can stammer out.

"You won't get the full effect barefoot," he says, dropping down on one knee and selecting a pair of Louboutins. He gently guides my bare feet into the mega-expensive emerald-studded heels.

I make my way to the mirror and all I see are dollar signs flashing like warning lights. I've never worn this much money before. I'm afraid to move. What if I ruin something and I have to pay for it?

"Now your hair. Let me see." He gently pulls my hair out of the short ponytail I tied it up in when Leah came to get us. He runs his fingers through it, shaking it out. "So much shine and volume. You must wear it down," he says. His fingers brush softly against my neck, and I feel myself blushing.

Matteo is definitely too close to me. I try to remember what makeover shows are like. Are the hosts usually this touchy-feely?

"No man will be able to resist you," Matteo whispers in my ear.

Okay, that sounds a bit unprofessional. And also, as Cindy would point out, aggressively heteronormative.

My brain is kind of glitching, because as I look at myself in the mirror, several irrelevant thoughts spin through my head.

I've never worn something so expensive.

Chase would die if he saw me in this.

Daniel would die if he saw me in this.

I might die if Daniel sees me in this.

Definitely can't limbo in this thing.

Remembering the competition jars me back to reality.

"Um, what exactly am I being styled for? Don't get me wrong, this is gorgeous. But I think I should wear something easier to move in. Is that an option?"

"Today's test won't require much movement," Matteo says vaguely. His hands are still working through my hair.

I frown. "Okay? So what is the challenge?"

"I'm afraid I can't say," he demurs.

I think back through Dante's *Inferno*. First there's Limbo, and they made us limbo. Next is the circle for lust.

There's something about what Matteo said—he used the word *test*, not competition or challenge. So today we're being tested on lust, and a sexy head of wardrobe that I've never seen before is suddenly putting me in a revealing ballgown and showering me with compliments?

"Ah, got it," I say. "Thank you. I think I'm all set."

Matteo blinks at me. "You're ready to go so soon? Weren't you enjoying that moment we were having?" he says, sounding nonplussed.

It might be my imagination, but he seems to have less of an Italian accent now.

"It was very nice," I say brightly. I'm speaking in my phone voice now, suddenly keenly aware that there is definitely a camera focused on me in this dressing room. "You're great at your job. Keep it up."

I hike up my skirts and hurry out of the room, heart racing. As hot as Matteo is, he isn't my type.

I collide face-first with something hard and slippery. I push away and look up, realizing that it's not a what, it's a who.

I've run into Daniel Cho, and my hands are currently resting on his bare, chiseled, oiled-up abs.

"Slayer," he says, tilting his head. "You good?"

"Why are you so slippery?" I blurt out.

"The stylist said she was going for a casual, beach-y vibe today," he says slowly, taking in my Disney Princess look. He clears his throat. "Uh, don't take this the wrong way, but why do you look like you're going on *The Bachelor*?"

"This is what my stylist recommended," I say dryly. Wait, was that a compliment? The girls on *The Bachelor* are all smoking-hot dental hygienists and marketing executives.

Daniel gives me the once-over a second time, opens his mouth, then closes it.

I can't stand this. "What is it?" I demand.

He blinks and shakes his head. "I'm having a hard time envisioning what kind of challenge we're going to face today if you're dressed like *that* and I'm dressed like *this*," he says, gesturing to the both of us, specifically the fact that he's in a pair of bright-red swim trunks and oiled up like a frying pan while I'm dressed for the Oscars.

Aha. So he hadn't figured it out. I revel for a moment in having the upper hand.

"The great Midas hasn't figured out the puzzle yet?" I taunt him, grinning.

"Puzzle? What?" His brow furrows, and I can see the gears turning in his head.

I have to keep myself from letting out a villainous laugh. I love it when he looks stumped. I spent all of high school chasing that look. Chasing the high of one-upping him, and rising to the challenge when he one-upped me.

He pushes his hair back and then snaps his fingers. "It was a seduction test, wasn't it? I thought she was a little too handsy with the oil."

"Bingo." I cross my arms over my chest and lean back oh-so-casually, but the damned Louboutins are an inch higher than my highest heels, and I falter. I feel myself starting to pitch backward, but Daniel catches me, pulling me in close as he steadies me.

I'm so close to him that I can feel the heat coming off of his bare chest and even catch the scent of the oil his stylist used on his abs—coconut. "Seriously, are you okay?"

"I'm fine," I say, and he lets go. "New shoes." I search for something else to say, something to cover for the fact that I nearly face-planted in front of him. My gaze falls on the tattoo on his bicep. "That's new."

"Oh, yeah. Got that in college."

"What does it mean?" I ask. The dashes are too specific to be purely for aesthetic reasons.

Daniel's mouth quirks up at the corners. "You can't figure it out?"

I frown at him. "If you're saying it's a puzzle, then I'm certain I can."

"I look forward to hearing your answer," he says. Oh, it's on.

I lift his arm, getting a proper look at it. He watches me with amusement as I manhandle him.

"Do you need a piece of paper? Shouldn't you be taking notes?"

"I have a very good memory," I snap back, dropping his arm abruptly. His tattoo is made up of four symbols, equally spaced out. Each symbol consists of a unique set of three black horizontal dashes, some with breaks in them, and some without.

"Daniel, can you explain what your tattoos mean?" a familiar voice cuts in.

I whip around to see Leah, Lex, and a cameraperson. How did I not notice them standing just ten feet away, capturing this entire conversation?

Oh, right, shirtless Daniel. That's why.

From the look on Daniel's face, he's caught off guard, too. I drop his arm and put some distance between us.

"What? No, keep going!" Leah looks around, her gaze calculating. "Actually, let's get the two of you into a confession room to really hash this out." Leah grabs the two of us, dragging us away from the "wardrobe department" and down the stairs.

Confession spots have been set up strategically around the beach, in the gardens, and in the house, so one is never far away if a producer wants to grab you and push you into baring your soul.

The closest one to us happens to be a nook set off of a hallway, in

a floral alcove with an oversized, rattan egg chair planted among jac-
arandas bursting with purple flowers. The chair's meant for one and
a half people, but that doesn't stop Leah from maneuvering both of
us into the cozy space. It reminds me of that night so many years ago
during regionals, when the two of us were lying close but not too close.

Leah claps her hands together. "I feel like I've hit the jackpot. It's not
every day that two cast members have history. You know, Alice, you
really come alive when you're talking to Daniel."

"Should I take that as a good thing?" Daniel asks, grinning.

"Absolutely not," I shoot back.

"Love this, keep up this energy." Leah flips to a new page in her
notebook. "From what I understand, the two of you are high school
friends—"

"Rivals," I correct. "We were *not* friends."

"—and you've been reunited on this show after nearly a decade
apart. What do you have to say to each other?"

"I don't have anything to say to him," I tell her. I know I have to stay
in Leah's good graces if I want to do well on this show, but something
about this line of questioning feels slimy. There's a narrative she's trying to craft, and I'm not sure what it is yet.

"I've got all day, darling." Leah jots something down. "Okay, let's
start with this. How do you two know each other? I want to hear the
whole story. And I'm going to be honest with you. If you don't give me
something, we'll make something up."

"Well," Daniel says, glancing at me. "We knew each other in high
school, but we went to different schools."

"Daniel, of course, went to a very fancy, very expensive private
school known as Charles Exeter Preparatory," I add.

"And Alice went to Eastridge High, a local public school. They came
in last place every year during Quiz Bowl—"

"No, we didn't!"

"Until Alice arrived on the scene. Suddenly, Eastridge started sweeping the competitions. By the time Eastridge faced Exeter, I'd already

heard about Alice. Her reputation preceded her."

"And you were scared shitless, right?"

Daniel looks me square in the eye. "I was impressed."

"Damn right," I say, grinning. I turn to face Leah and the camera. "The only thing you need to know about Daniel is that he has a tendency to lose when we go head-to-head."

Daniel snorts. "I'd say we're evenly matched in most things. Except athletics, where Alice comes up a bit short."

I'm about to snap at him for making a jibe about his height advantage—and did he forget the time I outmaneuvered him in the sudden death round of the District Finals with my amazing powers of strategic thinking?—when Leah's walkie-talkie comes to life with a burst of static and a sharp voice that sounds suspiciously like Dawn Taylor.

"Who's got eyes on Daniel and Alice?"

Leah fumbles with her walkie. "I'm here with both of them, Dawn Taylor. What's up?"

She tries to plug in her earpiece, but she isn't quite fast enough, because when Dawn Taylor replies, we can all hear her shouting, clear as day.

"Get them to the tiki bar ASAP! And I mean *now*, or heads are gonna roll."

STORY NOTES FOR EDITORS:
"DAWN TAY'S INFERNO: LOVE IS HELL,"
SEASON 1, EPISODE 2: LUST WEEK (CONT.)

Executive Producer(s): Dawn Taylor, Peter Dixon

DAWN TAYLOR, VOICEOVER: The competition heats up during LUST WEEK!

[B-roll footage: Bacon and Firefly making out at a picnic table at twilight.]

DAWN TAYLOR, VOICEOVER: Who will stay faithful . . .

[Footage: Mikayla and Trevor soulfully gazing into each other's eyes over the rainbow shots behind them.]

DAWN TAYLOR, VOICEOVER: . . . and who will be tempted?

[Footage: Close-up of Stylist Matteo's hands sliding down the hips of a female contestant, but the camera pulls away before her face is revealed.]

DAWN TAYLOR, VOICEOVER: And you'll never guess the twist ending!

[Footage: Alice puts her hands on the chest of an oiled-up Daniel.]

DAWN TAYLOR, VOICEOVER: Just another day in hell on *Dawn Tay's Inferno!*

Chapter Eight

Hell Is a Surprise You Didn't
Mentally Prepare For

The tiki bar is near the pool. It's an intense setup, complete with a wet bar, a built-in display rack, and of course a bunch of tiki torches. You can tell that whoever built this place was serious about having enough liquor to knock out a frat house because there's a door leading to a storage shed that must contain even more alcohol.

But when Leah positions me and Daniel in front of the shed, arranging us just so, I get the feeling that it's not to show us the expensive champagne.

"What?" Leah frowns as she presses her headset into her ear. Now that she's plugged her earpiece into her walkie-talkie, we can't hear anything. "Really? Dawn, I don't know. Are you sure you want to do it like this?" From the way Leah winces, I assume Dawn Taylor isn't happy with being questioned.

Leah grimaces, then sighs and rakes a hand through her curls. She says, "I'm—I'm really sorry about this. Open the door."

I hesitate, and my gaze goes to Daniel. He widens his eyes at me and lifts his shoulders in a tiny shrug. What kind of trap is this? Is there some kind of *Survivor*-style immunity idol challenge waiting for us behind the door? Is a celebrity preparing to prank us? Have the producers trained a viper to bite our faces?

Finally, Daniel steps in front of me, squares his shoulders, and throws the door open.

What's inside is a million times worse than a poisoned viper launched straight at my face. At least maybe I could've dodged that.

No, inside is Chase and Selena, looking like they're two steps away from having full-on sex in the supply room of the tiki bar. Her bikini is askew, his hair is rumpled, and they only look up when they hear me gasp.

"Ohmygod!" Selena wrenches away from Chase. "Shit. Shit. Fuck. Shit."

"Wha—" Chase looks around, bewildered. When he catches sight of me, he has the grace to look stricken. "Alice! I—"

He struggles to sit up, forgetting that Selena is straddling him, and instead lands in a heap on the floor, taking Selena with him in a tangle of limbs.

My eyes flick to Lex, who lowers the boom mic closer to us, just in case our regular microphones somehow aren't sufficient to capture this moment of stunning humiliation. I wouldn't say that I thought Lex and I were *friends*, but I do shoot them a look and Lex just shrugs—they're just doing their job.

I'm suddenly hyperaware of the cameras pointed at me and Daniel. There are multiple, because I guess they need to have footage of us reacting from every possible angle.

It's clear what our roles are right now: the jilted lovers. Half of me wants to scream, or run to the tiki bar, grab a drink, and throw it in Chase's face. But the other half of me knows all too well that this moment didn't happen on its own. Dawn Taylor told Leah to bring us here. They knew what was happening. They didn't stop it. Hell, they may have encouraged it. And now they're trying to get the most out of this moment by filming my reaction.

I should probably give in to what I'm feeling and let them have their big blowup. But part of me is too stubborn to play this part that they've written for me.

I can't stop the tears welling up in my eyes, but I can freeze my hands to my sides, fix my expression, seal my lips together. I won't let them have this.

Chase ducks his head in an "aw, shucks" gesture. Like he ate the slice of cake I was saving or forgot to fill the car up with gas again. Not like he just betrayed my trust, ended a three-year relationship, and threw away our chance at winning the one million dollars that I so desperately need.

My mind goes to very small, very stupid things. We're on a cell phone plan together. Neither of us can afford our current apartment on our own. We only own one frying pan. The logistics of breaking up are drowning me. Did he even stop to think about who would get the couch before he cheated on me? How is he going to cook without a frying pan?

Oh, who am I kidding. He doesn't know how to cook. He barely knows how to bake frozen pizza. For our entire relationship, I've been the one holding his hand. I should've gotten to choose when to let go. Not him. And not like this.

When Chase and I first got together, I wasn't thinking about forever. But as the years went by, I got used to how things were between us. I always knew exactly what he wanted for dinner, or what he felt like watching on TV, or what he liked in bed. And I knew that he'd always text me back, and that he'd remember my birthday and make a huge deal out of it, even if I asked him specifically not to. He was stable, consistent, safe. That's not terribly romantic, I know. But when you're someone who runs on anxiety and caffeine, having one less person to worry about is nice.

Once my mom got sick, when everything was crashing down around me, Chase was the one constant I could hold on to. Cindy and Tara were there for me, too, as were so many other people, but they all had their own lives. I didn't want to burden them too much with how crushing everything felt, how my world was falling to pieces.

Despite the sun beating down on us, I'm starting to go cold all over. I feel like any second now, I might throw up or pass out. The tears in my eyes are starting to spill over, and I turn away from Chase and Selena and this whole nightmare scene—and see Daniel, watching me, not Selena and Chase. He looks—I'm sure this can't be right, but he looks *worried*.

But then his gaze flashes to the cameras, and that look is gone. He turns to Chase and Selena.

"What the hell, guys? We were in a secret alliance," Daniel says, leaning into Lex's boom mic. Then, quietly to me, "You're not breathing, Alice."

He's right. I suck in a deep breath, and I feel a little bit less like I'm going to faint.

Just then, Dawn Taylor materializes at our side, summoned like some kind of sultry drama demon, with Seth right behind her.

"What a turn of events," she says in a tone that borders on sympathy but doesn't quite make it there. "Tell us what you're thinking."

"I'm sorry, Danny," Selena says, reaching across to grip his hand. He lets her touch him, but he doesn't take her hand, doesn't return the clasp. "We were just hanging out, and it was so hot, and this PA said we could cool off in here, and then—" She shakes her head. "I'm sorry."

"I think someone locked us in by accident," Chase says, scratching his head. "It was like seven minutes in heaven, or something."

"Alice, Daniel, this is your chance to get things off your chest," Leah prompts us.

I shake my head. If I talk, I might start crying in earnest, and I can't think of anything that would make this worse.

Dawn Taylor places a hand on my shoulder. "Alice, don't you have anything to say? Your fiancé just broke your heart—"

At that, Selena glares at Chase and hisses, "You were engaged?!"

She glances at my ring finger, and I realize she's seeing the engagement ring for the first time—which makes sense, because I wasn't wearing it yesterday.

Dawn Taylor is still going. "—and that's a pretty big betrayal. How are you going to move forward?"

How do I move forward? I don't. I can't. I feel frozen in this moment.

"Babe, I'm so sorry," Chase says, reaching out to touch my arm. "I didn't think—"

That does it, that destroys me. A sob escapes before I can stop it. I cover my mouth, willing myself to stop. Feeling. Anything.

"Hey, this sucks," Daniel says. Immediately, Dawn Taylor and the crew shift their focus back to him. "Selena and I only just started dating a month ago. She needed someone to go on this show with her, and I thought it'd be fun. We never talked about being exclusive, but obviously, I thought competing on this show together meant we'd at least see this through."

"Danny," Selena says, her own eyes brimming with tears.

"Daniel," he says. "Please call me Daniel."

"Daniel," she repeats. "I should've talked to you first. I really am sorry."

"I know," he says. He turns to Dawn Taylor. "Look, at the end of the day, we're all adults. I wish Selena the best. Yeah, I'm bummed, but I'm not going to go berserk and flip a table here or anything."

"Of course not," Dawn Taylor says, looking like she *definitely* wanted one of us to go berserk and flip a table. "We're all adults here."

"So what happens now?" Daniel asks.

The answer's obvious to me. How can we be in a competition for couples if none of us are couples anymore? I mean, maybe Daniel and Selena can stay together after this. It's not like they experienced a massive betrayal of trust like I did. But I can't stay with Chase. Not after seeing him with someone else.

I look down at my ring finger, at the discounted ring I made Chase exchange my original engagement ring for. Why did I even get engaged to him? Because my mom wanted me to, and she had cancer, and I didn't want to let her down. Did I really want to spend the rest of my life with someone who I couldn't count on, someone I was always cleaning up after? Maybe, in an alternate universe where none of this happened, he could've changed. But in this universe, I didn't care enough to make him change, and he didn't care enough to try.

Dating him had been easy. He'd asked me out, and I'd gone along with it. And I'd loved him. I loved that he was silly and fun and overflowing with this effortless, easygoing charm that made people want to be his friend. And when I was with him, I could convince myself that I was silly and fun and easygoing, too.

But I'm not. I'm anxious and overcompetitive and ambitious in a way that is deeply uncool. I work too hard and try too hard and want more than I've been given—and I don't think Chase has ever felt that way.

I look down at him. He's still on the floor, still tangled up with Selena. I say, "It's over, Chase. We're over."

Dating Chase had been easy. In the end, breaking up was easy too.

Dawn Taylor breaks into a bright, megawatt smile. This is what she wanted. Drama. Scandal. Emotional damage on all sides. Everything you could want in a tight sixty minutes of reality TV programming.

"Selena, Chase, I'm sorry to say that for you and your partners, your journey through hell is over." Dawn Taylor glances around. "Where's Freya? Anton? Someone, bring me a torch. This feels like a torch moment."

Freya sidles her way past the cameraperson. "Not yet. Peter Dixon wants to weigh in. He's in the war room."

Chapter Nine

Hell Is a Surprise Meeting
That Wasn't on Your Calendar

Dawn Taylor and Leah usher us to an upstairs parlor in the villa, which apparently the crew calls "the war room." But this space feels a world away from the one we've been living in. Gone are the tropical centerpieces and cream-colored sofas. We must be where the dirty work gets done, away from the cameras, because instead of opulent displays and high-end furniture, there's a long dining table strewn with half-full cups of coffee and schedules with scribbled notes in the margins, with mismatched chairs clustered around it. At the back of the room, a wall of monitors display footage of what's going on around the island, in real time and scenes from the last couple of days.

This room isn't meant for contestants, and I have a feeling that under typical circumstances, we would never have been allowed in here. Even though I'm out of the show, I can't resist trying to take advantage of the moment. I quickly scan the timelines and notes scattered on the table, channeling my teacher skills to read upside down and decipher the scrawled writing. Most of it is pretty mundane—contact sheets, catering schedules, headshots of the contestants—but I spot one piece of paper with each couple listed below their producer's name. And next to some of the names of the couples are initials. It takes me a second before I realize that the production crew is making bets. By the looks of it, almost half the crew is gambling on Daniel and Selena winning. No one is betting on me and Chase.

Well, I guess they weren't wrong, given where we are now. I don't have to look behind me to know that Chase is giving me sad, puppy-dog looks.

Peter Dixon is seated at the head of the table, lounging in a comfy-looking armchair. He doesn't look up for a moment, clearly absorbed in whatever's on his tablet. But when Dawn Taylor taps her nails on the table, he glances up and breaks into a broad smile. He sweeps the papers I'd been reading out of sight. Damn.

"Here we are, Pete. What do you want?" Dawn Taylor gives him an icy stare like she wants to either exile or murder him. Instead of taking a chair, she perches on a nearby filing cabinet, giving her the height advantage.

Peter Dixon chuckles. "Just give it a minute, DT."

I stay standing, arms folded, and Daniel falls in beside me. Chase sinks down onto a cardboard box, which sags under his weight. Selena finds a chic white stool and hops up onto it.

Minutes later, Seth storms into the room. Unlike Leah, whose outfits scream harried corporate mother of two, Seth wears an odd mix of high-end and low-key. He's sporting an oversized tie-dyed tee and Valentino jeans, paired with garishly colorful sandals, as if he got dressed inside a secondhand store in the dark. He doesn't look happy to be pulled into this meeting on short notice. Bryan is right behind him, looking far more serious than the last time we saw him.

"What did you do to my couple?" Seth demands, rushing up to Leah.

Leah rolls her eyes. "Cool it, Seth. How do I know that all of this isn't *your* fault? I saw you lurking around earlier."

"Hey now," Peter Dixon interrupts. Leah and Seth listen up. "Let's take the temperature down, guys. We have a really interesting opportunity here."

"And what makes you say that?" Dawn Taylor asks sweetly. She's smiling now, in a way that sends a chill down my spine.

"You have two couples here about to leave *Dawn Tay's Inferno*," Peter Dixon says, nodding at the four of us. "And the production assistants just let me know that both Naiah and Sage failed their Lust Challenge."

"Who?" I ask before I can stop myself. I tried to memorize everyone's faces and names yesterday, but some of them just didn't stick.

"They're the ones with the flower crowns. We met them last night while we were doing body shots," Chase says. Then he furrows his brow. "Oh, no, that was me and Selena."

"Yes, lovely people," Peter Dixon says. "Very insightful about auras. But not terribly committed to each other."

"So what?" Dawn Taylor asks. "We send all three couples home. It's perfect, actually. A scandal like this will be good for the show."

"DT, you know I value your instincts, and normally, you'd be right." Peter Dixon steeples his hands. "But I just got word from the FlixCast folks. Our Nielsen ratings for the season premiere were record-breaking. The execs ordered nine episodes. What happens if we cut three couples at once?"

"The math doesn't add up," I say. "The challenges are designed for a specific number of players, and the filming schedule requires an elimination for each circle of hell. If you get rid of us, you'll have to rework the challenges, and you'll be forced to fill time, instead of giving the viewers what they want."

"I'll also flag that if Selena and Daniel get eliminated now, we'll lose the Latino audience and a good chunk of the Asian audience," Bryan chimes in.

Great, so glad that's their reasoning. I catch Daniel grimacing at this. Selena also looks a little put off by what Bryan just said.

"So the math teacher can do math," Dawn Taylor says, her tone still ice-cold. "But the rules are the rules. This is a show for couples, and we're down three couples. That's reality TV, Peter."

"Ah, but you forget. We make the rules," Bryan says. "We just need the contestants to be coupled up."

"What," Dawn Taylor scoffs. "Are these two," she indicates me and Daniel, "going to get back together with their backstabbing, cheating partners who couldn't resist getting nasty next to a rack of Smirnoff Ice?"

"Hey now," Daniel cuts in. "I don't think we'll be getting back together, but I'd appreciate it if you didn't talk about Selena that way."

"And who says chivalry is dead?" Dawn Taylor says, throwing up her arms.

Bryan picks up his tablet again. "Leah, you noted that Alice and Daniel have chemistry."

I shoot a baffled look at Leah, who is carefully avoiding my gaze. I knew it. She was *up* to something. "That's correct," she says. "They met in high school. They have enough history to fill a textbook."

"And of course, Chase and Selena seem to have some chemistry too," Peter Dixon says.

"Yeah, they were fucking." Dawn Taylor narrows her eyes at him. I can almost see the lightning crackle between them. "Are you proposing that we swap the couples? And keep them in?"

"Got it in one," Peter Dixon snaps his fingers. He points at me and Daniel. "Ever wanted to be in a showmance?"

"What? No," Daniel says, while at the same time, I say vehemently, "Absolutely not."

"But Selena and Chase gave in to lust. They failed the test as couples," Dawn Taylor says.

"I respect the hell out of you, DT," Peter says. "But I'm going to have to disagree with you here. Every single one of these contestants passed the test with their stylist. What happened with Chase and Selena? That was the beginning of a beautiful new romance."

"But—"

Peter Dixon leans forward on his elbows, making eye contact with Dawn Taylor. "This is what we need to do to make this show a success. Don't you want *your show* to be a success?"

Dawn Taylor casts a look of venomous resentment at Chase and

Selena.

"Fine," Dawn Taylor says finally. "But you're forgetting something. The couples themselves have to agree to it."

"I'm in," Selena says right away, and leaps down from her stool to join Chase. She directs an apologetic look my way. "I'm sorry, Alice, but I need this show."

I nod. I'm pissed, but I can't exactly blame her when Chase was the one who betrayed me.

"Let me get this straight," Daniel says. "The only way for me and Alice to stay in the game is to compete as a couple?"

"That's the idea," Peter Dixon says.

"We'd have to really sell it," Leah says. She's already jotting notes in that notebook of hers. "We could say that a spark reignited between you and Alice when the two of you met again for the first time in years. Fate brought you together on the show."

What's being proposed is starting to sink in. The producers are all looking at me like it's the most obvious solution in the world, but I can't do this. I can't fake a relationship with my old rival. I know when I've lost, and the only thing for me to do now is make a graceful exit. I'm going to pack my bags and go home, newly single and nothing to show for it.

I glance at Daniel, and our eyes meet. God, I hate losing.

I find myself saying, "I need to make a phone call."

"Not allowed," Dawn Taylor says immediately.

Peter Dixon says, "Hey now. Didn't you read the contestant files? The kid's mom is having a hard time. You probably wanna call her, right?"

I nod.

Peter Dixon gives me a sympathetic look and offers me his phone. "Go ahead. Take your time."

I know my mom's number by heart—it's the only one I've ever bothered to memorize. I punch it in and retreat to the back of the room.

"Hello?" My mother's voice hits me like a sip of hot cocoa on a cold night.

"Ma," I breathe, slipping into Chinese for a moment. "How are you?"

"Alice! Do you know what time it is? You should be focused on your conference!"

Right. I just called my mom at one in the morning her time, and three in the morning in the time zone of my fictional teachers' conference. Oops.

"The conference hasn't been so great, Mom," I say. My voice catches in a sob. I want desperately to give her a kernel of the truth. "I'm not sure whether or not I should stay."

"Aiyah. Don't give up. I raised you to be stronger than that," she scolds, but her tone is soft and full of kindness. It's her version of a rousing pep talk.

"Are you doing okay without me?" I ask, biting my thumbnail.

"Yes. I'm doing great. Auntie Yee has been taking me to mahjong every day. I tell her, it's too much! But she needs a friend, you know, so I go with her."

Of course, in my mom's mind, she's the one doing Auntie Yee a favor, not the other way around.

"Have you been eating enough?" I ask.

"Tsk, I always eat enough. You need to go to sleep. Gargle with salt water if you're not feeling well, okay? I'll talk to you when you get back. I love you," my mom says. She hangs up before I can say anything else, and I'm left clutching the phone in my hand and blinking back tears.

Memories flash through my mind—my mom's face, lined and careworn. The post-op surgery room with all those monitors hooked up to her. The thick gray haze of smoke covering her apartment. The bookmarked cookbooks I have stacked next to the rice cooker. The three-hundred-dollar olive oil.

I went on this show, something I never would have ever done in a million years, for my mom. She's the one who was always there to wipe away my tears and hold me after a nightmare. Who worked over-time so I could buy a name-brand pair of UGGs when everyone else at school had them. Who told me over and over again that it wasn't my fault that my father left us, that my only job was to study hard and be happy.

Selena isn't the only one who needs this show. People—usually rich people—always say that money can't buy happiness, and money isn't everything. But when you've been swimming against the tide for as long as I have, just trying to stay afloat in an ocean of student debt and medical bills and rent and utilities, it sure feels like everything. And I want better for my mom. Hell, I want better for me.

I'm not ready to give up. I'm all in, no matter what it takes. I'll be damned if my cheating ex-boyfriend is going to crush my dreams of a better future.

"You're seriously asking us to fake a relationship," Daniel is saying to Leah when I rejoin everyone. "That's ridiculous. Right, Alice?"

Of course he would think it's ridiculous. It *is* ridiculous. The two of us are more likely to kill each other than to kiss. But I can't do this without him.

"I'll do it," I say, handing the phone back to Peter Dixon. I turn to Daniel, focus all my attention on him. "I want to keep competing."

"But why—" He shakes his head. "I'm lost, Slayer."

"I want to win. I can't stand doing things halfway." I'm not about to tell him my tragic backstory, but I don't need to. He already knows that I never give up without a fight. And I know that he can't resist ris-ing to a challenge, especially when it comes from me. I am his greatest rival, after all. I shift my weight, fold my arms, and plaster on my best shit-eating grin. "So are we going to do this or what? Unless you think you can't handle me."

"Dream on, Slayer." Daniel laughs. "I can handle you."

"So you're in," I say. I meet his gaze, and for one electric moment, it's just the two of us here in this room. He takes a deep breath and nods.

"I'm in," Daniel confirms.

I stick out my hand, and when he shakes it, elation floods through me. I'm back in the game. "You'd better keep up with me."

"You know I always have," Daniel says, cocking an eyebrow.

"Secret alliance is back, baby!" Chase shouts, pumping his fist in the air.

Selena gently takes his arm and lowers it. "Too soon. Read the room."

Seeing the two of them together, I wonder if Selena and Chase might actually, in the long run, be a good match. But what Chase did still hurts, and just thinking about it makes my stomach turn. Three years down the drain. Maybe it was time for our relationship to end, but what stupid way for it to happen.

The sound of applause jolts me out of my thoughts. Dawn Taylor is slow-clapping. "Well, isn't this adorable? I suppose I should thank the four of you for spicing this show up."

"Always happy to help," Daniel says dryly, but Dawn Taylor just nods as though he really means it.

"Seems to me like you've got the drama you wanted," Peter Dixon says. "Will you do the honors?"

"Of course," Dawn Taylor says. She brushes a perfectly curled tendril of hair behind her ear. "I'll give Naiah and Sage their send-off."

She stalks out of the room, her heels clicking on the tile. She pauses at the doorway. "Congratulations, all of you. Welcome back to hell."

STORY NOTES FOR EDITORS:
"DAWN TAY'S INFERNO: LOVE IS HELL,"
SEASON 1, EPISODE 2: LUST WEEK (CONT.)

DAWN TAYLOR: . . . I'm afraid that today, the couple that fell victim to Lust was Naiah and Sage.

> *[Footage: Naiah flirts with Stylist Matteo,*
> *making out with him in the dressing room.]*

> *[Footage: Sage is found with Stylist Emma, his pants down,*
> *starting to get hot and heavy before the footage blurs out.]*

> *[Dawn Taylor wearing a sexy devil costume standing*
> *in front of all the contestants gathered on the beach.]*

DAWN TAYLOR: Naiah and Sage, say your goodbyes. Your journey through hell ends here.

> *[Naiah, crying, runs off screen without speaking. Three vape pens*
> *and a blueberry-flavored condom packet fall out of Sage's pockets*
> *as he chases after her.]*

DAWN TAYLOR: Naiah and Sage weren't the only couple put to the test.

> *[Footage: Daniel opens the door to find Chase and Selena together.]*

DANIEL CHO: What the hell, guys? We were in a secret alliance.

SELENA RIVERA: I'm sorry, Danny.

CHASE DE LANCEY: It was like seven minutes in heaven.

[B-roll footage: Chase and Selena looking deep into each other's eyes, absorbed in conversation on the couch. Trevor and Mikayla egging Chase on as he does a body shot off Selena's stomach.]

[Pull-back shot of Dawn Taylor addressing the contestants inside Villa Paradiso.]

DAWN TAYLOR: Today, two couples broke up, and two new couples came together. A hot and heavy passion has burst into flame between Chase and Selena—

[Surveillance footage: Two figures moving together in the dark storage shed. Audio of moaning and heavy breathing amplified 4x.]

DAWN TAYLOR: —and a spark has reignited between Alice and Daniel, who reconnected on this island after eight years apart.

[Footage: Extreme close-up of Alice and Daniel in the hot tub together.]

DAWN TAYLOR: Welcome to Dawn Tay's Inferno, baby. You never know what might happen in the fires of hell. On this island, your love will test you, push you, and even change you.

[Gasps from the crowd, close-up shots of dropped jaws.]

DAWN TAYLOR: These new lovers made their case to me, and I've decided to give them a chance to prove their love to the world—and to each other.

[Interview footage: Ava and Noah (Co-CEOs).]

AVA DAWSON: To be perfectly frank, this is unfair. They failed to stay together as a couple. They should be out.

[Interview footage: Brittany and Jaxon (DTFarm).]

BRITTANY LEGARE: Oh, I'm not worried. I mean, these new couples *just* got together.

JAXON HILL: Yeah, we've been together for seven years. They won't be able to keep up with us. So let 'em stay. They won't last long.

[Footage: Brittany and Jaxon kiss and high-five each other over their heads without looking.]

[Interview footage: Selena and Chase (Naughty Hotties)]

SELENA RIVERA: I hate how things went down, but I talked to Daniel. We're all good. And I'm so excited to embark on this adventure with Chase.

CHASE DE LANCEY: Babe, I feel like a million bucks when I'm with you.

[Interview footage: Alice and Daniel (The Asians)]

DANIEL CHO: This isn't exactly what we expected, but life has a weird way of working out. I've always admired Alice, ever since high school. And the tension between us when we reconnected on the beach—well, you've seen it. It feels like fate, getting this second chance at a romance together.

ALICE CHEN: Yeah. A hundred percent.

DANIEL CHO: Sure, everything that went down today was a little crazy, but I'm choosing to see it as a blessing in disguise. *Dawn Tay's Inferno* brought us together, and I'm not going to take that for granted.

ALICE CHEN: Yep. Daniel and I are a couple now. We're together. Romantically. And physically.

Chapter Ten
Hell Is Breaking Up on Reality TV

The screen freezes on my face, and Leah taps on it with her fountain pen.

The last couple hours have been a whirlwind of announcing the partner swap, doing interviews, and now having Leah drag me up to the third floor to review my subpar performance. We're in the Video Village, where an army of PAs and editors huddle over a dizzying array of screens. Elaborate computer setups cover the rows of desks pushed together, lit overhead by sterile fluorescent lights.

The cramped room is packed with exhausted-looking people, and the recycling bin by the door is overflowing with empty cans of Red Bull. Lex and a few other members of the crew are there, presumably uploading audio or new raw footage. Someone is curled up on the floor in the back corner. "THE CRYING CORNER" has been written in Sharpie on a takeout menu taped to the wall.

I'm starting to feel like Leah brought me here to scare me into submission, and it's working.

"So, Alice, do you see the problem here?" she asks, tapping the screen again.

This must be what my students feel like when I ask them to stay after class to talk about their grades. It's not that I don't want to be a team player, but I'm still reeling from *my fiancé cheating on me five hours before*. Leah rewinds the footage back to a moment when Daniel is looking at me with an affectionate smile, his eyes crinkling at the corners. Meanwhile, I'm staring blankly ahead like one of the fish on ice at Pacific Market.

"You might not have heard of her, but our lead editor over there," Leah points at a slight woman massaging two fingers into her temple like she has a migraine from hell, "is Shawna Vasquez, one of the best in the biz. Shawna has all of our PAs combing through every second of footage that you're in. They're working around the clock to edit together something usable, and you are making it very hard for them."

Shawna certainly seems to be proving Leah's point. Her curly dark hair has been tied into a haphazard braid, and she wears a stormy expression on her face as she gives instructions to three PAs at once. Her stern scowl is at odds with the "be happy" written in retro psychedelic text on her tee.

I do a quick head count. There are about ten PAs stuffed in here, and sure enough, they're all watching some version of me on their screens. Aside from the crew member curled up in the corner, only one other person isn't eyeballing my face on a screen: the PA with slicked-back blond hair and sunglasses. He's decked out in a white polo that's open at the collar, salmon shorts, and a gold watch, and he's lounging on a pool chair on the balcony. Everyone else may be hard at work, but he looks like a finance bro on vacation. He guffaws at something playing on his phone.

Shawna notices, and with a very impressive middle-school-teacher voice, she yells, "Anton, get back to it, or I'm gonna throw your phone off that balcony!"

Anton flips her off but reaches under his pool chair to drag out a laptop.

"I'll do better," I promise Leah. "But can we address why Daniel and I are labeled the 'The Asians'?"

"Forget about that. It's a placeholder," Leah says. "Right, Freya?"

Freya looks up from her desk to our right. "Uh, no, I'm pretty sure that cut went out this morning—"

"Great. Thanks, Freya," Leah says, her voice dripping with sarcasm. Her fingers curl like she wants to strangle someone. "We'll update it in the next episode. How do you feel about 'Asian Sensation'?"

"Not a fan," I say.

"We'll workshop it," Leah says decisively. She lowers her voice. "Look, I'm not supposed to tell you this, but when Peter Dixon said our ratings were through the roof, he wasn't just stroking his own ego. *Dawn Tay's Inferno* is going to be huge. Way bigger than anyone expected. The network execs are promising to double our budget, and they're already talking about greenlighting season two. But if you screw this up, everything can go away just like that." She snaps her fingers. "We need you to get it together and make good television—"

"Leah, you're scaring her," a voice interrupts. It's Lex, leaning back in their chair to face us. "Alice, the reason your producer is so stressed—"

"Excuse you, I am *not* stressed, I am *thriving*—"

"Yeah, and my psych prescribes me Prozac for fun," Lex shoots back. "Look, this show has the production schedule from hell. Dixon's pitch for *Dawn Tay's Inferno* was that we'd have this cutting-edge AI editing software that lets us release episodes quickly with a skeleton crew."

"Absolutely deranged," Leah mutters.

"Spoiler alert, the software doesn't work. We have some bullshit program that splices together clips into unusable content. It's all a scam. So instead, the higher-ups are pushing our editors and production assistants to deliver episodes on par with much bigger productions like *Nepo House* and *Babe Getaway*, and it's gone about how you'd expect. We're crunched for time here, and Dawn Taylor wants results."

"And we're going to deliver them," Leah says. "Alice. I love you. If I could just stick my hand down your throat and make you say all the right things like an adorable little puppet, I would. I don't know if you realize this, but you've made a lot of enemies just by staying on the show. If the other contestants or the viewers at home can tell that you and Daniel aren't a real couple, you'll get booted from the show—and not even Peter Dixon can save you then."

"Understood," I say. Lex has gone back to their work, but I can tell they're still listening in on my conversation with Leah. "I'll work harder at it."

"It's not about working harder," Leah says. "It's about your chemistry with Daniel. This story we're trying to sell, that you and Daniel just happened to make a true love connection within minutes of Chase and Selena getting hot and heavy, it's ridiculous. It shouldn't work. But I've seen you with Daniel. When the two of you are going at it, it's like you can't decide if you want to jump his bones or, I don't know, challenge him to recite the periodic table."

"I don't want to jump his bones," I say automatically. But I still remember the feeling of his abs beneath my hands, the warmth radiating from him, and that—that's not helping.

"Leave room for Jesus, I don't care," Leah says. "But if you want to stay on the show, you have to at least look, act, and smell like a couple."

I think of the sapphic werewolf romance Cindy convinced me to buddy read with her last year, and how the werewolf marked her human with her scent. I shake my head—that's not what Leah is suggesting, and Daniel is not a werewolf. Get it together, Alice.

"—so this is me, warning you, as your producer. Figure out how to sell your chemistry and relationship with Daniel, or you're out."

"I will. I'll do it even if it kills me."

And it might. Even the thought of acting on some of the attraction between us—my mind helpfully rewinds back to his slicked-up abs—is enough to give me heart palpitations. But I've come this far, and I'm not leaving the island if I can help it. Plus, I can see how hard the editors and PAs in the Video Village are working. I don't want to make their lives any harder.

Leah lets out a bitter laugh. "I know I'm being on tough on you, but I'm in your corner. And hey, you know how Blake and Bella were in one of the private honeymoon suites? I snagged it for you and Daniel, so the two of you can work on your connection without any cameras around. You're welcome, by the way."

"Yes. Thank you. Amazing. Great news," I say. My mind is a jumble, trying to reconcile the contradictory feelings of never wanting to see Daniel's face again and being desperately curious about what he'll be like when we're alone.

Leah puts her hands on my shoulders, spinning me toward the door. "Daniel should be headed there already. Why don't you go meet him?"

....

My stomach twists into knots as I make my way toward the honeymoon suite. I keep playing with my ring finger. There's a faint tan line where I used to wear my engagement ring from Chase. I keep thinking that I've forgotten it or lost it, only to remember that I stashed it away in my luggage the moment I got back to the villa after everything went down.

I'm mentally drafting a Facebook Marketplace listing for all of the things I used to share with Chase that I want to sell off now—massage chair won in an office raffle, like new, fifteen knot-busting settings—when I remember that I have bigger fish to fry. I have to sell a whirlwind, fairy-tale romance with my high school nemesis to millions of viewers at home, plus my fellow competitors.

"We need to work on our chemistry," I tell Daniel as soon as I step into the suite.

"Hello to you, too," Daniel says, raising an eyebrow at me.

I glare at him. "Hello, *darling*," I say, "we need to work on our fake chemistry for our fake relationship so we can continue to stay on this reality show long enough to destroy the competition—which, by the way, includes our exes—and win a million dollars."

"Sounds like a tall order." He looks at me with an expression that I've never seen before. There isn't even a hint of a smirk, and his gaze holds mine for too long.

"What are you doing?" I ask, unsettled.

"I'm working on our chemistry, *dear*, just like you wanted," he says.

I groan. "This is the worst kind of group project."

The second those words leave my mouth, my brain kicks into overdrive. Of course, this is what I've been missing. Ever since I caught Chase in the shed, I've been playing defense, simply reacting to what's happening around me, and it's made for some pretty bad interview footage.

If I want to make this work, I have to approach it the way I approach every important project in my life—by crafting a highly detailed plan to play up our strengths and address our weaknesses. This really is a group project, one that just so happens to involve dating Daniel. We can overcome the obstacles of faking a relationship—a lack of shared background knowledge, our nonexistent chemistry, the fact that this is all for show—if we just make a plan of attack and stick to it.

"You okay there, Slayer? You look like that time during Mock Trial when you came up with an application of the plain view doctrine at the last minute."

"I have an idea for how we can improve our chemistry." I pause to consider fully what he's said. "And how do you know I came up with those arguments at the last minute?"

"You've got a tell." He taps the space above his eyebrows. "You wrinkle your forehead when you're thinking really hard. It's cute."

I snort.

"Anyway, I'm all ears," he says. "Please tell me this brilliant idea of yours."

I say, "What we need is a point-by-point plan to tackle the key facets of a relationship. If we cover all our bases, we'll be unbeatable."

Daniel laughs.

"You disagree?"

"It's not that. It's just a very Alice idea," he says. "That's a compliment," he adds when I make a face at him. "It makes a sense to treat this like a school project. If there's one thing I know we can do, it's nail an assignment."

"Absolutely," I say, pleased. He gets it.

"Now how are we doing this? Should we make a syllabus?" He raises an eyebrow, and I'm not sure if this is a joke or not, but I take it seriously.

"In an ideal world, yes," I say, and he laughs. "But I don't think we have time for that. We'll have to settle for a big-picture plan of attack. I wish I had my laptop or my phone or even paper and a pen. Are we honestly just supposed to wait around doing nothing until they need us for filming?"

"Yeah, Selena said it would be like this," Daniel says. "They want drama, and one good way of manufacturing drama is to make us desperate for entertainment. Either that, or they assumed that we would find *other ways* to keep ourselves occupied."

I know exactly what he means. On the surface, the island is the perfect setting for romance, with its pristine beach, deep-blue ocean, and summer villa. But given that Chase and I have been sleeping on cots alongside the other contestants, I haven't found the setting all that much of a turn-on. I guess Chase felt differently, though, considering he managed to hook up with someone else in a tiki bar shed. My heart twinges at the memory, but the pain is duller than I expected. Things have just been happening so fast that I haven't really had time to process.

"Well, *that's* not happening," I snort. "Whatever. I don't need paper. It'll be easy to remember. We've got three things we need to work on—intimacy, information, and entertainment.

I tick off the items on my fingers. "First, there's intimacy. We must convincingly hold hands, kiss, and act like we can't keep our hands off each other. Then there's information. We need to know the things that people in a relationship typically know about each other. What we like, dislike, what we studied in school, our goals in life, et cetera. Finally, there's entertainment. We've got to satisfy our audience and give them what they want. That means coming up with the perfect soundbites and providing romantic moments that will play well on screen. My vote is that we start out with information. Make sure we have everything we need to know about each other."

"I think we should start with intimacy," he counters. "People know we're a new couple, so we can get away with not having a dedicated mental file on each other. And it'll be easier to pull off soundbites and act like a real couple if you can touch me without acting like you want to challenge me to a duel."

"I don't act like that," I grumble.

"Remember that time we got stuck eating lunch together at the science fair, and you challenged me to an arm-wrestling match?"

"It was a strategic maneuver." I'd seen him charming the judges with his presentation on hydroponics that morning, and all I'd wanted to do was wipe that smug grin off his face. I try not to examine why that manifested in a demand to arm-wrestle. "Anyway, what about you? Can *you* even stand to touch *me*?"

Daniel doesn't answer. Instead, he steps into my space, close enough that I catch the scent of coconut from his sunblock. He lifts his hand, and I find myself tracking the movement, waiting to see what he'll do next. He brushes my cheek with the lightest of touches, and my pulse immediately ratchets up. I step back, my foot bumping into the bed behind us.

He smirks. "You were saying?"

Well, I walked right into that one. Point to Daniel.

"Okay, fine. We'll work on intimacy first," I concede.

"So how do you propose we do that?"

"You know the idea that small, harmless doses of poisons like iocaine powder can build up a tolerance to the lethal amounts?"

"Overlooking the fact that referencing the fictional science in *The Princess Bride* undermines your point, yes, I'm familiar with the idea. So like this?" He holds out his hand to me, his palm up.

I look at the lines and calluses that make up the landscape of his hand, the slight bend of his fingers.

"Well?" he asks.

Oh, right. I reach out my hand and tap my fingertips against his.

The feeling is electric, like when you're jumping on a trampoline and the static builds up, and the second you touch something, you get a tiny jolt. But I think it's just me. Daniel doesn't react—if anything, he's stone still. His skin is warm and rougher than I expected, and there's a small scar by his thumb. It's faded, like an old scar, but clearly deep enough to have left a mark.

I slide my fingers down his until my hand is fully resting on his. We're standing so close together that I can hear him breathe and see every flicker of his dark-brown eyes. I work to keep my own breathing regular as my heart thuds loudly in my chest.

"I think we've mastered handholding," I say lightly.

"There are probably some *other* things we should practice too," Daniel says. "If you think you can handle it."

"I can handle anything you throw at me," I say immediately.

He moves closer, taking my other hand in his, and I realize what's happening. We're playing a game of chicken, and whoever backs down loses.

I refuse to lose.

I free one of my hands to run my fingers through his hair, brushing it back. It isn't until I'm doing it that I realize I've always wanted to try this. His hair is so soft, even with the hint of product in it, and I resist the urge to muss it all up like he's my pet dog. I make eye contact with him, and is it my imagination, or does he look like he's trying a little *too* hard not to react?

In retaliation, he brings his thumb up and brushes it against my lips, and it takes everything I have in me not to shiver at his touch. Typical Daniel—of course he's good at this. But I can be, too.

I lean in just a little bit. Daniel's other hand skims down my shoulder, landing on my waist and pulling me in, so that we're flush against each other. My breath hitches, but I get it under control and place my hand on his chest. He dips his head, his lips coming so close to mine that I can feel his breath on my face.

In for a dime, in for a whole fucking dollar.

I close that last fraction of an inch between us to press our lips together. His mouth is warm and soft against mine, and it's fine. Nice, even. *I could do this in front of a camera*, I think, and I'm congratulating myself right up until Daniel tilts his head, parting his lips so that his tongue nudges mine open. A thrill races up my spine as I sink into the delicious heat of it, and I can't help letting out a small moan, my arms wrapping more firmly around him. There's no space between us now, and his hand slides along my back, sending another surge of heat through me.

I could do this forever, I think dizzily as the kiss deepens. My grip tightens in his hair, and I feel a shudder run through him. *I want*—but I don't let myself finish that thought. I break away. Daniel doesn't like me, and I don't like him. This is all pretend, and even if it feels good— too good—I can't get carried away. Eyes on the prize, I remind myself.

"I win," I say in the thick silence building between us.

"You win? You backed off first," he says, and does he sound breathless?

"But I initiated the kiss!"

"Oh, come on. That's not how this works. The first person to swerve loses."

"What happens if no one swerves?"

Daniel chuckles. "I think in this case, both of us win." He cuts a look at me, raising an eyebrow. "If you know what I mean."

"Very funny," I say, rolling my eyes. I try not to think about what exactly that would be like with Daniel. The way his body would feel moving against mine. "Anyway, I think we've made excellent progress. Kissing you was entirely bearable."

"Gee, thanks." Daniel folds his arms and looks at me, his eyes sharp. I recognize that expression. It's the same one he wore when he was about to point out an inconsistency in my argument during Speech and Debate. "Alice, if we're going to do this, I have to know something. Why do you want to stay in the game so badly? You said you don't back down from a challenge, but this isn't Quiz Bowl. It's a *reality dating show*. I don't even know why you're here at all. This isn't exactly your scene."

"Oh, and it's yours?"

"No, but it's Selena's. She asked me to come on the show with her, and I thought it'd be fun. But I'm a go-with-the-flow kind of guy. You're not."

"Maybe I've changed," I say.

"Not this much," Daniel says. "If you're here, there's a very good reason for it. You don't do things on a whim. And now we're faking a relationship. I need to know why you're willing to go this far to stay on the show."

He's right. I live for my routines and my to-do lists. I'm a math teacher at an underfunded public school. I call my mom every week, and crocheting at home while watching *Bridgerton* is my idea of a perfect Friday night. I'm not the type of person who drops everything to go on a reality dating show for fun.

But I can't tell Daniel about my mother's illness. After all:

1. This is my Achilles' heel. My mother has always been my weak spot, and I can't stand being vulnerable. It'd be like pointing out exactly where to find the gap in my armor.

2. I've barely talked to anyone about my mother's diagnosis. Chase knows that she's dealing with some type of cancer and Cindy knows she's dealing with a "health problem," but I haven't even told either of them that it's *stage 4 metastatic breast cancer*.

3. I'm pretty sure if I start to talk about this with anyone, much less Daniel Cho, I'll start crying. And the last thing I need right now is for him to see me in tears.

I know that I won't be able to get away with a lie. I decide on a partial truth.

"I need the money," I say finally. "I'm drowning in student loans."

Daniel drops onto the floor. He looks up at me, his gaze searching my face for a moment. He nods. "Okay."

"It's a long shot, but believe me when I say the money would be life-changing for me. So, please, we've got to be in this to win."

Daniel gives me a cocky half smile. "Alice, you should know by now that I always play to win."

"Yeah, yeah." I join him on the floor, bumping my shoulder against his. "And why are you still here? Your ex has someone else to compete with."

Daniel shrugs. "I still have a week of PTO left. And you challenged me. I don't back down from a challenge, especially when it's from you."

"Uh-huh. Now if only I could trust my sworn enemy to have my back," I muse, eyeing him.

"I don't recall becoming sworn enemies," Daniel says, tilting his head.

"It's implied. There isn't exactly a ceremony for it," I say, waving my hand like I'm starring in *The Princess Diaries*.

He laughs and catches my hand in his, turning my gesture into a handshake. "Alice Chen, I swear upon my honor that for the duration of this competition, I will have your back. I won't betray, sabotage, or malign you in any way. We're together till the end."

"Same," I say, but when Daniel raises an eyebrow at me, I add, "I swear, Daniel Cho, that for the duration of this competition, I'll have your back. I won't betray, sabotage, or malign you. Well, I might malign you a little, but only if you deserve it."

"I would expect nothing less," Daniel says solemnly and drops my hand.

We spend the rest of the night sitting across from each other on the floor, exchanging facts about our lives. I find out that his birthday is on New Year's Eve. He learns that when I was a kid, I had a pet goldfish named Miss Puppy because I'd actually wanted a dog. His favorite cartoon as a kid was *Jackie Chan Adventures*, while mine was *Avatar: The*

Last Airbender. His first charity event in law school was a 5K run, and that turned into a real love for running and hiking. I only run under duress, but love playing badminton. He's part of a remote D&D group consisting of his college roommates, and I watch K-dramas with Cindy, Tara, and my mom.

Weirdly, I find myself having fun. It's nice, being on the same team as someone who gets me. Chase never understood my competitive side, and I did my best to tamp it down when I was with him. He liked getting along with people. I liked crushing my opponents at board games and dominating at bar trivia.

But Daniel is just as competitive as me, and as the hours pass, we keep trying to one-up each other with facts we remember about each other and, at one point, a very spirited arm-wrestling match. In another life, I can see how Daniel and I could've been friends. Maybe we can still be friends.

Finally, as midnight approaches, I find myself yawning, which sets Daniel off yawning, too.

I stretch and climb to my feet. "I think that's enough for today. Let's get some rest. We need to be in top condition for tomorrow."

"Yeah, it's getting late. But we still need to discuss something."

"What?" I ask.

"There's only one bed, Slayer." He waves his hand at the center of the room, where there's a plush-looking bed, decorated with fluffy, heart-shaped pillows and a bedspread the blush-pink color of Valentine's Day bedding at Target.

Oh my god.

Of course there's only one bed. Leah did say that this was one of the villa's honeymoon suites.

"I'll take the floor," he says generously. Oh, hell no.

"First of all, *Daniel*," I say, "I'm just as capable of taking the floor as you are. Secondly, I don't see any reason why we can't both sleep in the same bed. It's huge."

"What if we can't keep our hands off each other, and we lose our-

selves to the throes of passion?" Daniel says. "I mean, after that kiss—
" He fans himself, and I snatch up a pillow to chuck at him. He dodges, laughing.

"You know, even with your hot new haircut and a tattoo, I think I can control myself," I say primly.

Daniel falls silent for a moment, and then simply says, "Tattoos."

"What?"

"Tattoos. Plural. I have two." Daniel shrugs. "Seems like something my very-not-fake girlfriend should know about me."

"Wait, where's the other one?" I ask.

He turns his body, angling so that I can see the back of his leg. The tattoo on his leg is tiny, small enough that I didn't notice it before. It's a frog wearing a jaunty little hat. A laugh bursts out of me.

"Okay, now that I've seen this little guy, I'll *definitely* be able to control myself in bed," I say.

"Hey!" Daniel protests, looking offended.

I plunge on. "Also, if anyone bursts into our room for whatever reason, it's going to look really suspicious if one of us is on the floor."

"Point taken. We should share the bed." Daniel pauses. "Are you sure?"

"Yes. Why are you being so weird about this?"

He looks in me in the eye. "Alice, we may be fake dating, but I'd like us to be real with each other in private. I don't want to make you uncomfortable."

I snort. "I'll be plenty comfortable. Have you seen the thread count on these sheets?"

With that sorted, we take turns in the bathroom. I rush through my skincare routine, brush my teeth, and hurriedly change into my pajamas. By the time we both settle into bed, I've built a pillow wall between us with all the heart-shaped pillows.

"There," I say, patting the pillows. "That should do it."

"Very nice, Slayer. No one will doubt we're a couple now," Daniel says.

"You know, there's a rising body of evidence that suggests that couples who sleep in separate beds are happier."

Daniel flops down onto the bed. "I'll be sure to cite that during our next confessional when the producers ask how it's going."

"Please do," I say. "Now go to sleep."

"Yes, ma'am," he says with laughter in his voice.

I roll over, turning my back to him. The bed is as soft as a cloud, and the cool sheets are smooth against my skin. As I close my eyes, shutting out the shaft of moonlight streaming into our room, the sensation of Daniel's lips on mine lingers. I hug one of the pillows tight and do my best to focus on falling asleep and absolutely nothing—and no one—else.

From: Peter Dixon (peterdixon@getrealproductions.com)

To: Shawna Vasquez (svasquez@getrealproductions.com),

CC: DTI Production Team (dtiproductionteam@getrealproductions.com)

Re: Memo from Peter Dixon

Hey folks,

Thanks to Shawna for flagging this. Please pay attention to the notes below. Today's episode got a little graphic. We need a trigger warning for anyone with a sensitivity to vomiting, gross stuff, food, etc.

—PD

Begin Forwarded Message:

Production Notes for Editors: "Dawn Tay's Inferno: Love Is Hell," Season 1, Episode 3: Gluttony

Content Warning needed before episode. Language can read: "This episode contains graphic depictions of vomiting."

Word choice? Mention bodily fluids, food sensitivity, or other related topics? LK please advise

Make sure any scenes are tastefully blurred before airing.

Chapter Eleven

Hell Is Sharing a Bed with Your (Hot) Nemesis

It must be Sunday is my first thought when I wake up. I can already tell it's going to be one of those pleasant, syrupy-slow mornings that makes you feel all warm and loose. I don't open my eyes because I just know, deep down, that I have all the time in the world. Mornings like these are rare, and I luxuriate in the feeling of sleeping in and cuddling with my boyfriend.

I have a hazy sense that I'm just emerging from a series of weird dreams, but his arm draped over me is a comforting weight. When I feel him stretch behind me, I push my hips back into his, so that we're spooned together. I can feel the satisfied hum he lets out, the sound reverberating through him as he shifts closer to me. His hand runs down my stomach to my thigh, and I arch into him, wanting—no, needing—him to dip his hand between my legs. A soft kiss is dropped on my neck, and I moan.

"Mmm, *Chase*," I say, turning in his arms, hands reaching up to curve behind his neck. I press into him and—

"Alice?" rumbles a bleary voice, and I freeze. Oh shit. This isn't Chase.

It's Daniel. In bed with me. And I'm all over him.

I shriek and push roughly back, shoving Daniel in the face with my palm and tumbling off the bed all in one go. I look up at the ceiling, my heart racing as I try to piece together the jagged edges of yesterday and last night into some semblance of sense.

Daniel peeks over the edge of the bed, throwing everything into startling clarity.

Chase is with Selena. I'm with Daniel. Daniel and I are pretending to be madly in love. And we shared the same bed last night.

"You okay? You nearly took my eye out."

"I— You—" I sputter. "What happened to the pillow wall?"

Daniel glances from me back to the bed. "The pillows are all at the foot of the bed. One of us kicks in our sleep," he says. "Pretty sure it's you."

Chase never mentioned whether I kick in my sleep, but he sleeps like a baby, and even if I was sleep-kicking enough to wake the dead, he wouldn't have noticed.

Not that it matters.

Because Chase isn't here. And not only has our entire relationship gone up in smoke, but I'm left trying to win this competition on my own. Everything I knew about Chase, every experience we shared, every little detail about him, right down to his sleeping habits and how much sugar he takes in his coffee, is irrelevant now—and I have to win this competition without that edge.

"It's okay if you kick," Daniel says. "I can overlook it for the sake of our fake relationship."

I throw a pillow at him.

Now that I'm fully awake, I discover that I'm ravenous. Luckily, we ordered room service yesterday since Leah had mentioned that filming was starting early today. There's a tray of food outside our door—microwaved breakfast burritos and little plastic cups of honeydew. I'd give anything for a mug of hot soy milk and a purple rice fantuan right about now, but I'll take whatever fuel I can get.

As I inhale my breakfast burrito, I flip open my suitcase.

"Is that what you're planning to wear?" Daniel asks as I pull out a Cindy-approved outfit.

"What's wrong with it?"

"Nothing, it's great. I just figure we should coordinate. You know, pretend to be on the same team?"

Fair point. I have to admit, matching will make Daniel and me look like we belong together. Like Tarun and Kendall's matching foodie outfits, or Brittany and Jaxon's cowboy boots. Maybe if we're lucky, we'll become "Reasonably Fashionable Nerds" instead of "The Asians."

"It's not a terrible idea," I admit. "We could try it."

"As always, your words of praise mean everything to me."

I ignore that. "Do I need to change anything out?"

"No. I have something that'll work," Daniel says, and he grabs clothes from his own suitcase.

He takes off his shirt, and I realize that I need to be anywhere other than here. I rush into the bathroom to change. When I come out again, Daniel is putting sunscreen on. He's dressed in white shorts and a blue-and-white-striped shirt that complements the deep-blue romper I've got on.

He glances over at me and breaks into a smile. "We look nice."

"Almost like we're a real couple," I say. "Ready to head downstairs and flaunt our new relationship?"

He takes my hand, and I'm proud of how steady my heartbeat is as I lace my fingers with his. "Ready when you are, *darling*."

⋯⋯⋯⋯⋯⋯

I must have slept in later than I thought, because Daniel and I are the last contestants out of the villa. Leah is already waiting for us at the bottom of the winding staircase, tapping her toes impatiently on the pristine marble floor.

"There are my winners," Leah says when she spots us. "How was the suite I snagged for you? Did you get a chance to *connect*?" she asks, looking over the two of us.

"Working on it," I say at the same time that Daniel says, "Never been closer."

"Okay, maybe work on *that*," Leah says, circling her index finger in the air between us. "But hey, you're dressed nicely and holding hands. I'll take it."

Daniel and I walk hand-in-hand the whole way down to the beach, and thanks to our practice yesterday, I manage to relax into it and just enjoy the sun on my skin as we make our way over to the rest of the contestants.

"Oh, so it's true," Ava says, eyeing the pair of us. This is the first time we've been seen together since Dawn Taylor's announcement yesterday, and it feels like Ava is staring daggers at us. Daniel squeezes my hand.

Game on. I squeeze Daniel's hand back and plaster on my best "talking to parents at Open House" smile. "Yep," I say breezily. "I can't believe it either. I feel like I'm in paradise."

"I think it's wonderful that you two found true love from the ashes of heartbreak," a lilting voice says. "I'm Firefly," the woman adds when I glance at her. I realize I've seen her before—or at least, I've seen the back of her head before. She was the one making out with her partner on the first night. Today, she's wearing a sari that matches the bright green of her hair. She still has on the black combat boots and the fingerless black gloves from the first day.

When she sees me taking in her clothes, she makes a face. "My producer asked me to wear a sari today. I guess they're playing up the 'we have an Indian contestant' angle. Something about trying to bring in the *Indian Matchmaking* demo? But I'm not going to throw away the rest of my style." She links arms with the handsome Black man next to her. "Oh, this is Bacon, by the way."

He's still in full Burning Man–style desert gear, with a black vest and black goggles on his head. "Hey," he says.

"*Bacon?*" Ava asks. The judgment is dripping from her voice.

"Because he's so hot and tasty," Firefly deadpans, and then bursts into laughter.

"She's 'Firefly' because she's the light of my life," Bacon says. "Also, she likes to light things on fire."

"We like to go by our Burning Man names," Firefly explains. "It started out as a bit, but then it just stuck. Anyway, we're totally rooting for you and Daniel. It's giving true love, you know?"

"True love?" Ava says with a snort. "More like a true loophole. I know you guys got together so you wouldn't be eliminated. Normally, I'd file a complaint, but you're not worth the effort."

With that, she stalks away from us. Bacon shakes his head. "Don't let it get to you. There's always going to be people who doubt your love. Firefly and I had a hard time when we first got together too."

Daniel makes a sympathetic noise. "Yeah?"

"My parents were convinced that he wouldn't be able to get Bengali culture. And his parents thought I was a bad influence." Firefly smiles up at him. "But you like my influence, don't you?"

"I never would have discovered welding—and myself—without you," Bacon says, punctuating it with a kiss. Firefly bounces up on her toes and pulls him in for a longer kiss.

And we've lost them. They're full-on making out again, oblivious to the people around them. I glance up at Daniel, who scrunches his nose at me. I let out a quiet laugh and turn back to the challenge at hand.

Two long tables have been set up in shallow V formation. Each table has twelve plates covered by red domes painted with flames. In retrospect, maybe eating that breakfast burrito was a bad idea. I drop Daniel's hand and start jogging in place, hoping that I can hurry along my digestion and make room for more.

Once the producers explain our cue to us, Dawn Taylor arrives in a swirl of filmy red fabric, and filming begins.

"Hey, babes," she says, blowing a kiss to the camera. "It's Dawn Taylor, and this week we're descending to the next circle of hell—gluttony!"

The cameras circle us as we step up to the seats labeled with our names. There are four couples at each table, and three plates in front of each pair of us. Tarun and Kendall are to our left, and next to them are Brittany and Jaxon. And to our right are Selena and Chase. I turn away, unwilling to look at Chase. It's too soon, and I have to push down the flickers of anger and grief I feel just hearing his voice. Out of the corner of my eye, I see Daniel shift so that Chase is blocked from view.

"This week," Dawn Taylor continues, "each of you must work with your partner to finish every last bite of food on the plates before you!"

"Wait, the gluttony challenge is to participate in gluttony?" I say under my breath. "Shouldn't we be *not* eating if this is the circle for people who overeat? She does realize that Dante's *Inferno* wasn't, like, an instruction manual, right?"

"I'll level with you, I'm not sure Dawn Taylor has actually read the source material," Daniel says.

Dawn Taylor gestures, and eight crew members dressed as waiters step up to the table. "We've got three delectable dishes for you. Feel free to eat them in any order and however you want. The only rule is that each couple must clean their plates. The last couple with food remaining on their plate is out. Now let's take a look at what's on the menu."

The crew member closest to me whips off the cover of the first and smallest plate, revealing several wrinkly peppers.

"Chiles rellenos de queso de cabra," Dawn Taylor says with careful enunciation. "In other words, peppers stuffed with cheese. Our chefs have added habanero chilies to the mix. A real treat . . . if you can handle the heat."

"Ooh, my grandma made these for me once!" Selena says, clapping her hands together.

"I can do those, easy," I say to Daniel. "My mom raised me on her homemade garlic chili oil."

"Yeah, but I've been eating my grandmother's buldak since I was a baby," Daniel shoots back. "And she does *not* hold back on the spice."

Dawn Taylor flourishes her hand at the second round of dishes. "Next up, we have . . . cow eyes!"

The second cover is lifted to reveal a plate with a single raw cow eye staring back at us. I'm viscerally reminded of high school biology class. Except I'd much rather dissect the eyeball than put it in my mouth. There's a puddle of something slimy beside the eyeball, and I really don't want to know what it is.

"We've had cow eyes before, sweetie. Remember the tacos de ojos?" I hear Kendall tell Tarun.

"That was at a Michelin-starred restaurant in New York," Tarun hisses. "These are raw and prepared by rank amateurs, Kendall!" Their designated "waiter" glares at them.

"And last but certainly not least, I hope you've saved room for dessert," Dawn Taylor says.

Off comes the final cover and there, sitting on the largest plate, is a huge, skull-shaped chocolate cake. It's big enough to serve an entire class of voracious eighth graders. It's the kind of cake that one kid in *Matilda* had to eat as a form of torture.

As we're all staring in shock, the crew members light each cake on fire. There must be some kind of liquor soak on them, because the skulls ignite instantly. I hear Brittany squeak, and Noah swears at the flaming cakes. Firefly, on the other hand, is in her element. She starts twirling and waving her hand over the flames.

"And as a special prize, whoever finishes first will be treated to a four-course meal with wine pairings from a personal chef. And whoever finishes last is out of here. Your time starts now—give 'em hell!"

Daniel turns to me. "So, how do you want to do this?"

My gaze snaps to Chase. He's already dug in and is covered in chocolate frosting. But here is Daniel, strategizing with me. I could get used to this.

"We should start with the peppers to kill our taste buds," I begin. "Swallow the cow's eye whole. Then split the cake."

"Not a bad strategy."

"But?" I prompt.

"But, what if one of us ate the cow eye and the peppers, and the other one ate the cake?"

I narrow my eyes. "Is this some kind of misguided attempt to spare me from eating the peppers and the eye? Because I could do both of those right now without breaking a sweat."

Daniel taps the plate of cake. "We should minimize our risks. Your plan splits the load evenly, which would be great if every dish had the same challenges. But the peppers and cow eye test your spice tolerance and gag reflex, while the chocolate cake is a simple matter of volume. If we both ate the peppers and cow eye and started feeling a bit off, eating the chocolate cake would be that much more difficult."

Right. Battling nausea from eating something raw that we don't eat every day, or indigestion from something spicy without any drinks to wash it down, could make finishing off the cake tricky, and we can't afford that.

"I can handle the peppers and the cow's eye. Can you handle the cake?" he asks.

"I told you, I can handle anything. I could do this entire challenge myself."

"Okay, then handle the cake," he tells me, then grabs the peppers and downs them like it's nothing.

"*You* handle the cake," I snap at him. Screw the strategy. I snatch up the cow's eye before Daniel can react and swallow it whole. It's slimy, raw, and extremely gross, but I'm able to choke it down with a few deep breaths. Years of chugging horribly bitter Chinese herbal medicine has trained me for this, and when I'm sure I've kept the eyeball down, I flash Daniel a peace sign.

He gives me an exasperated look, and then we both turn to the cake.

I realize that production has very intentionally not given us any utensils. I use one of my hands to scoop up a handful of moist chocolate cake. Daniel follows my lead. The cake is so over-the-top sweet that I almost gag, but at least it's masking the taste of the cow's eye.

"Chase is taking that cake *down*," Dawn Taylor observes as a camera zooms in on Chase wolfing down handful after handful.

Beside him, Selena is almost finished with her peppers, but she offers the last bite to Chase. "Babe, this is delicious. You have to try it," she says.

Chase doesn't hesitate before he takes a bite—and I know exactly what will happen next, because Chase can barely handle my mom's mildest chili sauce. Almost immediately, Chase's face goes red and his eyes bulge. "That's fire," he chokes out.

Dawn Taylor swoops in. "Selena, you might want to help him out there. Get that cow eye, girl!"

Selena looks like she had absolutely no intention of eating the cow eye, but now that the camera is focused on her, she delicately picks up the eyeball. She plugs her nose and pops it in her mouth.

"Get it down! Get it down!" Dawn Taylor chants. Selena chews and shimmies to the beat of the chant. For a moment it looks like she's going to spit the whole thing out, but then she swallows and opens her mouth for Dawn Taylor to inspect.

"You're good! You got it," she tells Selena.

As I shovel another handful of cake into my mouth, I try to distract myself by looking around at the rest of our competition.

Brittany and Jaxon, once again wearing matching cowboy looks, have clearly started with the peppers. While Jaxon seems fine, tears are streaming down Brittany's face.

"I don't think those peppers wanted to be eaten," she croaks hoarsely.

"Meanwhile, Daniel is *flying* through the dessert!" Dawn Taylor cheers.

The cameraman swivels over to Daniel, who's digging in with both hands. I take another bite, upping my pace. No way am I going to let it look like Daniel carried the team on this one.

"No, no, no," Tarun moans to my left. "This cumin is killing my palate! I'm not going to have any taste buds left after this."

"You still there, Slayer?"

The name jolts me back to my own partner. I look at Daniel, who's licking some frosting off of his fingers.

"Yes. Doing great. Fantastic," I say, but with my mouth full, it comes out more like "Mmmphfgh."

He tilts his head at me. "You've got a little—" He gestures at me, which is hilarious because I'm literally covered in chocolate cake. What's less hilarious is when he reaches up and uses his thumb to wipe away a bit of chocolate from the corner of my mouth, brushing my lip again for the second time in twenty-four hours. The brief touch is enough to send a bolt of heat skittering through me.

"There," he says, like he's actually done me a favor.

What the hell was that?

I glare at him as I take another bite. I'm definitely regretting the burrito I ate this morning. Now I'm fighting for every fraction of an inch of space in my stomach.

"Done! We're done!" someone cries behind us.

Everyone turns to the power couple, Ava and Noah. Their plates are clean, and their mouths are open to prove that they've finished the job. They look like baby birds waiting for their momma bird to regurgitate into their mouths.

Dawn Taylor saunters over to them. "Amazing work! Babes, you have officially won our Gluttony Challenge."

Noah and Ava high-five each other. As the rest of us double down on eating, Dawn Taylor takes the chance to interview them right there on the spot.

"Why do you think the two of you came out on top today?" she asks.

"I knew I couldn't let Ava down," Noah says. "It's just like this in our real lives back home. We both work over sixty-hour weeks. We're hustlers. We're up at five in the morning, hitting the gym before work, answering emails through breakfast, that kind of thing. But we do it for each other."

Ava wraps an arm around him. "It's true. I see how hard he works, and it makes me want to work that much harder."

"I'd do anything for Ava," Noah says with an intensity I can't help but find a little chilling.

Or maybe that's just the competition jitters. I focus all my energy on wolfing down the chocolate cake.

Across from us, Mikayla and Trevor are arguing about who's going to eat the cow eye.

"Trevor, you should do it. Remember how good you were at the cinnamon challenge?" Mikayla is saying.

"Mikayla, I threw up for hours after the cinnamon challenge!"

"Yeah, but like, *after*. All you have to do is keep it down long enough for Dawn Taylor to check our plates and then you can throw up as much as you want!"

I look down at my own plate. I've only got a couple bites left. We're so close to second place, I can taste it—and it tastes like chocolate. I cram another bite into my mouth. Daniel scoops a big handful for himself. We both glare at each other as we frantically chew, each of us trying to finish before the other.

I swallow a fraction of a second before Daniel. I lightly punch his shoulder and point to my mouth. Daniel swallows and calls out, "Dawn Taylor, can we get a check over here?"

Our host sails over. "Second place! Congratulations!"

I'm so full I could burst. I flash a weak thumbs-up.

"Hello? Congratulations?" Dawn Taylor prompts us, and I realize that Daniel and I are meant to celebrate as a couple. I turn to him, raising my hand for a high five, just as Daniel goes in for a hug. I try to adjust to his hug, but Daniel switches to a high five, the combined effect of which is that Daniel ends up batting my face with his hand.

"We'll work on that," Daniel says with a grimace, turning the smack into an awkward head pat. I really hope they don't air that.

"So, how does it feel to finish your first challenge in hell together as a couple?" Dawn Taylor asks.

"It feels amazing," Daniel says, smoothly sliding into his interview voice. "I'm so glad I could step up for Alice and be the kind of partner that she deserves. We might be the newest couple here, but I think we showed everyone that we're a force to be reckoned with."

"A force of love," I add. "Because we're lovers." Off to the side, Leah smacks her forehead with her hand. We're spared having to elaborate more on our fake relationship when the next couple finishes.

"Done! We're done!" Mikayla calls out, waving Dawn Taylor over.

Trevor lets out a wet burp, but he's able to open his mouth and prove that the cow eye has gone down. The two of them slide into their post-competition soundbites without missing a beat.

"We really just wanted to do this for all of our followers watching along at home and rooting for us," Mikayla says.

"Yeah, we never want to let our fans down," Trevor adds. "Hashtag Trekayla, hashtag couples of Instagram, hashtag *Dawn Tay's In*-freak-ing-*ferno*! Get into it!"

Chase and Selena finish next. They celebrate by leaping into a chest bump. Chase asks for shots to celebrate, which Dawn Taylor absolutely loves and a PA immediately provides.

Brittany and Jaxon finish next, and right after them, Dominic and Zya raise their hands and roar like gladiators in the Colosseum.

"Yeah! That's how it's done!" Dominic shouts over Zya's hoots.

Then it's down to Tarun and Kendall versus Firefly and Bacon.

"We've got this," Bacon says. He pounds the table as he chews the cow eye.

"*You've* got this," Firefly replies, rubbing his shoulders. "Remember when our ice chest got a crack in it at Burning Man, and we lost all our food and we ended up eating that unflavored protein whey for three days? This is just like that!"

Kendall is struggling through the cake. "This is a culinary atrocity."

"Would you rather be eating the raw cow eye?" Tarun shouts back at her, holding up his plate.

Kendall looks at the half-eaten mess he's left. "You said you had it *handled*!"

"I did, but I—" Tarun tries to finish, but nothing comes out.

Or rather, no *words* come out.

Instead, he clutches at his stomach briefly, and then half a cow's eye erupts out of his mouth and plops onto the sand.

"Ohmygod!" Brittany says, jumping back to avoid it.

Jaxon isn't as lucky, and some of the eye splatters onto his boot. "Shit," he chokes out, and then he dry-heaves once before projectile vomiting.

"Selena? Babe?" Chase says behind me. There's a sheen of sweat on Selena's luminous golden skin, and she's starting to turn green. Chase braces her, but he isn't looking too hot either. Both of them start to double over, Selena gripping the table's edge and Chase stumbling next to her.

"Make sure you get this!" Dawn Taylor yells, pointing a camerap-erson to our table.

The threat of Chase and Selena joining Jaxon and Tarun in this im-promptu group activity is enough to send everyone scattering.

Ava and Noah are trying to make their escape when Selena hurls directly in their path, bits of the Gluttony Challenge splashing all over their Birkenstocks.

"Ew, ew, ew!" Ava moans.

"Hey, get over here and start cleaning!" Bryan shouts at the PAs. They race to grab cleaning supplies—all except for one.

"Anton, you've got to help too," Freya says, prodding him with a mop handle.

"No way. I didn't sign up for being on the cleanup crew," he says with a laugh.

"Seriously, you're not going to help us out?" Noah asks, gesturing from Anton to himself and Ava. "This is your chance to step up and show your bosses that you're good in a crisis. People remember that kind of thing when it's time for promotions or bonuses."

"Nah, I'm good here," Anton says. He pats one of the PAs on the shoulder as he leaves. "Have fun, buddy."

The PA he ditched mutters, just loud enough that I catch it, "Fuckin' asshole."

"Alice, you need to get out of here," Daniel says urgently. He shuts his eyes as if he's in pain.

"What's happening? Are you feeling sick, too?"

He nods. "It's not going to be pretty. Go save yourself."

The thought is tempting, but Daniel looks so miserable. And we're a team—I mean, we shook on it. I can't leave him here to barf on camera.

"Come on, we're going," I say.

I take his hand. He really must not be feeling well, because he doesn't put up a fight as I steer him back toward the villa. In the chaos, no one tries to stop us.

We've gone another few yards when he pulls back.

"I can't take another step," he says.

"Good thing you don't have to." I point at the trash can I've led him to, not too far from the catering tent. After I nudge the trash can closer to Daniel, I stand in front of it to shield him from camera view. Then I politely study a palm tree a few feet away and ignore anything I hear for the next couple minutes.

When I turn back around, Daniel is releasing a breath slowly out through his mouth.

"Better?" I ask.

He winces. "Sort of. Should we go back? They technically haven't cleared us to leave."

"It's fine. The challenge is over. I'm guessing Tarun and Kendall are probably going home," I say. "And you look awful."

Daniel chuckles. "Thanks, Slayer. You really know how to make a guy feel special."

"You need to rest," I say, taking his arm. "Everything else is secondary."

We make our way back to the suite. Once inside, I push him toward the bed.

"Go lie down," I say.

"Whatever you say," he says, crawling into bed.

"It's so weird that you're just listening to me," I say. "Maybe you should have food poisoning more often."

Daniel just groans into the comforter. I try to think of what might help him recover, but I don't have any of my usual go-to's with me. Back home, I'd have peppermint tea or ginger candies on hand.

Chase liked to tease me whenever I popped a ginger candy. Unlike me, he never got stomachaches or had trouble with indigestion or nausea. He can clear out leftovers from our fridge that have been hanging out in the back for over a month. I've seen him eat old gas station sushi and potato salad that's been sitting out in the sun without a problem. He has an iron stomach. But somehow he's the one throwing up and I'm the one who's completely fine.

I take a seat on the bed beside Daniel. It's strange to see him like this. I'm used to seeing him at his best—handsome, charming, and way too smug for my liking. But right now, he looks unguarded, vulnerable. His hair falls across his forehead, and without thinking, I brush it away gently.

I draw my hand back when he cracks one eye open at me. "Sorry," I say.

"No, it's nice. I like it," he mumbles. "I was just surprised."

"That I can be nice?"

"That you can be nice to *me*," he clarifies. "I always got the impression you hated me."

I roll my eyes. "Don't be dramatic. I don't hate you."

"Your exact words to me at District Finals were 'I hate you,'" Daniel reminds me.

"I can't be held accountable for the things I said as a teen," I retort. "And don't lie, you hated me, too."

"No, I—" He closes his eyes, searching for the right word. "I never hated you. Sure, I was annoyed that I kept losing to you—"

"Damn right."

"But I think, more than anything, I was in awe of you." Daniel flips over to face me. "You rolled into Quiz Bowl like it was your job to take me out."

Had I done that? I know I was going through some pretty bad times back then, and all I'd wanted to do was push my feelings down so far that they ceased to exist. And the way to do that was to focus on competing.

"So what?" I say. "That's why I was there. To win."

"It's not like I wasn't there to win," Daniel says.

"You sure? Because you always seemed like you could take it or leave it. Like you could brush off any loss."

"Maybe I just had a better poker face," Daniel says. "Seriously, I want to know. Why did you hate me, specifically?"

He's clearly not going to give up on this—and now that we're on the same team, I feel like just maybe, it wouldn't hurt to tell him the truth.

"It's because I had to give up everything to win. I spent all my time studying. I didn't go to school dances. I didn't hang out with my friends after school. I didn't have hobbies. All I had was Quiz Bowl, and Speech and Debate, and Mock Trial."

"Don't forget Science Fair."

"And Science Fair," I add. "I had to try so hard. But you—you did it without breaking a sweat. You had everything. Friends. A life. Two parents." I don't mean to let that last part slip out, and I put a hand up to my mouth as though I can catch the words and cram them back in.

"Yeah?" Daniel's voice is soft, understanding. It's hard to put up a defense to it.

I find myself continuing. "My dad left the summer before I met you," I say, closing my eyes. The sharp edge I felt in the time directly after has long dulled, but the words still hurt.

"Ah," he says quietly. "I can see how I'd be annoying to you, when you were going through all that."

"The great Daniel Midas Cho admits that he can be annoying?" I laugh.

He winces at the nickname, like it's a sharp jab.

"Happy now? I answered your question." I lift the corner of a blanket and drape it over him. "Now rest."

"Mm" is the only thing he says, his eyes shuttering closed. After a minute or two, his breathing evens out.

Now that he's asleep, I leap off the bed and pace around the room, mapping out my priorities for the rest of the afternoon. At the very least, I need to find some Gatorade for Daniel. After this morning, he's going to need the electrolytes.

The villa is unusually quiet as I search for the kitchen. There must be one in this sprawling mansion—the catering has to come from somewhere. When I find it, I head straight for the sleek, industrial-sized fridge. It's fully stocked, but only with alcohol—not a bottle of water or Gatorade in sight.

I sigh and shut the fridge door. If I'm going to get Daniel something that'll help hydrate him, it's not going to be from here.

I turn around and nearly collide with Chase.

"Whoa!" he says, steadying me before I fall over. He's still looking a little green, but he's upright at least.

"Oh, hey," I say casually. I try to lean against the wall, also casually. I'm so casual right now and absolutely not hurt that the guy I dated for three years backstabbed me on television. But when Chase sways on his feet, I ask, "Are you okay?"

"Babe. I mean, Alice. I feel terrible about what happened. I mean, I also feel terrible from puking about twenty times, but I feel even worse about what happened with us," he says, and as much as I want to cast him as the villain of my story, I can tell that he means it.

I'd planned to be calm and collected around Chase, to pretend like I didn't care. But now that I'm alone with him, the words tumble out of me. "Why. God, *why*, Chase? Why would you do this to me?"

Chase winces like I sucker-punched him. "I don't know. I didn't mean to. I know it isn't an excuse, but I was just so drunk. Bryan kept taking shots with me, and he was asking me all these questions about—" He looks away from me.

"About what, Chase?"

"About our relationship! Okay? He was saying all this stuff about how he couldn't believe we were together. That you've got your life together and I'm kind of a fuckup."

"He said that about you?" I say, shocked.

"I mean, he didn't call me a fuckup, but I could tell that's what he meant." He smiles sadly. "I bet that's what you think of me, too."

"I don't—" I shake my head. "I don't think of you as a fuckup." But then I'm remembering all the times I've had to pay Chase's credit card bills for him, and how I had to explain the concept of jury duty to him after I realized he'd been recycling his summons. It's like he doesn't live in the real world. And normally, that would have consequences. But I was always there to cover for him. Maybe Chase isn't a fuckup, but I'd always felt he relied on me more than I was able to rely on him.

Chase says, "It's okay, Alice. If there's one thing I've learned from being with you, it's that I was lucky to have you in my corner. I know you cared about me. But I don't think you've ever really taken me seriously—I mean, *I* don't even take myself seriously—but you're a serious person. So is Daniel. I've seen the way you and Daniel talk to each other. It's like watching two supercomputers do space math together."

"That's not really a thing—"

"Exactly. Daniel probably knows that's not really a thing too." He sighs. "Look, I know what I did wasn't okay."

"It really wasn't," I agree.

"But I was having so much fun with Selena, and then—" Chase groans. "I wasn't thinking."

"I know." That was the problem. Chase never looked before he leapt. Probably because for his whole life, his parents cleaned up after him. And then, when we started dating, I took over that role.

I remember when my mom said Chase made me complacent. I didn't get what she meant by that, but I think I do now. When you spent your childhood translating for your parents at school, at the doctor's office, and even at the grocery store, it's almost second nature to take care of other people. To shoulder responsibilities that you have no business taking on. Helping Chase out had come so easily, and I'd thought that was just what being in a relationship meant. But I never felt like I could truly lean on him the way he leaned on me.

I can't even completely blame him for it. I never asked to lean on him. It was just simpler to deal with things myself.

"I'm sorry, Alice," Chase is saying. "You've done so much for me, and I was so shitty."

"It's fine," I say automatically, and then correct myself. "Actually, no, it isn't fine. But you're just going to have to live with it. And for what it's worth, you and Selena make a cute couple."

Chase brightens at that. "Right? She's so funny and hot and—"

"*Dude.*"

"Sorry." Chase grimaces. "I get that it sounds like I'm just trying make excuses, but I really do think you and Daniel are great together. And I—" Chase's eyes go wide. "I think I'm gonna hurl again."

I leap out of the way as Chase charges past me, heading for the nearest bathroom.

I take a beat to recover from that conversation. We're in a crazy situation here, and being separated from Chase feels like I've had my legs knocked out from under me. But after that talk, I'm starting to feel more grounded.

Focus. I still need hydration materials. I remember the war room. If there's a place that would be fully stocked, it's the place where Dawn Taylor and Peter Dixon have all their big meetings.

At the bottom of the stairs, I see the war room door is open, and I walk in, bypassing the conference setup for the two doors at the back of the room. The first door opens into a fancy, well-lit bathroom with shelves of expensive makeup and a floor-to-ceiling mirror. Dawn Taylor must use this for touch-ups.

The second door leads to a gigantic walk-in pantry. It's probably bigger than some apartments in New York. I step inside, and wow, the execs have been holding out on us. There's everything in here. It's like if you took the entire snack aisle of a high-end grocery store and crammed it into one room. I grab some saltines and survey my drink options—there's bottled water, seltzers, juice, bottled lattes, and Gatorade.

As I grab several bottles of yellow Gatorade, I hear a pair of familiar voices—Leah and someone else. Seth, I remember, Selena and Daniel's producer before they broke up.

It sounds like they're coming this way. Immediately I shut the door as quietly as possible. Technically, no one said I *couldn't* be here, but I have a feeling this place is off-limits. Both producers come into the war room, their voices growing louder.

"—hardly in a position to be acting like a saint after the shit I've seen you pull over the years," Seth is saying.

"What I do to motivate my contestants is my business," Leah says. "This time you went too far."

"Easy, Gleeson. You think I did it just for kicks?"

"Yeah, Seth, you're a fucking psychopath."

"Takes one to know one." There's the squeak of a chair. They must be settling in. "Look, I had my marching orders. I was told it was on me to guarantee that we got some Grade A vomit shots to go after the *Fear Factor* audience, or it'd be my job on the line. And I delivered. You're welcome."

"You poisoned them."

"I put a very, very small dose of ipecac in the peppers, plus some homeopathic stuff I got off eBay. That's it. They'll be fine. What was I supposed to do, say no, I don't feel like it today? I would've had my ass handed to me. But by all means, if you want to hold the line on ethics, step right up."

"Whatever. You've made it very clear that you'll do whatever it takes. But if you fuck with my couples again, I'll rip your head off," Leah says, her voice steely.

"Same goes for you, cupcake."

"Go die in a hole." A pause. "You got any gum?"

"Yeah, it's in my locker. I left it open."

They head out the door, shutting it behind them.

I stay in the pantry room for another minute, still reeling from what I overheard. I didn't expect going on a reality show to be a cakewalk—Cindy and Tara had made sure that I knew what I was getting into. But poisoning the contestants? That's so far beyond anything I expected. And it explains why Chase had thrown up, when normally he can keep down everything he eats.

Trying to win this competition with a brand-new boyfriend that just so happens to be my high school rival was daunting enough. Now I've got to do it with the producers going the extra mile to mess with everyone? I might have Leah in my corner, but what if Seth sets his sights on me and Daniel? What if he does *whatever it takes*?

But I'm not scared—I'm mad. I'm here to win, no matter what sketchy shit the producers get up to.

....

I storm back to my room and throw open the door. A bit too late, I remember that Daniel is supposed to be sleeping, but luckily, he's sitting up in bed, looking slightly better than before. I toss the water and Gatorade on the bed.

"Whoa, Slayer. What did the door do to you?" Daniel says. I check that the hallway is clear before I shut the door behind me.

"I just found out that that your old producer Seth used ipecac to poison the peppers. You know, for drama."

"So that's why you didn't get sick," Daniel says. He groans. "What the hell. Why—"

A knock at the door interrupts us. When I open it, Lex is on the other side. I can't think why they're here, but then I remember all the drinks I stole.

"Lex? If this is about the Gatorade, I'm sorry," I say. "Actually, I'm not sorry. Daniel needed to rehydrate."

Without a word, Lex reaches around me to disconnect the mic pack I'm still wearing. They do the same to Daniel. I meet Daniel's gaze, and he shrugs.

"First of all," Lex says, "I don't care about the drinks you lifted from the war room. I love petty theft. Second of all, if you're wearing a mic pack, assume that someone is listening to you."

"But I thought they only record when we're filming." Even as I say this, I recall the live camera from the first night we were here, when filming had wrapped for the day and the producers had told us we were only getting our pictures taken.

"That's a good one," Lex laughs. "Next time, make sure to take off your mic packs before you head back to your room."

"They can't—" I shake my head. "Can they do that? I guess this *is* a reality show."

"We signed the waivers," Daniel says, rubbing his eyes, and Lex points at him.

"Bingo. Look, it's not my job to babysit any of you. But I'll tell you right now, making accusations about the producers while your mic pack is on? Not the move."

"You heard us," I say.

"I tapped in for a second just now," Lex says. "It's my job. And you're lucky I was the one listening in, and not someone else."

"Right, lucky," I echo. I don't feel lucky. "But what about Seth poisoning the cast? That's not normal, right?"

Lex grimaces. "No, I've been on a lot of shows, and I've never seen the producers go *this* hard. But I can't do anything about it, and neither can you. I'm warning you, just don't make any trouble. It's not worth it."

"But this isn't right," I insist. "There's got to be someone we can talk to." And I'd do it. When I found out that the new social studies teacher was telling students that the earth was five thousand years old and that girls should only wear skirts that hit below their ankles, I went straight to the principal and got his ass fired—which is to say, I've never been afraid of a fight.

But Lex doesn't know that. They say, "I wouldn't risk it. We may not be friends, but—"

"We could be friends," I put in. "You're giving us advice. That feels friendly."

"—that doesn't mean I want to see you get screwed over by this show," they conclude. "Just watch your back, okay?"

Before I can ask any more questions, Lex turns on their heel and walks out. I'm left staring at the door, still clutching a bottle of Gatorade. I can't shake the feeling that there's something seriously wrong here.

[Interview footage: Solo talking head—Daniel.]

DANIEL CHO: It might seem sudden, Alice and I getting together, but we're really just picking up where we left off in high school. I've always had so much respect and admiration for her. I guess you could say I had a huge crush on her, even back then.

[Interview footage: Solo talking head—Alice.]

ALICE CHEN: In high school? I hated Daniel. The best part of my week was when I got the chance to beat him at something and wipe that smug smile off his face. Oh! But everything's different now. I'm so happy we're together. I mean, it's a fine line between love and hate, right? Both such passionate feelings. Hahaha. Ha.

[Interview footage: Solo talking head—Daniel.]

DANIEL CHO: Who wouldn't like Alice? She's smart as hell and one of the most caring people I know. And we've always been a good match. She's the ultimate competitor and strategist, and she never holds back.

[Interview footage: Solo talking head—Alice.]

ALICE CHEN: Why did I fall for Daniel? Okay. I mean, he's hot—you know he's hot. You have eyes. He looks hot. He even sounds hot. Oh god, why did I say that? Can you cut that? No? Well, um, he's just so sweet and disarming—even when you don't want to be sweet and disarmed at all.

[Interview footage: Solo talking head—Daniel.]

DANIEL CHO: Going into today's challenge, I'm ready to take on anything with Alice by my side. We came in second yesterday, so hopefully we can keep up that momentum.

Chapter Twelve

Hell Is the Prisoner's Dilemma

The next day, I wake up to the covers being violently yanked off me.

"Up, up, up!" Leah drops them on the floor. "Looks like you two got cozy overnight," she observes.

As I blink away the dazzle of morning sun, I realize that my head is tucked into Daniel's shoulder, and his arms are wrapped around me. I let out a squeak and roll away, but it isn't easy. Our legs were tangled together, our bare skin touching in a way that I really don't have time to think about right now.

Daniel clears his throat. I jump out of the bed. We both don't look at each other.

"Guess I spoke too soon." Leah heaves a sigh. "Come on, we're already late."

I check the digital clock on the bedside table. "What? We're early."

"Dixon's pet PA, Anton, botched the call sheets. Plus, we have a lot of catch-up to do since we lost so much time dealing with the vomit fest yesterday." Leah unzips my suitcase and starts flipping through my clothes. "Cute, but given your new story arc with Daniel, what you have isn't going to cut it. Here, try this." She reaches into her own bag and produces a red sundress that she tosses to me.

"Uh." I hold up the dress. It's fire-engine red.

"Just try it on," she says. "I know, it's very look-at-me, and your wardrobe is more about blending in with the walls, but it'll help viewers remember who you are. And the editors will have an easier time with the color balance in your scenes."

"Got it," I say, ducking into the bathroom. Once the dress is on, I check myself out in the mirror. With the plunging neckline, barely-there straps, and flared skirt, this is the kind of look that Cindy would call a "fuck-me" dress. I'll admit that it does look good, especially paired with my jade necklace.

I emerge from the bathroom to find Daniel wearing dark jeans and a maroon button-down with the sleeves rolled up to show off his forearms.

"Hey there," Daniel says, turning to me, and then his eyes widen.

"What is it?" I smooth my skirt down. "Did I get toothpaste on myself?"

"No, you—" He blinks, then reaches for my hand. His voice drops, taking on a slight rasp. "You look perfect."

"You're not so bad yourself," I say.

"All right, save the flirting for when the camera's rolling," Leah says, herding us out of the room.

"We're not flirting!" Daniel and I yell in unison, and Leah cackles.

As we follow Leah down a winding staircase, then past the living room where the other contestants have been sleeping and a stunning bay window that looks out onto the ocean, I ask Leah about our wardrobe people. She laughs at that, telling us that our "stylists" were only here for the Lust Challenge. Apparently our producers are expected to do double duty as our wardrobe people.

From the set of her shoulders, it's clear that Leah is feeling the pressure of landing that extra budget from FlixCast. There's a lot riding on the next few episodes, and the stakes couldn't be higher.

"What about breakfast?" I ask.

"I've got you covered," Leah says. Then she sees Anton at the end of the hall, lounging against a wall, and groans. "Let me guess, Anton. You didn't get the smoothies I asked you to fetch for our lovely contestants."

"Didn't feel like it," Anton says, yawning.

Leah glares at him with a fire hot enough to melt lead. "Anton. Do you see how busy everyone is? Can you at least pretend that you're here to do your actual job?"

Anton pushes off the wall and heads to the kitchen, but not before calling over his shoulder, "You know, technically I don't report to you!"

"Technically, every single person on this set outranks you!" Leah yells back.

We end up back on the beach, where a whole new setup has been constructed. The crew has built bamboo walls to hide what the challenge of the day is going to be. Eventually we're escorted around the walls, where we're greeted with the sight of two empty barrels in the sand, one painted red and one painted blue. The camera crew is standing at attention, covering every possible angle of the barrels. Behind the barrels is a small trailer painted with bright red and orange flames, looking like it blasted out of Flavortown.

I'm puzzling over what the competition could possibly be when Seth runs up with our smoothies.

"I asked Anton to get those," Leah says with a frown. "You can't keep bailing that kid out. He already acts like he owns the place. It doesn't help that you're always jumping in every time he flakes."

Seth shrugs. "I had a free minute, and we both know Anton wasn't going to do it. Do you want your contestants to starve?"

Daniel and I lock eyes for a second before we try the drinks, and I can tell we're both thinking the same thing—did Seth mess with these drinks and are we about to get food poisoning again? But no, that would be way too suspicious, and Seth has no reason to pull the same trick twice. Right?

"Drink! Fast!" Leah barks at us, and we obey.

I only have time to take a few sips of the tropical blend of coconut, pineapple, and strawberries before Leah snatches the cup out of my hand.

"Time's up. Alice, you go first," Leah says. "Daniel, you're going to wait over there inside the trailer."

Leah guides me over to the barrels.

"What about the other contestants?" I ask Leah as she fluffs my hair.

"Different format today. You're all going to do the challenge separately," Leah says.

Several feet away, Peter Dixon perches in a director's chair, attended by a handful of producers and production assistants.

"I think we're good to start the first take. Where's DT?" Peter Dixon says.

Right on cue, Dawn Taylor emerges from her own trailer, looking stunning in a skintight crimson dress, her perfectly blown-out hair topped with two cute devil horns. The cameras immediately train on her, and one of the producers signals for her to start.

"Welcome to the Greed Challenge! Today we're putting your greed to the test," Dawn Taylor says. She turns to face me. "In front of you are—" Fireworks explode behind her in a shower of red sparks. A loud series of pops immediately follows, and she shrieks.

"What the *fuck*?" She whips her head around, murder in her eyes.

"Dawn!" Peter Dixon jumps out of his chair and rushes over to her. He grasps her shoulders. "Are you okay? Shit, didn't the PAs tell you we were doing fireworks for this challenge? I told Anton to keep you in the loop."

She gives him a withering look. "No, he didn't mention it."

"I'll talk to him. This is unacceptable," Peter Dixon says, shaking his head. "Do you need a moment? Should we cut?"

"No, I'm fine. Keep rolling." Dawn Taylor pastes a smile back on. She walks back to her mark and nods at the cameraperson.

"Today, we're putting your greed to the test," she says again. This time, when the fireworks shoot off behind her, she spreads her arms and throws her head back. "Mwahaha!" She laughs as the sparks rain down around her.

"I'm here to present you with a choice," Dawn Taylor announces. "If you want to, you can drop out of the competition right here, right now. And I'll give you *twenty thousand dollars* to do it."

I can't help it, I gasp. That kind of money is more than I make in six months.

"Yeah, I know," Dawn Taylor says. "Here's the catch. If you take the money, your time here ends, and your partner gets *nothing*. And if you're thinking you can do something cute like splitting the cash after the show's over? Dream on. We've built into the terms of agreement that you absolutely cannot share the money. I'm making this offer to every contestant today, and only one person is going to hit the jackpot."

She gestures to the barrels. "Now I'm about to start a timer. Inside each barrel is a bucket. If you want to stay in the competition, fill the blue barrel up with water from the ocean. If you want the money, fill up the red barrel. Whoever fills the red barrel the fastest will win a cool twenty thousand dollars and leave the competition. Whoever fills the blue barrel the fastest will win a romantic ride on my personal yacht at sunset. Understood?"

I nod. My mind is racing. Twenty thousand dollars. I'm starting to sweat at the thought of pocketing that much money. Twenty thousand would be enough to cover all the hospital bills we owe currently. It would be enough to have some money left over to put toward any future treatments my mom would be facing. It would mean I could breathe easier again.

"Your time starts *now*!"

I have to think this through. I know staying in the show and winning would result in a bigger payout. It's one million dollars compared to twenty thousand. But then again, there's no guarantee that Daniel and I are going to make it to the final challenge, much less take home the grand prize.

But winning the twenty thousand dollars isn't guaranteed either. If I'm not the fastest to fill the red barrel, I'll lose. And I'm doing this challenge alone. I can't rely on teamwork to carry the day. Even if I try my hardest, I'm not the strongest or the fastest one here. My chances of beating every other competitor who decides to fill the red barrel is low.

Maybe I'm thinking about this all wrong. It's not just about me. I have to take Daniel into consideration. Sure, we've agreed to a truce. We're even kind of getting along right now. But he's been my rival since high school, and he has no reason to be loyal to me. Why wouldn't he go for the twenty thousand dollars?

And to complicate matters, there's the question of what Daniel thinks I'm going to do. He knows I'm here for the money, and it's not like we're in a real relationship. Of all the couples here, we're the most likely to flip on each other and take the cash. If he thinks I'm going to flip, then he'll flip too—and try to beat me to the punch.

Part of me wants to believe in Daniel, believe that we'd stick together until the end. I glance toward the trailer where Daniel is waiting.

I shake my head, dislodging that train of thought. Enough wasting time. I'm here for my mom. The rest is just noise. My course of action is clear. I grab the bucket from the red barrel and start racing down the beach.

Thanks to the crash course on island-based competitions Cindy and Tara had put together for me, I knew there was a good chance that I'd be doing some kind of water transfer challenge—a classic on the show *Operation: Bikini*. The trick is to assess the distance and account for how much water is going to spill out of the bucket. In this case, there's about fifty yards between the barrel and the ocean, which means that each trip is going to be time-consuming and exhausting. If I rush, I run the risk of spilling most of my water and flaming out. My best shot is to go slow and fill my bucket to the brim so that I can cut back on the number of trips I take.

When I tip my first bucket of water into the red barrel, it sloshes at the bottom, barely making a dent. This is going to take forever. I look down at the barrel as if it can tell me its secrets. Then I realize, technically, there's no rule against moving it closer to the ocean. I brace myself against it so I can tilt the barrel onto its bottom edge and half push, half roll it toward the water.

There. It's much closer.

But it's still a large barrel. After five minutes, I'm covered in sweat. After ten, I'm starting to get blisters. After twenty, I can't even feel the blisters, so at least that's something. And after almost thirty minutes, on my last trip, my arms are shaking, and my fingers can barely maintain their grip on the bucket. I stumble forward, nearly dropping it, but manage to catch myself and dump the water in.

Immediately behind me, a spray of red fireworks goes off.

"Crap!" I yelp. Okay, I get why Dawn Taylor didn't like that.

"Alice, you've made your choice," Dawn Taylor says solemnly. "Now you wait."

....

The waiting is its own form of torture. After the challenge, I'm taken to what I can only describe as a party room, with a fully stocked bar and plenty of plush armchairs facing a view of the dense forest behind Villa Paradiso. It's absolutely gorgeous, but despite the luxury I suddenly find myself in, my mind is a mess. I'm already kicking myself for wasting precious minutes making my choice. Of course, Daniel is going to make the same decision, and knowing him, he'll do it with twice the speed and strength that I have. Damn it.

When the door swings open, my heart leaps. I'm expecting it to be Daniel, but instead Selena bounds in.

"Alice, hey! That was a tough one today, huh? But we did it!" she says, holding up a hand for a high five. I hesitate, and she lowers her hand. "Too soon? Sorry."

"It's cool." I manage a weak smile. "I mean, it's not. But that's between me and Chase."

"That's fair." Selena sighs, sinking into one of the armchairs beside me. "It's just, I don't know. I wasn't thinking. I guess I just assumed when I saw you with Daniel that you and Chase weren't exclusive. I really had no idea that the two of you were engaged." Selena shakes her head. "Not my best moment. I am so, so sorry about how things went down, and I really regret hurting you like that."

She might just be a good actor, but to me she sounds genuine. Still, that doesn't mean I want to be having this heart-to-heart with her right now.

"We really don't have to talk about this," I say.

"But hey," Selena says, brightening. "You and Daniel are hot together. I can absolutely see the chemistry between you two. The way he looks at you—girl, let me tell you. He never looked at me that way."

"We really, *really* don't have to talk about this," I repeat. I contemplate climbing out the window to escape this line of conversation. "Can we talk about literally anything else?"

Selena laughs. "Okay, I hear you. How about mimosas?" She doesn't wait for me to answer before she leaps up, snags two flutes, and starts pouring.

"Selena, when you said it was a tough one today, do you mean you had a hard time deciding, or that you had a hard time filling the barrel?" I ask.

"Filling the blue barrel, duh!" she says. "Don't get me wrong, I'd love some cash right now, but I'm on this show for my career. Dropping out won't do me any favors." She casts me a sideways look. "And I know what he did was wrong, but I feel like I have a real connection with Chase, you know? Just like you have a real connection with Daniel."

"Mm," I say. I don't correct her, but I do take the mimosa she hands me.

The magnitude of my choice is starting to sink in. Did I make the wrong call? There's no way Daniel decided to fill the blue barrel. But what if, for some bizarre reason, he did? How am I going to face him? To distract myself, I take a sip from the champagne flute, focusing on the sensation of the bubbles and the tart orange juice sliding across my tongue.

Selena raises her flute and takes a huge swig. "Ugh, I needed that. I don't think I could've handled much more today. I barely slept."

I take a real look at her. She's so gorgeous, almost impossibly so, that it hadn't really occurred to me that she might've had a rough night and not be looking or feeling her best. But there are bags under her eyes, dark enough that her makeup doesn't quite mask it, and her hair doesn't have its usual shampoo-commercial sheen.

"Rough night?" I ask.

"It was awful. Chase and I had to keep getting up to barf." Selena rubs her temple. "I'm not usually someone with a weak stomach. I mean, usually I can mix tequila with wine and eat jalapeño poppers all night! This felt way more like a bad case of food poisoning."

I'm about to tell her that she was literally poisoned, but the mic pack digging into my back reminds me of what Lex said yesterday.

"Maybe having everyone eat raw cow eyes that were sitting out in the sun all day wasn't the best idea," I say instead.

"I know, right? You're so lucky you didn't get sick."

The door opens, and I'm spared having to make any more small talk. Brittany bounces in, fanning herself.

"Howdy, y'all! Whew, that was wild!" she says, taking off her cowgirl hat and shaking out her hair. She looks around. "Hey, where's Mikayla? She should've finished before me."

"She's probably in a different waiting room," Selena guesses.

"Ah well. Her loss," Brittany says, and makes grabby hands at the mimosas. "Now let's get this party started!"

Selena hands Brittany a flute. "Drink up, girl. I have a feeling we're going to need it."

It's another two hours before we're summoned back to the beach to film the conclusion of the Greed Challenge. The producers keep the couples separated, and I end up sitting between Brittany and Selena.

"Here we are," Dawn Taylor says, for once solemn. "I wish I could say that all of you chose to fill that blue barrel and stay true to each other. But that's not the case. In fact, one of you filled that red barrel so fast it made my head spin!"

We all look around uneasily.

"Daniel," Dawn Taylor says, and my heart leaps into my throat. "Do you think Alice was the one who did it?"

Daniel looks at me and smiles. "No way. Alice and I, we're a team, and we're in this together. And she'd never walk away from a competition, even for twenty thousand dollars."

His words slice through me. Normally, he'd be right. But he doesn't know about my mom or the medical bills I've left unopened on my kitchen table. He doesn't know that I've spent hours on the phone with her health insurance, trying to convince them to lower our costs. He has no idea how much time I've spent in hospital waiting rooms, grading exams and hoping for the best.

"Isn't that sweet?" Dawn Taylor says, looking from me to Daniel. "And Alice? Do you think Daniel betrayed you?"

"He would never." I hope I sound convincing. "When he gives me his word, he means it."

Dawn Taylor makes her way down the row of contestants, asking each of the couples the same question. Finally, she returns to the center of the group. It's time to put us out of our misery.

"It's the moment of truth. The person who filled the red barrel the fastest did it in less than fifteen minutes!" Dawn Taylor announces.

Fifteen? Fifteen means it wasn't me. I had a slow start, and even with moving the barrel, I took way longer than that, thanks to my noodle arms.

"And that person is"—she pauses dramatically—"Bacon."

We all gasp. Firefly's hand flies up to cover her mouth as she turns to Bacon in disbelief.

"Bacon! How could you?" Firefly demands.

"It's twenty thousand dollars! You know what I can do with that kind of cash. It'll change everything. I can get a 12V Cummins Diesel, full solar!" Bacon says. "That thing'll be luxury when we're on the open road!"

Firefly shoves him. "Seriously? We were supposed to win this competition to show my parents we were serious and didn't need them! I can't believe you just made this decision without me!"

"I figured we'd talk it out later," Bacon protests.

"Oh, we have a *lot* to talk about, *Barry*." Firefly throws up her hands. "This is what I get for falling for an Aries."

"Fiona, baby," Bacon shouts as Firefly turns her back on him. "Don't do this."

She whirls around to jab a finger at his chest. "We're getting a divorce—"

"We're not married!"

"—and I'm taking the sourdough starter!"

Dawn Taylor cuts in, coming between them. "Bacon, make sure you read the fine print on that cash. You can't use it on anything that will benefit Firefly. So don't even think about trying to buy your way back into her good graces. Now, I'm sorry, but your journey through hell ends here."

Bacon is crying now, tears tracking down his cheeks as Firefly storms off. We're all quiet in the wake of their departure. Firefly and Bacon had seemed so genuinely in love, but it hadn't been enough to withstand Dawn Taylor's test. I just hope that they can get through this.

Relief and disappointment surge through me as the cameras circle Firefly and Bacon like vultures. I wanted that twenty thousand dollars. But I'm still in the game, and I still have a chance to compete. I grab Daniel's hand and squeeze it.

He squeezes back and tilts his mouth toward my ear. When he speaks, his breath rustles my hair. "Good thing we made that deal not to betray each other *before* this challenge happened?"

I pull back. "Don't tell me it didn't cross your mind."

He turns more fully toward me, his gaze serious. "No, never. We're teammates, Alice."

Now it's guilt that's flooding my system. If Daniel is telling the truth, then he didn't betray me—not the way I did, after we literally made a pact to support each other in this fake relationship.

But we're not the same as Firefly and Bacon. After this, we don't have a life to go back to together. Plus, I remind myself, it's entirely possible that Daniel's lying, and what happened was that he filled the red bucket and just didn't beat Bacon's time. But going by our past together, I can't recall a time Daniel's lied to me.

For a second, I contemplate coming clean to Daniel. But when I picture the look on his face, the hurt and the judgment—well. Maybe I'll tell him later, when this is all in our rearview mirror and we can laugh about it. And anyway, he doesn't have the full picture of what I'm dealing with. He wouldn't understand.

"Now for our winners today, the fastest to fill the blue bucket was—can you guess?" Dawn Taylor waits a beat before announcing, "Dominic!"

"Fuck yeah!" Dominic roars. He lifts Zya on his shoulders, and they're racing down the beach together.

"As for the rest of you," Dawn Taylor says, facing us, "you've survived to descend into the next circle of hell. The stakes are higher than ever, so you'd better get ready. The inferno is only going to get hotter."

The end of her speech is punctuated by a blast. Fireworks explode behind her once again. This time, there's more than just a burst of sparks—this is an entire show. I clap my hands over my ears as the fireworks just keep erupting, growing louder and brighter.

Then everything goes wrong. One of the fireworks zooms right past Dawn Taylor and explodes on the sand in front of us.

Dawn Taylor screams, and then we all scream.

A dozen more fireworks roar to life, whizzing straight for us. The smoke is thick in the air now, and I'm frozen. It's too much like the day I found my mom on the floor, flames licking up the wall behind her stove. I have to move, but I can't seem to summon the will. Despite the heat of the sun, I'm cold again, and time seems to slow to a trickle.

Dawn Taylor ducks for cover behind a cameraperson. Everyone, crew and cast, are scrambling to get out of the way. Someone shoves past me, and I go sprawling face-first in the sand. I'm pushing to my feet when I see it. One of the fireworks is headed for me.

Then Daniel tackles me, and I'm being slammed into the sand again. It feels like I've been punched as we both go down. But that's the last coherent thought I have before a firework explodes next to us, spraying us with sand. For a moment, I can't move. There's sand in my mouth and a faint ringing in my ears.

Then I realize why I can't move. There's a weight on top of me, a body. It's Daniel.

Daniel, who tackled me.

Daniel, who shielded me.

Daniel, face down, the outlines of a burn on his side.

"Daniel!"

Chapter Thirteen

Hell Is Your Academic Rival Saving Your Life

Turns out, it doesn't matter whether you're sitting on a stackable chair in a dimly lit room that reeks of antiseptic or a cushioned rattan chair in a tropical villa—waiting for someone you care about sucks.

Not that I care about Daniel.

I mean, I need him functional to continue the competition, of course, and I would never wish him harm—I'm not *evil*. ("You think you're lawful good, but you're secretly chaotic good" is how Tara once put it.)

And he threw himself into the firework's path to protect me. He saved me. He's hurt because of me.

I can't quite wrap my head around this new reality where Daniel Cho, the guy I spent my high school years locked in academic combat with, would take a firework blast to his side just for me. *Maybe he just has a hero complex*, I tell myself. But I know that's not it.

In the aftermath, Peter Dixon took charge, directing the crew to call our on-site medics. A very harassed-looking medical team arrived shortly after and whisked Daniel back to the villa, where they created a makeshift hospital room for everyone who suffered burns or cuts or bruises.

I've spent far too much time this year in waiting rooms. I jiggle my knee, trying to get some of my nervous energy out, but it doesn't help. I need to know if Daniel's okay.

Someone emerges from the room, and for a moment, my heart leaps, hoping against hope that it's Daniel, whole and unharmed. Instead, it's Lex, looking rumpled and exhausted.

For once, they don't have a boom mic attached to their hand. They're clearly about to slink away to do whatever sound techs do in their free time, but I leap up to intercept them.

"Any news? What's going on in there?" I ask.

I can see Lex check to make sure I'm not wearing my mic pack, but we've already taken them off for the day.

"What a shitshow." Lex scrubs at their face. "This is the most dangerous set I've been on, hands down."

"You mean most reality shows don't include explosions and burn wards?" I hazard.

Lex laughs bitterly. "Like I told you before, I wasn't kidding when I said that you need to watch your back."

The way Lex is glancing around nervously gives me pause. "You don't think this was an accident," I say slowly. "What really happened, Lex?"

"I don't know," Lex says. "All I can tell you is that Mom and Dad are fighting, and we're about to be collateral damage."

"Dawn Taylor and Peter Dixon aren't getting along?"

"Oh, they play nice when the crew's around, but I know for a fact that they don't agree on anything. It doesn't help that the stakes are higher than ever. The network execs are loving the show, but they haven't signed off on a bigger budget. Dawn Taylor and Peter Dixon are desperate to prove to them that this show is worth the investment." Lex makes a face. "Which means we're killing ourselves trying to manufacture a hit with nowhere near enough money or crew or resources."

"Sounds like a case of bad planning."

"I'll say." Lex shakes their head. "Most sets would get shut down after the number of 'accidents' we've had. We're breaking all kinds of union rules here. No one's happy. But Dawn Taylor wants us to go bigger. More drama. More extravagance. More everything."

"God, I'm sorry they're putting you through all this," I say. The crew and staff don't deserve this. "Is there anything I can do to help?"

Lex snorts. "Thanks. You're the first person to ask that. You really don't belong here, do you?"

"What?"

"It's not an insult. I'm just saying, it's obvious that you're not here to boost your follower count or land a sponsorship deal. You're not even on social media."

"I am, too," I protest. "I'm just not public." I make it very hard to find my account online. I don't want my students following me. It's weird enough when I run into them in the grocery store sometimes.

"Every other contestant here is ready to cut throats and hide the bodies if it means getting their moment of fame. But you? You can walk away at any time."

"That's where you're wrong," I say. "I can't walk away. I need the money. I have to stay in."

"Well, ask yourself this. Is all this worth it?" Lex gestures at the door behind them where Daniel is being treated. "That could be you in there next time. Are you really willing to risk everything just for a chance to win a million dollars?"

"I've got bills to pay. What about you? Why are you still here, if you think it's so dangerous?" I counter.

"Same as you. I've got bills to pay." Lex scratches at their arm, a grim look on their face. "But I can take care of myself. I've worked these kinds of jobs before. I'm used to no one caring about the crew. As long as I keep my head down, I'll get through it. But you're new to this, and you've been pushed into the spotlight. This show is going to eat you alive if you don't watch out."

"I'm tougher than I look," I say.

"I hope you're right."

I hope I'm right too. But after nearly getting hit by a rogue firework, I'm not so sure that I am. I don't want to let Lex know that, though. They have enough to deal with.

Then I realize that Lex must have been with the medics for a reason, and that reason is staring me in the face. A bandage covers part of the sleeve of tattoos on their arm. "But wait, are *you* okay?" I ask.

"What?" Lex glances down at their arm. "Oh. Yeah, I'm fine."

"Are you sure? Do you need me to get anything for you?" I ask. "I know where all the good snacks are. Not because I was sneaking around the villa without permission or anything."

Lex pantomimes zipping their mouth closed. "Kid, I don't want to know."

"Look, I know you have this whole 'grizzled veteran of the industry' thing going on—"

"Thank you," Lex says proudly.

"But that doesn't mean you can't ask for help. You told me I need to watch my back, but maybe we can watch each other's back."

Lex scoffs. "And how do we do that?"

"Well, you know what's going on behind the scenes with the crew. And I don't have anything to do except spend time with the other contestants. We can compare notes, piece together everything that's happening on this island. You said it yourself, this is the most dangerous set you've ever been on, and we don't know who we can trust. Having all the facts can only help us."

"You know, I have an actual job to do," Lex says skeptically. "I don't have time to be playing spy with you."

"And I have a show to win," I say. "We should team up. Exchange information. Look out for each other. What do you think?"

"I think you're a people pleaser, and you just want to be my friend because you're in a new and confusing place," Lex says.

"You're not wrong," I say, grinning. "But this is also a mutually beneficial arrangement that makes sense strategically."

Lex gives me a considering look. "You know what? Sure. My therapist did say I needed to be more open with other people."

"Yes, listen to your therapist," I say.

"Sure, great, can't wait to get an A in therapy," Lex grumbles, but I can tell their heart isn't in it.

"Thank you, *friend*," I say in a singsong voice. "Hey, if we're going to team up and go sleuthing for information, we need a catchphrase. Like, *it's all adding up*. Or *the math checks out*!"

"All right, that's enough out of you. I'm regretting this already," Lex says, shaking their head, but I catch a half smile on their face. They leave without another word.

I'm left alone in this sunny, beautiful excuse for a waiting room, but with Lex gone, I've run out of patience. I give it another ten minutes, and then I approach the door—and nearly get run over by Dawn Taylor.

"Watch it," she snaps at me as I leap to the side.

A medic rushes after her. "Ms. Taylor, don't you want the pain meds?"

"Don't give me that shit. I need to be sharp for filming," Dawn Taylor says over her shoulder. "I can't believe this happened. I could kill those PAs."

"But your burns—"

"I said I'm fine!"

Dawn Taylor disappears down the hall, but not before I glimpse white medical gauze wrapped around her leg, spanning from her knee to her ankle.

The medic sighs. "I wasn't trained for this," she mutters.

"You weren't?" I ask.

The medic glances at me. "Big problems are supposed to be sent to the mainland. But there's a huge storm rolling in, so we're stuck treating people here. It's not exactly ideal."

The medic heads back into the makeshift hospital room, and I take the chance to follow. The first person I see is Leah. She's pacing back and forth in front of Seth, who's perched on the arm of another rattan chair. Bryan is leaning against the wall, looking grim.

"I'm sure I saw Anton setting up those fireworks," Bryan is saying.

"Figures. Everyone knows that he half-asses everything." Leah is chewing her gum with a vengeance as she speaks. "I don't know how he even got this job. He has none of the qualifications, and his attitude is garbage."

"He's a lazy shithead," Seth says. "But we already knew that. The problem is now he's gotten half the cast and crew injured. Did you see the staff breakroom? It looks like we're extras on the set of *ER*."

"Hey, what are you doing here?" Leah says, noticing me. "You didn't get hurt too, did you? I swear, I'll murder that trust-fund ass—"

"I'm fine," I say quickly. "I just wanted to check on Daniel."

Bryan snorts. "You can drop the act, Alice. None of the producers really believe you instantly fell in love with Daniel the second Chase hooked up with Selena."

Ouch, I guess Bryan's buddy-buddy side is only for Chase.

"Don't talk about my couple like that, you dick," Leah spits. To me, she says, "Ignore him. Daniel's over there." She gestures behind her to a cot in the far corner before turning back to rip into Bryan.

I head to the corner to find Daniel lying on one of the cots, his eyes closed. His shirt is off, and there's a bright white bandage around his torso. Before I can stop myself, I reach out to lay my hand on his forehead, but then he cracks an eye open.

"Daniel!" I jump back like I've been scalded. "You're awake."

"I was trying to eavesdrop," he whispers to me.

"Are you okay? I mean, of course you're not. Does it hurt? How are you feeling?"

"I'm horribly wounded, Slayer," he says with a dramatic sigh. "Survival is uncertain. Remember me as I was. Perfect and stunningly handsome."

This guy. Why was I so worried about him? I give him my sternest teacher glare.

"Yikes, point that death stare at someone else." Daniel pats the bandage on his side, then winces. "It hurts like hell, and it's going to scar, but I'll be okay, Alice. Don't worry."

"I wasn't worried," I say, folding my arms. "Who said I was worried?"

"I can see it in your face. You've got that little worry line," he says. He reaches up and presses a finger to my forehead. "You used to look like that when your team was falling behind."

"Did not," I say automatically. But Cindy's pointed out the same worry line before. How did he notice?

Daniel tries to sit up and groans. "Ow, fuck. You know, I read the waiver, but I didn't think I'd actually get hurt."

"Has anything like this happened before to Selena?" I ask. Despite Lex's warnings, I wonder if maybe this is actually pretty standard.

"No, not that I know of," he says, frowning. "But she's been on a lot of shows."

"Was Selena the one who pushed you to apply?" I ask, thinking of how Chase had all but signed the papers for me. It would make sense if Selena was the one who got them on the show. For all that Daniel is competitive, I can't really imagine him deciding to go on reality TV. He's never avoided the spotlight, exactly, but he never struck me as someone who wants to be famous.

"Applied? Selena was recruited. Someone from production reached out to her on Instagram," Daniel says. "She said yes and asked me to join her. We'd only been dating about a month at that point, but it sounded fun. At least, it did at the time." As if proving his point, he winces as he shifts to sit up more.

That cot can't be comfortable. "I'm going to get you out of here," I decide. I head back to Leah and the others.

"—this entire thing is going to set the schedule way back, not to mention the storm," Leah says, pacing the floor.

"Can I take Daniel back to rest in our room?" I interrupt.

"I'm ready to get out of here," Daniel contributes from behind me. He's already grabbed his shirt. He goes to pull it back on and lets out a hiss of pain.

"Here, let me." I help him tug the sleeves over his shoulders, my fingers lightly grazing his bare skin. It's hot where we touch, and I remind myself to ask the medic for an ice pack, extra bandages, and antibiotic ointment just in case.

"Thanks, Slayer," he says.

Guilt surges through me again. Just hours ago, I chose to betray him, and I assumed he would betray me too. But instead, he stayed loyal to me and, worse, jumped in harm's way for me.

"Fine, go," Leah says, all business. "I'll send someone to check on you later. Get some rest."

Once we're out of hearing range of the producers, I take Daniel's hand. "You didn't have to do it," I say softly. "Jump in front of me, I mean."

He looks down at me. "I didn't do it because I thought I had to," he says, just as quietly.

"Then, why?"

Something flashes in his expression that I can't quite parse. He's silent for a beat before he finally says, "It happened so fast, I don't even know. It was just instinct, that's all."

"Instinct," I echo.

"Yeah, spur of the moment," he says. "You ever do something just because? Or is it all bullet points and five-year plans with you?"

"There's nothing wrong with a solid five-year plan," I say primly. It's clear I'm not going to get anything else out of him, so I tug him around to face me, look him in the eye, and say, "Thank you, Daniel."

I watch as he swallows and looks away, his ears reddening just the slightest bit. "You're welcome, Alice."

STORY NOTES FOR EDITORS:
"DAWN TAY'S INFERNO: LOVE IS HELL,"
SEASON 1, EPISODE 4: THE STORM

*[Footage: Dark storm clouds roll over the villa
as thunder booms ominously.]*

MIKAYLA MOORE: I thought this would be, like, a cute little getaway for me and Trevor, but it's getting really crazy out there.

[B-roll footage: Heavy winds bend palm trees nearly in half.]

ZYA CLARK: I'm sure most of these girls are too busy worrying about ruining their manicures to get their hands dirty with storm prep, but not me, bitch!

DOMINIC ROSS: That's what I love about you. You're just not like the other girls. Hey, think I can carry five of these sandbags at once?

[Footage: Several of the cast work assembly-style to make sandwiches.]

*[Footage: Contestants move to strategically place buckets
under leaks in the roof.]*

CHASE DE LANCEY: Guess we should've checked the weather, huh? I just want to get back to competing with my girl Selena, but I'm kind of glad this is happening. It's nice that we're all coming together now to get through this wild storm.

*[Footage: Together, Chase and Alice position a bucket
to catch a water leak. They smile at each other.]*

Chapter Fourteen

Hell Is Having to Make Small Talk

Leah is standing on a ladder with a Stanley cup full of water that she's slowly pouring onto the floor a few drips at a time. The cameraman focuses on me and Chase as we place a bucket under the "leak." Lex has a boom mic lowered close to us, presumably to catch the sound of falling water.

Chase asks, "Hey, are you okay after the fireworks? I saw you go down, and I got worried."

"Oh, yeah," I say, shoving another bucket under the fake dripping water for lack of anything better to do. "Daniel pushed me out of the way. You don't have to worry."

"I'm glad he was there," he says. Then after a beat, "I hope you know you'll always be important to me, Alice."

"You'll always be important to me too," I say, but as I say it, I can see how in my head I've already started to reconfigure our relationship.

The grief and anger I felt when I saw Chase tangled up with Selena is still inside me, but after the talk I had with Chase, it feels muted, almost distant. Here on the island, every day feels like a week because of how much is happening and how much I'm experiencing. That and I've been so busy focusing on selling this relationship with Daniel, I haven't really had time to think about it all.

Or maybe it's the sleep deprivation.

I'm spared having to say more when Dominic and Zya burst into the room, covered in mud.

Leah takes this as a cue to change things up. "All right, let's move over to the kitchen and show you all, I don't know, checking the refrigerator? Locking the windows? Just look busy."

We head into the kitchen, which is a complete mess thanks to our rushed efforts to make "emergency sandwiches." As we enter, the power in the villa flickers and then goes out, plunging us into darkness.

"Chase!" Selena comes racing in. She looks around, her eyes wild. "Chase, there you are. What's going on? Why did the power go out?"

"Ran out of electricity?" Chase shrugs. Selena grips his arm, genuine terror on her face.

Daniel walks in, carrying a box of flashlights and candles. A few of the production assistants and crew members start lighting candles, and soon the room is awash in the warm glow of candlelight. I grab a flashlight and pass another one to Selena.

"Thank god," she mutters, switching her flashlight on. "I know it's stupid, but I really, really hate the dark."

"Aw, babe," Chase says, rubbing her shoulders. "You can rough it for a couple days, right? It's like camping, but we're indoors."

Selena glares daggers at him. "I had to deal with enough of that shit when I was a kid. My dad didn't pay the power bill half the time, and me and my sisters were always freezing our asses off in the dark. I'm not doing that again."

"You don't have to," Daniel says calmly. "There's a backup generator."

"Really? How do you know?" Selena asks.

"Saw it earlier," Daniel says. "I went outside to help the crew get the film equipment put away. Looks like it's a big one—should be enough to get us through the storm. The lights should be back up soon."

Sure enough, the lights blink on within minutes.

"Thank you, universe," Selena cheers, and does a silly little jig around the room. I almost miss the cozy glow of the candles, but I'm relieved that we don't have to ride out this storm without power. And even if Selena's my competition, I wouldn't wish the darkness on her.

....

Later in the day, the storm starts to slow. Through the window, I can see that instead of lashing winds and sheets of rain, there's just a gentle fall of raindrops. Though the clouds are still a stormy gray, there are small pockets of sky blue where sunbeams stream down, like an idyllic and dynamic computer background.

"I think we've reached the eye of the storm," I observe to Daniel when he comes back to our suite. "Why are you wet?"

"I set something up for us." He shakes like a dog, sending droplets of water flying. He heads to the bathroom to towel off and change his bandages.

"Oh?" I was lying on the bed, musing about where I'd gone wrong in life, but at this, I prop myself up on my elbows to get a better look at Daniel. "And what exactly do you have planned?"

"ACBA," he says.

"Huh?"

"Our accelerated chemistry building activity," he says grandly. "Also known as a date. I'm taking you out, Slayer."

My heart rate speeds up at that, traitorous thing. "And how are we supposed to go on a date during a storm? Didn't the producers ask us to stay inside?"

"We'll sneak out," Daniel says, grinning. "Come on, this is the perfect chance. Aren't you tired of being cooped up in here?"

I have to admit, I am getting pretty bored. With nothing to do, I've resorted to reorganizing everything in my luggage and folding all our bedsheets into neat squares.

"All right," I say finally, and take his outstretched hand.

We put on our shoes, and he peeks outside the door, checking that the coast is clear. A small thrill shoots through me when he turns back to me, a mischievous smile on his face, and pulls me through the doorway with him.

"Come on," he whispers, and soon we're running through darkened corridors, my heart pounding as we slip past Seth and Anton talking in the kitchen, and creeping by the wing with the Video Village. I'm not sure where we're going, but we seem to be taking a winding route toward the back of the villa.

"Are we going outside?" I ask. Too late, I realize I've forgotten to whisper. Daniel's eyes widen comically as we dart around a corner, and he presses me into the wall. We hide in the shadows, waiting for two PAs to pass us.

When they're gone, he says, "One, I won't ruin the surprise, and two, Slayer, what part of 'sneaking out' makes you think you can talk at normal volume? You out of practice or what?"

Being out of practice implies I was ever in practice. Which I most definitely wasn't.

While Cindy was learning the finer points of sneaking around to hang out with our friends in the 7-Eleven parking lot at night, I always begged off. Cindy didn't need me there to have fun, and to be honest, I preferred spending the late hours with my mom. We'd watch the latest K-dramas, singing the theme songs together and drooling over the lead guys. I never felt the draw of escaping my family. Especially when we only had each other.

I shrug sheepishly and mime zipping my mouth. He squeezes my hand, keeping me close until we finally reach the back door.

The rain soaks us the minute we step outside, but it's warm and I hardly mind. Daniel leads us confidently toward the jungle behind the villa and points out a curated path cut through the trees. Following it, we soon reach a tropical cabana. The roof is thatched with braided palm fronds, and bougainvillea vines lush with color cascade around the pillars. Despite our sketchy electrical situation, fairy lights twinkle up in the eaves, and at the center of it all is a picnic table.

"How did you find this place?" I marvel.

"I've been keeping an eye out for the right spot," he says. "And then I added a little magic."

When I spot the spread that's been laid out, my jaw drops.

"No. How?" I turn to him.

On the table are two flickering candles and a pile of snacks. There's Korean rice cakes, bars of strawberry Hi-Chew, packets of dried squid and seasoned nori, and—I can't believe I'm really seeing this—haw flakes.

Daniel grins. "My luggage was mostly snacks from H Mart. Sorry it's not a four-course meal, but this was the best I could do under the present circumstances."

"How did you know?" I touch my finger to the haw flakes, which Daniel has made the centerpiece.

"That they're your favorite? An informed guess." He shrugs. "Do you know how many times you'd pop one of those in your mouth, and then go on to completely destroy my argument in Mock Trial?"

"That doesn't answer why you just so happened to have them in your luggage," I point out.

"You made them look so good, I always wanted to ask for one, but I didn't have the guts. So when I went shopping for snacks to bring on this trip, I snagged a pack." He raises an eyebrow at me. "You know, objectively, they aren't that great of a snack. There are better ones."

"They're cheap and crumbly discs that I'm fond of for nostalgia reasons, all right? I won't hear a word against them," I say, wrinkling my nose at him. "Anyway, I didn't make you buy them."

"It's cool. I'm glad I did." Daniel lifts a hand to squeeze my shoulder. It feels so natural, so right, that I lean into it. "It's nice to have something familiar when you're away from home. Or at least that's how I've always felt."

He picks up a Tupperware with a red lid and opens it. Inside are what look like rice rolls coated with chopped nuts. Daniel offers me one. To my surprise, it's delightfully warm.

"Oh, wow. What is it?" I ask.

"Tteok. I made it," Daniel says. "My grandmother used to make this for me on competition days. She always put nuts in the ones she made for me."

"Your grandmother?" I ask. I search my memory, and an older woman in colorful floral cardigans comes to mind. She came to some of Daniel's competitions, but I don't recall his parents ever being there—just her.

"Yeah, she taught me how to make these before she passed away last year."

I never formally met Daniel's grandmother, but learning that she's gone is enough for me to feel a twinge of sympathy. "I'm sorry. Were you close?"

Daniel looks away for a moment. The fairy lights illuminate his face, enough so I can see him tearing up a bit. We sit in silence for a few minutes, and then he says, "My parents are both lawyers. They usually had to work late. My grandmother lived with us, so she was the one who'd pick me up from school, make dinner every night, and scold me when I did something dumb, like skin my knees skateboarding."

"Did that happen a lot?"

He chuckles softly. "Constantly. I was always getting into scrapes, even when I was really little. But my grandmother was always there, ready with Band-Aids. And when I had nightmares, she was the one who chased them away with folktales and midnight snacks."

It's hard to imagine Daniel as a kid. Before this, I only knew the high school version of him, all angles and obnoxious confidence. It's strange to think of him being young, vulnerable, the kind of kid who wakes up with nightmares.

I take a bite of my tteok, and it melts in my mouth while still staying crunchy. I close my eyes to savor it, and immediately want another one once I'm done. I hold my hand out, and Daniel obliges.

"You made this?" I ask.

Daniel looks embarrassed. "I made a big bag and froze some before we came here so I'd have some comfort food. It was a bit of a gamble that I'd be able to warm them up in the kitchen, but they turned out okay."

"They're good! Really good," I say. "You must be a pro."

"Nah, it's just a hobby, and not one that I have much time for."

I wave my piece of tteok at him. "Then how did you get into making these?"

"Hmm, let's see." Daniel tilts his head, considering. "I guess, growing up, my grandmother always took me grocery shopping with her at H Mart. Every trip, she let me pick out something new to try. Then when we moved to the Bay Area in junior high, I had a hard time making friends."

"Really?" I peer at him. "I kind of thought you were always popular."

Daniel shrugs. "I wasn't as outgoing back then. But at lunchtime, when everyone else was eating spaghetti marinara and mushy green beans, I had these amazing meals that my grandmother packed for me, plus a ton of snacks. And when I offered to share, well, everyone wanted to be my friend after that."

"So you bribed your peers into being your friends."

"If it works, it works," Daniel says grinning. "Once I'd figured out that my lunches were the key, I asked my grandmother to teach me how to cook. And after a while, I just fell in love with it. There's something so wonderful about getting to see the people you love eating food that you made, you know?"

"That's pretty cool," I say.

Damn, no wonder Daniel was so popular in high school. While I was busy reading *Inuyasha* and whatever other manga I could get my hands on at the local library, he was learning entire skill sets to win over his classmates.

I realize that despite our study date the other day, I never got around to asking him what he actually does for a living. We were too busy memorizing each other's birthdays and other basic stats like that.

"So, is that what you do now? Something to do with food? You seem so passionate about it."

"No, actually, I just finished up law school at Berkeley, and I'm a lawyer now."

I give him a look.

"What?" he asks.

"You hated Mock Trial," I say before I can stop myself.

He wrinkles his brow. "I did?"

"You never took the lead role," I say. "You did the pretrial case senior year, presumably so you could leave practice after the opening argument."

I pause, unsure if I should keep going.

"And?" Daniel prompts me. "I know you have at least one more data point, Slayer."

"And you never beat me at it," I say. "Which tells me you weren't really trying."

"Oh, I was trying," Daniel says, his mouth quirking. "You were just better in that particular realm of competition." Daniel meets my gaze, his voice lowering. "But I always gave it my all when you were involved."

I feel myself blushing at that. From day one, from the moment I met Daniel, he was my rival and my nemesis. I wanted nothing more than to beat him, and that drive kept me going through high school. When I made Cindy quiz me during lunch or studied far too late into the night, it was because I was hell-bent on wiping that smug grin off his face and reveling in his defeat. I relished competing against him—and most of all, I relished winning.

Daniel had always played it cool. I'd assumed our battles hadn't meant anything to him—that I was just an afterthought. But hearing this, I have to wonder if maybe I was wrong about that. Maybe I'd meant just as much to him as he did to me.

"You're right, though," Daniel says, "Mock Trial wasn't my favorite."

"So what made you go into law?" I ask.

"It just made sense," Daniel says, shrugging. "Going into law was what my parents wanted for me. Both of my older siblings are lawyers, too. I didn't want to disappoint my parents, so I took the path of least resistance."

I nod, understanding the need for parental approval, even though my mom's desire for me to pursue medicine wasn't enough for me to do something I didn't love. At the end of the day, I knew she'd support me choosing my path, so that's what I did.

"What's it like, being in a family of lawyers?" I ask.

"You have no idea," he laments. "Every meal is like a cross-examination." Then he laughs. "Not that it's a bad thing. Debating is basically our way of showing we respect one another. And competing with one another is basically our love language."

"So much about you makes so much more sense." I'm starting to wonder if maybe, just maybe, Daniel and I have far more in common than I initially thought, when we hear a loud boom.

"What was that?" I ask, jumping to my feet. I look around for the source of the noise, my heart racing.

"Can't be anything good." Daniel is already up. "Come on, we should get back."

Together, we make our way toward the villa. By now, the sun has set, and the light is fading quickly. The storm is starting to pick back up again, and the wind whips the trees as we're pelted by raindrops. The trek through the trees isn't as easy as it was an hour ago, and my flimsy sandals snag on a root.

"Crap!" I nearly hit the ground, but Daniel catches my arm.

"I've got you," he says. He takes my hand, intertwining our fingers together, and doesn't let go even when we make it back to the packed dirt path leading to the villa.

I'm wondering how I'm going to clean all the mud off my sandals when Daniel stops short, and I realize that we have much bigger problems.

The villa is dark. The windows aren't lit from within, and the pool we've been walking beside is an inky black, no longer glowing with the shimmering blue of the pool lights.

"Did the power go out again?" I wonder. I tug us forward, but Daniel drops my hand and starts jogging toward the side of the villa. I run after him as he follows the perimeter of the wall.

"There," he says, stopping at last. He points at a huge metal block with pipes running along the side and a vent in the front. The metal is dented, and even in the rain, smoke is billowing out from it.

Daniel says, "The generator. That's what that boom was. I think it blew out."

There's an acrid scent in the air. A hefty tree branch is stuck through the vent, as if it had speared the generator through. I prod the branch. It sparks, and I jump back. We look down at the ground, and something black oozes from the generator. In this light, it looks like blood, and I shiver in Daniel's arms. He tightens them around me.

"Maybe it's oil?" Daniel wonders. He nods at the branch. "I'm guessing the storm must've caused the branch to jam the generator, and it sprung a leak."

We both look up, but the nearest tree is over twenty feet away.

"But the wind wasn't that strong when we heard the generator go," I say slowly. Lex's warning echoes in my mind. First the fireworks and now this? Maybe this wasn't a freak accident caused by the storm. Maybe this was intentional.

"Yeah, I don't know," Daniel says scanning the trees. "Let's go inside and report it."

We turn—and run straight into Leah.

"Shit!" Leah yelps. "You scared me." She shines her flashlight on us. "What are you two doing out here? You should be inside!"

"We went out for a walk when the rain let up," Daniel says. "You coming to check on the generator? I think it's busted."

"Damn it." Leah goes to push her stringy, wet hair out of her face, but her face pinches in pain as soon as she lifts her arm. "Fuck," she hisses.

"Are you okay?" I ask.

"It's fine. I'm fine. I just slipped earlier. Must've strained a muscle when I caught myself." She points her flashlight at the generator. "Well. That thing's dead. It's just one accident after another here."

"When it rains, it pours," Daniel quips.

"Save it for the cameras, Cho," Leah snaps, but it's half-hearted. She pulls out her phone and snaps a photo of the generator. "Come on, I don't want you guys hanging around here."

Leah strides away, and we hurry after her. As we near the front of Villa Paradiso, lightning strikes, a bolt of white in the night sky. In that split second, a flash of movement catches my eye—a streak of something blue and a shadow stark against the walkway for the briefest of moments. But then the darkness returns, and all I can see is the spindly outline of branches.

"Alice?" Daniel touches my arm.

"Did you see that? There's someone else outside." I say, squinting into the distance.

"Probably an animal," Leah says. "Everyone's inside, except you two." At the villa, she holds the door open with her good arm. "At least there's one bright spot in all this," she says as she follows us in.

"What?" I ask.

"Our cameras are working just fine, so we can keep filming."

With the power out, the inside of the villa is also pitch-black. Leah's flashlight is the only light we have to guide us as we make our way through the halls. As we pass one of the tall bay windows, I see the line of trees surrounding the beach, and I'm reminded of the branch plunged into the generator. It could've been an accident, but I have a creeping feeling that something—or someone—happened to that generator.

EXCERPT FROM THE *REAL TALK WITH EDEN AND MIN* PODCAST

EDEN: Ba da da da daaa! You're here with Eden—

MIN: And Min!

EDEN: And we're breaking down all the reality TV drama for you today.

MIN: Okay, first we have *got* to talk about *Dawn Tay's Inferno*.

EDEN: I absolutely love this show. It's giving drama, it's giving train wreck, it's giving ethics violations. I'm obsessed.

MIN: You aren't alone. I think people derive a certain amount of schadenfreude from watching couples fall apart, and *Dawn Tay's Inferno* exploits the hell out of it. This show is killing it in the ratings game right now. Last night's episode had more viewers than *The Bachelorette* did at its peak. Can you believe that?

EDEN: I can believe it. Between a once-in-a-lifetime freak tropical storm and the nonstop relationship drama, this has it all. Reality TV is my sport, and *Dawn Tay's Inferno* is my Super Bowl. Plus, this is coming from Peter Dixon. If you've been paying attention in the reality TV world, Peter Dixon's career is on fire.

MIN: True, but it could just be he has a killer casting department for finding the right people to really bring the drama.

EDEN: Of course he's got a team to support him, but Peter Dixon just gets how to make good TV. Problematic, and often lawsuit-worthy, based on the last couple court cases to come his way, but good TV nonetheless. We have to respect the hustle. Combine that with an icon like Dawn Taylor and a bunch of hot couples rolling around on the beach and, well, it's not going to disappoint.

MIN: To be honest, it's a little contrived for me. Like, don't you think that relationship swap was totally planned in advance? I'm not even sure this "storm" is real.

EDEN: The storm is so real. I've been tracking it—don't laugh.

MIN: Who's laughing? Not me.

EDEN: Uh-huh. Anyway, normally I'd agree with you on the swap being scripted, but I've been through enough breakups that I can sniff out genuine heartbreak. You can, like, see the exact moment when Alice's heart shatters into a million pieces. Apparently, they've been together since college, which—woof.

MIN: Ugh. I felt so bad for her. Alice, throw the whole man away!

EDEN: Seriously. Chase has got that golden retriever himbo thing going for him, but Daniel is definitely an upgrade for Alice. I swear, whenever he looks at her, he's got cartoon heart eyes.

MIN: Right? Finally, some good fucking food. I'm rooting for Alice and Daniel, and I hope Chase *literally* breaks a leg from a palm tree falling on him. Or maybe Dominic will step up and actually do something useful and throw Chase off a speedboat or something.

EDEN: Min!

MIN: I said what I said.

Chapter Fifteen

Hell Is a Slumber Party with No Pizza

The fragrant tropical breeze and the sweltering hot weather is a thing of the past. Between the torrential rain and the howling wind, temperatures have plummeted.

The producers have sent the contestants into the living room, where we're collectively sharing a single battery-powered space heater. The cots are pushed against the walls, and everyone is huddling around the one source of heat. Blankets and pillows, commandeered from the rest of the villa, are scattered on the floor. It's like a high school slumber party—except none of these people are my friends.

I rub my arms for warmth and feel a weight settle on me as Daniel drapes a steel-blue blazer over my shoulders. I inspect the fabric. It's surprisingly soft, and there's a smart little handkerchief tucked into the pocket.

"Is this your suit jacket?" I ask.

Daniel offers a wry smile. "Yeah, it's all I've got. Wish I had a hoodie with me, but I didn't pack for a major storm and a blackout."

I tug the blazer tighter. "It's perfect. Thanks."

I catch one of the cameras swiveling toward us, and I plaster on a smile that I hope looks adoring and not like I'm experiencing rigor mortis. Daniel settles beside me.

"Aren't you cold?" I ask. He's changed into dry clothes—shorts and another button-down.

"I'm good. And you'll keep me warm, right?" he says, winking. Because we're being filmed, I don't chuck a pillow at his head. Instead, I lift my arm up for him. For a moment, he hesitates, and then he scoots over to join me. Even now, he's so warm, and I find myself snuggling closer to him, seeking out the comfort of his body heat.

I rest my head on Daniel's shoulder. He drops a kiss on my temple, his lips pressing against my skin for the span of a heartbeat. My face heats at the contact, and I will myself to not react any more than that.

If you'd told high school me that I'd be voluntarily cuddling with Daniel Cho in paradise, I'd have told you to get lost. Well, first I'd grill you on the mechanics of time travel, and then I'd tell you to get lost.

"Aw, you guys are so cute," Zya drawls. She's curled up next to Dominic by the space heater, clad in an oversized plaid shirt. "You two sure got together quick after you were cheated on and dumped."

Dominic smirks. "Level with me here. Were you that desperate for a rebound or are you just in it for the competition?"

"We're in love," Daniel says coolly.

I can feel the rumble of Daniel's voice, and it grounds me enough to simply say, "If you have a problem with us, take it up with the producers."

"What, you gonna snitch on us?" Zya taunts.

"Oh, shut up," Selena says from where she's cuddled up with Chase. "Who we date isn't any of your business."

"Girlie, the four of you are fucking with my chance to win a million dollars, so I'd say it's very much my business," Dominic sneers.

"Hey now, let's take down the temperature," Chase says, holding his hands up. He's got an affable smile on, the kind he'd wear to break up a bar fight. Beneath the friendly expression, though, I can tell even he's starting to get pissed. "We're just trying to ride out this storm, okay?"

"Sure. Whatever." Dominic focuses his attention back on me, and my skin crawls as he says, "I don't know what your game is, but you'd better sleep with both eyes open."

I'm spared having to tell Dominic to go fuck himself when Trevor enters the room carrying an armful of throw pillows and a giant comforter.

"Did Mikayla come through here?" he asks us. We all exchange blank looks.

Daniel answers, "No, haven't seen her tonight."

"Weird," Trevor says. "I told her I'd pack up our stuff to come down here. Figured she'd be here by now."

"Give your girl some space," Jaxon says. Ironically, he's got his head in Brittany's lap as she crochets an elaborate lace top. "You'll be just fine if you're apart for more than five minutes."

"You don't get it," Trevor insists. "This is our brand. It's what Trekayla is all about. We're always together."

"*Always?*" Jaxon repeats skeptically. "Even when you're takin' a dump?"

Brittany prods him with her crochet hook. "Don't be gross, honey."

"I get you, Trevor," Selena says. "Everyone is different. Some people want space, and some people don't. Plus, for content creators, your identity is your brand, and that's how you make your living. You have to take that seriously."

Trevor shoots her a grateful look. "Yeah, exactly. We've got the followers, but that doesn't always translate into dollars. Which is why we're here, to take our relationship and our platform to the next level."

"Oh, I know," Selena says. "I love your reels. I watched your announcement video on the boat ride over before Seth took my phone away."

"God, what I would give for my phone back," Jaxon groans.

Ava and Noah arrive just then, dragging their hardshell suitcases behind them.

"Jesus!" Noah glances at the rain sleeting past the window. "I'm sick of this weather. You guys know where the food is? I need to fuel up."

"You don't want to see what he's like when he gets hangry," says Ava. "He's like the Hulk, if the Hulk managed to keep his shirt on. One time he broke the Peloton."

"Sounds like an anger management problem, not a nutrition issue," I mutter to Daniel.

Selena says, "We've got sandwiches on the table over there if you want. They're looking a bit sad from sitting out, though."

"I'll take it." Noah immediately walks over and inhales a sandwich, then makes a face. "Guys, no offense, but how can you screw up sandwiches this badly?" he asks.

"Yeah, it's sticking to the roof of my mouth," Ava says. She's chewing like a dog trying to eat peanut butter.

"Oh, is Miss Gaslight Gatekeep Girlboss too good for sandwiches?" Zya asks in a mocking tone.

Ava rolls her eyes and turns her back on Zya. It's clear that we're all sick of whatever Zya and Dominic's deal is.

"At least Tarun and Kendall aren't here to see this," Daniel says.

"Pour one out for the homies," Chase says solemnly. He waves Ava and Noah over, and soon we're all gathered around the heater in a circle. I get the distinct feeling that someone is about to ask if we should all play truth or dare.

Brittany speaks up. "I've got a question," she says in a hushed tone. "What do you think happens to the losers?"

"Murdered," Daniel deadpans.

A hush falls over the group for a second before everyone bursts into laughter.

"Nah," Chase says, "Bryan told me they get put up at a fancy hotel on the other side of the island."

"Wish we were there," Jaxon grumbles. "I bet they have power. And room service."

"What I wouldn't give for my mom's chopped salad right now." Selena sighs dreamily. "She makes the best salad dressing."

"Forget salad. How about real food? After these past few days, I'm starving for a sausage pizza and an IPA," Zya says. She smirks. "I just can't stand girls who don't eat real food."

"God, you're so hot," Dominic says, caressing her thigh.

"We get it, you're 'not like other girls,'" Selena says acidly. "But you know, hon, you don't actually have to put other women down all the time. There's no cameras here. What are you trying to prove?"

"Sorry, I don't do girl drama," Zya says, waving a dismissive hand at Selena, who looks like she wants to strangle Zya. I shoot Selena a sympathetic look, and she widens her eyes at me.

"I'm not sure how anyone can eat anything after the Gluttony Challenge," Brittany says, redirecting the conversation. "Are y'all feeling better after yesterday? That food poisoning was so intense."

"Yeah, I don't think I've ever had it that bad. I've eaten sidewalk fries before, and nothing happened to me," Chase says.

"Sidewalk fries?" Brittany tilts her head. "Like, street food?"

"Like he picked fries up off the sidewalk and ate them," I clarify.

"I bet it was because they didn't store the cow eyes properly. I mean, how do you even *store* cow eyes? Isn't there a food safety person on staff?" Brittany wonders.

"Probably not." Given what Lex has told me about how short-staffed the crew is, I seriously doubt it. "And for what it's worth, I don't think it was the cow eyes. I ate the eye for my team, and I was fine."

"I reckon it's gotta be the peppers then," Jaxon puts in.

"Can't believe I was betrayed by one of my favorite foods!" Selena says mournfully.

"I get the feeling there's more going on here than we're seeing," I say.

"Elaborate, please," Ava says. All eyes are on me suddenly. My hand goes to my hip, just to triple-check I'm not still wearing my mic pack.

"Well, things keep going wrong," I say. "The fireworks. The food poisoning. The backup generator blowing out. It just doesn't seem . . ." Remembering Lex's warning, I choose my words carefully. "Well-managed."

"My money's on the tight production schedule," Noah says. "You can't create a good end product without sufficient resources."

"Do you think the set is cursed?" Brittany asks, darting a look around the room. "Because this has 'curse' written all over it."

"What are you, five? Don't be stupid," Zya says, and Brittany glares at her.

"Well, I just hope our luck turns around," Trevor says firmly. "Mikayla and I need this show to be a hit."

"You're not the only one," Ava says. "But I wouldn't worry. Doesn't matter how badly this show is run, it's going to do numbers with Dawn Taylor on board. That's why Noah and I applied."

"Eh," Jaxon says with a shrug. "I didn't even know who Dawn Taylor was before we came here."

"Nuh-uh, you know who she is," Brittany interrupts. "She's Krista from *Cocktails & Confessions*!"

"Hate to break it to you, honey, but I didn't watch that show for the plot. I was just hoping a certain sorority girl would give me the time of day—and it worked, didn't it?" Jaxon says, and Brittany cuffs him lightly on the shoulder with a laugh.

"I can't believe you're here for *Dawn*. She's so old," Zya cuts in.

"She's only in her forties," Ava says, and it's clear by the sneer on Zya's face that she does not find that a compelling counterpoint.

"Exactly, she's basically decrepit," Zya says. "There's a reason she's clinging so hard to this show. When was the last time you saw her in anything?"

"But that was because of the whole thing with her stalker," Selena points out. "She stepped back from public life for her safety."

"I heard that was made up for the drama," Brittany says. "I love Dawn Taylor, but I wouldn't put it past her. She knows exactly what she's doing."

My mind summons the memory of Dawn Taylor when I ran into her the other day outside of the villa's makeshift hospital room. Her leg had been wrapped in bandages, and she'd looked incandescent with rage at someone causing problems on her set. This show must mean everything to her, especially after so many years out of the spotlight.

I shake my head, trying to ignore the chill that goes down my spine.

"Women that age aren't *decrepit*," Brittany is saying. "It's just that Hollywood hates casting older women. Once you turn forty, suddenly the only roles you can play are grandmothers and evil stepmothers. If you're lucky, you get to play a rich but perimenopausal woman about to get cheated on by your husband in some thriller."

"It's not a crime to only want to see hot people on TV," Zya says.

This time, it's Selena shooting me a look that clearly says, *can you believe this girl?*

"You know, you're going to be that age one day," Ava retorts.

"Yeah, but I'll still be hot," Zya says.

Ava shakes her head. "Okay. Stay delusional. Brittany, to answer your question, if there's a curse on set, its name is Anton."

"Ugh, not him," Brittany says. "You're right. He's such a creep!"

"Wait, did he try anything?" Jaxon asks, his eyes flashing with anger. "Do I need to have words with him?" He cracks his knuckles.

"It's just that I've caught him staring at me, and I swear he was following me on one of my walks the other day," Brittany says. "I don't like it, but I don't think he's worth getting in trouble over. If it comes down to it, I'll punch him myself."

"Well, I'm not surprised," Noah says. "Word is that guy massively fucked up the fireworks. I don't know if Anton's incompetent or just lazy, but everything he touches turns to shit. And in a place like this, that can be dangerous."

As if to punctuate his words, a crack of thunder reverberates through the room. The door swings open with a crash.

It's Mikayla. She's soaked to the bone, her usually picture-perfect red hair in wet clumps.

"Oh! Uh, hey everyone," she says weakly.

"Sweetie!" Trevor rushes over to wrap her in a blanket.

"Thank you, Trevie," she says, melting into his arms. She takes a few steps inside, tracking mud in behind her before she realizes what she's doing. "Oh crap. I'm so sorry." She tugs off her shoes and dumps them by a planter.

"Where were you?" asks Trevor. "You said you'd be down here."

"I just stepped outside for a bit. I thought I left one of my gratitude journals out on the patio. But I couldn't find it anywhere."

"You go get warm. I can go look," Trevor says, but Mikayla tugs him back toward the blankets.

"No, it's okay. I looked everywhere. It must've blown away."

We make room for Mikayla and Trevor so they can warm up by the heater. With a confidence I can only admire, she doesn't hesitate to strip down. When they announced filming was done for the day, the rest of us immediately changed into comfy casualwear like leggings or sweatpants, but when Mikayla strips out of her muddy shirt and pants, she's wearing a matching pink satin set with black lace trim underneath. In the dim glow of the candlelight, she looks ready for the Victoria's Secret runway.

"So, what'd I miss?" Mikayla asks, glancing around at all of us. "Any hot goss?"

"The set is cursed, Dawn Taylor's hell-bent on making sure the show goes on no matter what, and Selena's seen your reels," I say, listing things out on my fingers.

"Aw, I knew I liked you," Mikayla tells Selena, who blows a kiss back at Mikayla.

Mikayla only has a few minutes to try—and regret trying—a sandwich before Leah appears in the doorway. Like the rest of us, Leah's in her own pajamas, a cozy flannel set. Bryan and Seth flank her, both in loose T-shirts and pajama shorts. Several camerapeople follow them in.

"Loving the sleepover vibe," Leah says, surveying us. "But let's make this a party so we have something to send to the editors tonight. How's that sound?"

"Should I change or . . ." Mikayla begins, reaching for her clothes uncertainly.

"No way," Seth says immediately. "You look amazing. I mean, it'll be perfect for the cameras. We can blur anything, uh, untoward."

"Drinks!" Leah decrees. Anton and Freya arrive, carrying two platters of drinks.

Zya makes a face as Anton hands her a fruity mixed drink. "Are you kidding me? I'm not one of those girls who always has to have something pink and sugary. I want whiskey. Neat."

"You heard the lady," Dominic says, shoving the glass back at Anton so hard that it sloshes all over him.

Anton looks down at his shirt. "What the hell? We're not your waiters, you 'roided up clown."

"Oh, it's on," Dominic says, his face contorting into a gleeful expression. His hand snaps out to grab Anton's shirt. He pulls Anton up off his feet, winding up to punch him out.

"Don't do it, Dom! We'll get sent home," Zya says, grabbing his arm.

Dominic hesitates. He looks from Anton to the cameras that have swarmed around him to capture this moment. Even though Anton is a member of the crew, drama is drama.

"Don't let him ruin our plans!" Zya insists.

Dominic lets out a forced laugh and drops Anton. He shakes his hand out, as if he actually did throw that punch. "This isn't over."

"Anton, get out of here," Bryan says, stepping between them. "You've caused enough trouble."

"Don't tell me what to do," Anton sneers, but it's clear he's shaken. He hurries out of the room without so much as a backward glance.

"You know what," Leah says, looking around at all of us. "I can't deal with this. I need an aspirin. Let's call it a night."

Chapter Sixteen

Hell Is Having to Be Vulnerable

*C*LANG! CLANG! CLANG!

I jolt awake, flailing around in my makeshift bed on the floor until someone pulls the blanket off my head.

I look up blearily at Daniel. Even though it's still dark out, he somehow looks refreshed and put together, with his hair swooping over his eyes just so. It's infuriating.

At some point during the night, the power must've come back on, because the intricate gilded chandelier at the center of the room is once again blazing with light.

"Good morning, darling," he says. I can barely hear him over the ringing of the bells.

"What is that noise?" I shout back.

"If I had to guess, I'd say the producers decided to interrupt our beauty sleep," Daniel says. Then he crouches down, smiles warmly at me, and brushes the hair back from my face ever so gently. "Not that you need it, sweetheart. You're gorgeous."

My stomach flips. I've never seen Daniel act this way—I mean, not to *me*. My mind does a speedrun montage of everything that happened last night. Why is he caressing my face like that? And did he just call me *sweetheart*? I'm not against it, but the way he's looking at me, I have to wonder if he's been abducted by aliens and given a brain transplant.

But as I search for a response, I realize that his smile looks just the tiniest bit forced. His gaze darts to the right, and yep, there's a camera pointed right at us. Apparently the crew is here to capture the chaos of a bunch of exhausted couples waking up at the crack of dawn.

"Darling," Daniel says again. "Are you with me?"

Crap. I need to sell this moment for the cameras. The other couples are already suspicious of us, especially Dominic and Zya. But I'm too tired to come up with the right thing to say. I lean in and kiss Daniel.

Our lips connect, and at first he stiffens. I make to pull away, but then he relaxes into it, wrapping his arms around me and deepening the kiss. This isn't the warm, familiar feeling of kissing Chase. It's more like holding a live wire, every part of my brain screaming that this is Daniel Cho who's swiping his tongue across my lips and pulling me back into my nest of blankets. I curl my fingers in his shirt and feel him groan, the sound reverberating through me. All I want is to keep kissing him, keep feeling his body on mine, keep pressing into him until he does more than slot his knee between my legs.

But then Daniel pulls away. He rests his forehead against mine, and our breathing mingles together as I come back to myself—and realize that the cameras have captured everything. Right, that was what this was all about.

I'm finally awake enough to know what to say. I tuck my hand into Daniel's and look at him with an expression that I hope is sufficiently sweet and loving. "Whatever we're doing today, I know we can win—together."

"That's the Slayer I know," he says, pressing a kiss to my forehead. I feel my cheeks heat, and this time, I don't will the blush to go away.

In short order, we're hustled out of the villa and taken on a ten-minute trek down to the beach, where a massive wooden structure has been erected. The walls of this structure are easily thirty feet tall and are painted with a variety of colorful symbols. We pass by one of the entrances, and a quick peek inside confirms that our challenge involves a labyrinth.

Dawn Taylor is striking a pose at the top of the structure. Despite the early morning chill, she's in a bright-orange leather bikini with sparkling spikes on the cups, like she's auditioning for a role in a glitzy remake of *Fury Road*.

"Welcome to the Wrath Challenge!" she shouts, and pyrotechnics shoot off behind her, lighting up the dark sky. "Babes, I hope all of you are well rested."

We're not.

"It's time to put your love to the test. Love is patient, love is kind, blah blah blah. The truth is that love is easy when everything's going right. But what about when everything around you is going to hell? Well, you're about to find out."

A crew member ducks past the cameras and puts down a giant treasure chest.

"For the Wrath Challenge, each couple must navigate my infernal labyrinth . . . but I'm not making it easy. One of you will be blindfolded, and one of you will have your hands tied behind your back. Communication and cooperation is the name of the game here. The first couple who escapes the labyrinth will win the chance to get hot and heavy in a luxurious hot tub date. The last couple to finish is, well, you know the drill. Have fun . . . and try not to lose your cool."

Dawn Taylor blows a kiss, and we're off. Noah and Dominic race over to the treasure chest, jockeying to be first. Dominic shoves Noah roughly out of the way and wrenches the chest open. Inside is a stack of blindfolds and coils of rope.

"Dominic, you've got to *listen* to me if you take the blindfold," Zya insists, trying to grab his arm and stop him from putting one on, but Dominic just brushes her off.

"You should wear the blindfold," I say to Daniel when he comes back with our supplies.

"Yeah?" he asks. "Go on, let's hear it. I'm sure you've got a list of reasons."

"You know me so well," I say sweetly. "Number one, I think it's safe to assume that the labyrinth will involve some physical challenges. And even without your sight, you'll be better equipped to tackle it if your hands are free. You've clearly got more upper body strength than I do."

He raises an eyebrow.

"It's an objective fact. Don't let it go to your head," I say. "Plus, you're about five inches taller than me, which gives you an additional physical advantage. Number two, I'm better at giving instructions than you are."

"And how do you know that?" he asks.

"I'm a teacher," I remind him. "And number two, you're still healing from getting burned. Having your hands tied behind you would probably stress your wound."

He raises an eyebrow. "I'm sore, sure, but I don't think being tied up will necessarily be any harder than whatever I'll have to do blindfolded."

"Number three, I just really don't want to be blindfolded," I tell him.

Strategically, it makes sense for me to give the instructions. But honestly, I just hate the thought of groping about, unable to see where I'm going. The idea of giving up that control, trusting someone else to tell me where to go and what to do—it's enough to give me hives.

"Fine by me," Daniel says. "I can take the blindfold." Once we have our blindfold and rope, he makes quick work of tying my hands behind my back. His touch is gentle but sure.

"I hope that was as good for you as it was for me," he says, putting his blindfold on. I laugh, and it loosens the knot of anxiety that's been lodged in my throat since the start of the challenge.

Then it's time to enter the labyrinth. Pair by pair, each of us are led to a different entrance.

"Babes, it's time!" Dawn Taylor's voice booms from a megaphone. "Get ready . . . get set . . . and go!"

On her mark, Daniel and I venture into the labyrinth. It's not much darker inside than it is outside. Although the labyrinth is open to the sky, the sunlight streaming in is half blocked by the towering walls on all sides. The crisscross of scaffolding above us serves as catwalks for the camera crew. I spot Lex up there, along with a squadron of camerapeople following along as we navigate.

Before us, the path is illuminated by electric torches that cast a warm, flickering glow over everything, creating a haunting atmosphere. It feels like we're adventuring archeologists traversing unexplored catacombs. Or, you know, like we're in line for the Indiana Jones ride at Disneyland.

The crew must've spent weeks constructing this labyrinth before we arrived on the island. I feel bad for the set designers—the labyrinth is an incredible set piece, but it didn't fare well in the storm. I can see where some planks from the catwalks have fallen and paint has been washed away.

Just making our way through the labyrinth itself is slow going. The packed sand paths have transformed into long trenches of mud. Our shoes squelch as we walk—or at least, as I walk. I turn back to see Daniel with his hands outstretched in front of him, tentatively edging forward. We don't have time for this.

"Daniel, reach out in front of you," I say. I maneuver so that my bound hands are in front of him, and he takes them.

We continue slogging through the mud like this until we make it to the first obstacle. A space has been cleared, and on the floor is a mound of huge blocks. Letters are painted on each block. Gaps have been cut into the wall, clearly designed to hold the blocks. Above the gaps is a riddle.

"It's a giant word puzzle," I say, my mind already racing to come up with a strategy. "There are these big blocks here, five in total. It looks like we're going to have to slot them into the wall to spell something to answer the riddle."

"Gotcha. Where are the blocks?" Daniel lets go of my hands and starts feeling around—and accidentally puts his hand on my face.

"Hey!" I headbutt Daniel's hand and he loses his balance, pinwheeling his arms before landing flat on his butt.

"Sorry! Sorry," Daniel says as he struggles to his feet.

I glance up to see the camera crew and Lex up on the scaffolding, and sure enough, they've caught everything. I can tell Lex finds it hysterical, because they have their hand over their mouth so they won't ruin the audio quality.

I point Daniel to the blocks, and he attempts to lift one. "Geez, these are heavy. Good thing I work out," Daniel says, flexing.

"Good for you," I snort. "Okay, the riddle is: What has two hands, two eyes, and four legs?"

"A centaur?" Daniel guesses.

"We have to spell the answer with the letters on the blocks," I say, surveying the scene. "Let's see, we've got AL, EL, DA, NI, and ICE."

"Think it has something to do with Dante or the *Inferno*?"

I shake my head before I realize that Daniel can't see me. "Maybe. I wouldn't bet on it. I think we're pretty far from the source material here."

"Any other clues around here? Anything you see that could be a hint?"

I look around. "Nope. There's the riddle on the wall, but that's about it. The riddle's been painted in red, but it's sort of faded and peeling off, probably because of the storm."

"What color is the paint on the blocks?" Daniel asks.

"It's red, like the riddle," I say. I look from the wall to the blocks on the ground. "Except the paint on these blocks is bright red, like it's new."

That could mean anything. Maybe the blocks weren't stored outside, or maybe someone thought to throw a tarp over them. Or maybe the blocks were painted just moments ago. The paint looks fresh, and the letters look a little slapdash, as if someone were rushing through it.

My jaw drops. "It's us! What has two hands and two eyes and four legs? Alice and Daniel."

"Because I'm blindfolded and you're tied up," Daniel says.

"Exactly. I bet once they knew which entrance to the labyrinth we were stationed at, they painted the letters."

At my direction, Daniel heaves the blocks into their slots, one by one. The moment we finish, one of the walls to our left shifts with a grinding rumble. From where we're standing, I can see Freya and Anton laboring to move the wall, but the camera captures it at an angle where it looks like the wall is moving on its own.

After another slog through the mud, we make it to the next challenge. A gleaming ornate key hangs above a vine-covered wall.

"This one's pretty straightforward," I say, taking it all in. "We're in front of a fifteen-foot climbing wall with a key at the top, and there's a door we have to unlock."

"Climb the wall, got it." Daniel steps around me and onto the crash pads laid out by the wall. He reaches out to touch the wall. "Ow! What was that?"

"Sorry," I say. "Forgot to mention. The wall is covered in spiky vines."

"I thought you said this would be easy!"

"I said it would be straightforward," I say. "As in, our objective and how we accomplish it is clear. I never said it would be easy. Now put your hand on your nose."

"Is this a prank?" he asks. "Because as much as I love a good shenanigan, I don't know if this is the time."

"Just do it."

"All right, I trust you," Daniel says, and I know he's just saying it for the cameras, but my mind repeats it back to me like it means something. *I trust you.*

"Now straight out from where your hand is now, that's where the first handhold is. It's like a little rubber ledge the size of your hand, the kind they have on rock-climbing walls. So just reach straight out by about a foot."

Daniel doesn't hesitate, immediately reaching out and grabbing onto the handhold.

"Got it," he says. "Now what?"

"There's another one about forty-five degrees up and to the right, one foot from the first one," I say.

With that, he has enough leverage to lift himself up. I continue navigating him along the wall, and he manages to hoist himself up without too much trouble. Even though it turns out that Daniel is great at climbing, I try my best to pick the easiest moves so he won't aggravate his burns. At the top, he gropes about in the air as I shout directions, and finally he pulls the key free.

"You did it!" I cry.

Daniel puts the key into the lock and the door swings open with a click. Once Daniel is back down, we step through into the next part of the labyrinth.

What I see on the other side makes my heart sink. In large letters painted on the wall are the next set of instructions.

"*One can see and one can do. Now it's time to wear the other shoe. Blindfold off, hands free. Time to switch which one you'll be.*" I groan. "We have to switch."

I take off Daniel's blindfold. He blinks as his eyes adjust to the light.

"Whoa," he says, taking in our surroundings for the first time. "The writing on the wall feels a little serial killer, doesn't it?"

"No comment." As much as I don't want to, I push my hands toward Daniel. "Untie me."

Once I'm free, I tie the blindfold loosely around my head, pushing it up so I can tie Daniel up.

I try to be gentle. "Is this okay? Does your side hurt?"

"Nah, I'm fine," Daniel says, shrugging it off, but I can see him wincing.

"I'm sorry," I say.

Daniel laughs. "Slayer, don't worry about me. It's too weird. You're going to scare me."

I laugh too, and that carries me through the terrible moment of pulling my blindfold on. I take a moment to adjust to the sudden and complete darkness.

"You good?" he asks.

"Let's get this over with," I grit out. I hate this. I want to tear off the blindfold and run out of here. Then Daniel takes my hand and squeezes it. When my foot catches on something, he's able to steady me before I can even begin to lose balance.

"I've got you," Daniel murmurs, quiet enough that I almost don't hear it.

"Where are we going?" I ask, desperate to distract myself. "I need information."

"You're not missing much," Daniel says. "We're walking through a narrow hallway. I'm making sure you don't bump into the walls, but if you reach, you can feel it."

I touch the wall briefly, run my finger along the smooth wood, and it helps.

"Turning," he says.

I hate this. "How did you make this look so easy?" I grumble.

"It wasn't easy," Daniel says simply. "But I trusted you to guide me."

There it is again. Trust. Daniel trusts me.

"You didn't think I was going to run you into a wall or anything?" I ask.

"Well, no, because that would be detrimental to our success as a team," Daniel says. "And I know you wouldn't do anything to hurt me. We might've spent high school on opposite sides, but you were always an honorable opponent."

That's true. And if I'm being fair, Daniel was always an honorable opponent in turn.

"I keep thinking I'm going to crash into something or fall on my face," I admit.

"I wouldn't let that happen to you," Daniel says, his voice low. There's something comforting and strangely intimate about hearing his voice when I can't see anything, and the only connection I have to the rest of the world is through his touch. It makes me want to keep talking, for better or for worse.

"I know," I say. "It's just that I hate relying on other people. If you want a job done right, you have to do it yourself. That's how I was raised. And I don't trust just anyone to have my back."

"But I'm not anyone. I'm *Daniel Midas Cho*," he says. I don't have to see him to know that he's directing a shit-eating grin at me.

"All the more reason to distrust you," I declare.

I'd thought I could trust Chase because I had him all figured out. But it turns out, I'd been wrong on both counts. For a moment I wonder what my life would've been like if I'd dated Daniel instead of Chase. As much as I'm loath to admit it, I have a feeling he would've been a good partner. In high school, he was the guy who showed up fifteen minutes early to every competition in a freshly pressed suit and somehow managed to charm all the parents and teachers. And from what I've seen of him on the island, he's still that guy. He takes care of the people around him, and he steps up when something needs doing.

I return my focus to putting one foot in front of the other. Daniel directs us around another corner and then stops abruptly, his grip tightening—but it's too late. I pitch forward and bring him down with me. We end up in a heap together in the mud.

"Shit! I'm sorry," he says, doing his best to pull me to my feet with his bound hands. "We turned and then we turned again and . . . there's a drop-off here. And a slime pit."

"A slime pit," I repeat.

"Yep, the slime's neon green, in case you're wondering. There's a pillar at the end of the pit and at the top is a rope with a handle. I'm going to guess that one of us has to go into the pit, climb the pillar, and pull on the rope to lower the drawbridge so that both of us can cross over."

"And I have to go in the pit," I say as I picture what's before us. "Because I'm the only one who can climb the pillar."

"If it's any comfort, the pit isn't that deep. Maybe five feet."

"Great. Fantastic. Amazing." I face the pit, or where I think the pit is. Daniel gently turns me slightly left.

I take a deep breath and ease myself into the pit, and immediately, it sucks me in. Ugh. The slime oozes over me as I sink into it, my shoes slipping as I struggle to find purchase on the floor of the pit. When I'm finally standing, the slime comes up to my shoulders. My eighth graders would love this, but personally, this is my worst nightmare.

"Just go straight!" Daniel calls out. "You've got this."

I'm still not over how surreal it is for Daniel to be cheering me on, instead of his own teammates. His voice has always carried during competition, loud and brash and confident. Once upon a time, I found it grating. I resented that he and his teammates were always hyping each other up, while I had to singlehandedly drag my own team to victory, with only Cindy there to root for me.

But now, I don't know. It's nice.

"Stop!" Daniel shouts, and I try to, but end up splatting forward into the slime. Yech. "Okay, reach out directly in front of you. There are handholds on either side of the pole. Use them to climb up, and be careful. You've got about ten feet to go."

I reach out and the handholds are exactly where Daniel said they'd be. I heave myself up and out, and the slime makes a gross sucking sound as it reluctantly releases me.

I pull myself up, one rung at a time. Daniel shouts encouragement. At one point, I suspect he breaks into a song and dance routine.

"Alice, you can reach the rope now. It's just above your head!"

I wave my hand above my head, and once I feel the rope hit my hand, I grab it and yank. There's a raucous crashing sound and the whoosh of something falling past me.

"That was the bridge!" Daniel calls. "You can climb back down now, but it's probably faster if you jump."

The seconds are ticking by, and I can tell that it's going to take me way too long to climb down the pole. I think of Daniel, how sure he sounded when he said he trusted me. Everything is screaming at me not to jump, but we're in a race against the clock and the other couples. If I want to stay in the game, I have to do it. I have to trust Daniel.

I turn around, take a deep breath, and jump.

The slime welcomes me with a horrible *squiiiiiisssshh*. I flounder for a moment, but then I hear Daniel shouting directions.

"A little to your right! Just follow the sound of my voice," he calls.

Wading through the slime as fast as I can manage, I make my way back to Daniel, who guides me to another rope that I use to pull myself out of the pit.

"You all right, Slayer?"

I nod. I've lost my left shoe, but I'll deal with that later. Right now we need to get out of here.

Daniel takes my hand. It squelches in a way that is distinctly not romantic. "Now we run."

He leads me across the bridge and through a series of twists and turns. I'm almost crushing Daniel's hand now as we hurtle through the darkness, but he doesn't seem to mind. Then we come to a stop.

"Hey, open up!" Daniel shouts.

I hear the rattle of a door. Together, we step over the threshold.

"Drop your blindfold!" someone says. I tug it off, and for a moment the light is too bright for me to see anything.

"Are we in time?" I ask, panting. "Did we make it? Did we get eliminated?"

My eyes adjust, and I can make out Dawn Taylor in front of me, with everyone—Peter Dixon, the camera crew, the producers, Lex— surrounding us in a semicircle.

"Eliminated?" Dawn Taylor holds out two glasses of champagne. "You not only survived my Wrath Challenge, you won!"

Chapter Seventeen
Hell Is When Shit Hits the Fan

Dawn Taylor is beaming at us like we just presented her with an Emmy Award, and Daniel is saying something corny about how we strengthened our love in the labyrinth. But I'm still processing that we didn't just survive, we came in first.

Leah is ecstatic as she leads us a few feet away to get our reaction interview.

"You two nailed it," she says. "How are you feeling? Ready for some quality time together in the hot tub?"

Daniel and I lock eyes, and for a split second I think I see panic on his face, but it's quickly replaced with his usual easy smile.

"We can't wait," he says, winking at me.

Another couple staggers out of the labyrinth moments later. It's Noah and Ava, quickly followed by Mikayla and Trevor, who are loudly bickering.

"Looks like there's trouble in paradise," Ava wryly observes.

Then Jaxon arrives, hand-in-hand with a slime-covered Brittany, who does the Electric Slide to celebrate. We all laugh as Selena and Chase charge through next, screaming at the top of their lungs. Somehow, both of them are drenched head to toe in slime.

And then, finally, Zya and Dominic straggle through last, looking miserable. Gone is any sense of camaraderie as Zya tears off her blindfold and hurls it in Dominic's face.

"You didn't listen to a single thing I said," Zya accuses Dominic. "It's not my fault you got dick-punched by that wall!"

Dawn Taylor glides over to meet them. "Zya, Dominic, your journey through my inferno is at an end. It's time for both of you to get the hell out of here."

Dominic looks like he's about to spontaneously combust. A vein is popping on his forehead, and he's breathing like he just ran a marathon. But then he glances back at the labyrinth and all the fight drains out of him. "Fuck this. I didn't want to go on this show anyway."

Zya and Dominic stalk away in silence with Seth and a cameraman hotfooting after them to get their soundbites. Daniel tugs me away from the crowd as the producers descend on the others.

"So, Cinderella, where did you leave your shoe?" Daniel asks me.

"It fell off back in the goo." I eye the scene in front of us. "Think anyone'll notice if we go back and grab it?"

"Nah," Daniel says. "Come on."

"Let's get a group shot going in ten," Peter Dixon is saying as we scuttle back into the labyrinth. "A clip of the slimed contestants together will make a killer promo."

As we turn the corner into the labyrinth, I see my shoe sitting at the edge of the slime pit. Daniel picks it up and guides it onto my foot, his touch at once gentle and firm. Ignoring the butterflies in my stomach, I look anywhere but at him.

That's when I see the body.

There's someone lying by the slime pit, limbs splayed out, in a puddle of something dark.

"Daniel, look," I say, tugging his arm as he straightens up. Then I call out, "Hey, are you okay?"

"Shit," Daniel breathes. His hand finds mine, and together, the two of us make our way across the drawbridge, carefully at first, and then we start sprinting.

I rush to over and kneel in the mud. Whoever this person is, they're not breathing. The dark puddle is blood, and a lot of it.

"Oh god," I say. I want to be anywhere but here. But I force myself to breathe through it as my next steps fall into place. I'm trained in first aid and CPR—I had to be for my teacher's license—but before anything else, I have to call for help.

I reach for my phone and realize it's not there.

Damn it.

"Daniel," I say, "I'm going to try to do what I can. I need you to—"

"I'll get someone," Daniel says, immediately understanding. He's off and running, but I don't watch him go. I have to try to save this person.

I'm shaking as I turn them over.

My hands fly to my mouth.

It's Anton.

WAIVER AND LIABILITY RELEASE

I, the undersigned, release from any and all liability GET REAL productions, including but not limited to the entities of PETER DIXON, DAWN TAYLOR, and all unnamed members of the production crew and cast.

I understand that my participation in DAWN TAY'S INFERNO is conditional on my acceptance of reasonable and unreasonable risks either inside the challenges or outside of the competition. I release GET REAL from any liability for physical, mental, emotional, or intellectual damage, including but not limited to dismemberment, brain damage, stroke, heart attack, death, or permanent impairment. I forever relinquish the right to seek legal action against GET REAL productions.

I acknowledge that GET REAL is not responsible for my physical care during the competition, including if medical attention, such as CPR, the use of emergency medical equipment, or emergency transportation, is needed and not provided in a timely manner.

Chapter Eighteen

Hell Is Finding a Dead Body

Looking at Anton's body, I know CPR's not going to save him, but I try anyway. As I pound on his chest, my mind starts categorizing every small detail: Anton's wide-open eyes, the shocked look on his face. How perfectly styled his blond hair is, still fresh with gel. The bloody bruise around his eye. The mud caked on his shoes and along the hem of his pants. The way one of his hands is scraped and bloody. How still he is, even when I try to breathe air into his lungs. The tacky sensation of blood on my knees where I'm kneeling in it.

My eyes fill with tears for this person I barely know. The last time I saw him alive, he was pushing one of the walls of the labyrinth with Freya. Well, more like he was letting Freya do most of the work while he pretended to push. Not to speak ill of the dead, but from the little I saw of him, it didn't seem like he got along with either the cast or the crew. But he was a living, breathing person less than half an hour ago. That counted for something.

After several minutes, I sit back and just look at him. How did this happen?

Above us, the walls of the labyrinth frame a perfectly clear sky divided up by a network of scaffolding. During the competition, I'd done my best to forget that an entire film crew was up there, capturing our every move and every stumble—but I know Leah had been up there at one point, and most likely the other producers and production assistants had been following their own couples.

Anton, I realize, must've been up on the scaffolding too. It was the quickest way for him to move from one place to another in time to help move the walls or report to a producer. One of the beams making up the walkway is splintered, jagged bits of wood breaking up the neat symmetry of the paths overhead.

Anton had to have fallen from there.

"Alice!"

Almost as soon as I hear my name, Daniel is pulling me to my feet and embracing me, and I hug him back as tight as I can. The thrum of his heartbeat grounds me, and when he lets go, he takes my hand. I twine our fingers together, desperate for the contact.

Behind him, several members of the cast and crew come running in, stopping only when they see the body. For a moment, no one seems to know what to do, but then one of the medics breaks through the crowd and starts checking Anton's pulse. I bury my face in Daniel's shoulder and breathe deep as his hand rubs circles into my back.

"I'm here, Alice," Daniel murmurs.

When I finally look up, I accidentally make eye contact with Dawn Taylor, who's standing at the back of the crowd. Her heels put her above almost everyone else, and she's watching the scene with a detached expression. She doesn't seem to notice me. Her gaze wanders, and when it finally lands on the body, her lips curl in disgust.

Above the din, Peter is getting everyone's attention.

"That's a wrap for today," Peter Dixon says, his voice hoarse with emotion. He's blinking back tears, but he soldiers on. "Everyone back to your rooms. Let's let our medical staff do their jobs, okay?"

Anton is carried out on a stretcher.

....

We're all hustled back to the villa and told to stay inside until further notice. When Daniel and I are back in our suite, I start pacing the floor, my feet sinking into the plush carpet with each step.

"Anton—" I can't even say it. "He's—"

"It's okay, Alice," Daniel says softly. "It's going to be okay,"

But it won't be for Anton.

I barely knew him, but I'm shaking with grief and horror. All I can think about is how senseless Anton's death is. Everything that made Anton who is he and every possible path he might have taken in the future, it's all gone now because of an accident.

"Alice."

There's a moment where Daniel and I just look at one another. Then we come together like magnets drawn to each other. He wraps himself around me, solid and certain. I rest my face in the crook of his neck. All I want right now is to feel connected to someone tangible and real and alive. He holds me tight for a moment that stretches into a small and precious eternity.

Then I pull back, my gaze searching his face. His fingers brush my cheek, and I can feel myself falling into him.

"God, I just—" I start. Then I flinch back at the knock on the door. I swipe at the tears tracking down my face while Daniel goes to open the door.

Lex is standing in the doorway, a grim look on their face.

"Lex! Are you okay?" I ask.

"Not really," Lex says. They look tense and jittery, more unsettled than I've ever seen them before. Their eyes dart over me, and I lift my arms.

"I'm all clear. We left our mic packs with the producers," I say. "What's going on?"

Lex folds their arms. "We shouldn't even be talking. We should be packing our bags and getting on the first flight out of here. But Dawn Taylor is insisting that 'the show must go on,' as if a death didn't just happen on set, and Peter Dixon is backing her up. I tried to make contact with my union rep, but the signal is shit right now. There's nothing getting in or out from this side of the island, thanks to the storm. No flights, no calls."

"We're trapped here." I sink onto the bed.

"Yep, we're trapped," Lex confirms. "I have a meeting with Shawna in ten, so I don't have much time. You wanted to exchange information? Let's exchange information."

"I'll tell you everything. But first, sit." I lead Lex to the suite's only armchair and push a pile of yesterday's clothes off of it.

"Let me get you some water," Daniel says. I take a seat across from Lex on the bed. Daniel hands Lex a bottle of water we'd squirreled away from catering, then sits beside me.

Lex takes a sip, and I can see their hands shaking. That's enough to make *me* nervous.

"I lost my shoe during the challenge. Daniel and I, we went to look for it. But then we saw someone on the ground." I squeeze my eyes shut, and there, in the darkness, is Anton's body, blood pooling around him.

The image is seared into my mind. I can recall every gruesome detail with horrifying clarity, and I know I'll be having nightmares about finding Anton for years to come. I make a mental note to search for an in-network therapist when I get off this island.

My heart starts to race as I struggle to find the words for what happened. Daniel presses his shoulder against mine, and I take a deep breath.

"He was on the other side of the pit. We crossed the bridge, and we found Anton. I tried to give him CPR, but it was too late."

Lex is almost vibrating with tension. They lean forward. "Do you know how he got there? He should've been outside with the other PAs."

"He must've fallen. One of the walkways was broken, probably from the storm," I say, thinking back to the scene of Anton's death. The jagged bits of wood above me. The fathomless blue of the sky. The metal bars that made up the scaffolding.

"Alice?" Daniel says, his gaze on me. "You look like you're puzzling something out."

I shake my head. "I just don't get it. The walkway planks had splintered, but there wasn't enough of a gap for someone to fall through. And the scaffolding had safety rails. There's no reason he couldn't have hung onto the railing and made it across."

"Could he have jumped?" Daniel asked.

I picture the way Anton's body was sprawled out on the ground, face up. "I don't think so. The way he landed, I just don't see it." I focus on the memory of his eyes, wide open and—I may just be imagining it—fearful. "He had a bruise around his eye."

"Anton didn't have a black eye when we saw him last," Daniel muses. "And there wasn't anything he could have hit on the way down that would've given him that kind of injury."

Something clicks for me. "It looked like someone punched him."

"There were also signs of a struggle," Daniel adds. Then, when he sees the look I give him, he adds, "Hey, I took forensics for a semester in undergrad and a few criminal law classes in law school."

I hold up my hands. "I didn't say anything."

"Alice can correct me if I'm wrong," Daniel says, "but I think there were tracks in the mud around his body. Like someone had been dragging him."

"Look at you, Nancy Drew, Esquire," I say.

"Thanks, I loved playing the Nancy Drew games as a kid," Daniel says.

"Same. My favorite was *Ghost Dogs of Moon Lake*," says Lex.

"This is very cute, and I love this for our friendship," I say, waving between Daniel and Lex, "but can we get back to the topic at hand? The fact that Anton's dead and maybe . . ." I don't want to believe this could happen, but I have to admit the possibility. "Maybe someone killed him."

"There's a nonzero chance," Daniel agrees. "Whatever the case may be, whether it's negligence or murder, we need to involve the authorities at this point. Get a real investigation started so the chain of custody on any evidence is airtight."

"Didn't you hear me?" Lex says. "Nothing and no one is getting off this island. Help isn't coming."

The three of us fall silent.

Finally, I say, "We may be trapped, but we're not helpless. We can do something about this. We have to. For Anton."

"Anton's dead. It's over for him. We need to make sure that we get off this island alive," Lex says. They sag back into the chair, the shadows below their eyes deepening. I wonder how much sleep they've been getting.

"These goals aren't mutually exclusive," I reason. Now that I have a purpose, a plan is forming and I'm back on familiar ground. "Step one: We figure out if Anton was murdered, or if he died because of a massive OSHA violation. Step two: If Anton was indeed murdered, then we make a list of suspects."

"That won't be easy," Lex says. "I can tell you for a fact that everyone hated Anton, including the whole crew. He was an asshole."

"Doesn't help that he got a lot of people injured with those fireworks he botched," I agree. "Even Dawn Taylor got hurt."

"Hang on," Daniel says, looking from me to Lex. "Are we sure this is a good idea? You're proposing that we play detective."

"It can't be that hard. I've watched all of the Benoit Blanc movies, and I was the best individual contributor during our Escape the Lab teacher team-building exercise back in October," I say. I drop the false bravado and look Daniel in the eye. "But seriously, it makes sense. We've had too many 'accidents' on set, and at this point, I'm fairly sure all of those were intentional. If we want to stay safe, we need to know if there is a murderer loose on the island—and if so, who."

On that cheery note, Lex's walkie-talkie lets out a burst of static, and we all jump as Leah's voice tells Lex that she's en route to the villa to pick up the contestants.

"Sounds like you're being summoned," Lex says, rising. "I gotta go."

"Be careful," I say, and Lex nods. They slip out, closing the door silently behind them. Barely a few minutes later, Leah arrives, her face pale with exhaustion.

"Anton didn't make it," she says bluntly. "We're filming a memorial in ten. Get ready and meet me outside."

"Wait, Leah," I say, grabbing Leah's arm.

She hisses, her face contorting in pain. I snatch my hand back. I forgot she'd been hurt the other night during the storm. "Sorry, Leah. I just wanted to ask if we could sit this one out. I just don't think I can stomach filming right now, after what happened."

Leah looks almost sorry when she says, "Order from the top, Alice. You don't get a choice. Put on something dark, okay?"

We file down to the beach in silence. The sparkling blue of the ocean and the verdant green of the palm trees feel at odds with the sober atmosphere of our procession.

While we were cooped up in our rooms, the production crew must've been hard at work setting up the memorial. A circle of candles—the same ones that were used on our first date night on the beach—have been placed in the sand, and there's a bonfire going in the middle. Lit by the firelight is a heap of things—a pair of aviator sunglasses, a tie-dyed bucket hat, and a duffel bag. In front of it all is a sign that reads "In Memory of Anton Brophy" in Times New Roman font.

It's clearly designed to be a camera-ready moment, and honestly, it's not even a good one. The whole thing is obviously staged so that it can be fed straight to *US Weekly*.

"This sucks," I say, but I don't know if it's about the cheapness of the effort, the entire murder situation, or Anton's actual death.

Daniel says, "Bet they're doing this so they can flash 'In Memoriam' at the end of this episode."

Some of the crew are wearing black uniforms, but that's the closest to funeral attire that we get. All of us couples are dressed for the beach. After all, that's what we packed, though some people have made an attempt to don something appropriate. Chase is wearing his dark-blue shark shorts instead of something in a brighter color, and Selena has changed into a black sports bra and leggings. Jaxon is holding his cowboy hat in his hands.

"Any reason there's trash on the ground?" Noah asks, and Ava shushes him.

Seth is the one who answers, "That's Anton's stuff. It's for inspiration. To help you with your eulogies."

We have to give eulogies? I shoot a look at Daniel, who grimaces. Bringing out Anton's belongings feels macabre, but I guess it makes sense. The only thing the cast knew about him was that he was the PA most likely to ignore orders and get caught hiding behind a palm tree while scrolling through Instagram—not exactly the kind of reputation that lends itself to a heartfelt speech. And from what people said last night while we were huddled around the space heater, there was no love lost here.

But would any of us kill him?

"This is just so sad. I—" Mikayla is openly sobbing now. Trevor wraps her into a hug, but that only makes her cry harder. "I can't believe this happened!"

"Oh, honey," Brittany says sympathetically. "He's in a better place now."

"Doubt it, unless he's got Wi-Fi," Noah cracks, and Ava subtly steps on his foot. "Ow! What was that for? We all know he was an asshole. The guy didn't do his job. Dying didn't magically make him a good person."

"Seriously?" Brittany shoots a glare at Noah. "I mean, okay, I didn't like the guy either. I found him following me around—twice! And right after that, some of my stuff went *mysteriously* missing."

"Britt, maybe now's not the time?" Jaxon mutters.

"I know, Jaxon, I'm not a child!" Brittany shrugs Jaxon's arm off her shoulder. "What I'm saying is, he may have been a creep and an asshole who used a gallon of hair gel, but that doesn't mean that he deserved to die—"

"All right! Let's get started," Dawn Taylor calls. We fall quiet as she walks over to join us, resplendent in a skintight black dress with a silver statement necklace draped around her neck. "As some of you may have heard already, we've had a tragic accident on set. Anton, one of our production assistants, fell to his death from a section of scaffolding that was damaged during the storm, and our medical staff was not able to revive him," Dawn Taylor says, like she's reading off a script. Then she claps her hands. "Now! Who wants to go first?"

No one wants to go first.

"DT, go easy on them. Why don't you kick us off?" Peter Dixon says.

A flash of anger crosses her face, but it quickly smooths into a solemn look. She looks squarely at the camera and says, "We're gathered here today to say farewell to Anton Brophy, a valued member of our hardworking crew. He was taken from us in a tragic accident, but his memory will remain in our hearts forever."

Dawn Taylor bows her head, and a single tear tracks down her face. For a moment, we all listen to the crackle of the fire and the roar of the ocean behind us.

"Great, are we done here?" she says briskly. "Do we need another shot of me crying?"

"I think we're good in the crying department, DT. But could you share a memory you have of Anton real quick?" Peter Dixon asks.

"What do you want from me, Pete? All I know is he never got my coffee order right," she snaps.

Peter Dixon shakes his head. "We can do better than that for him. This'll mean a lot to his parents."

Dawn Taylor turns back to the cameras. She's quiet for a moment. "He . . . he always showed up," she says victoriously, like she's one of my students announcing what they think is the right answer to a tough math problem—only to get it completely wrong. "Pete, you should reach out to Chris and see if he'll give us a soundbite for this."

"I don't think that's going to fly, given the circumstances," Peter says.

"Hold up," Noah interrupts. "Who are we talking about?"

"Anton's related to one of the good Chrises," Dawn Taylor explains. I'm not sure which one she's even talking about, but everyone else seems to be in the know and takes this in stride.

"Ohmygod," Mikayla breathes. "He was a *nepo baby*!"

"Sweetie, we talked about this," Trevor mutters to her. "You can't be using slurs. It's bad for the brand."

Dawn Taylor insists on doing another crying take for the camera, and then points at Ava and Noah. "Go on, your turn. Let's hear it."

"Gimme a sec." Ava clears her throat, putting on an appropriately mournful look. "We're devastated. We didn't have much of a chance to get to know Anton, but it was clear that he was a valuable team player."

Noah is nodding along, like he wasn't talking shit about Anton a mere fifteen minutes ago. He says, "Anton's death really shook me to my core. It reminded me that we only have this one life to live. That's why I always start my day at five in the morning, to make the most of the time that I have. Thank you, Anton, for that reminder."

The camera moves on to the next person. Soon it'll be my turn, but my mind is completely and totally blank.

I squat down and survey my options—designer sunglasses, a bucket hat, and an unzipped duffel bag, the contents of which are spilling out onto the sand. Maybe there's something here that I can use in my eulogy. Inside the duffel bag is a pair of Crocs. A small bottle of gummy vitamins that I suspect are actually edibles. A small, worn-down pocket-sized notebook.

I pick up the notebook. It's a nice one, not one of my trusty Mead Five Stars or Composition notebooks, but an honest-to-goodness Moleskine, and—*that's not important*, I tell myself, and start flipping through. It's a mix of to-do lists, food and drink orders for catering, and the occasional drawing of a dick. I leaf through most of it, and then my eye catches on my name written in the back:

NOTES
Alice—totally faking it with Daniel, thinks she's smarter than everyone else, mom sick, probably desperate

What the fuck? But I don't have time to be outraged because there are more names and more notes:

> *Kendall—suing Get Real*
> *Mikayla—cheater, hounds the crew members for info on challenges*
> *Jaxon—fake accent, actually from NYC*
> *Brittany—takes prescription pills. should we "lose" them for her?*
> *Selena—daddy issues. desperate for approval, afraid of the dark bc of childhood*
> *Chase—head empty, thinks with his dick if smashed on jell-o shots*
> *Dominic—very short fuse. rage issues, has history of disorderly conduct*
> *Ava and Noah—would kill anyone who gets in their way. snuck in a secret phone (can use this)*

There's a line drawn under this list, dividing up the page. Below it, the notes continue.

> *Leah—unable to function without a fatal amount of caffeine in her system, nose job*
> *Freya—sleeping her way to the top*
> *Peter—enough botox to kill a horse*
> *Dawn—washup, trying to make a comeback with her show. will shell out if she thinks that*

I don't get to see what Dawn Taylor's going to shell out for because the next couple of pages have been ripped out. The notebook is blank after that, but I can make out faint lines where Anton pressed his pen too hard while writing. I trace the grooves, wishing I had a number 2 pencil I could use to color the paper and reveal the message, like a kid from a detective novel.

I angle the notebook, but all I can read is a number: 398

"Hey, what's all this crap doing here?" Bryan asks, spotting me by the duffel bag.

"Dawn Taylor told me to set up the memorial," Seth says. "Figured Anton's stuff would make for a good visual."

"All of his belongings should go to his next of kin," Bryan snaps. "Pack it up."

"Fuck off, Bryan," Seth says, scowling. He gestures at the filming in progress. "I can't, not until after they're done. Unless you want to take responsibility for borking the continuity?" Seth must be having a bad day—his hair is sticking up every which way, and there's gauze wrapped around his right hand.

Before anyone can notice I've been paging through Anton's notebook, I quickly drop it in the sand and straighten up. My mind is going a mile a minute as I process what I just read. I'd suspected that Anton was murdered, but this is confirmation. He was gathering blackmail material. It can't have been a coincidence that he ended up dead, with a black eye and a scraped-up hand.

But who did it?

Most of the cast and crew already had a reason to dislike Anton. If you mix that with the pressure to succeed—either on the contestants to win or on the crew to make *Dawn Tay's Inferno* a hit—then almost anyone could be a suspect. The producers, for instance, were already willing to poison and endanger us to manufacture drama. What if they went too far?

And why are there pages ripped out of the notebook? Did Anton do that for a reason, or did the person he was blackmailing do that to cover their tracks?

I drift over to Daniel's side and tune in to what Mikayla is saying.

"Anton will greatly be missed. His aura was too bright for this world," she says, looking mournful for the camera.

It's nine-thirty by the time Dawn Taylor claps twice, calling us all together to wrap things up.

"Thank you for coming out to remember Anton. I know you all need to catch up on your beauty sleep, so I won't drag this out any longer," Dawn Taylor says. "I just want you to know that this cast, this show is everything to me. You are all my top priority, and we will be reevaluating our safety measures to ensure that all of you feel safe and supported on set. Rest assured that I'm going to be personally looking out for all of you. All of the fame, money, and success in the world isn't worth anything if even *one* of you gets hurt on the path to stardom."

Dawn Taylor presses a hand to her chest, the rings on her fingers glinting in the firelight. "I would stop this show in a heartbeat if I thought there was even the *slightest* chance that any of you are in danger."

We all nod like we believe her. Leah even wipes a tear from her eye.

But I get the feeling that the only one buying Dawn Taylor's bullshit right now is Dawn Taylor.

r/Dawn Tay's Inferno
"Wrath" [Post-Episode Discussion S01E05]

Babes, welcome to the Dawn Tay's Inferno live discussion thread!

NOTE: I know everyone is excited about the latest episode, but PLEASE keep threads consolidated here under this post. We don't need fifteen different live discussion threads. THANK YOU!

TOP COMMENTS:

u/realitybites787

Love Dawn Taylor, so glad she's making a comeback. But I'm so sick of the IG girlies on there like Brittany and Mikayla. Trevor and Mikayla caught major drama for being in an MLM right before they went on the show. The producers should have vetted their cast better.

> Reply: u/SlutForMothman
> wait which mlm? was it the 2-in-1 nutritional supplement / vaginal douche that's going around? if so, trekayla is responsible for so many yeast infections

> Reply: u/unending-possum-scream
> Doesn't seem like they vetted the cast, period. Dominic is where the Venn diagram of toxic masculinity and fragile masculinity intersect.

u/lonelyoens

Gang who are we all rooting for? I want Brittany and Jaxon to stay in, mainly because seeing the two of them wear cowboy boots on a beach is absolutely sending me lol

> Reply: u/glammygirl123
> i'm all in for chase and selena. don't @ me about chase, i know he sucks. but he is legit hilarious, that man has not a thought in his head. and i read in an interview that selena went to san jose state on scholarship + financial aid and she's putting her baby bro through college too. we truly love to see an underdog thrive

Reply: u/SlutForMothman

step on me selena

Reply: u/lonelyoens

Sorry OP, but I'm rooting for everyone except Brittany and Jaxon. They're so fake! I googled their "farm" and it's basically a bed-and-breakfast that Jaxon's parents run.

Reply: u/glammygirl123

Damn that's wild. I'm also a sucker for Daniel. He seems like a sweetheart and he's hot. IDK why don't they show more of the math girl

Reply: u/fizzfuzzbizzbuzz

she's def getting a purple kelly edit.

Reply: u/SlutForMothman

?? what's that

Reply: u/fizzfuzzbizzbuzz

sorry it's a survivor reference. it's when the editors erase a player for no stated reason. idk, maybe she's terrible in interviews or she pissed off someone in production. but they're definitely going out of their way to ignore her, which is weird for a character who's been at the center of so much drama and has made it this far in the game.

Reply: u/510153029402

Don't forget these are actual people, not just "characters"

Chapter Nineteen

Hell Is a Pop Quiz You Didn't Study Enough For

Like so many things in this reality-based TV show, it doesn't feel real that Daniel and I go straight from the beach memorial to something as mundane as brushing our teeth together. Sharing the small space of the bathroom with Daniel feels almost too easy, as if we've been doing this dance of moving around each other our whole lives. In some ways, I guess, we have been. I try not to think about what it would be like to do this together for more than just a few days.

"You were right, Alice," Daniel says.

"What?" I say through a mouthful of toothpaste. I spit into the sink. "Run that by me again?"

"Anton was killed." Daniel furrows his brow. "What you said earlier about the list of blackmail material you found, I think that seals the deal. Someone murdered the guy. And I overheard the producers when they were cleaning up the memorial. It's like Lex said, we're stuck here. The storm caused a lot of problems along the islands. An accident on a reality TV set isn't even close to the top of the list for local law enforcement or the medical office. Backup isn't coming anytime soon. We're on our own. We have to figure out what's going on here if we want to make it through this."

I nudge Daniel aside to rinse out my mouth, and he tosses me the dental floss.

"Told you," I say.

"We'll have to play it safe, though. You said the blackmail list included cast and crew. That means we don't know who we can trust. Anything we figure out, we share between us and Lex, and no one else."

"Agreed. Stay sharp, Midas."

"Same goes for you. Stay sharp, Slayer."

Less than a week after I arrived at *Dawn Tay's Inferno*, I find myself on the water again. First thing after breakfast, Leah and the other producers ushered us onto a fleet of speedboats that are taking us who knows where. The ocean spray is bracing, and I lean into it, not caring if the cropped floral tank that Leah foisted on me gets wet.

After yesterday's challenge, I'm hoping that today's challenge isn't too out there, but those hopes are violently squashed when we're split from our partners, escorted onto a floating platform, and positioned on a beam that extends over the water.

"Are we sure this is, like, safe?" Mikayla asks as she peers over the edge of the beam. "I mean, after what happened to Anton."

"It's safe," Leah assures her. "We tested it on the PAs earlier today."

"They'd better be getting hazard pay," Daniel says, but Leah is already gone, shouting orders at the production assistants. They're hard at work attaching buckets of slime to ropes hanging down from a wooden beam, suspending one bucket over each of our heads, but the vibe is different now. They're working silently, not a smile to be seen. It's clear that everyone is nervous and on edge. It feels like the calm before the storm.

"It certainly seems like the slime budget has skyrocketed," I observe.

"Unless they're just reusing yesterday's slime," Selena says. "Then it's free-ninety-nine."

There's an edge to Selena's voice today. The sunny smile she usually wears is gone. The other contestants look haggard and tense. Are they freaked out by Anton's death, or feeling guilty for murdering him?

Mikayla in particular looks more frayed than usual. She's managed to chew through an immaculately manicured nail, and her shoulders are hunched in, like she's trying to shrink away from Trevor's arms around her.

Jaxon and Brittany seem the least changed. They're decked out in their standard cowboy getups, and their matching poker faces seem entirely focused on winning. I wish I could borrow some of that calm.

Soon enough, Dawn Taylor arrives on her own speedboat, a beacon of color in a flowy, bright-yellow pantsuit with matching yellow sunglasses.

"Babes, it's time to play!" she says, whipping off her sunglasses theatrically. "Today we're in the sixth circle of hell: Heresy. And we're putting you all to the test to see how well you know your partner! You'll each get a board to write on. I'll ask either the men or the women a question. Your goal is to mind-meld and write the exact same answer as your partner."

As the producers pass out whiteboards, Dawn Taylor continues, "For each mistake you make, our lovely assistants will pull a lever and drop a bucket of slime on you. You can make three mistakes, but on the fourth, you and your partner will be dropped into the ocean—and the first couple who hits the water is out of the competition. Welcome to Heresy, bitches!"

"I'm starting to think I didn't need to read all of Dante's *Inferno* for this," I say.

"SparkNotes is always the way to go, babe," Selena says.

"Wait, this is based on a *book*?" Mikayla says. "No one told me that!"

An airhorn blasts, and more than a few contestants jump at the sound.

"Let's get started!" Dawn Taylor says. "First question. Ladies, what's your greatest fear? Gentlemen, I want each of you writing down what you think your partner will say."

Oh god. Daniel and I never talked about this. There's no way he could possibly know what my greatest fear is. *I'm* not even sure what my greatest fear is. Failure? Losing my mother? Going back to high school, but I'm naked? I have a lot of fears. It's part of the package deal that comes with being a naturally anxious person.

I just have to game the system and think about what Daniel might guess about me. I'll pick something generic that most people are afraid of. Snakes? Snakes. Everyone's afraid of snakes, right? I mean, probably not zookeepers or veterinarians or those people who keep twenty snakes as pets. But it's as good an answer as any.

Mikayla is apparently afraid of cacti, which makes no sense, but who am I to judge? Trevor pumps his fist in the air when he gets it right.

Ava puts down "yellow jackets," and Noah nails it.

Selena writes "power outages," which I think we all knew after the night of the storm, but Chase somehow totally misses the mark and instead puts "racoons."

"You said their little hands were creepy," Chase objects.

"Creepy, not *scary*!"

I'm looking forward to seeing Chase get slimed, but of course he enjoys it, laughing and pretending to take a shower in it, which makes the entire crew crack up.

When it's my turn, I turn my board around: "Snakes."

Daniel makes a face as he turns his board around, and I see his answer scrawled onto the whiteboard: "Losing."

"Ouch. Extra sad, given that this answer brings you one step closer to losing," Dawn Taylor says. "Sorry, Daniel, it's slime time!"

An assistant yanks on a rope, and a bucket flips over, dumping slime all over Daniel. He chuckles good-naturedly and shakes it off.

The game continues.

"Ladies, how many kids does your partner want to have?" Dawn Taylor asks.

Selena turns her board around: "0"

Chase reveals his: "5"

Selena shrieks as the bucket of slime is dumped on her head.

Then it's my turn again.

"Alice, you put, let's see. Two and a half?" Dawn Taylor asks.

"The statistically average number of children—never mind, it was dumb," I say, scrubbing my board clean.

But then Daniel flips his board around, and by some miracle, there it is: "two point five." Daniel sees my shocked expression and winks.

For the next few questions, our strategy of cramming about each other pays off. I correctly identify that Daniel's parents are lawyers. He remembers that my best friend is Cindy. Not everyone fares as well. Jaxon and Brittany end up on the brink of elimination along with Selena and Chase.

As the challenge progresses and I fall into the rhythm of competition. When I'm waiting my turn, I take the chance to observe the people around me. Most of the crew members, including Lex, just seem burned out or angry, probably because they're being forced to work through a tragedy. I notice that Seth seems more focused on his couples than ever, intently watching Mikayla and Trevor like he's trying to telepathically send them the right answers.

Finally, a question about how Jaxon really feels about Brittany's parents knocks the two of them out. She thinks he adores them, but Jaxon thinks that his mother-in-law "looks and acts like if Cruella de Vil was a vegan."

"Ooh, I'm so sorry, but it's curtains for the two of you," Dawn Taylor says.

"Wait, no!" Brittany cries, but the plank drops out from under her. She plummets into the water below, with Jaxon just behind her. We hear Brittany's shriek as she hits the water.

"Jaxon and Brittany," Dawn Taylor says, even though they can't hear her from where they're treading water, "your time in my inferno is over. Get the hell out of here!"

A boat whisks Brittany and Jaxon away, and all that's left of them is a lone cowboy hat bobbing along in the ocean.

"Now let's heat things up," Dawn Taylor says, doing a little shimmy. "Gentlemen, what's the hottest part of your partner's body?"

What part of my body does Daniel find the hottest? Oh god, just kill me now. It doesn't help that I've racked up three mistakes at this point.

"Eyes," I write, praying that it's a generic enough answer to work.

We flip our boards.

Daniel has written "brain."

"Because you're so smart," he explains weakly.

"Brains aren't a body part, they're an internal organ! That doesn't even make sense!"

The plank beneath me gives away, and suddenly I'm plummeting into the water like a cartoon roadrunner, my legs and arms flailing frantically. I make a little squeaking sound as I smack against the surface butt first.

The ocean water is deceptively cold and sharp, and I flounder for a moment before I break the surface. I paddle over to the platform and pull myself up alongside Daniel.

"You okay?" I ask, my hand going to the now-soaked bandages.

Daniel places his hand over mine. "I'm fine. You're freezing."

He puts his arm around me and pulls me close. As always, he's warm, and the heat of him starts seeping into me almost immediately. I press closer to him, and not just for the cameras.

"Good effort, Slayer," he says, and offers me a fist bump.

"We live to fight another day," I say. I hate losing, but with Daniel, somehow, he takes the sting out of it.

Chase and Selena drop into the water after us, so we all end up on the losers' bench together.

"Hey, secret alliance is back at it again," Chase says cheerfully, completely missing the fact that we're united in being at the bottom of the competition.

"Speaking of secrets, I've got some hot goss," Selena says, leaning in. "Mikayla said that she heard Peter Dixon and Dawn Taylor really going at it, screaming at each other. But last night I saw Peter Dixon walking by with a fancy box of French pastries. Like croissants and madeleines and stuff. I think he was headed to Dawn Taylor's suite, so I guess they made up?"

At that point, we hear a scream, followed by a splash. It looks like Mikayla and Trevor were dropped into the water. That makes Ava and Noah the winners. They've won a romantic night toasting s'mores and getting cozy by the fire pit at Villa Paradiso, plus the dignity of not getting dunked in the ocean.

The temporary break in the storm ends sooner than expected, and we end up cresting over choppy waves that make our speedboat shudder and shake. My fingers are wrapped so tight around the safety bar of the seat in front of me that my knuckles have gone white. After a particularly brutal jolt, I nearly lose my grip, but then Daniel wraps an arm around me, his hand covering mine.

"Can't lose my partner to the ocean just yet," he tells me.

I smile up at Daniel, but then my heart catches in my throat. Behind us, over Daniel's shoulder, I spot Trevor glaring at us. He's mad, and I'm not sure why—until I realize that he's sitting alone. Mikayla has opted to sit with her producer, Seth, and with the boat being tossed around violently the way it is, the two of them are clinging to the safety bar and each other. They're arguing about something, but I can't quite make out what. Anton's messy scrawl pops up in my mind's eye.

Mikayla—cheater, hounds the crew members . . .

The boat fights another wave, shuddering and breaking my train of thought.

"We'll have to stop the boat up over here," the speedboat driver shouts back to us. He drops us off over by the labyrinth. As the rain picks up, we make our way across the beach toward the villa.

I glance back at the labyrinth. Despite the storm, several members of the crew are working to dismantle it.

"They're taking the labyrinth down already?" I ask Leah.

Leah shrugs. "They've got to strike the set. Half of it's going to be reused for tomorrow, but it needs a complete overhaul."

I've watched enough detective movies to know this is bad news. The scene of the crime is being disturbed. The back of my neck prickles as we walk farther and farther away from the place where Anton was killed.

Chapter Twenty

Hell Is a Fakeout Makeout with Someone You Maybe Want to Real Make Out with

Once we've been divested of our mic packs, we all retire to our rooms. I'm exhausted from the challenge, but also wired and jittery. My mind keeps playing my memories of the last few days on loop: The messy scrawl of handwriting in a notebook. Anton's body, lying prone in the sand. The bandage snaking around Dawn Taylor's leg. Seth and Mikayla arguing on the speedboat.

To calm my nerves, I force myself to take a blisteringly hot shower. I step out feeling a little bit more human.

"Shower's all yours," I call, walking back into the bedroom, and stop short.

Daniel is arranging some plates on the coffee table in our room.

"Hey, come and eat," he says. He's laid out an entire feast—a bowl of perfectly ripe honeydew and watermelon, fresh green Cobb salad, and fried chicken.

"Where did you get all this?" I marvel.

"Stole it," Daniel says. "I engineered an entire heist from craft services while you were showering."

I could kiss him, I think. I really could. Daniel steers me into a chair and I take a huge bite of the chicken. It's perfection—just a little bit spicy and fried to a crisp.

Daniel says, "Okay, now you can tell me what's on your mind."

"How do you know there's something on my mind?" I say between mouthfuls. I'm practically inhaling the food now.

"Alice, you're always thinking about something, but even I can see that your brain is working overtime right now. Why do you think I brought you food? You haven't eaten all day, and I know you don't eat when you get stressed before a competition. Same principle." Daniel pushes the bowl of fruit toward me, and I spear a piece of watermelon. "Now talk."

"You know how the crew is taking down the labyrinth?"

"I don't like where this is going."

"I want to go take a look at where Anton died."

Daniel rubs his face and groans. "Alice, that's a big risk."

"But we need to check the scene of the crime before it gets completely destroyed. We know someone out there killed Anton, probably because he was trying to blackmail them. The sooner we figure out who that someone is, the better."

"I'm going with you," he says. "No arguing."

I'm about to do just that, but then I nod. "Fine," I say. Having backup and another set of eyes could be helpful.

As I finish my food, a warm, contented feeling steals over me. My mind is no longer the churning whirlpool of questions and worries and to-do lists all clamoring to make themselves heard. Instead, I feel like I can take on whatever is ahead of me.

I look over at Daniel, who's stealing bites from my Cobb salad. There's something comforting about having him here. Why does it feel so good to be working together?

It must be because I trust Daniel.

I actually trust Daniel.

The sky is overcast when we make our way back to the labyrinth from the Wrath Challenge, and everything is eerily quiet. There's only the lapping of the waves on the beach and the rustle of the trees as the wind picks up.

If the weather were like this back home, my mom would say that the wind was rising—a sure sign that it's about to rain. We'd rush out to the balcony to pull the laundry off the clothesline, and hours later, a downpour would arrive—but by then, my mom and I would be settled in around the kitchen table. She'd be cracking watermelon seeds into a bowl and watching a K-drama with Chinese subtitles on. I'd be picking at a plate of sliced fruit and grading papers.

As Daniel and I step into the shadows cast by the looming wooden structure of the labyrinth, I wish I were home now, cozy and safe. But that's not an option for me. I found Anton's body. I tried to revive him. I saw the dark bruise around his eye, how his arm dangled lifelessly off the stretcher. Someone on this set is a murderer, and I can't let this problem go unsolved.

Daniel's hand tightens on mine, and I realize with a start that someone is slumped over just inside the entrance. For a moment a spike of fear goes through me, until I realize that it's one of the crew members, and he's not dead, just snoozing.

He jerks awake with a snort when we approach. "Hey! Contestants aren't supposed to be here."

This crew member is a burly guy in his forties, with a buzz cut under his hard hat and a reflective yellow vest tucked sloppily into his jeans.

I zero in on his name tag. "Gill, it's lovely to meet you." I look up at Daniel, playing the part of a friendly and forgetful girlfriend. "I'm so sorry about this. I dropped my sunglasses in there. I should've gone back yesterday, but after Anton . . . after he . . . ." I blink really hard and start to sniffle.

Playing along, Daniel tugs me close to him. "Just breathe, sweetie." To Gill he says, "Look, man. I won't tell anyone if you don't. Leah said we needed them for our interviews—you know, for continuity. She's on a tear right now, so I'd appreciate it if you'd let us run in and get them real quick."

"Sure, just don't get in the crew's way," Gill says gruffly. He's looking anywhere but at me, obviously uncomfortable with seeing me fake cry. A crashing sound reverberates through the enclosure, and Gill is gone, shouting, "Jeff, I told you not to stack those so high! They're not fuckin' Pringles!"

"Nice work," I say to Daniel, nudging him with my shoulder.

He quirks an eyebrow. "Rare praise."

"Yeah, you should get it embroidered on a pillow."

We navigate the labyrinth, retracing our steps from yesterday. But this time, there's no camera crew in the scaffolding above us, and we easily make it past the wooden walls and scattered blocks. Finally, we reach the point where we had exited the labyrinth, and Daniel and I cautiously enter.

"Try not to disturb anything," Daniel advises me.

"Thank you, counsel," I say with mock seriousness.

We stop just a few feet shy of where we found Anton's body. The blood has been scoured away, and the path is clean now. The slime pit has been partially emptied. We squint up at the scaffolding, which is the same as it was yesterday.

"See, look at the walkway," I say, pointing at the splintered wooden beam above us. "It's got a break in it, but . . ."

"But it's not big enough gap for someone to fall through," Daniel concludes.

"And the railing seems fine," I say, eyeing it. If the scaffolding had given way, Anton could have grabbed onto the metal railing for balance and simply stepped over to a more solid part of the walkway. "It's like I told Lex, he couldn't have fallen. And there's no reason for him to have a black eye, either."

"Shit." Daniel surveys the area grimly.

We knew what we were dealing with, but seeing the proof before our very eyes, that feels different. This isn't just the set of *Dawn Tay's Inferno*. This is really and truly the scene of a crime.

"Let's take a look around—" I start, but I snap my mouth shut when a burst of laughter filters through to us. Then there's the rumble and clank of equipment being moved and footsteps approaching.

I glance toward the exit, but it's too far for us to make a break for it. We had an excuse for being in here, but we promised to be quick, and we should've been long gone by now. I'm panicking, trying to come up with a reason we're still here. Maybe I dropped my sunglasses in the pit, or just couldn't find them. The sounds of the crew are growing louder and louder, and there's no escape.

I feel a hand on my elbow. It's Daniel, his face half in shadow and half lit by the meager sunlight breaking through the clouds above us. He tips my chin up, his gaze intense on mine, and all he says is "Alice."

I swallow. I know exactly what he's trying to ask, and my heart's already starting to race at just the thought of it. I nod, and then he's sweeping me into his arms and pushing me back against the labyrinth wall, pressing his body against mine.

By the time the sound gets closer, he's kissing me deeply, his hands going through my hair, his thigh slotted between mine, and we're doing a very, *very* good impression of being locked in a passionate make-out session.

Maybe too good of an impression. The threat of being caught heightens everything, sending a rush of adrenaline surging through me. I can feel a spark igniting everywhere we're touching as I lose myself in the kiss, my hands running over the expanse of his back. When Daniel's fingers trace the gap of exposed skin beneath my shirt, I gasp at the touch and nod. His hands leave a molten trail of fire as they skim under the band of my bra.

I start to I surrender to the sensation of his fingertips pressing into me, but at the sound of heavy footsteps, my eyes fly open, and I can see the brown Timberland boots of a crew member barely within my peripheral vision.

"Hey! Get a room!" Timberlands laughs.

Daniel pulls away from me and looks over his shoulder at the crew. He's covering me with his body still, and thank goodness for that, because I'm not sure I want the crew seeing me like this. I fight to steady my breath. Part of me just wants to drag him back to our suite and keep going, keep hearing those little desperate noises he was making, keep feeling the hard length of him pressed against me as he touches me everywhere.

"Did you find your sunglasses?" Another member of the crew—Gill, I suspect—calls.

"Not yet," Daniel says. He turns around and, still blocking me from view, says calmly, "Sorry, we got a little distracted."

"No shit," Gill says. "We're heading out for dinner, but I don't want to see you two when I get back. This is a demo site, not one of your sexy cabanas."

The sounds of the crew retreat, and Daniel steps away from me. I adjust my shirt and decide the best course of action is to act like nothing happened.

"Let's split up the area around Anton's body to see if we find anything. You cover the area from the pit to that wall, and I'll do the same on this side."

And we start searching. The rain probably would've washed away any marks, but the walls and scaffolding seem to have preserved the site. I can see faint drag marks from where Anton was. I keep searching. At first there's nothing, just the debris of construction and the footprints of the workers around the site, but then I notice a strange pattern in the shoe treads.

"Daniel, check this out," I say. "The footprints here look different from the rest."

Most of the footprints are clearly from the rounded Timberlands that the construction crew are wearing. But there's a single set of footprints that don't match up. They're narrow with a distinct pointy tip.

"These are leading away from the body. You said that someone tried to drag Anton away, but obviously they failed. They must have had to make a quick exit once I came back, and this must be the route they took," I deduce.

We track the footprints as they lead into the shadows of the labyrinth. Our silence is punctuated by our shoes crunching in the sand and the cry of birds in the distance.

"Damn," I say when the already faint shoeprints trail off into a dark corner. "Dead end."

"Maybe not." Daniel studies the wall, then pushes it. It gives a little, opening a crack and revealing itself to be a door.

"Whoa, how'd you see that?"

"I saw the hinge. Most of them were painted black, but someone missed this one," he says, pointing at a silver hinge close to the ground. "I imagine this is how production got in and out of the labyrinth when they were setting up all the puzzles."

"Good job," I say, and we open the door.

Or we try to. It seems a little broken, and I realize something's caught at the corner of the door. I reach down to where some rocks and debris have been kicked up and start clearing them away so the door can move. That's when my hand brushes against something crumpled and half buried by the sand. It's a piece of paper.

I smooth it out. Something's been printed on it, the ink faded by the elements. "I think it's a photo."

I look around and spot a fake, battery-operated lantern on the wall. After switching it on, I hold up the image to the halo of light it provides.

"Is that—" Daniel squints. "Mikayla?"

There, looking away from the camera, is Mikayla, wearing her lingerie outfit from the night of the blackout and straddling someone's lap.

And that someone isn't Trevor. I point at the man beneath Mikayla. He's got one hand between her legs and one cupping her breasts.

"Look at his hair," I say. The man's dark hair is peeking out from beneath his hat. "Do you know who that is?"

"I don't—"

"Hey!" A voice cuts off whatever Daniel's saying. "You shouldn't be here."

I know before I turn around who I'm going to see.

There's something menacing about how Seth is pacing toward us. I take a step back, suddenly desperate to put more distance between us. Seth looks tense, even more so than the last time I saw him. His jaw is clenched, and he's holding his hand carefully, a fresh bandage wrapped around it.

"You should be in your rooms," Seth snaps. "Does Leah know you're here?"

"Does Leah know *you're* here?" I retort. It's not the smartest response, but it's all I can think to say in the moment.

"I dropped something yesterday. Came back for it," Seth says, adjusting his hat. My gaze leaps to the crinkled picture I'm still holding and the identical blue cap on the man's head. "And Leah's not my keeper. I don't answer to her. But you do."

The puzzle pieces are slotting together: The blue hat I've caught glimpses of around the villa. The figure standing stock-still beneath the palm trees when we first landed on the island. Seth sitting with Mikayla on the speedboat while Trevor fumed. Mikayla disappearing during the storm and then returning to the villa soaking wet.

Mikayla isn't cheating in the competition. She's cheating on Trevor.

And Seth's bandages aren't wrapped around his entire hand. They're wrapped around his knuckles. Like he punched somebody.

"What happened to your hand?" I ask quietly.

But Seth has noticed what I'm holding. "Give me that photo," he says, dropping all pretense of being the friendly producer we're used to.

"Let's talk about this," Daniel says firmly. "Why don't we go back to the hotel first? I'm sure Leah's waiting for us."

"Not until you give me that," Seth says, pointing at the photo.

"No," I say evenly. "I think it's evidence. I think you met with Anton yesterday because he'd printed this incriminating photo of you and Mikayla. I think he tried to blackmail you over it, and instead of handing him money, you punched him . . . and maybe you even threw him off the scaffolding—"

"That's not what happened!" Seth screams. He lurches toward me, trying to grab at the paper again.

"Hey!" I yelp, and then Daniel's pulling me behind him. Seth takes a swing at Daniel, aiming for his head, but Daniel simply ducks under Seth's fist and, with ruthless efficiency, tackles him to the ground.

Holy shit, Daniel can *fight*?

Now prone, Seth lashes out. Daniel dodges, jerking back and cursing as the punch glances off his cheekbone.

"You need to cool it," Daniel orders, but Seth answers him with another fist, this time landing a hit on Daniel's side. Daniel jerks back in pain, his hand going to where he was burned not too long ago.

Seth scrabbles away, but I'm ready for him, and I piston my arms forward, shoving Seth off-balance. Still wincing, Daniel wrenches one of Seth's arms and twists it behind his back.

"Get off me," Seth yells and bucks against Daniel, his legs kicking out and colliding with the scaffolding.

There's an ominous, drawn-out *creeeeaaaaaak*.

The scaffolding around us is wobbling. I hear a loud clang in the distance as a beam slides out of place and plunges into the sand.

"We've got to go!" I shout, and pull Daniel up. He grabs my hand and we sprint for the exit. The sound of metal on wood crashing together follows us as we navigate the labyrinth in reverse. Seth is staggering behind us, clutching his arm.

Daniel pushes me through the doorway first, then glances back to check on Seth.

"Come on!" he roars, and Seth puts on a burst of speed just as another beam plunges down, just inches away from him.

"Alice! Daniel!" Leah is running toward us, her hand on her earpiece. "What the hell are you guys doing here?" She glares at Seth. "You couldn't have called this in? And why are you limping?"

"Seth tried to attack us," Daniel informs Leah.

"What?" She looks at each of us, then taps her earpiece. "Security, come down to the villa." To us, she says, "I don't know what's going on here, but we're taking this to Dawn Taylor."

Chapter Twenty-One
Hell Is a Real-Life Whodunit

When we arrive at the villa, Leah takes us straight to the war room to meet with Peter Dixon and Dawn Taylor. Security shows up to meet Leah, but it turns out that "security" just means a really burly PA who opens the door when Leah waves at him.

I follow as Leah pushes Seth and Daniel into the room. This time around, it feels less like going to the principal's office and more like preparing for a day in court. Dawn Taylor is sitting at the head of the table, with Peter Dixon to her right. They certainly look like they could be in reality TV court. She's making a sleek black jumpsuit look like this season's hottest fashion trend, and his charcoal blazer is impeccably pressed.

On the other side of the table, I know that we must look like a wreck. Seth and Daniel look like they've wrestled with a tree and lost, and I can feel the dust in my hair that was kicked up when the labyrinth self-imploded. None of us opt to sit down.

"What's going on here?" Dawn Taylor demands.

"Sorry to bother you guys, but Seth and Daniel got into it at the labyrinth site," Leah says. "Dawn, I told you Seth's had it in for my contestants. This is crossing the line."

Peter Dixon cuts in. "Boys, you know that fighting on the set is prohibited and could be considered a breach of contract—"

"The hell with the rules. What the fuck were you thinking, Seth?"

Dawn Taylor says, rising out of her chair. "You *punched* Daniel? Are you trying to ruin the show?"

"He came after me!" Seth protests.

"And why would he do that, Seth?"

"Because . . ." Seth trails off. In front of Dawn Taylor, Seth no longer seems menacing. He looks deflated, like a corporate lackey getting a bad performance review. His shoulders are slumped, and he's looking down at his square-toed boat shoes, which are weathered and worn down from overuse. Seeing him like this, I almost feel sorry for Seth.

Dawn Taylor turns to Daniel. "What, did he fuck Alice or something?"

Daniel's eyes turn steely. "Don't talk about Alice like that," he says, his voice cold.

"I wasn't the contestant Seth was sleeping with," I say. "That would be Mikayla."

"You're hooking up with Mikayla?" Leah asks, incredulous.

"No! No, that's bullshit," Seth says, sputtering. "Yeah, I'm with Mikayla all the time, but I'm her producer—"

I slide over the photo we found in the labyrinth, and Seth trails off. Dawn Taylor snatches it up, eyebrows shooting up as she pores over it.

Dawn Taylor snaps a finger at Leah. "Go get Mikayla. Now."

"On it," Leah says, heading to the door.

"Come on, Dawn, we don't need to get her involved—" Seth protests.

"Seth, for once in your pathetic life, please shut up," Dawn Taylor says. She turns back to me. "So, is that why Seth and Daniel were fighting?"

"Not exactly, no." I look at Daniel, a silent question in my eyes. When he nods, I continue, "I set him off. I accused him of murder. I don't believe Anton's death was an accident."

Peter Dixon whistles. "Wow. You really do belong on reality TV, Alice. Any particular reason for this accusation?"

"I overheard him admitting that he poisoned the contestants during the Gluttony Challenge," I say. Peter Dixon shoots a startled look at Seth. "And as you see in the photo, we know that he's been sleeping with Mikayla. I think he punched Anton to keep him quiet about his relationship with Mikayla."

"But I didn't kill anyone—" Seth insists.

"All I'm saying is that you punched him. Anton had a black eye, and you have an injured hand. I think we can do the math. And it's clear that you had cause to be angry with him. The question is, were you angry enough to kill him?"

Just then, the door slams open. Trevor bursts in, trailed by Leah and Mikayla.

"What's going on? Is Mikayla in trouble?" Trevor demands.

"We're asking Seth a few questions. Alice here thinks he killed Anton," Dawn Taylor summarizes.

"Okay, I didn't say that I was a hundred percent on that," I interject. "It's just a theory."

Mikayla's hands fly to her mouth. "Seth? No, he wouldn't do that."

Trevor casts a scornful look at Seth. "You know, I had a feeling that there was something off about him."

Mikayla's eyes land on the paper Dawn Taylor is holding, and I can see the moment she recognizes what it is. Her expression shutters as she drops her hands from her face. Taking a deep breath, she steps away from Trevor and says, "Seth didn't kill Anton, I'm sure of it. He told me that he only punched him, and I believe him. He did it for me."

"Sweetie pie," Trevor says. He reaches out a hand, but Mikayla brushes him off. "What are you talking about?"

"You should probably see this," Dawn Taylor says, showing the photo to Trevor. She looks a little bit too happy to be breaking the bad news. Trevor's eyes widen, and he stumbles back like he's just taken a blow to the chest.

"You—" Trevor shakes his head. "You were cheating on me?"

"Trevie. Trevor. I'm sorry," Mikayla chokes out. "I didn't mean to. It's just, after we got in that argument on the first night, I didn't know who else to talk to."

Trevor jabs a finger at the photo. "That's a lot more than talking, Mikayla!"

"Let's get back to the part where Seth decided to punch everyone on my set," Dawn Taylor cuts in. "Care to explain yourself?"

"Anton caught me with Mikayla the other night. He said he'd tell Trevor, hell, the whole cast. Then he started blackmailing us," Seth says. "At first, Anton just asked me for dumb stuff. Like making me do his grunt work for him, so he could kick back. That kind of thing."

I think back to Seth bringing us the smoothies that Anton was supposed to get. "And that 'dumb stuff' was enough for you to punch him?"

Seth rubs his eyes. When he answers, he sounds utterly defeated. "A couple nights ago, he told me that he wanted us to pay up. But I'm not rolling in it, and Mikayla shares a bank account with Trevor. So I tracked him down during the Wrath Challenge for a chat."

"Some chat," Daniel mutters to me.

"I wasn't planning on hitting him," Seth says. "Believe me. But you know Anton. He can really get on your nerves. And yeah, I lost it. I hauled off and punched him. After that, he said he'd lay off, that he had bigger fish to fry anyway. Then we heard someone coming, so I got out of there. But Anton was alive and working on the set when I left him, I swear. You can ask any of the crew where I was after that."

"God, you're such a loser," Leah says, shaking her head. To Dawn Taylor, she says, "I think he's telling the truth. I saw him and Anton later at different points during the Wrath Challenge. I did notice he had a shiner, but I assumed he'd gotten high on set and walked into something."

"I'm telling you, I'd never kill a kid like that," Seth says, his voice pleading. "I know I shouldn't have hit him, but the things he said, the way he was ready to ruin Mikayla's life—I couldn't let him do that to her."

"*You* couldn't let him do that to Mikayla?" Trevor cuts in, his voice shaking with rage.

Trevor moves faster than I've seen him move in any of the challenges. In an instant, he's grabbing the collar of Seth's garish Hawaiian shirt.

"Trevor, no!" Mikayla shouts and flings herself at Trevor. "Please, don't do this. Let's just talk, okay? I'm sorry, baby, I'm so sorry."

Trevor takes one look at Mikayla's face and shoves Seth hard against the wall. Then he backs off, chest heaving.

Dawn Taylor stands up, surveying the scene with disdain. "Seth, I'm taking you off your assignments. Leah, can you take care of Trevor and Mikayla?" She says this with a pointed look which I take to mean "make sure you get their messy and inevitable fallout on camera."

Leah nods and leads Trevor and Mikayla out, talking to them in low, soothing tones.

Peter Dixon clears his throat, getting everyone's attention again. "Obviously, we're facing a serious issue here. Seth, we'll need you to talk to the authorities. Once they can make it to the island, that is." He runs his hands through his hair, looking conflicted. "I don't know, DT. Maybe this is all too much. Maybe we should stop filming."

Dawn Taylor folds her arms. "No, absolutely not. We've got way too much momentum to stop now. And there isn't a problem here. One little affair isn't going to derail *my* show."

"Wait, what's this about the authorities?" Seth says, sounding panicked. "I didn't kill Anton. You believe that, right?"

"Of course," Peter Dixon says. "But he's dead, and we know that you punched him—you admitted as much yourself. Until we can clear you, you'll have to sit tight."

Moments later, a couple more burly crew members arrive. "Seth will need to be confined for the duration of our stay here," Peter says to them. They nod without questioning this bizarre order, which makes me wonder how bizarre the orders around here can get before anyone blinks. "It's just for now, Seth."

Silence falls over the room once Seth is gone. Finally, Dawn Taylor crumples up the photo and chucks it into a nearby trash can.

"Well, that was more drama than I was expecting for one evening," Dawn Taylor says. She moves to sit back down, favoring the leg that didn't get burned during the fireworks. "Alice, thank you for bringing this to our attention. We all want the show to be the best it can be, and what Seth was getting up to with Mikayla—that was unacceptable. I'm glad we sorted that all out."

It sure doesn't feel like everything's been sorted out.

"But what about Anton?" I ask.

"What about him?" Dawn Taylor says. "He's dead. It's unfortunate, but it is what it is."

I can't believe what I'm hearing. Dawn Taylor is just brushing off the fact that someone on her set was murdered. For her, all that matters is that filming continues.

And it's clear that even if Daniel and I uncovered one mystery on set, we haven't solved the case. I remember the shoeprints in the labyrinth, how they were pointed. In addition to what Leah said about seeing Anton and Seth throughout the Wrath Challenge, Seth's shoes weren't pointed. Someone else dragged Anton's body through the sand, and I'm a hundred percent sure it wasn't Seth. So who was it?

"Someone killed Anton," I say, looking Dawn Taylor and Peter Dixon in the eye. I need them to acknowledge this.

"You really think so?" Peter Dixon says, looking concerned. "DT, I know you said no, but we should really consider pausing the shoot. If there's any chance that Anton's death wasn't an accident, we can't keep on like this. We have to think about our cast."

"I am thinking about our cast," Dawn Taylor says heatedly. "And the best thing we can do is to continue filming. Our contestants didn't come all this way just to be mired in some controversy. The press will have a field day over this."

"I don't know, DT," Peter Dixon says. "I think we should take this seriously—"

Dawn Taylor throws up her hands. "Pete, what do you want from me? I can't believe you're even saying this."

It's like we're not even in the room right now. I look at Daniel, and he nods at the door. We start to sidle out as Peter Dixon and Dawn Taylor continue to argue.

We're all the way down the hallway when I hear Dawn Taylor yell, "This is my show, Pete, and you better fucking remember it!"

r/Dawn Tay's Inferno
"Memorial" [Bonus Web-Only Content 003]
Okay, we have to talk about the memorial clip going around. You might have noticed that Episode 6 was "Dedicated to the Memory of Anton." If you go to the bonus content tab on their network page, there's a fifteen-minute clip with the cast and crew talking about how this guy died on set . . . and filming is STILL going?

TOP COMMENTS:

u/lonelyoens
Someone died? I smell a lawsuit.

> Reply: **u/capybaraMoon2334**
> Clip was edited weirdly too. Production is covering something up
>
> Reply: **u/SlutForMothman**
> probably covering up a huge osha violation. capitalism kills!! u/capybaraMoon2334, what's the tea re: editing
>
> Reply: **u/capybaraMoon2334**
> The memorial clip doesn't include Dawn Taylor in it anywhere. Usually the show would have her speaking first to set up whatever's happening. Instead they have Selena doing a voiceover, for some reason. Could be that they didn't like the take Dawn Taylor did and couldn't reshoot. Or, and this is my theory, Dawn Taylor's trying to distance herself from this . . . because it wasn't a "tragic accident."
>
> Reply: **u/ glammygirl123**
> If they stop filming I'm going to literally die.
>
> Reply: **u/SlutForMothman**
> literally die is what Anton did :(

Chapter Twenty-Two

Hell Is Mud Wrestling with Your Ex

Leah keeps a close eye on us for the rest of the day. She claims that she's just looking out for her favorite couple, especially since Daniel is still recovering from his injury, but I overheard Dawn Taylor on Leah's walkie-talkie telling her to watch us like a hawk.

Still, we manage to get a moment to ourselves when Leah heads off to "take a fuckin' shower and lie face down in bed." Lex swings by the moment our producer's gone.

"Thought she'd never leave," Lex says, glancing back at the hallway before shutting the door. "You two are really on Dawn Taylor's shit list now, aren't you? What the hell happened?"

We quickly update Lex on the Seth situation.

Lex lets their head tip back against the wall. As they contemplate the ceiling of the suite, they say, "Let me get this straight. Anton was blackmailing Seth and Mikayla. Seth punched Anton during the Wrath Challenge . . . but we don't actually know who killed him."

"Correct," I say. "Whoever the murderer is, they're still out there."

"What a nightmare." Lex casts a sidelong glance at me. "Are you sure you want to keep looking into this? It sounds like Dawn Taylor wants to keep this show going no matter what. She won't appreciate you stirring up trouble. And if she's fine with her producers poisoning the cast, there's no telling what she'll do."

"We'll manage," I say firmly. "So how's the crew taking everything?"

"I think everyone agrees that we're not being paid enough to deal with this shit," Lex says. "But what else is new? Oh, and I heard that some of the PAs had to clear out Anton's stuff from his room. Apparently it was a 'disgusting rathole.' They're missing his work laptop, though, and they can't get into his crew locker."

At my puzzled look, Lex explains, "The crew lockers are where we stash our valuables. It's all underground. Not remotely convenient to get to, so I don't bother."

"Wait a sec. What do you mean, underground?" Daniel asks.

"Oh, right, they never gave you the tour." Leah points at the floor. "There's a whole underground bunker beneath the beach. Part of what makes this island a prime location for filming reality shows."

"Why can't the crew get into his locker?" I ask.

"They didn't find the key in his stuff. But they're not searching very hard. Filming is still our top priority."

"We need that key," I say. "I bet Seth and Mikayla weren't the only people Seth was blackmailing. If we can get into Anton's locker, we might find more information on who might have wanted him dead."

Lex laughs. "Or we just find his stash of edibles."

"It's worth a try," I insist. Searching the labyrinth was a dead end, but the crew locker sounds like a promising lead.

"I'll ask around," Lex says. "But you two need to lay low. Act like you're just happy to still be on this show."

"We *are* still happy to be on the show," I say.

"Uh-huh," Lex says. "Try to act normal. Daniel, if anyone starts getting suspicious of you two, just do that thing where you look completely in love with Alice. You're good at that."

"Roger roger," Daniel says, his ears reddening. I wonder if it's that embarrassing for him to pretend to like me. I resolve to make it up to him if—no, when—we get out of here.

Around noon the next day, the remaining couples—me and Daniel, Selena and Chase, Trevor and Mikayla, and Ava and Noah—are herded out of the villa. Seth is nowhere in sight. I wonder if he's been packed off to wherever the losers are or sent off in a small dinghy to fend for himself in the ocean.

We're escorted past the tree line and into the jungle. Even though we can still catch glimpses of the ocean from here, we're not on the beach anymore. We pick past fallen branches and knobby roots erupting from the earth before ending up in a clearing. At the center of the clearing is a series of mud pits dug into the dirt. Narrow beams just barely wider than my thigh are suspended above the mud pits, like a tic-tac-toe grid. Oh god, we're going to have to balance on those and fight above the mud pits, aren't we?

"At least it's not slime this time," Daniel murmurs to me.

We're kept waiting for what feels like an eternity in the stifling humidity, until even the producers start looking worried and whip out their phones to tap out messages. My fingers twitch, just itching to get my hands on one of those phones. I would give anything to hear my mom scold me about not wearing enough layers, or to tell Cindy about everything that's happened on the island. Being completely cut off from the rest of the world has only made this strange experience even stranger.

Just when Trevor asks if he can go piss in the trees, Dawn Taylor arrives, clutching a latte in one hand and a bottle of aspirin in the other. She's wearing a white leather romper with a backless top for this challenge, which seems like a bad idea given the mud pits. The moment the cameras train on her, she hands off the latte and aspirin to Leah and turns to the rest of us.

"Well, well, well," Dawn Taylor says, eyeing us. There's something about her delivery today that's a little bit stiffer, like she's reading from a script instead of gossiping over brunch with her friends. "It looks like we're down to four couples now, and babes, it's only going to get harder from here. This week, we'll be putting your relationship to the test with another fiery challenge. I hope you're ready for *violence*!"

Bryan points at us, cueing us to cheer like we're super pumped for violence. It's clear who's picking up the slack now that Seth and Anton are gone.

"For this particular circle of hell, you'll be fighting for your lives in a mud pit, gladiator style The only rule is no head shots. Other than that, anything goes in my battle royale from hell. The first couple to fall is eliminated. The last person or couple standing wins *five thousand dollars cash*! Now, get ready for the fight of your lives!"

We're each given a helmet, kneepads, and elbow pads, as well as a huge wooden staff that has padded orbs at each end. Our safety equipment comes in cardboard boxes with one of our names hastily scrawled on each one. Everything is gleaming and new, and exactly my size. I pull the kneepads and elbow pads on, then reach for the helmet.

I'm half thinking about the challenge, so I don't see it until the helmet is in my hands. A snake slithers out from between the helmet straps, its yellow and black bands clearly a bright warning sign against predators and prey alike.

"Shit!" I chuck the helmet. When it lands with a soft thump in the grass, the snake slithers out and makes its way toward the tree line.

Leah comes sprinting over. "What's going on?"

"There was a snake," I say, pointing into the jungle. By the time Leah glances over, the snake is long gone.

"I don't see it," she says.

"I saw it," Daniel cuts in, his voice serious. "I want to know what the hell a snake was doing in the safety gear."

"I'm sure it was an accident, but I'll let production know," Leah says briskly, and then she's off, barking orders at a PA.

Daniel retrieves my helmet and turns it over and over in his hands, checking it everywhere.

"All clear," he says. His fingers brush mine as he hands it back to me.

When everyone's geared up, the producers position us around the mud pit.

I tap Daniel's shoulder. "Our best strategy is to hang back and let the first wave fight it out themselves. Stay out of the way and stay alert. Got it?"

"Got it." He bumps his shoulder against mine.

I'm not feeling all that confident about my chances. The staff is heavy in my hands, almost too heavy for me to lift and swing effectively. And having to balance on the beam while holding the staff does not sound like a walk in the park.

Dawn Taylor raises a hand. "Babes, square up! Ready, set . . . *fight*!"

Trevor darts out first, moving to put himself between Mikayla and the others. Noah takes the bait, charging forward to sweep his staff at Trevor's legs.

"Agh!" Trevor loses his balance and pitches forward. He just barely manages to grab onto the beam.

Then Ava nimbly leaps past him to get to Mikayla. She whacks Mikayla in the stomach with the padded end of the staff.

"Trevor, help!" Mikayla shrieks, seemingly unaware that Trevor is literally dangling over the mud pit and hanging on for dear life. "Trevor!"

Trevor swings himself up and is immediately forced to bring up his staff to keep Noah from knocking him over again. As they grapple, Ava goes after Mikayla hard, lunging forward and causing the other woman to fall on her butt.

Mikayla scrambles backward on the beam, screaming, "Trevor, help!"

Trevor grits his teeth and shoves Noah back, long enough to turn and dive for Ava instead. He throws his staff at her, catching her feet and sending her tumbling into the mud pit below.

Before Noah can get back to Trevor, Chase and Selena join the fray, both going straight for him. They launch a well-coordinated attack, Selena going high as Chase goes low, and Noah goes flying.

One couple down. I lock eyes with Daniel and nod. Time to get off the sidelines. Daniel and I charge out together. Trevor and Mikayla are the closest to us, and already winded from the fight, so we go after them.

Daniel takes a swing at Trevor that clips him in the shoulder, but Trevor manages to maintain his balance and return the favor.

Daniel dodges, almost losing his balance. I dart over and steady him.

"Thanks, Slayer."

"You're welcome," I say. I really could get used to being on the same team as Daniel. We work well together, and that knowledge makes me almost giddy, confidence bubbling up in me like a fizzy soda. I look around for Selena.

"Secret alliance?" I mouth at her. Selena winks at me. Together the two of us turn on Mikayla, swinging our staffs at her.

"Trevor, stop them!" Mikayla squeals as I jab at her. "Why aren't you helping me?"

But Trevor is busy grappling with Daniel and Chase. He yells, "I'm a little busy right now, Mikayla!"

"Well, hurry up!" she yells back as Selena and I close in on her.

"Goddamnit," Trevor grinds out. He's on the defensive now, his staff raised to block blows from Daniel and Chase. "Did you see how Alice helped Daniel? Did you ever consider trying to help *me* instead of just needing me to bail *you* out?"

Ducking, Trevor dodges out of Chase's reach, elbows past Daniel, and in two bounds he's on us. But instead of saving Mikayla, he ever-so-gently bops her foot, sending her sprawling into the mud pit.

Selena and I gape at Trevor.

"That still counts, right?" Daniel asks no one in particular.

"What the hell!" Mikayla wades over, wiping the mud out of her eyes. "Trevor, why would you do that to me?"

"Why would I do that to you? Why would you cheat on me?" Trevor shouts down at her. "After everything I did for you! Remember the Barbie-themed picnic I set up for your birthday with the pink ombré balloon arch and the backyard movie projector? What about when I woke up at five in the morning to make you cotton-candy-flavored rolled ice cream from scratch on Valentine's Day or when I planned an entire beach weekend for you as a surprise anniversary trip? I was the perfect boyfriend! I raised the bar for perfect boyfriends!"

"Ohmygod," Mikayla says. "Be real for once, Trevor! You didn't do any of that for *me*. You did it for the views, for the likes, and for the engagement. You totally got off on people saying what an amazing boyfriend you are and how lucky I am to have you. And you know what, I don't even *like* Barbie!"

"It was a sponsored post! It paid for our kitchen renovations!" Trevor says, throwing his hands in the air. "Of course everything I did was to build our brand, but that was still for you, too. For us. Because we're Trekayla."

"I don't think I want to be Trekayla anymore," Mikayla says, tears starting to well up in her eyes. "I think I just want to be Mikayla."

Trevor sinks to his knees, like she's mortally wounded him. Daniel takes advantage of this moment to swoop in and smack Trevor in the chest.

Trevor makes a "gahhh" sound as the wind gets knocked out of him, and he tumbles down into the pit next to Mikayla.

The producers are loving every second of this. I can see multiple members of the film crew vying to get the best angle as Mikayla reaches for Trevor and he shrugs her off. They're both completely covered in mud now, and watching them split apart from each other is kind of like watching the tragic breakup of two swamp monsters. Still, I feel for them. Their whole brand was their relationship, but now they'll be known for how they broke up.

Now it's down to Selena and Chase versus Daniel and me.

"Looks like it's the battle of the exes!" Dawn Taylor calls out.

It's time to end the secret alliance. Chase turns his staff on Daniel as Selena pivots to face me. Taking the initiative, Daniel swipes at Chase, trying to sweep his legs out from under him—but Chase jumps back, his own staff swinging wildly.

"Ow!" Selena yells as one of Chase's haphazard swings bops her, nearly knocking her off. Getting his balance back, Chase lunges to make a swing at Daniel that misses, and in the process, the back of his staff hits Selena in the face.

"Sorry!" Chase yells, ducking out of range. He stumbles back—which brings him level with me.

He locks eyes with me, and for a split second, I wonder if he's going to go easy on me. If seeing me reminds him of all our times together. When he watched a viral video about roof running, and then broke his leg trying to do parkour, and I had to leave fourth period to take him to the hospital. When I made him his favorite Jell-O cake, which was literally just Jell-O shaped like a cake, for his birthday. When he proposed to me in an Arby's.

But it turns out, Chase isn't experiencing a montage of our past together. His deep-green eyes don't reveal even a flicker of conflict as he drops to his knees and swings at my legs, screaming, "Witness meeeee!"

I leap over his staff, then pivot back to face him. I swing my hardest at him, whacking him firmly in the chest. He pinwheels for a moment, dropping his staff to keep his balance.

"Nice one, babe," Chase says.

And then, without missing a beat, his hand snakes out, and he yanks on my outstretched staff, throwing me off balance.

I can't help the undignified yelp that escapes me as I plunge off the beam and into the mud. I take some small consolation in the fact that Chase ends up in the mud right after me, thanks to Daniel.

"Oh, hey," Chase says casually, like he hangs out in mud pits all the time. "No hard feelings?"

I scoop up a handful of mud and chuck it at him, which makes me feel a lot better. Moments later, Daniel lands in the mud next to me with a huge splat. Above us, Selena lets out a victorious cheer.

"*Selena* got you?" I ask incredulously.

"Nah, I just thought I could use a facial," Daniel jokes, and smears a handful of mud over his cheek. "But hey, good work. We stayed in."

I close my eyes, ignoring the sensation of mud squelching all around me, and let the relief wash over me. We made it. We're still in the game. Hell, we came in second. Now if only we could catch the murderer loose on the set.

After we've showered back in Villa Paradiso, Leah orders us to put on our swimsuits and come outside for our belated Wrath Challenge prize.

"We didn't have time to do this after, well, you know," Leah says. "But better late than never, right?"

She leads us over to a gorgeous, secluded spot on the beach where a wood-paneled tub sits nestled in an oasis of greenery. Vines of beautiful tropical blooms twine around the trees surrounding us, and there's a view of the glimmering ocean in the distance.

The tub itself resembles a gigantic wine barrel. There are two glasses of champagne and half a dozen chocolate-dipped strawberries set out on tray nearby. My mouth starts to water at the sight of it all.

It's the picture of a perfect romantic getaway—except for the film crew stationed all around us. I try to ignore everyone, and that goes about as well as imagining everyone in their underwear during a public speech—which is to say, terribly.

We get the go-ahead from Leah and step into the hot tub. Sinking into the hot water is pure bliss, the heat soothing my aching muscles. Before I started preparing for this reality show, the most exercise I did on a daily basis was going out for what Tara likes to call "a load-bearing mental health walk." These physical challenges have been hell on me, and I've been so sore.

Daniel hands me a glass of champagne, but before I can take a sip, Leah stops us. "Let's get a shot of you two clinking glasses and giving a toast."

"Sure." Daniel lifts his glass. "To love."

"To winning," I add.

"Alice, why don't you feed Daniel a strawberry?" Leah says. It's really more of a command than a suggestion.

I pluck a strawberry from the tray. "Come here," I say. Daniel is a polite distance from me. "Why are you so far away?"

The water sloshes in the hot tub as Daniel scoots closer. I slide the strawberry into his mouth, my fingers brushing his lips.

"Delicious," Daniel says. He's starting to turn red, from either the sun or the heat of the water.

"Did you put on sunblock?" I ask him.

He gives me a strange look. "Of course."

"Good, just checking," I say, popping a strawberry into my own mouth. Damn, these are good. The tangy bite of the strawberry cuts perfectly through the creamy dark chocolate. I could eat ten of these, easy.

"Okay, enough talking. Let's get some shots of you making out," Leah says—a very normal thing to expect two people to do on command.

I lean in to kiss Daniel, and Leah makes a displeased noise.

"That's not going to convince anyone," she says. "This is your moment to really sell this. Are you in love or not?"

I couldn't even be convincingly in love with Chase when I *was* in love with Chase. How can I possibly pull this off with Daniel?

But just as I'm starting to panic, Daniel gives me an encouraging smile. He clearly thinks he's got this, and if he can handle this, surely I can, too.

At my nod, Daniel's hands find my hips, and he pulls me fully into his lap, my thighs straddling his as the water laps against us. I expect him to kiss me, but instead he rests his forehead against mine.

"Relax, Slayer." His voice is quiet, low, just for the two of us. "We practiced for this, remember? Albeit, I *did* have the upper hand back in our room."

I know what he's doing. He's trying to bait me into being so competitive that I forget my awkwardness.

And it's working.

I wrap my arms around his neck and pull him in, my fingers tipping his face so his mouth meets mine. It's a different angle from our other kisses, and I'm pleased by the leverage I have on Daniel. And then he gasps and leans into the kiss, stoking the heat between us, sucking the taste of the strawberries right off my lips. We press closer together until there's no space left between us, and there's only his skin against mine, and the slosh of the water against the tub as we move.

I'm not sure how much time goes by. It could be seconds or hours, but there's nothing I care to think about more than Daniel's hold on me, tethering me to our moment.

"Damn," Leah says, and I jerk out of the kiss so abruptly, I push off Daniel's lap, sending a wave of water slopping over the edge of the tub. "Shawna's going to be thrilled with this footage."

Daniel doesn't move to pull me back, and it feels like a bucket of cold water falling over me. I'm disoriented, having completely forgotten about the cameras. But Daniel doesn't look even remotely frazzled. Was it all just for the cameras for him? Of course it was. But part of me wishes we could have kept going.

"That looked cozy," someone says, and the thought of doing more with Daniel flies out of my head.

It's Dawn Taylor, and she's handing me and Daniel luxuriously fluffy waffle-knit robes like she's a PA. Freya hovers behind her, clutching a clipboard.

"Leah told me about the snake," Dawn Taylor continues, making a face like I'd just complained there was a fly in my champagne, or something equally trivial. "I'm so sorry."

"There's been a lot of safety issues on set," Daniel says.

"And I apologize for that," Dawn Taylor says, sounding not one bit apologetic. "It won't happen again, I guarantee it."

"Thank you," I say, tugging on the robe and stepping out of the tub. I really don't feel like being half naked in front of Dawn Taylor.

"Anyway, I wanted to personally tell the two of you that I'm so impressed by how well you're doing, especially for such a new couple,"

Dawn Taylor says. "I think you have a real chance at winning."

Dawn Taylor takes my hands. "So my advice, and I hope you take it seriously, is that you just focus on the competition. Don't worry about anything else. No more getting into fights with my producers or playing detective, mmkay?"

I can feel the tips of her manicured nails dig ever so slightly into my palms.

She says with a sweet smile, "I'd hate to see any of the contestants get hurt."

Dawn Taylor Interview Debacle Resurfaces

BY MAXINE DEAN, GLAMGOSSIP.COM

Hollywood, CA. Internet sleuths have resurfaced footage of an interview Dawn Taylor gave fifteen years ago while promoting her indie film flop *Women of Power*. The interview begins with Dawn Taylor sitting down with Kyle Wesgrave for his podcast, *Among the Stars*. Wesgrave first compliments Dawn Taylor on her sundress, which makes Dawn Taylor visibly uncomfortable. Wesgrave then transitions into talking about the fashion in Dawn Taylor's upcoming film, which focuses on one of the first female chefs to earn a Michelin star.

Wesgrave proceeds to ask Dawn Taylor why she didn't stick to chick flicks and reality TV, areas where she's seen a lot of success. "Clearly, your fans aren't interested in this recent career pivot. The box office is speaking, and it's saying that people want to see you in a bikini getting wasted."

At that point, Dawn Taylor removes her microphone and hurls it at Wesgrave, nailing him directly in the forehead with the battery pack and breaking his glasses.

The video continues to film as Dawn Taylor leaves the frame, but we see Wesgrave's assistants rushing in as Wesgrave clutches his head. The podcast host goes on to label Dawn Taylor a "crazy bitch" who "is out of control."

Viewers have since weighed in on this resurfaced clip. One fan posted on a forum, "I don't support violence, but Kyle was being a total ass."

Another more critical take pointed out that Wesgrave was indeed correct about the film's performance: "Dawn Taylor's film flopped. She can't just assault everyone who points that out!"

RELATED ARTICLES

REALITY TV: Where to watch Dawn Tay's Inferno

REALITY TV: 10 Shows Like Dawn Tay's Inferno to Watch After Season 1 Ends

REALITY TV: Dawn Taylor or Selena Rivera: Who Wore It Better?

Chapter Twenty-Three

Hell Is Uncovering the Truth

H oly shit. Was Dawn Taylor trying to threaten me or warn me?
I'm still pondering this when Leah and Bryan drop us off like
we're kids being left at day care.

"Go change and then meet us in the kitchen for dinner," Leah instructs us.

I switch out of my swimsuit as quickly as possible. After what Dawn
Taylor said to me, I can't shake this jittery feeling that something is
terribly wrong, and I'm desperate to do something with myself to burn
off the nervous energy. When Daniel emerges from the bathroom, he
catches me pacing around the room and swinging my arms back and
forth, like I'm one of those old Asian uncles getting their cardio in at
the local park.

"Everything good?" he asks.

"Yeah, I'm fine. Just peachy keen. The bee's knees. Absolutely nothing wrong here." I'm babbling now, and I have to stop. "Let's go, everyone's waiting for us."

We're headed down the corridor leading to the kitchen when Daniel
says, "Hang on." He tugs me to a stop, then pulls me into a storage
closet and closes the door behind him.

He leans in toward me, and like clockwork, my heartbeat starts
picking up. Is he about to kiss me? He's so close, and I tip my head
back just a bit to meet his lips, but then he says, "Alice, are you okay?

Dawn's little pep talk back at the hot tub . . ."

"Yeah, that was weird," I agree, though my mind isn't on Dawn Taylor. It's dark in the storage closet, and I'm being crowded into Daniel by a mop and a stack of buckets. "I think she's just annoyed with me for, you know, accusing one of her producers of murder."

Daniel sighs, and I feel his breath in my hair. "I don't like that there was a snake in your helmet. Our names were on the boxes, Alice, and the equipment looked brand-new," he says. "And you'd just said in the challenge that you were afraid of snakes. This feels personal."

"It might've been an accident. We are right next to a jungle," I say. "Or maybe it was a dumb prank from one of the producers to stir up drama."

"I think it's more than that, Alice," Daniel says somberly. "I think someone sees you getting too close to the truth, and they're trying to threaten you."

I shiver. From the way he's speaking, I can tell Daniel's dead serious about this. It's one thing to chase down a murderer. It's another thing to consider that a murderer has you in their sights. My blood runs cold at the thought of what might happen next.

"Well? I'm waiting for you to have three to four objections to my reasoning," he says. "I'm ready, bring on the bullet points."

I laugh at that, and the laughter eases the tight feeling in my chest. I swat at Daniel. "I don't disagree with you just for the sake of disagreeing with you!"

"You're disagreeing with me right now," he points out. Given how dark it is, he can't see me stick my tongue out at him, but I do it anyway. And almost end up licking him.

"So that's what this was all about?" I ask. "You pull me into a storage closet to issue dire warnings?"

"Just adding a little spice to our relationship." Daniel chuckles, then sobers. "But seriously, Alice, be careful."

"Okay, well, if we want to be *careful*, we'd better come up with a good reason why we're late to dinner, especially if someone catches us stepping out of a storage closet."

"Come on, Slayer. That's easy. You know why we're in here." His voice is quiet and teasing, and I immediately get the message. My whole body flushes hot at the thought, and I'm already reaching for him. The memory of how he felt beneath me in the hot tub is still fresh, and I want more.

"Hurry up, Midas. We don't have all day," I say, and his lips find mine.

I know we're only supposed to make it *look* like we've been going at it in here, but then he nips at my lower lip, and my tongue darts out to soothe it, and just like that, all logic goes out the window as his tongue tangles with mine. I rise on my toes to arch into him as the kiss turns slick and heated, every move sending sparks skittering down my body and back again. When his mouth leaves mine, I let out a sound of protest, but then he's kissing down the column of my neck, the hot press of his lips sending a jolt of pleasure through me.

When we break apart, he's breathing harder, and I'm almost certain there's a hickey on my collarbone. My lips are tingling in a way that just makes me want to kiss him again.

Instead, I ruffle his hair. "Shall we?"

We throw the door open—and nearly slam into Freya.

"Watch it!" she says and scurries off. I feel a twinge of sympathy for her. There's likely no love lost among the other production assistants, but coping with the death of someone you worked with can't be easy.

In the kitchen, Ava looks us over, her gaze catching on Daniel's ruffled hair and the hickey on my neck. "Young love," she snorts, as if she's not basically our age.

Then the producers arrive, and we're directed to crowd around the kitchen island like we're all one big happy family.

"Let's hear some reactions to all that craziness today!" Leah prompts us.

One of the production assistants sets down several platters of fruit, baby carrots, and celery sticks for us to nibble on. By now we know that we won't really get to eat dinner until filming's over. Feeling just a tiny bit rebellious, I dunk a baby carrot into a tub of hummus and crunch into it.

"Selena, can you kick us off? Ask the others how they feel about Trevor and Mikayla imploding," Bryan says.

Selena immediately shifts into her role, saying, "Guys, can you believe Trekayla's meltdown? They were, like, my favorite Instagram couple. I've taken so much emotional damage. I feel terrible for them."

"Mikayla's cheating blew up in her face," Ava says pointedly. "She was always relying way too much on Trevor to carry her anyway. A real partner steps up and shares the load."

I scan the room, looking at all the contestants and crew members here, wondering if one of them is guilty of more than corny platitudes. When I get to Bryan, I realize he's staring at me. There's something about the way he's looking at me that I don't like. Chase's friends are usually fun, good-natured guys, but I'm realizing that Bryan is a different breed.

"Alice, you've been quiet," he says. "Share your thoughts with the class?"

"Dawn Taylor said she was going to put our relationships to the test," I say. "It seems like she's really delivering." I give myself a mental pat on the back for saying all of that with a straight face.

"Buckle up," Daniel says to the others. "Tomorrow's probably going to be crazy."

"Do you know what's the theme?" Ava asks. "Not all of us had the time to read up on Dante before we got here."

"Fraud," I supply.

Daniel says, "And if this was what they did for Violence, I can only imagine what they're going to put us through for Fraud."

"Well," Ava says. "Shit."

....

The next morning, I drag myself out of bed when Leah comes barging in to take us to the day's shoot.

"Leah, it's still dark out," I protest. I'm used to waking up early to teach zero period, but I'm getting really sick of being dragged out of bed at the actual crack of dawn.

"Weather app says this is the only break in the rain today," she says cheerfully as she presses a banana and a granola bar into my hands. "Eat. Quickly."

We pass by the living room, which has been cleared out. With Trevor and Mikayla's departure, there's enough bedrooms in the villa for each couple to claim one. It's strangely quiet without all the other couples here, a marked difference from when Chase and I were crashing with everyone else. Gone are the heaps of laundry, the unmade beds, and the scattered luggage.

"It's starting to feel like a ghost town around here," I whisper to Daniel as we walk through the halls.

"We're in the endgame now," he says, and it hits me for the first time that we could actually win this. I'd gone into the competition determined to win, but that's a far cry from actually being so close that I can taste it.

I squeeze my eyes shut for a moment and imagine coming home with the money. Walking up the stairs to my mom's apartment and showing her a huge novelty check. Well, they'd probably just do a wire transfer or something like that, and I know that my winnings will be taxed to hell, but a girl can dream.

I can tell it's going to be a wild day when it starts with us getting into a helicopter.

"We have helicopter money?" I ask Leah as people start climbing in.

"As of a few days ago, yes," Leah says. She turns me to face her. "Here's the deal. Just keep your head down and focus on making it to the end. I'm pulling for you and Daniel."

"Aw, you're just saying that," I say, but it's nice to know someone is in our corner, even if that someone is a cutthroat reality-show producer.

The view below is dizzying, and I find myself gripping Daniel's arm as the villa falls away from us. It looks like we're headed to the very center of the island.

"Is it really safe to be flying with the storm still going?" I shout to Leah over the noise of the helicopter.

She shrugs. "I'm sure they wouldn't do it if it weren't safe."

That makes me feel a little better.

"This helicopter's way too expensive for them to risk it," she adds.

My mind jumps off from that point, trying to calculate the cost of the helicopter—fuel plus the pilot's hourly fee plus maintenance. But then Daniel nudges me.

"What?" I mouth.

"Look," Daniel mouths back and points out the window.

We're high enough up that the helicopter is no longer climbing. The water below us is a maelstrom of bright blue, sea green, and sapphire, with gleaming sparks of sunlight and white crests of waves. I'm mesmerized by how stunning it all is as the helicopter turns sharply and the view of the ocean gives way to the greenery of the trees on the island, foliage so dense that you can't see the ground, just palm fronds and vines layered on top of each other, all racing to climb up to the sky.

I glance over at Daniel, and the corners of his eyes crinkle when he looks back at me. He mouths *isn't it amazing?* and I find myself genuinely grateful that he told me to look, and that I didn't just waste the entire ride thinking about how much it cost or what could go wrong. I wonder what else I've been missing.

Soon enough, we land on a flat spot next to a bridge. The bridge is a classic stone and concrete arch, reinforced with steel, with what I'd estimate is a six-hundred-foot drop to the ground below. The crew has already set up a technical rig of metal, harnesses, and ropes, which I have a distinctly bad feeling about.

I can understand why, from a production standpoint, we're here. It's incredibly cinematic, and I can see a drone camera circling above us as the helicopters touch down and drop us off.

As someone who might have to do a stunt on this bridge, though,

I'm not a fan. I inhale deeply while counting to four, then hold my breath for seven seconds, then exhale for eight seconds. I'm doing my best to calm my nerves, but as the panic sets in, I can tell it's not about to work.

Then Daniel takes my hand, squeezes it briefly, and says, "You've got to be kidding me. Is this really a good idea after what happened to Anton?" He's addressing Leah, his voice deceptively mild. "Do we know if the bridge sustained any damage in the storm?"

"It wasn't my call, I can tell you that, but the PAs checked over all the equipment, and we surveyed the bridge. You're perfectly safe."

When filming starts, the three of us remaining couples are stationed on the bridge, positioned against a waist-high railing that serves as a safety barrier. Across from us, there's a huge, white screen.

"You know, I didn't think I was scared of heights," Selena says, peering over the edge. "But maybe I am."

Noah scoffs. "That's the point. They want you to be afraid."

"Next time I go on a reality show, I'm going to tell them I'm afraid of large sums of money and puppies," I mutter.

"At least they haven't figured out how to weaponize my true fear—parental disapproval," Daniel mutters back.

Dawn is the last to arrive, in her own helicopter. When she disembarks, the cameras follow her as she walks toward us like the bridge is her runway, and we're the peanut gallery at Paris Fashion Week.

Despite the way she's taking on the catwalk, there's something off about Dawn Taylor. It might be the gale-force winds or the early hour, but her hair just isn't quite as glossy as it usually is, and she looks pale and just the tiniest bit haggard, even with her makeup on. Her outfit, a red jumpsuit with a white belt, seems a little rumpled, as if whatever magic she possesses that keeps her looking camera-ready is starting to wear off.

"Babes, welcome to the semifinals," Dawn Taylor says, striking a pose. "I've got a devilishly difficult challenge for you today. You're looking down the barrel of the Fraud Challenge."

By now we know our cues. Selena gasps, everyone looks shocked, and I arrange my face into a suitably horrified expression.

"I know some of you have been very, very bad," Dawn Taylor says in a sultry tone. "And it's time to come clean. For the Fraud Challenge, you'll be playing a twist on Two Lies and a Truth. I've personally picked out three revealing statements about your partner. You'll be on the hook to guess which statements are true and which are false. Fail to guess correctly, and you'll be taking a plunge."

She gestures at the steep drop below us.

"Whoever makes the most mistakes is getting the *hell* out of here. Now, without further ado, let's get into it!"

The crew members help us into the harnesses and secure them. A bungee operator comes around to check that all the straps are correctly attached. Then Freya and Bryan come around to do a second check, testing our cords and adjusting as needed.

Once we're all standing on the edge of the bridge, Dawn Taylor fills us in on the rules.

"The game is simple. I'll list three facts about your partner. For every statement you correctly guess as true or false, you get one point. If you get two questions wrong, you get pushed off the bridge into a terrifying bungee free fall. The couple with the most cumulative points wins a hot couple's massage back at the villa in the Sunset Suite. The losing couple is getting the hell out of here. Ties will be determined by who answers the fastest, so stay sharp, babes!"

A cameraperson pans across the row of us on the bridge, and I try not to think about how high up we are.

"Noah and Ava, step onto the platform," Dawn Taylor calls out, and Noah and Ava cautiously climb over the safety rail. All that's left between them and the fall into the water below is their bungee cords. Dawn Taylor joins them on the platform, positioning herself so she's closer to Noah. "Okay, Noah, you're up first. Let's see how well you know Ava."

"We caught footage of Ava checking out Daniel and Chase by the pool. True or false?"

Noah laughs. "True. Who wouldn't check out these guys? They're pretty easy on the eyes!"

Noah gets the point, then scores one more for knowing that Ava cheated on her vegetarianism with a taco last week. When the round is over, the two high-five each other over earning three points.

"Now let's see if our next couple can go three for three! Alice and Daniel, it's your turn."

Daniel helps me over the safety barrier as we step onto the platform together. My stomach lurches as I glance down toward the water below. I take a deep breath to steady myself. I can do this.

Dawn Taylor says, "Daniel, true or false? Alice chose to betray you during the Greed Challenge."

Shit. I never told him, I realize too late. Why didn't I tell him right after it happened?

Oh, right. Because I didn't trust him back then, and I'd made my choice for good reasons. And then by the time I felt like I could trust him, I'd kind of forgotten about it. I was busy with the mystery of Anton's death, after all.

"False. Alice would never back down from a challenge or betray a teammate," he says with so much certainty that I feel like I've been sucker-punched in the gut.

"Oooh, looks like there's trouble in paradise," Dawn Taylor says, and with a click of a button, the white screen lights up with a projection of me during the Greed Challenge, racing to fill the red barrel. "Daniel, Alice chose to betray you."

Daniel looks over at me, his expression carefully blank.

"I'm sure it was a strategic move," he says, going for upbeat but coming across stiff.

I grimace and try to mouth *sorry* at him, but he's no longer looking at me.

"Okay, Daniel, this is it. One more wrong answer, and you're taking the plunge. True or false? In one of her confessionals, Alice told us that she secretly thinks you're an egotistical know-it-all."

"True," Daniel says instantly.

"Are you sure, Daniel? You don't want to think about it?" Dawn Taylor says.

"She's practically said as much to my face," Daniel says, shrugging. "Trash talk is her love language."

"I'm *so* sorry, Daniel," Dawn Taylor says. She rests her hand on his chest and then shoves.

Daniel teeters for a moment, and then he's gone, plummeting away into the distance.

"Daniel!" I can't look away from the sight of his disappearing figure. But just as it looks like he's going to smash into the ground, the bungee cord snaps back, sending him rocketing up. Our eyes lock for just a moment as he comes almost level to the bridge, and I can't read his expression.

"Zero points for Alice and Daniel," Dawn Taylor says, moving on to Selena and Chase. "Chase, true or false? Selena still sleeps with a night-light."

Chase not only fails that question—it was true—but also his second—that Selena secretly hates Mexican food (which, come on, even I knew that was false). I suspect getting both questions wrong secretly delights him, because I can tell by the way he's looking over the edge of the bridge that he actually really wants to go bungee jumping.

When Dawn Taylor pushes him over, he screams "Cowabungaaaaa!" into the void like he doesn't have a care in the world. She waits for Chase to get reeled up before she begins her pitch for the second half.

"Okay, round two, babes!" Dawn says, fanning herself with the question cards.

Like Noah, Ava crushes hers, although she's miffed at finding out Noah lied about the number of girlfriends he'd had before her. They end up with a grand total of six points.

Then Daniel and I are up again.

"Ready, Alice? Daniel admitted in confessionals that you aren't as good of a kisser as Selena is. True or false?"

"False," I say. "Not that I think I'm a better kisser than Selena, but Daniel would never say something like that about his girlfriend on camera."

Dawn claps her hands. "Correct! You're on the board with one point!"

Finally. I try not to think about the fact that the choice I made during the Greed Challenge may be ultimately what sends me out of the competition. I have to focus.

"Next question. True or false? Daniel had a crush on you in high school."

I laugh so hard I snort. "False!" I say confidently. "We were always at each other's throats. There's no way."

"Sorry, babe, that's actually true!"

What? How? When? This must be something Daniel lied about in an interview to make our fake relationship seem more plausible, right? But I don't have any time to process this, because Dawn's already asking me the next question.

"True or false? Daniel let Selena win during the Violence Challenge."

"I realize it might've been hard for Daniel to take Selena on, especially given their recent breakup, but I also know that he's very competitive and he always plays to win," I say, glancing sidelong at Daniel while I talk. He looks miserable, and my gut twists. "So I think that's a lie."

"Locking that in?" Dawn drawls.

"Locking it in," I say. I'm not entirely sure, but even if I'm wrong, at least I can be fast, which might benefit us in a tie.

Behind Dawn, the projector clicks on.

We see Daniel and Selena square off. He raises his staff, about to go after her with the padded end, but I can tell something is wrong. Selena isn't looking like she's in any condition to fight. Instead, she looks tense and unhappy, and when she lifts her staff, she nearly fumbles it. When Daniel sees the look in her eyes, he freezes and lowers his staff. Then

Chase comes barreling in, and Daniel whips around to knock him out with a single swing. By then, Selena's recovered herself and knocks Daniel out in turn.

I was wrong. Daniel let Selena win.

"Sorry babe," Dawn says as she rests a hand on my shoulder. "Only one point for you and Daniel this round!"

At first, I think Dawn's hand is on my shoulder to comfort me, but then she gives me a shove, pushing me off the bridge.

For a second, my body can't catch up with the knowledge that I'm in free fall, but then I can feel the lift of my stomach, the nerves from looking down from such a great height transforming to unbridled joy.

I try for a second to avoid screaming, but then I give in. I keep yelling even as the bungee cord starts to reach its end. But then, instead of the cord snapping me back, I keep falling.

Something's not right.

I'm plunging farther than the other contestants. Any elation from the free fall turns to pure terror.

As I plummet to the earth, countless memories flit to the surface: my mom teaching me how to make dumplings, the fragrant scent of duck egg congee, the evenings I spent studying for exams with Cindy. Chase is in there too, and I remember our first kiss, sweet and hesitant beneath the awning of the dining hall. And finally there's the taste of haw flakes on a rainy day with Daniel by my side.

Then my harness tightens around me, and I'm shooting back up into the sky, the wind whistling in my ears. My heart is in my throat until the bungee operators reel me in.

When I look back at the bridge, I spot Dawn Taylor and Leah talking to Daniel. They're trying to be quiet, but their raised voices still carry.

"—the conditions on this set are unacceptable. This is gross negligence and extreme disregard for safety," Daniel is saying.

"Look, I get it, you're upset. Of course you'd be. But that's why we had the backup harness," Dawn Taylor says, calm, reasonable. "She was never in any danger. I know you were all set to go jumping in after her, but we had it handled."

"Did you?" Daniel asks. "Because it sure doesn't seem like it to me."

"I need to film," Dawn Taylor says. "If you have more concerns, talk to Leah."

When I'm back on the bridge, Daniel rushes over to me and envelops me in a hug. "Thank god," he says.

"I'm okay," I say to him, but he only hugs me tighter.

"You—" he begins. "I thought—" He shakes his head. He looks at me with an anguished expression, and it hurts, seeing that. All I want to do is make all that fear and worry go away. So I do.

I tilt my head up to kiss him fiercely. He loops an arm around me, leaning into the kiss as he runs his hand through my hair. It's *good*, too good, and I don't want it to be over. When we pull away from each other, I search Daniel's face for signs that he's as affected by all of this as I am. The color in his cheeks is heightened, but that could just be the wind at this elevation.

It's Selena and Chase's turn next, and after the bungee operators quadruple-check their harnesses, filming resumes.

"Now Selena, if you get two points here, you and Chase could be in the finals . . . and Daniel and Alice will be out," Dawn says solemnly.

Fantastic. My entire financial future has come down to how well my ex and his new girlfriend know each other.

Selena bounces on the balls of her feet, shaking out her arms.

"True or false? Chase didn't pay taxes for the first two years after he entered the workforce."

I know this is true because I'm the one who taught Chase about taxes. But Selena, assuming Chase is a functional adult, guesses it's false.

"Next question. We caught Chase on camera saying he's still in love with Alice. True or false?"

"False," Selena says happily, but then she darts a worried look at me.

My heart sinks, because I know she's right. Chase, who cheated on me? Who's been draped all over Selena this past week? Who broke up with me on a reality TV show? He can't still be in love with me.

But I also remember another version of Chase. One I would have confidently said was my partner for life. A man who brought me lattes when I was stuck at the hospital, who proposed to me simply because he knew it would put a smile on my mom's face, who always had a smile for me, even when I was spiraling from anxiety or cranky after an all-nighter grading exams.

Dawn clucks her tongue. "True," she says. And the clip plays on the big screen. Chase is sitting in a confessional chair, holding a mai tai with a bright-pink umbrella in it, and he looks drunk and sad.

"I don't know, man. Selena is amazing. But. Damn. I think I'm still in love with Alice."

"Chase," Selena says, managing to put so much hurt into the one syllable of his name.

Then Dawn Taylor sends her flying off the bridge, and Selena screams all the way down.

I look over at Chase, but he won't meet my eyes. What the hell was he thinking, saying all that? How could he cheat on me and then say he's still in love with me?

"I'm so sorry, Chase and Selena," Dawn says after Selena gets reeled back up. "You came in dead last, with zero points. Your time in hell is over."

My heart is in my throat as Selena and Chase make their exit. I can only imagine the talk they're about to have. And for me, there's no goodbye, no explanation, no closure.

Too much has happened—in the last thirty minutes, the last day, the last two weeks—and I don't know how to feel right now. Beside me, Daniel is silent. After that challenge, we both have a lot to think about.

Leah and the crew come up and start taking off our gear. As I go through the motions of working with the crew to take off the bungee cord that got dislodged and the harness vest that saved my life, I glance over at Daniel. He seems quiet, closed off. I see him strip down to his regular clothes, methodically taking off each harness and carabiner and letting them drop onto the blankets we're standing on. Then he strides right up to Leah.

"Leah, a moment?" Daniel says.

"Yeah, shoot. What's up?"

"Well, half the cast got food poisoning. A fireworks malfunction injured dozens of people. We lost both the main power lines *and* the backup generator in one night. Alice's bungee cord broke. And there's the small matter of a death on set," Daniel says. "Did I miss anything?"

"We talked about this. Accidents happen," Leah says.

"An *accident* is forgetting to charge the mic packs overnight," Daniel says, his tone taking on an edge. "This is criminal negligence. If you can't guarantee our safety, maybe we should leave the show."

"What?" I stare at Daniel, but he's not meeting my gaze.

"You can't!" Leah cries. "The contract—"

"I'm sure I can find a loophole in the contract, given everything that's happened," Daniel says.

Leah's voice is a hushed whisper when she speaks again. "Okay, let's not be hasty, Daniel. I know you're not feeling too hot about everything going wrong on set. But nothing else is going to happen, okay? I guarantee it."

"Somehow I find that hard to believe," Daniel says, folding his arms.

"Okay, look. This stays between us," Leah says. "But those accidents were manufactured. The food poisoning. That was all Seth, fucking dumbass. And the generator blowing up was, uh, engineered, let's say."

"Why do all this?" I ask, but I think I already know the answer.

"Drama! Spicing things up! Sometimes it isn't enough to leave these things to chance," she says. "And it's working. The show's a runaway success."

"What about the fireworks and Anton's death?" I say.

"Well, those were actual accidents. Anton half-assed everything he did, and he picked the wrong time to not properly secure the fireworks. For all we know, he was busy swiping right on Tinder when he fell to his death."

"Okay, then what about the snake?" Daniel asks.

"I can't control wildlife, Daniel! And with Seth gone, I have twice as much work to do around here. I can't double-check everything for creepy crawlies." Leah sighs. "I'm sorry about the bungee cord. I nearly shit myself when that happened. But look, the people who were screwing things up on set are either done or locked in the pantry, and the show's almost over. There won't be any more accidents, I promise. I'm looking out for you. I've been looking out for you from day one, remember?"

I weigh Leah's words in my head. Most of what she said seems plausible, and I know for a fact that she's telling the truth about Seth being behind the food poisoning.

Daniel doesn't look ready to drop this, but just then, someone shouts for us to board the helicopter. Leah gives us both two friendly pats on our shoulders, only wincing a little as she does so, and sends us toward the chopper. Daniel climbs in first and holds his hand out to me.

When he helps me in, for a second, I meet his eyes.

He's still unhappy about what happened earlier.

I don't know what emotion, if any, he must see in mine. Shock, maybe. I can't believe that Daniel would threaten to leave. How could he walk away from this? From me? We'd made a promise to each other to stick this out.

But there's no opportunity to talk over the din of the helicopter as it ascends into the stormy sky.

Chapter Twenty-Four

Hell Is the Consequences of My Own Actions

The weather has taken a turn for the worse by the time as we circle the island. The rain is falling in sheets, and the wind is whipping so hard that I can practically feel the helicopter fighting the wind. But it manages to stay in the air, even as we're all starting to question whether it's safe to be up here.

By the time we're deposited just outside the villa, the feelings that have been simmering inside me have come to a boil. Lingering fear from nearly plummeting to my death. Confusion over Chase's confession. Doubt about Leah's promises of safety. Anger at Daniel for letting Selena win and then threatening to leave the show. And worry that Daniel was right to do so.

I hate feeling this vulnerable, and I can't get the sensation of falling, the shriek of the wind whistling in my ears, the complete and utter loss of control, out of my mind. It's easier to embrace my anger at Daniel than to think about that.

Daniel and I both manage to keep our shit together until we make it to our room. Then I turn on him.

"You let Selena win?" I get up in Daniel's face, letting my fury carry me. I know the moment I stop being angry, I'll crumble from all the fear and anxiety I have bottled up in me.

"*That's* what you're mad about?" Daniel folds his arms. "That I couldn't bring myself to toss my ex-girlfriend into a mud pit? I'm not ashamed of holding back."

"Chase pushed me in, and I was fine," I say furiously. "We could've lost because of you!"

"Because of me?" Daniel scoffs. "What about you? We made a deal to work together, and you sold me out for the chance to win twenty thousand dollars."

I deflate a little at that.

"All I did was, like, lightly betray you," I say, but my heart isn't in it anymore.

"And here I thought you were all in," Daniel said.

"It was the logical choice. Going after the twenty thousand dollars versus the uncertainty of staying in the game."

Daniel rakes a hand through his hair. "I know, but that doesn't mean the betrayal doesn't sting, Alice."

"I'm sorry. But I'm not ashamed of my choice," I say, echoing Daniel. I'm just ashamed I didn't tell Daniel sooner. "I told you, I really, *really* need the money. You don't understand."

"I want to understand, Alice," he says, laying a hand on my arm. His gaze is on me, and he looks so open and vulnerable that I can't help but actually want to tell him.

The thing is, I didn't even tell Cindy how bad the diagnosis was, and we're best friends. At the time, it had all felt so terrible and overwhelming that I hadn't wanted to acknowledge it. I did what I always do. I acted like I was fine, like everything was going to be okay, and just handled things myself. Fortunately, even without knowing how bad things were, Cindy could tell I was struggling, and she was there for me.

I should've trusted Cindy. Maybe now, I can trust Daniel—with the truth, with my friendship, and maybe even more.

I stop thinking and start talking.

"It's my mom. She has cancer. Stage four metastatic breast cancer. The treatment has been brutal, and we don't have good insurance. It's not just my student loans, Daniel. These medical bills, I'm being buried by them. And I need the money to get my mom the best possible care that I can. I want her to be able to stop working and just rest."

I lapse into silence, dropping my gaze. I've run out of steam, and I'm ready to just crawl into bed and never come back out. Then I feel Daniel wrap his arms around me.

"I'm sorry, Alice. I'm so sorry," Daniel says. "You're right. I didn't understand."

I crumple against him, feeling everything—all my anxiety and fear about leaving my mother to come here, my powerlessness to do anything real to help her, my guilt for betraying Daniel over twenty thousand dollars.

His embrace is soothing and warm, and we're pressed so close together that I can hear his chest rumble as he says, "Thank you for telling me."

"When you were talking to Leah—" I lift my head to look at him. "Would you really have left the show?"

"No, not without you," Daniel says. "I was mostly bluffing. I know we can't really walk away, legally speaking. The contract is pretty airtight, and we don't have any hard evidence to give us cover."

I nod, but I don't ask the question that I really want to ask. The question that my mind keeps circling back to, like a cut in my mouth that I can't help probing with my tongue. Did Daniel let Selena win because he's still in love with her?

Because it would be totally reasonable if he is. It hasn't been that long since their breakup. And Selena is amazing—she's gorgeous, she's funny, and she's incredibly cool.

Not to mention the fact that my relationship with Daniel is completely manufactured for reality TV drama. Just thinking about how none of this means anything, that he's just being sweet and considerate because I'm his fake girlfriend—it hurts.

As if he can read my mind, Daniel says, "For what it's worth, I'm sorry about letting Selena win. I should have talked to you first."

I take a deep breath and force myself to pull away from him. "It's okay. You don't have to say you're sorry. You don't owe me anything."

"Alice." Daniel takes ahold of my shoulders, his gaze intense. "Of course I owe you that much. We're in a relationship."

"A fake relationship," I remind him. "This has always been a business arrangement. An act to stay on the show. You have every reason to still care about Selena. To love her. I don't get to ask for more from you." I turn to leave. I don't want him to see the tears welling up in my eyes. I'm furious with myself. This is all fake. Why am I crying?

Daniel catches my hand.

"I'm not in love with her," he says quietly.

"You don't have to say that." My voice is starting to wobble.

Now he takes my other hand, turning me so we're fully facing each other. I'm finding it hard to look directly at him. I pray that my tears don't start spilling over, but I think it's too late.

"I'm telling you because it's true," Daniel says. "I went easy on Selena because, well, Selena grew up in a violent household. She's talked about it on other shows before, so it's not a secret, and she's gone to therapy to deal with her trauma. But when we were competing over that mud pit, I could tell that the whole situation wasn't good for her. I didn't want to make things worse."

"Oh," I say. I remember how shaken Selena looked on the bridge, the way she froze up. "So it wasn't because . . ."

Daniel sighs. "Selena and I just got together, remember? I had fun with her, and I like to think we'll stay friends after this. But I don't have any deep attachment to her. Not like you and Chase. The two of you were engaged. I'm sure you still have feelings for him, especially after hearing how he feels about you—"

"No," I say. I can sense the truth of my feelings rising to the surface, and I'm done being afraid. I'm done being in denial. I look out the window at the beach outside, as if the view could give me courage. "I mean, I still care about him, but I'm not in love with him anymore."

Daniel's thumb comes up to swipe a tear from my cheek, and I finally meet his gaze.

"Really," he says, almost a whisper. "And what changed?"

"I did, in a way," I say quietly. "Because I've come to realize something."

I'm leaning into him, and suddenly we're both moving into each other, Daniel's hands coming up to frame my face. His eyes flick down to my mouth, then back up to meet my gaze. There's that unreadable look on his face again, the one I keep seeing at random moments—when I'm telling a bad joke, or when we're brushing our teeth together, or—oh god—when he's about to kiss me.

I hadn't known before what that look meant, but now I do.

"What did you realize?" he prompts.

"I don't actually dislike you," I whisper.

I don't know who moves in first, but I do know that Daniel laughs into our first kiss, our first real kiss between us, a light touch of my lips to the generous curve on his. One of his hands stays on my cheek, sweetening the angle, while the other curls around me to anchor us together at the small of my back. We stay there for a moment, warmth rushing to my cheeks.

"I don't actually dislike you either," he murmurs. "Quite the opposite actually."

There's something fragile and secret in the close space between us, and it's so unbelievably easy to lift my mouth to his again, to tilt my head, to pick up where we left off.

My brain is usually an unending stream of thoughts and worries, but with every press of his mouth against mine, my world narrows down to only Daniel. With his hands sliding down my waist, I barely notice how my clothes still cling to me from the rain, and the shiver that runs through me is not from the cold air on my damp skin but from his body pressing me into the wall, a solid weight warming me through and through.

"Alice," Daniel breathes as he breaks the kiss. I try to catch my breath before he takes advantage of our new position to kiss my throat and down to my collarbone, turning his warmth into fire. "Is this okay?" he whispers into my skin as he nudges the strap of my sundress off my shoulder.

I nod, and he starts alternating between blisteringly hot open-mouthed kisses and tantalizing nips, driving me wild as he follows the slope of my neckline to my chest and up again, leaving a blaze in his wake. He sucks a love bite into my neck, and I'm suddenly desperate to touch him, to return the favor and make him feel even a fraction of the heat inside me.

I can't let Daniel win, I think dizzily, and it's the best kind of competition now. I slip my hands under his shirt, greedily sweeping my hands along the planes of his back and over his broad shoulders. He, in turn, peels my sundress down past the dip of my waist and over the curve of my hips. I angle my head up again to capture his mouth, and he moans into the kiss, tracing a single sensual line down my spine.

This isn't enough.

I push at him. "Off, off, off," I chant frantically, tugging his damp shirt from his shorts. His mouth chases mine as I tear his shirt off him and toss it behind us. He's kissing me again before I can even thumb the button open on his shorts. Our ability to multitask is really tested when we both fumble with the rest of our clothes—the zipper of his shorts and the hooks of my bra—but we succeed eventually.

Daniel's gaze sweeps over me, and for a brief moment I feel self-conscious. How can I possibly compare to whoever's in his past? But he smiles gently, his hand coming up to cup my cheek.

"Is this okay? We don't have to do anything if you don't want," he says.

"But I *do* want," I protest, and his returning smile is slow and full of promise. "It's just, you're you, and I'm me."

"That's kind of the point," he murmurs into my neck. "You're so fucking perfect, Alice."

The uneasiness inside me evaporates, replaced with the warmth of his touch and his words.

There's a beat where we just stare at each other, and then suddenly we're crashing together with purpose. He catches me up in his arms, and we fall back onto the bed in a tangle of kisses. I land on top of him, and I capture his mouth again for the sweetest, deepest kiss yet. We stay there, slow and languid, almost indulgent, until the sweetness sparks into something hotter. Daniel moves his head lower, his breath fanning warmly over my chest.

"Okay?" he asks, almost a whisper.

I'm still nodding my enthusiastic consent when his mouth presses a series of kisses down my body. He lavishes attention on one breast and then the other until I'm writhing. His hands move further down, to the inner corner of my thigh and up to my center, teasing me.

I'm lost in this moment of the pleasure, of having Daniel worshiping every inch of me. All my usual anxieties threaten to crowd in, but I focus on his touch. I want to be present for every precious second of this.

Beneath the press of his fingers, I can feel myself unraveling, until it's all I can do to ask breathlessly, "Condoms?"

"In my suitcase," Daniel says. His suitcase is only across the suite, but it might as well be on the moon.

"Suboptimal," I say, kissing his collarbone to get his attention back, and he laughs into my neck.

"Well, I hadn't anticipated this turn of events," he counters. In retaliation, I reach down to his length to stroke him once, twice. His eyes shutter with pleasure.

"Daniel, don't you know you're supposed to put things in their proper place?"

"Alice, you're killing me here," he says. He lets out a moan when I lean forward and rock against him, reaching the nightstand.

"And the proper place for condoms is where bed activities happen, so therefore—" I yank the drawer open and push past the melatonin gummies in my sleep kit to pull out a foil package triumphantly. "Here."

"I can't believe this is a turn-on," Daniel murmurs, watching me rip open the condom.

"Organization is very sexy," I say as I work it onto him.

"*Alice*," Daniel groans.

I move above him and start to sink down. The desperation on his face contrasts with the gentleness of his grip on my hips as he guides me onto him. He closes his eyes again as he fills me, his hands reverently tracing up my spine until he's as deep as I can take him.

"Alice, you feel so good," he says helplessly, and the words spur me to move, heat coiling tightly inside me. I *need* him. Daniel seems to understand this because suddenly he flips us, taking over with a passion that makes my toes curl. He presses me into the mattress with one long, searing kiss, and I lift my hips up to meet him with every thrust, faster and faster until it's unclear who's spurring the other on.

If I'm being honest, I'd always known there was a connection between us, a push and pull that's been all-consuming and, up until recently, infuriating. But now we're moving together, perfectly in sync. It's intoxicating, the shared rhythm of our desire, and when we both tip over the edge into bliss, it's Daniel's name that's coming off my lips.

....

Afterward, we climb into the shower together, letting the hot water wash over us as Daniel massages my sore muscles, and I do the same for him.

He looks almost wistful as he bends to kiss me.

"I can't believe that happened," he whispers, his voice barely audible over the stream of the shower.

"You mean, because we used to be mortal enemies?" I ask.

He chuckles. "You've never been my enemy."

"Okay, fine. Academic rivals, then."

"Alice Chen, I've had the biggest crush on you since the first day we met."

I give him a look. "Very funny."

"I'm not joking, Alice." Daniel's fingers tangle in my hair as he moves on to massaging my scalp. God, that feels good.

"Then when you said that in an interview—"

"I was telling the truth," Daniel admits. "It helped sell our relationship, sure, but I wasn't lying."

"But—" I close my eyes for a moment, trying to take this all in. "Why?"

"Alice Chen," Daniel says solemnly, "you've always known exactly what you want, and you go after it so fiercely and fearlessly. From the moment I met you, when you beat me in our very first competition together, I couldn't take my eyes off you. Whenever we competed against each other, it felt like it was just you and me in our own world. I had a crush on you in high school, and when I went away to college, I realized it was maybe even more than that. Without you around, every victory rang hollow."

I close my eyes for a moment, remembering how I felt when Daniel left. "I know what you mean. It just wasn't the same."

"It wasn't," Daniel says. "And then I go on this show, and you're here, of all places. Seeing you again, seeing you strategize and compete and be yourself, it made me fall for you all over again. You push me in ways that no one else can. And you're not just competitive—you're smart and funny and you're almost nice to me when I'm on the verge of death."

I swat his arm playfully, but he catches my hand and holds it.

He looks into my eyes. "Alice, I'm my best self when you're around. You make me want to challenge myself to be better, just to prove to you that I can keep up and sometimes even win. You're so driven—not just to win, but to help other people. To do right by them. To speak out when something's wrong. You're smart, you're razor-sharp, and you're so brave." Daniel chuckles. "I've never been to bar trivia with you, but I'm sure you crush the competition every time."

"Correct," I murmur, nestling into him. My fingers trace gently over his tattoo, the sequence of lines that Daniel never explained to me, and then it clicks.

"It's the Korean flag!" I say, gripping his arm.

He raises an eyebrow at me. "Please elaborate."

"The Korean flag depicts the four trigrams for sky, water, earth, and fire. But they're in a different order on your arm."

"That's part of it."

"I think," I say, considering, "the marks look like binary. Four digits. A birthday?"

"My grandmother's. I had it done when she passed," Daniel says. "I wanted to keep a piece of her with me."

I circle the marking with my hands. "You said she raised you? I can't imagine what that was like, losing someone that close to you."

"It was rough," Daniel says. "She was such a big part of my life for so long. But, in a way, her passing ended up being a catalyst for getting to know my dad. Growing up, I just didn't have anything in common with him. To me, he was this stern, distant figure."

Daniel sighs. "Losing my grandmother hit my dad hard. He took a month off of work to grieve. We ended up spending a lot of that time together. We even started meeting up to go running. We still do, every Sunday." His mouth quirks in a crooked smile. "We're going to do the Tokyo Marathon this year."

"That sounds like fun," I say quietly.

Daniel hesitates, and then says, "I'd love for you to meet him."

"As long as I don't have to run, I'd love that," I say, and it feels like a promise. "So what about the other tattoo? What's the story behind the frog in the hat?"

Daniel laughs. "I just like frogs. He's my little guy."

I laugh with him. I'm enjoying our new intimacy on more than one level. I lean in, kissing the spot where his jaw meets his ear, my hand wandering down to trace his abs.

Then I yawn so hard, I hear my jaw crack.

"We'd better go to bed," he says. "We'll need our rest if we're going to survive this show."

"I hate it when you're right," I grumble, my hands passing one suggestive stroke down his body before I reach to turn off the water.

Once we've toweled off and brushed our teeth, we ease into the bed.

I know I'm a goner as soon as my head hits the pillow. Daniel crawls in next to me, and I indulge in the lazy satisfaction of tangling our legs together as we warm up the bed.

"There's one thing I don't get," he says drowsily.

"What is it?" I murmur, already half asleep.

"It's about our last challenge. You *really* never called me an egotistical know-it-all?"

I snuggle closer to him. "I mean, I don't think I used that *exact* phrasing, so it's probably more of an issue with semantics."

"Those bastards," he murmurs, dropping a kiss on my temple. Something in me thrills at how casual the gesture is. I suppose we've been getting in plenty of practice.

Daniel pulls me close so that I can wind my arms around him and put my head on his chest. I grip the top edge of the comforter and pull it over us. And together, with his hand on the small of my back, we fall asleep.

Chapter Twenty-Five
Hell Is the Morning After

I drift awake, still tangled in Daniel's arms. I slide out to get a drink of water, yawning, but once I'm up and moving, I'm wide awake—and all the fears and worries I had before come flooding back. Without Daniel to distract me, I'm suddenly keenly aware of how little time we have left. We're racing toward the finale of the show, and we're still no closer to finding out who killed Anton.

I'm determined to stay on the show and see this through. A million dollars is on the line, after all, and I came here for a reason. But that doesn't mean I fully buy whatever Leah was trying to sell us back on the bridge. Her assurances are little comfort considering how many accidents—not to mention an entire murder—have happened.

I pace the room, listening to the patter of rain outside accompanied by the rise and fall of Daniel's breathing. It would be so easy to just crawl back into bed with him and forget about all this. But I've never been able to let a problem go unsolved—in the classroom and out of it. And with Anton's killer still loose, we're all sitting ducks.

I just wish I had more information. Leah filled in some of the blanks for us, but that brings us no closer to the truth. She said the generator broke down because of her, and the food poisoning was all Seth.

But wait. I remember what Seth said, that time I was hiding out in the war room. He'd made it seem like he'd been given orders to poison the cast, not that it was his own idea.

Leah had said that everyone who was screwing things up on set was either done or locked in the pantry. I'd thought Leah was just saying things off the cuff, but what if she was serious? What if Seth's really been locked up somewhere in the villa?

I can't shake the thought that Seth might know more about Anton's death than he was letting on. And now that I'm thinking about all this, there's no way I can go back to sleep. I grab my sweatshirt and pull on a pair of jeans before I quietly slip out the door.

It's early enough that I don't encounter anyone in the hallways or dining room as I pass through. It's also dark, but thankfully the storm has cleared a bit, and I can see the full moon in the windows. It's enough light to see my way by.

In the empty war room, I turn on the lights and go straight for the pantry.

When I get closer, I see it's been locked from the outside with some knotted bungee cords, and my hopes soar. I go up to it and knock lightly.

"Seth? Seth!" I whisper into a small gap where the doors meet.

"Who's there?"

"It's Alice Chen."

"Oh *great*, Scooby-Doo's here," Seth mutters. "Fuck off. I'm sleeping."

"Wait," I call quietly. What can I say to get him to talk to me? I try, "I'm sorry they locked you in here. It's so messed up. They could have at least given you a room in the villa."

Silence.

I try a different tactic. "I talked to Leah today. About how you poisoned the peppers. She said it was all your idea."

More silence.

I add, "Oh, and she called you a dumbass."

"Well, she's a chronically online megalomaniac who eats toast plain," Seth snaps. Bingo.

"Is she lying?" Though it's not strictly true, I say, "She also said that you were behind all the accidents on set. I mean, all the nonfatal ones."

"God, she's such a bitch," Seth says. "I didn't do any of that."

"Are you sure?" I remember how sick Daniel and the rest of the cast were after the Gluttony Challenge, so I feel only a tiny bit guilty when I say, "Given your history, it's pretty easy to believe that you were behind everything that went wrong on set. Sounds like you'll be on the hook for any lawsuits that happen after this show wraps."

"But—" I hear the scrape of a chair. "I can't believe this shit. I was just following orders."

"Whose orders?"

"Who else? Dawn." Seth laughs. "Man, I thought you were *smart.*"

"At least I'm smart enough not to sleep with someone who's taken," I say. My mind is racing with this revelation, but Seth's not done.

"Of course they're trying to pin everything on me. They've already thrown me under the bus, so why not make everything my fault? Leah and Dawn are trying to come out of this clean, but their hands are just as dirty as mine. Make no mistake, Dawn is the one calling all the shots. All the producers answer to her."

"But it's her show. Why would she want things to go wrong?" Before I even finish asking the question, I know the answer. For the drama, just like Leah said.

"Believe it," Seth says. "She told me to poison the peppers because they're one of Selena's favorite dishes."

"Wait, Selena?" I ask. Then everything starts falling into place. "So when the generator broke . . ."

"Leah took out the generator because Selena's afraid of the dark, and Dawn wanted to scare her. Oh, and you'll love this, Dawn's the one who came up with the idea of pushing Chase and Selena together. She roped Bryan into helping her."

Judging by Seth's sneering tone, he probably thinks he's managed to land a blow on me. But after my night with Daniel, it's hard to be all that upset. I say calmly, "Why was Dawn targeting Selena?"

"You're really not in the industry, are you? Selena's hot."

"Uh, okay?"

"I mean, everyone wants a piece of her right now. People loved her on *Hottie Havana* and *Operation: Bikini*. Rumor has it that Selena's in line to replace Dawn as the show's host, and Dawn is *pissed* about it."

"How would that even work? The show is named after Dawn Taylor." I shake my head. "Never mind. Did she do anything else to Selena? Or anyone else on the cast?"

"I don't think so." Seth pauses. "It was all just diva shit. Like fighting with Peter over how to run the show, pushing us all to work around the clock when we're already spread thin. Did you know she threw a tin of cookies at Freya?"

This rings a bell. "Cookies?"

"Or madeleines, whatever," Seth says. "Fancy ones, dipped in chocolate. Don't know what her problem was. I wish someone would send me madeleines."

Something about this feels familiar, but I can't put my finger on it. I change tacks. "Do you think Anton's death was really an accident?"

"Who knows? I didn't kill him, if that's what you're asking," Seth says. "But if someone did, he had it coming. He was fucking insufferable and an absolute nightmare to work with. And I'm sure I wasn't the only one he was blackmailing."

I think back to the notebook and the half-written sentence about Dawn Taylor. "Do you think he was blackmailing Dawn Taylor?"

"No idea. I mean, she was acting a little unhinged right before Anton died, but what else is new? She's always been like that. That's her whole thing."

I remember how angry Dawn looked after the fireworks accident. If Anton was blackmailing Dawn Taylor, that changes everything. But of course, I can't just march up to Dawn Taylor and go, "Hey, girlfriend. Anyone been blackmailing you lately?"

It's sounding more and more like the key to all of this is, well, Anton's locker key. I need to know more about what Anton was up to and who else he blackmailed. Lex said that the production assistants hadn't found his laptop yet. I'm willing to bet that the laptop is stashed away safely in his locker. And if Anton thought the laptop was important enough to hide away from his co-workers, then I want a good look at it.

But if his key wasn't in his room, where else could it be?

"Do you know where Anton spent most of his time?" I ask.

Seth laughs. "You're really playing detective, aren't you?"

"Someone has to," I say in my best no-bullshit teacher voice. "Answer the question, Seth."

"How would I know? The guy was everywhere. Not doing his actual job, mind you. Just fucking around and creeping on people. Even when it was all hands on deck in the Video Village, he was trolling on Reddit or posting thirst traps to Instagram."

Ohmygod, the Video Village. When Leah dragged me over there, I'd seen Anton on the balcony in his own little world while everyone else toiled away inside.

"Thanks, Seth," I say, and then I'm hurrying away, back into the dimly lit maze of the villa. I head straight to the Video Village, navigating by memory. When I step inside, it's just like I remembered it—screens everywhere, editors and production assistants hunched over keyboards even at this late hour. Shawna's there, combing through footage with Freya.

Shawna looks up, squinting at me. "Alice? What are you doing here?"

"I, uh, wanted to light some incense for Anton," I say. "It's a Chinese thing. I heard he used to hang out here a lot?"

Freya tilts her head. "Were you two, like, close?"

"Oh, yeah. Definitely. Super close. He was always making me smoothies and I just wanted to, you know, manifest some gratitude?"

Luckily, she doesn't think to check if I'm actually carrying incense or matches. I squeeze by her and go out onto the balcony. It's a small space, but it's got a stunning view of the ocean. From over the railing, I can also see the courtyard several stories below.

It seems like no one has touched the space since Anton died. The pool chair is still there, covered in a blanket that smells strongly of weed. On the ground is a laptop charger, but the laptop itself is nowhere to be seen. There's a metal table with two chairs pushed into the corner, and a terra-cotta pot with a hibiscus plant in it.

I don't really want to touch this gross, crumpled blanket, but I hold it up with two fingers and shake it out. Nothing. I glance back to check no one's watching me on the balcony. Fortunately, everyone inside the Video Village is laser-focused on their screens, their backs to me.

I continue my search, scouring the floor of the balcony by the light of the moon. I check the ashtray on the table, look over the chairs, and even run my hand through the gap between the railing and the balcony. It's slow going in the darkness of night, and I wish I had my phone with me to shine a flashlight on everything.

I don't know how many minutes have passed, but my knees are aching by the time I decide to call it. The key isn't here. I straighten up—and something glimmers out of the corner of my eye. I move my head, and there it is. A glint of moonlight being reflected back at me. It's in the planter, just the tiniest speck.

I go over to the pot, and sure enough, there's a corner of something metallic poking out of the dirt. I dig in the soil, and a small key with a key chain comes away in my hand. I dust off the dirt and pocket it quickly, my heart racing. I've found it. I can't believe my good luck.

I'm so distracted by finally being able to get more information on Anton that I almost miss the sound of someone sliding the door open.

"Hey, sorry I was just—" I start, but whoever it is doesn't wait for me to make up an excuse for still being out on the balcony.

Before I can turn, I feel hands on my back, and one hard shove sends me tumbling over the balcony rail into the darkness below.

Chapter Twenty-Six
Hell Is an Emotional Roller Coaster

I'm in free fall.

For a split second, I'm not sure which way is up or down. The wind is cold and biting, and I get the funny feeling you get when you're in an elevator going up, like my body can't quite catch up to what's happening. I reach out for something, anything, and manage to grab onto a metal rail.

My entire body shudders as I stop falling with a hard jolt. I'm holding on to the rail of another balcony, a couple stories down. I try to yell, but nothing comes out. I try to breathe, but I'm not taking in much air. It's only on the fourth attempt that I can get enough air into my lungs to shout, "Help! Someone!"

The quiet that stretches out after my plea is long and terrifying.

Can't anyone in the Video Village hear me? But then I remember that most people were wearing headphones and focused on their work. Is anyone else awake? I shout again, to no avail.

No one is coming, I realize. I feel tears start to slip down my cheeks in fear and frustration. My hands are shaking, and I know it's not going to be long before my grip slips.

"Help! Help! Please!" I yell with everything left in me, shouting and shouting until my fear threatens to choke me.

Then there's a scuffle and the sound of a glass door scraping open. For a split second, I'm afraid I'm going to see a stranger, whoever pushed me, come to finish the job.

But instead, it's Daniel's face that peers over the balcony and Daniel's arms that pull me up and into the villa. I throw my arms around him, probably soaking the soft fabric of his sleep T-shirt with my tears of relief. Together, we sag onto the rug on the floor.

Daniel strokes my back, his arms tight around me. I'm pressed to his chest, and I can feel his heartbeat, steady and strong.

When he finally speaks, his voice is raw. "Are you okay?"

I nod. My pulse is still jackhammering away, but the rush of terror is fading now as I breathe in Daniel's scent.

"Alice, what happened? Where did you go?"

"I couldn't sleep," I explain. "And then I remembered what Leah said about Seth, how it was his idea to poison the cast. But I knew that wasn't true, so I went and talked to him."

"You talked to Seth in the middle of the night," Daniel says flatly.

"And then I remembered that I'd seen Anton on the balcony of the Video Village, and I had to check it for his key." I reach into my jeans pocket, and for once, I'm grateful for the uselessly tiny and tight pockets on women's pants. Anton's key chain is still safely tucked away. I take it out and hold it up triumphantly. "And look! I found it."

But Daniel doesn't celebrate with me. Instead, he says, "That doesn't explain why I found you seconds away from falling to your death. For the second time in twenty four hours."

"Someone pushed me over the railing of the Video Village balcony," I say, and it still doesn't feel quite real. Someone just tried to kill me. "Thank you, by the way. For saving me. How did you find me? I thought you were asleep."

"I woke up when Leah knocked on our door to get us for filming," Daniel says. "But you were gone. I was headed to the kitchen to check if you were there when I heard you yelling."

"Good thing you did," I say.

"I ran, Alice," Daniel says. He pulls back to look at me. "I ran faster than I've ever run in my life. If I'd gotten to you just a few seconds later

. . ." He takes a long, shuddering breath. "You could've died."

I don't want to think about that. If I do, I'll fall apart, and I can't afford to, not now. We're so close to the finish line in this competition. And I have Anton's key. I'm closer to finding out the truth than ever before. I had a plan to solve Anton's murder, and I'm going to follow it to the end.

"I'm fine, Daniel," I say gently.

Daniel rubs his hands over his face. "We can't keep going like this. Whoever killed Anton, they aren't going to just let us waltz in and out of this place alive. You're being targeted, Alice. Yesterday, your bungee cord broke, and today I find you dangling from a balcony. Someone wants you dead."

"And we can catch them," I insist. "I have the key now. We just have to get it to Lex—"

"No, Alice," Daniel says harshly. His voice softens. "Please, we have to drop out of the competition."

"What? No!" I take Daniel's hands. "I know it's dangerous. But I'll be careful."

"Careful isn't enough!" Daniel looks away for a moment, and I'm struck by how tense his shoulders are. He says, his voice ragged, "Do you know how scared I was when I realized you'd disappeared? This isn't a fair fight, Alice. We have no idea who we're up against. You aren't safe here, and I can't protect you."

"I don't need you to protect me," I snap. "I can handle things just fine by myself."

"Seriously?" Daniel huffs out a laugh. "What happened to all that talk about working together and looking out for each other when we were with Lex? This isn't a solo mission, Alice. I'm here, too."

"I know," I say, frustrated. "But we're so close to the end. And my mom needs this."

He shakes his head. "Your mom needs *you*. Alive and with her."

"She's going to have that and a million dollars."

"Alice, look at me," Daniel says, taking my hands. "Would your mom really want you to do this? To risk your life for a chance at winning?"

"You have no idea what my mom would want," I say, shaking him off. My expression hardens. "I'm not quitting."

I'm furious now, that he would seriously suggest leaving the show, when I have Anton's key in my hand and a million dollars just out of reach.

And the worst part is that I know he's right. My mom wouldn't want me to do this. She doesn't even like the idea of me walking home at night by myself. If she knew what I was doing, she'd order me to leave right away and then scold me for hours while angrily cooking me a feast.

But I owe everything to my mother. If I can't do this for her, then what use am I? All the terror from today is thrumming in my veins, and I need to do something about it. I need to regain control of what's happening. I need answers.

"Daniel, I—" I'm about to promise Daniel I'll be careful and convince him that we should stay when the door swings open. Light floods in from the hallway.

"*There's* my star couple," Leah says. "I've been looking for you guys everywhere. We're five minutes late for call time."

"Now's not a good time," Daniel says tersely. "We need a minute."

"We don't have a minute! You two need to be down at the beach ten minutes ago," Leah says. "This finale is extremely time-sensitive. You guys need to go, go, go."

"We're not going to be in the finale," he says, standing.

I clamber to my feet after him. I just need time to reassure Daniel that we can make this work. But instead of time, I've got Leah and a camera crew in my face.

"Can you just give us a moment?" I say. "We'll be right with you. We're doing the finale, don't worry."

"No." Daniel steps away from me. "I have something I have to say." In an instant, I know exactly what's going to happen. I've competed against him too many times to not recognize the calculating expression on his face. I've left him exactly one way to get what he wants, and he's going to take it.

Once, before my dad left, we went to Great America as a family. It was my first time, and I only had eyes for the biggest roller coaster. I had no idea what to expect, but for a fraction of a second before the first big drop, I felt my stomach tighten and my breath catch in my chest before I was screaming in gut-wrenching terror.

This is that feeling again, except instead of a roller coaster, it's Daniel doing this to me. Daniel, who I thought was starting to actually care about me. Daniel, who I just hooked up with. And yet, it's still Daniel, who knows how to beat me at my own game.

I watch, unable to move, as Daniel pivots to the perfect angle for the cameras. "Alice," he says, and in that moment, I hate the sound of my name on his lips. "This just isn't working out. Yesterday, we all found out that Chase is still in love with you. And seeing that made me realize that I'm still in love with Selena. The truth is, I can't stop thinking about her."

"Daniel," I begin, but nothing else comes out. I don't know how to stop this.

He continues, "I'm sorry, but I can't be with you. I'll always look back fondly on the time we shared together, but the more I get to know you, the more I realize that we just aren't compatible. You're not the kind of person I can see myself with."

My stomach lurches like I'm in a free fall, and I feel lightheaded as I take in what Daniel's saying.

The moment Daniel turned to the cameras, I'd anticipated what was coming. But I hadn't anticipated how much it would feel like a gut punch. Tears spring to my eyes.

I know he's lying about being in love with Selena. He said himself that they'd only just started dating, and he barely seemed bothered when they broke up.

But he could be telling the truth, too—not about Selena, but about me. Maybe I'm not the kind of person he can see himself with. After all, from the beginning to the end, this was all fake. Our goals were temporarily aligned, that's it. But I was stupid enough to get caught up in the heat of the moment and actually start falling for him.

And then, when he wanted out, he found a way to make it happen.

It's clear that I can't count on Daniel the way I thought I could. But it doesn't matter. I'm used to being let down—by my father, by Chase, by college classmates who wouldn't pull their weight during group projects, by school administrators who didn't believe in my students, by doctors who pretended my mom's accent was too hard to understand. A thousand disappointments, big and small, accrued over a lifetime.

When the chips are down, I know I can't count on anyone other than myself and my mom. It's only ever been us against the world, and this is just further confirmation.

Looking at Daniel, the way he can just smile at the camera while my heart breaks into so many pieces, I realize that we really are done.

....

Leah disappears to talk to Peter Dixon and Dawn Taylor. I can't bring myself to say anything to Daniel, especially with the cameras still in the room with us.

When Leah returns, she drags us off to give our confessional interviews.

"It was just such a whirlwind," Daniel is saying from the other side of the room. He's seated in a rattan chair by the window. "My feelings for Alice were real. I mean, this island is so beautiful, it's impossible not to fall in love with whoever you're with. But now that we've been together for a week, I can see that this was just a rebound for both of us. I was heartbroken over Selena. Alice was heartbroken over Chase. We were able to comfort each other, especially because of our shared history. But I think we were both starting to see that this wasn't going to work out in the long run."

I disappoint Leah for the last time with my interview. I can barely speak for the tears threatening to pour out and drown me. I'm not even sure what I manage to say.

"That's fine. That's good. We can use it," Leah says, though I can tell she's just letting me off the hook. She puts a hand on my shoulder, which is probably meant to be comforting, but I feel nothing inside. "Alice, sweetie, you're going to be okay. America loves an underdog. Everyone's going to hate Daniel for what he did, and they'll love you. You're going to come out on top, I guarantee it."

I'm pretty sure I've hit rock bottom, but I nod anyway. As if the opinion of strangers online is at all relevant to me.

Afterward, we're sent back to our suite to pack our bags. Our cameraperson stays to film us collecting our things, and later, two more camerapeople arrive. It must be a slow day on the rest of the island if they're this focused on getting footage of me stuffing my bras into my luggage.

"I'm sorry it ended this way," Daniel says as he zips up his suitcase.

"Mm." I don't trust myself to speak. I'm not sure if he means our fake relationship or the competition. I stomp on my luggage to pack it down, which makes me feel a tiny bit better. I start categorizing my things to distract myself.

Toothpaste. I've lost my chance to win a million dollars. Hairbrush. I'll never find out who killed Anton. Socks. I'll never learn who almost killed *me*. I slam my suitcase shut with so much force that the bed bangs against the wall.

Daniel tries to say goodbye to me, but I push past him with my luggage. I want to put some distance between us. Hopefully they won't make us take the same shuttle away from the villa. Probably a naive hope. I'm sure they'd much rather film us sitting together in stony silence. Hell, they'll probably have us share a room and a bed wherever we're going, just for kicks.

But as I storm through the villa, Freya intercepts me.

"Peter Dixon wants to talk to you," Freya says. For all that Freya looks fragile, she's much stronger than I expected. Her fingers close on my arm like a vise, and I let her steer me to one last meeting.

Peter Dixon and Dawn Taylor are there in the war room, waiting for me. But I'm done playing nice.

"What do you want?" I demand, throwing my bag on the ground and crossing my arms. I know I'm acting like a child, but I relish letting loose for once.

"Good to see you too, Alice," Dawn Taylor says. "You're a smart girl. You tell me why I wanted to see you."

"I have no idea," I say stubbornly. "Can I go?"

"I think you'll want to stay for this," Dawn Taylor says, her lips curling into a smile.

"We've got a problem here," Peter Dixon says, folding his hands. "We've got a finale to film, but we need two couples for that to happen. We were planning on bringing Selena and Chase back, but . . ."

"They just broke up," Dawn Taylor says. "Apparently, Selena didn't like that Chase is still in love with you."

"So you see the pickle we're in," Peter Dixon says. "But Chase wants a second chance."

My breath catches in my throat. "Wait, does that mean—"

I hear a soft, uncertain voice behind me.

"Hey, babe."

Chase stands in the doorway. Chase, with his horrible *Rick and Morty* T-shirt over a pair of truly atrocious cargo shorts. His hair is sticking up at all angles and he looks like he's been through hell.

"Babe, I'm so sorry," Chase says. "I don't know who I am anymore. All I know is that I just want to be with you again."

"Don't blame yourself," Peter Dixon says kindly. "It's the producers. They're great, don't get me wrong. We've got some of the best in the biz. But sometimes they go too far."

Dawn Taylor scoffs. "They know how to get a good show out of people. That's all."

"Let me guess, Chase," Peter Dixon says, sighing. "They pushed you to drink and then said all kinds of things to you to manipulate how you felt." He pinches the bridge of his nose. "DT, I thought I told you that we weren't going to be doing that on this show."

"What?" Dawn Taylor looks outraged. "Oh, come on—"

Chase raises his hand, looking penitent. "It's okay. I don't blame the producers. It's not an excuse for what I did. Alice, I want you to know that I take full responsibility."

It's true that Chase cheated on me, and I haven't forgiven him for that. But Dawn Taylor directed her producers to make it happen, all because she wanted to eliminate Selena. She messed with my entire life for this. The more I think about it, the angrier I get. I have to call her out on it. I don't think I could live with myself if I just bowed my head and let Dawn Taylor walk all over me. What do I have to lose at this point?

"Chase, yes, you made a mistake," I say, infusing calm into my voice, "but we were both pawns in a much bigger game. Dawn Taylor has been pulling as many strings as she can to get Selena eliminated."

"Great. Here we go," Dawn Taylor says, rolling her eyes.

Peter Dixon steeples his hands. "Is that so?"

"She ordered the producers to poison the peppers specifically so that Selena would get food poisoning. Then she had them kill the generator during the storm to scare Selena. And of course, she had her producers push Chase and Selena together to get Selena eliminated." As I recount what Dawn Taylor's done so far, I wonder what else she could have been doing behind the scenes.

The woman in question huffs out a laugh. She settles back in her chair, clearly shifting from "caught" to "owning it" in real time.

"Fine. You got me. I'd do anything to make this show a hit," Dawn Taylor says. She turns a withering glare on Peter Dixon. "And please, Pete, don't play innocent here. You've made it beyond obvious that you want to replace me with a hot young thing who'd take a fraction of my salary and never say no to you. I know Selena's been gunning for my job since she got on set, and it's all thanks to you."

"Now, DT, that still doesn't excuse what *you* did."

"Well, *Pete*, we're both professionals. We both know what it takes to make good TV. I heard what happened on the set of *Matchmaker Mayhem*. That show makes everything I did look tame in comparison. And if I were a man like you, the fact that I'd be willing to do whatever it takes would be applauded," Dawn Taylor says. She glances at her phone. "Look, we can take turns dragging our skeletons out of the closet, or we can go film this finale before the set literally melts down."

Peter Dixon looks conflicted, and I can almost see him weighing the thought of dragging Dawn Taylor through all the things she did against getting the finale filmed.

"You're right," Peter Dixon says finally. "We're on the clock. If we don't wrap filming in the next hour, everything the crew spent all night setting up will be ruined. Let's stick the landing here, and then we can hash this out later."

"Deal." Dawn Taylor nods.

"So how about it?" Peter Dixon turns to me and Chase. "Want another chance at winning a million dollars?"

"I'm in," Chase says eagerly. "If Alice is, of course."

"Yes," I say quickly. Warning bells are going off in my head, but I ignore them. I have to seize this chance to get back in the game. "Let's do this."

I reach for Chase's hand, but he's already barreling toward me. He tackles me in a bear hug.

"Save it for the cameras!" Dawn Taylor snaps. She raises her walkie-talkie. "Can we get some cameras in the war room? Yes, now!"

Within minutes the camera crew bursts in, but Chase doesn't wait for them to set up the shot. Before I can stop him, he sweeps me up in his arms.

"I love you, Alice!"

I glance over at the cameras. Here we go again. "I love you, too," I say back, forcing a smile.

Am I in over my head? Yes. Am I still going to power through and keep going? Of course. It's all I know how to do.

Chapter Twenty-Seven

Hell Is Reuniting with Your Ex
to Go Rock Climbing

I'd hoped to find a chance to hand Anton's key off to Lex, but we're told by the producers that instead of filming some extra footage of the final two couples, we're going to start shooting the finale immediately.

"There's a break in the storm and this could be our last chance for hours," Leah informs us.

She takes us through the jungle outside the villa and then down a side path.

Chase holds my hand as we walk together. The camera crew has gone ahead to set up for the big finale, and it's just the two of us, trailing a distance behind Leah.

"Chase," I say quietly, "can we take this slowly? I mean, I want to work together for this final challenge, but after this, I'm not sure."

"Of course," Chase says, squeezing my hand. "We're doing this for your mom, right? So let's get this bread!" He drops my hand to pump his fist in the air.

I laugh. Because even in these circumstances, Chase can make me feel like we're in a comedy and not a horror movie. Maybe we are. Maybe everything is going to be just fine.

And then our final challenge comes into view.

Holy hell, it's a volcano. A huge, four-story-tall volcano rises in front of us. There's smoke and lava pouring out of the top.

I know it's all fake, but it doesn't lessen my sense of dread. There's probably a million ways they can make someone die on this kind of set and have it look like an accident. At least Daniel isn't here to say "I told you so" about this whole thing being dangerous.

Ava and Noah are already at the base of the volcano when Chase and I get there.

"Man, you're like a cat with nine lives, aren't you?" Noah says, high-fiving Chase. "You just keep coming back."

"You know it!" Chase laughs. I don't join in. I'm too busy staring up at this giant volcano, trying to figure out how I can possibly strategize a win for a challenge that involves an entire volcano.

One of the cameras pushes in on me and Chase. From the sidelines, I see Leah gesturing for us to kiss.

Chase takes the hint and sweeps me into a kiss. I kiss him back, aware of the cameras on us, but I feel nothing as I press my lips to his. Even though I'm furious with Daniel right now, all I can think about is the last time I kissed him, how good it felt to let go of all my worries and just sink into the feeling of his mouth on mine.

I break away from Chase just as a rumbling sound fills the air and the ground beneath us starts to shake.

Bright red and orange lava erupts from the volcano. Dawn Taylor emerges from the back of the volcano's rim. Her hair and makeup are perfect, and her floor-length, skintight red gown is gorgeous.

"Welcome to the final circle of hell, babes. It's the Treachery Challenge, and we've saved the best for last!" Dawn Taylor flashes a dazzling smile at the nearest camera.

If I hadn't been watching Dawn Taylor so closely for the last ten days, I probably wouldn't have noticed it, but her smile seems a little stiff. Is it just nerves over the finale? Or does she know something bad's about to happen because she's planning to kill one of us off in the finale?

"First, you'll race to the top of this volcano. The first couple that makes it to the summit will get the chance to make one final choice to determine the winner. Whoever completes the challenge first wins *one million dollars!*"

Leah comes over to talk to us while we're each fitted with a safety harness intended for rock climbing.

"If you end up falling into the volcano during the challenge, just hold your breath while you're in the lava," she instructs, tightening my harness. "There's a chute in there that goes down and out of the volcano. So, yeah, it'll be messy. When you reach the bottom of the chute, one of the PAs will be there to help you out and escort you through an underground tunnel and back to the beach for final filming."

"Got it," I say.

Leah gets someone to inspect my equipment, then fastens my helmet for me. When she's done, she pulls me into a tight hug. "Good luck, Alice," she says. If I didn't know better, I'd swear she's a little misty-eyed. "I'm rooting for you."

The producers give us a few minutes to stretch and say some last words before the challenge. I leave Chase to give the soundbites and sidle up to Lex.

"Psst, Lex," I hiss, switching off my mic pack.

Lex says quietly, "What now? I can't believe you're still here after what happened during the Fraud Challenge. You should've left with Daniel."

"And leave you to fend for yourself? Never," I say, and Lex rolls their eyes. "Anyway, check this out. I found the key to Anton's crew locker!" I palm the key into Lex's hand.

"Where did you find it?" Lex frowns, examining the key. "Never mind. Not important. I've got a moment, so I'll head there right now. Just stay safe, okay?"

"I will. You stay safe, too," I say.

"I'm not the one with a target on my back," Lex says. "See you at the finish line. Good luck." They make a subtle shooing motion at me, then slip back to join the small army of camera crew filming B-roll. I switch my mic on and make my way over to Chase.

"There you are," he says, squeezing my hand. "One of the PAs was asking for you. I told her you were probably peeing in the woods."

"Yep," I say distractedly. "Just answering nature's call." I've wasted precious time handing off the key to Lex, and now I've got barely any time at all to study the Treachery Challenge course.

The crew has outfitted this giant fake volcano with a rock-climbing wall. All the way up the volcano face are handholds and footholds in red, blue, and green at varying heights. About one-third and two-thirds of the way up, there are narrow platforms that it looks like we're meant to climb onto. Each of the platforms has a console with levers, buttons, and a wheel.

That's all I manage to gather before Leah signals us to face Dawn Taylor. The cameras sweep across us, and then we're filming one last time.

"Get ready. Get set. Get the hell up there!" Dawn Taylor cheers, and we're off.

Ava and Noah rocket forward, their legs pumping in tandem. I'm still studying the wall, trying to figure out what's the best route for us.

"Come on, babe! Don't get left in the dust!" Chase yells. He's picked a handhold at random and is hoisting himself up easily. Damn it. I have no choice but to follow Chase's ascent.

About two feet up, I glimpse a small warning label on the wall with a red radioactive symbol. It makes the volcano look like it's a toy made for kids and not a Godzilla-sized TV set.

I test my weight on the next toehold. When I go to reach for the corresponding handhold, I notice that it's bright red, just like the warning label. At the last second, I swerve for a blue handhold instead, straining my arm to grab it.

"Chase!" I yell up at him. "I think something bad happens if you touch the red handholds!"

"What?" Chase yells down at me—just as he steps on a red foothold. Gooey lava explodes out of a nearby vent. Chase yelps as his foot slips, but he manages to use his weight to swing onto another foothold.

It looks like his climbing harness holds, and I pray that mine will, too, if I slip.

I try to dodge, but a shower of lava—which is really just gelatinous red glop—hits me in the face with a horrible splat. Ugh. I don't think I'll be able to eat Jell-O ever again.

"Sorry, babe!" Chase shouts. "Don't touch the red handholds!"

We continue to make slow progress upward. My muscles are screaming at me, but I ignore the pain and focus on pushing myself to keep going.

Ava and Noah are just above us, and before long, they reach a narrow platform jutting out from the volcano, marked by a colorful green flag. As soon as both Ava and Noah set foot on the platform, a confetti cannon goes off.

"Ava and Noah have reached the first milestone!" Dawn Taylor's voice rings out from speakers somewhere nearby. "For those following along at home, that means Chase and Alice need to watch out! Every milestone gives our intrepid couples a chance to make it harder for their competition to keep climbing."

On the platform, Ava and Noah have taken hold of what looks the wheel of a ship, and they're turning it counterclockwise.

A rumble reverberates through the volcano. Oh shit.

The green handholds on our route retract, disappearing into the wall. I scramble to push off of the green ledge I'm on and just barely manage to clamber up onto our own platform. There's no confetti for us, and when I try our wheel, it does nothing.

I look up to chart our next move and my stomach sinks. With the green handholds gone, it's going to be much harder to scale the volcano.

"Ready to keep going?" Chase asks. "Or do you need a break?" I'm hunched over, trying to catch my breath as I assess the situation.

"No time," I say, squaring my shoulders.

We continue climbing, but it's slow going, at least for me. Chase loves hitting the climbing gym with his friends, so of course he's scaling the wall easily, even now. But without the green handholds, I'm struggling to keep up. We're falling farther and farther behind, and if Ava and Noah beat us to the next milestone, we're toast.

"Chase!" I shout. "Stop waiting for me! You need to get to the next milestone before Ava and Noah!"

Chase hangs off the wall to throw me a quick salute, then starts scrambling up. He's fast, even faster than Ava and Noah, and with a strategic jump, he's able to get to the second milestone just seconds before Noah. Chase spins the wheel, and their blue handholds disappear into the wall—and more handholds appear on our route.

"Did it, babe!"

"Nice work," I call up. "Keep going!"

It's taking all my concentration to continue scaling the wall. I force myself up, willing my hands to keep grabbing each ledge and pulling myself up, pushing with my legs. My arms are shaking now, and I can feel the harness digging painfully into me.

"Babe! Need help?" Chase calls down. He's clinging to the side of the volcano, perfectly at home dangling high above the ground. For a second, I consider letting him come back down to give me a hand. But it's too risky and our strategy is working. I don't need help. I just have to push through.

"I'm good," I yell, despite being the furthest thing from good. For the millionth time in this competition, I wish I'd taken up weightlifting, or done push-ups in the teacher's lounge, or something. I force myself to think of my mother. Of that fucking olive oil. Climb, Alice, climb.

Noah and Ava are right behind me, and I can't slow down for even a single second.

Every one of my muscles is screaming, but I grit my teeth and heave myself up. But I don't have it in me to go any farther. I tell myself to move, but I just can't. It's like my body's stopped taking directions from me.

If I want to win, I have to do what I hate most. I have to rely on someone else.

"Chase!" I yell. "Help me up!"

"I got you," Chase calls, and he reaches out a hand. I take it, and he hoists me up that one last stretch.

Together, we stand up straight. The summit is actually a huge platform that rings the glowing mouth of the volcano. I didn't realize this space was so big from down below. It's easily thirty feet wide, which is just enough space to accommodate all the production crew, the cameras and dollies, and the climbing equipment. A giant crane towers over us, and we're surrounded by fake foliage. There's even a very fake-looking rock formation behind us forming the backdrop for this scene. Lit tiki torches ring the area, their fire giving everything an ethereal glow.

This is it. We're at the top. We did it.

Confetti cannons blast all around us. We're showered with colorful, glittering confetti.

"We won!" Chase yells, slinging an arm around my neck.

It doesn't feel real.

I can hardly believe that I'm seconds away from winning the money and figuring out what happened. My mind flashes to my mom, and I can just see the shock and then relief and pride on her face when I tell her the news. I imagine going out with Cindy and Tara for hotpot to celebrate and taking a hiatus from my job so that I can spend the whole year taking care of my mom. And neither of us will have to worry about money as we binge K-dramas and chug down expensive bone-broth soup.

Chase keeps yelling "We won!" over and over until I hug him back, and then we're jumping up and down, shouting and cheering and laughing. Leah flashes me a thumbs-up from the sidelines. I look around for Lex. I know they're on the job right now, but I want to share this moment with them.

But Lex is nowhere to be seen.

Lex should've been back by now. They said they'd see me at the finish line. As I scan the faces of the crew, more carefully this time, I still don't see them. If they're not here, then something must be wrong.

What if something happened to Lex on their way to open Anton's locker?

Is this how Daniel felt when my bungee cord stopped working on the bridge? It was easy to brush off the danger when it was just me, but being on the other side, knowing that someone I care about might be hurt—it's a terrible feeling. I search the crowd of crew members again, desperate to see Lex's sardonic smile. I need to make sure Lex is okay.

I'm going into full panic mode over Lex's disappearance when Dawn Taylor starts clapping.

"Congratulations, Alice and Chase. The two of you have been through hell to get here," Dawn Taylor says. "But I'm afraid your trials aren't over yet."

Of course. Things just can't be easy.

"As you know, the theme of this finale is Treachery." Dawn Taylor waves a hand over the bubbling volcano. "And I've decided that there can only be one winner in my inferno. The first person to throw their partner into the volcano wins . . . and gets one million dollars!"

They can't change the rules on us now, can they? Did the fine print ever guarantee two winners? This has to be a test. We're being tested on our loyalty to each other.

I glance at Chase, who's looking at Dawn Taylor with a puzzled expression. I can practically see the gears turning in his head as he makes sense of what she's saying. Then he breaks into a smile.

"Oh, I get it," Chase says cheerfully. He takes both of my hands, looking me in the eye. The cameras focus on him as he speaks. "Alice, I love you. I really screwed up with you, and I told myself that I'd make it up to you someday. It looks like that day has come. The money's all yours, babe."

"I—" I gape at Chase. "What?"

Chase spreads his arms and tosses back his head. "I'm ready! Push me in!"

It would be so easy to throw Chase into the lava. But once again, Daniel's right. Trying to win is a fool's errand. Dawn Taylor can change the rules as much as she wants. The producers can manipulate how I feel and what I do. The editors can give me the hero edit or the villain edit.

I've been trying to play their game this whole time—say the right words, wear the right clothes, kiss at the right cue. But I have no power here. And what's worse, someone on this island wants me dead. I'm completely at the mercy of not only the show, but also Anton's killer. And I'm not Michelle Yeoh. I'm not some action hero who can keep getting lucky and surviving. I'm just Alice Chen.

The only way to win is to stop trying to win at all. Leah said that the volcano lets out into an underground tunnel, which is where the crew lockers are. Lex is missing, there's a murderer among us, and time is running out. I know what I have to do.

I take a deep breath and jump.

....

For a split second, it feels like jumping into a pool on a hot summer's day. But then the fake lava swallows me, and it's surprisingly cold and sort of gloppy. Some of the lava gets in my mouth. It tastes like feet.

I flail for a moment in the lava, but then as I sink, I make contact with a solid, smooth surface, and then I'm speeding down an enclosed slide. I'm going fast, too fast, and suddenly I'm afraid that I'm about to die a very, very stupid death.

Then I crash out of the slide and land in a huge pool of more lava. I'm sinking like a rock, and I struggle to swim upward, still holding my breath. But the pool is deep, and my clothes are dragging me down, making it hard to move through the lava. I'm running out of air, and my movements grow more frantic as I try to break the surface. No PA comes to pull me out.

I'm going to die. I'm going to die on a reality TV show, covered in bright red goo, inside a fake volcano.

Oh god, Cindy's going to have to explain to my mom what happened to me. I'll never talk to them again, or find out the truth behind

Anton's murder. Another thought bubbles up: I'll never get to see Daniel again. I'll never get to kiss him, or tease him, or find out what life might be like with him.

I'm going to die, and my last thought is of Daniel? This really is hell.

Then a strong hand grabs mine, and I hold on for dear life as I'm hauled out of the pool. I wipe the glop from my eyes and look up at—

"Daniel?" I whisper, shocked.

He hasn't let go of me, and when I say his name, he pulls me into a tight hug. I'm covered in fake lava, but he doesn't seem to care. I feel him take a deep breath, and then he releases me.

"I couldn't leave you," Daniel says, cupping my face. "When I found out that you weren't getting eliminated with me, I snuck away to come back for you. But you were already climbing the volcano. I was too late."

"No, you were just in time," I tell him. I'm not sure it was an accident that no one was around to get me out of the pool. Daniel saved my life. Again. "You saved me."

He laughs. "Validation from Alice Chen. I can die happy now," he says, pulling me close.

"As sweet as this is, can we move things along?" says another voice, one I'm immensely relieved to hear.

"Lex!" I say, peering around Daniel. Lex limps up to us, waving to me before promptly sitting down on the floor. Their hair is a mess, and their shirt is ripped. "Oh, god, what happened to you?"

"You explain your part first," Lex says, gesturing to Daniel. They lean back against the wall again, looking exhausted.

Daniel says, "Alice, when I realized that you weren't leaving set with me, I escaped from production and ran back. By the time I got to the villa, everyone had left. But then I overheard Freya talking to Bryan on her walkie-talkie. He was telling her to make sure you went into the volcano, no matter what."

"He was trying to kill me," I say, realization dawning on me. "Leah said one of the PAs would be here to help me out of the pool, but there was no one there."

Daniel nods, his mouth a grim line. "I booked it to the volcano, and when I saw one of the crew members open up a trapdoor to go underground, I put two and two together. I went into the tunnels, hoping to head Bryan off . . . but I was too late. I found a PA knocked out in the hallway."

"The PA who was supposed to come get me," I surmise.

"I think so," Daniel agrees. "And then I ran into Bryan and Lex. They were fighting."

All along, I'd thought Bryan was just a dick, but it turns out he was dangerous, too.

"Bryan caught me on my way to the crew lockers. He knew I was supposed to be with the crew," Lex says, their voice raspy. "Next thing I know, he's shoving me against the wall like he's some high school bully. Sprained my ankle trying to get away. Then Superman over here swoops in and kicks the crap out of Bryan."

"He got away," Daniel says. "But I didn't want to risk going after him, especially with you possibly going into the volcano. I'm glad I made it just in time."

"Thank you, really," I say. "But are you okay? Did Bryan hurt you?"

"Alice," Daniel says, taking hold of my shoulders. "Don't worry about me. Worry about yourself."

"Don't tell me what to do," I say stubbornly. I crane my neck, trying to check Daniel over for any injuries.

"Fine, then about how about this," Daniel says, taking my hands. "You can worry about me, and I'll worry about you. Deal?"

"Deal."

"Again, this is very cute and all, but we're on a deadline," Lex says. They reach into their utility jacket breast pocket and produce Anton's key. They toss it to me. "You need to get to the crew lockers. Find out what's going on."

"What about you? We need to get you looked at," I say.

"I'll be fine," Lex says. "You'll have to go without me. With my ankle like this, I'm only going to slow you down."

"But Bryan—"

"I'm tougher than I look. The only reason Bryan had me on the ropes was because I didn't see him coming. And he's needed on set, so he won't be coming back anytime soon," Lex says. "Just head back down the tunnel and you'll find the locker room."

"Are you sure? I don't want to leave you," I say.

"Trust me, Alice, I can take care of myself," Lex says. "Now go!"

Daniel and I sprint off. The fluorescent lights flicker overhead as we hurry through the tunnel, casting a sickly glow on our surroundings. We pass countless closed doors and a handful of dark rooms that look like they haven't been aired out in decades. Eventually, we spot a piece of paper taped to the wall with the words "EMPLOYEE CHANGING ROOM" printed in black Sharpie. We take a left and step inside.

There are rows and rows of faded blue lockers. A few have stickers or writing on them, and each one has a little silver plaque with a number and a letter. The key has 398 written on it, but the numbers here only go up to fifty.

"There's always trial and error," Daniel says as he kneels and starts with the first locker, labeled 1A.

I study the key. "Each locker has two sides," I point out. "Try 39B." In addition to his many other sins, like having a taste for blackmail, Anton had sloppy handwriting.

Daniel moves over to 39B and tries the lock. The door creaks open, revealing a hoodie that says "Amiri" on it, a small wireless camera, a sheaf of notebook pages, and—as we clear aside the papers—a laptop.

"Yes!" I pull out the laptop and power it on.

"Do you know his password?" Daniel says. We've sat down on the locker bench, and he's perusing the notebook pages while looking over my shoulder at the screen.

"No, but I can guess," I say. I type in a few different passwords, and on the third try, we're in.

"Wait, what was it?"

"It was 'admin.' I figured Anton wouldn't have bothered to change his password from the default."

"Wow. At least his laziness is working in our favor," Daniel says. He holds up the notebook pages. "I'm assuming these are Anton's notes. This page has a list of timestamps correlating to dates that go back to the first day of filming." Daniel shuffles through the papers. "And this page looks like he was brainstorming ways to blackmail people. Dawn Taylor's on here too. Something about a stalker?"

I ponder that. "This is proof that Anton was planning on blackmailing her, too. But I'm not sure what the timestamps and dates are for."

"They look like video timestamps. Check the files on the laptop."

Anton's desktop is a mess. Just looking at it stresses me out. There are countless docs and folders, along with quite a few SpongeBob memes, for some reason.

"Try that one," Daniels says, pointing at a folder labeled "nothing to see here."

Inside the folder are video clips, dozens of them. I click on one, and it starts playing. The video starts off with a partial view of one of the party rooms. The camera angle is not great: The view is from a low point, and a curtain covers the top third and side of the screen. Daniel holds up the notebook page, and we match the date with a timestamp. When I scrub through to the timestamp, Anton walks into view, followed by Peter Dixon.

"—that's your plan to get rid of Dawn? Seriously?" Anton is saying.

"Keep it down," Peter Dixon says quietly.

"Relax, man. No one comes over here. I scoped it out, remember?" Anton says, and then, of course, winks directly at the camera. Luckily for Anton, Peter Dixon doesn't notice. "So you want me to sabotage the fireworks? Like set them off in the wrong place, or what?"

"I don't care how you do it. Just scare Dawn," Peter Dixon says. "I want her shaking in her four-inch heels. By the time filming's done, renewing for season two will be the last thing on her mind."

The clip ends there.

"Blackmail videos." Daniel squints at the papers in his hands. "And blackmail notes."

I glance at the locker, where the wireless camera is sitting. "Anton must have stolen one of the on-set cameras and placed it strategically to get blackmail footage."

We click on another video. In this one, there's another camera shot of the floor, but the voices are unmistakable.

"No, not those. They have to be madeleines," Peter Dixon says, sounding irritated.

"And how am I supposed to get madeleines in the middle of a storm?" Anton demands.

"Bake them if you have to. She needs to think that her stalker is here, and he's found her again. If that doesn't convince her to quit, I don't know what will."

"Ohmygod." I turn to Daniel. "Peter Dixon wasn't trying to make up with Dawn. He was trying to scare her."

I click on yet another video. This one is partially obscured by a spider plant. Bryan walks into frame, talking to Freya.

"—Peter said to hide them," Bryan says. "Anton says she's on a walk right now, so just go into Brittany's room when she's not there and take her meds. It's not that hard."

"Are you sure this is legal?" Freya asks.

Bryan snorts. "Of course it's not legal, but Peter wants us to do it. Are you going to tell him no? Besides, we'll give them back. It's just for the week. She's not going to die. Look, if you don't want to do it, I'll send Anton."

I can't stop watching. I click on the most recent video, and a clip opens of an overhead view of Peter and Anton at the back of the villa.

"—a stubborn old bitch, I'll give her that," Peter is saying quietly. "But she's still got to go. I don't care what we have to do."

"What if we can't scare her off?" Anton asks.

"If she doesn't back down by the finale, then we'll have another fireworks accident on set. A fatal one." Peter Dixon chuckles. "And since you did such a good job with the fireworks last time, I'll leave it to you."

"What?" Anton looks around. "Jesus, you can't be serious. I'm not committing *murder*. I am not being paid enough to do that."

"The time for backing out was a long time ago."

"Hey. I've done enough of your dirty work that I could make things very difficult for you, if I had to," Anton says. "I don't want to, of course. I just want a little extra cash. Come on, you've got money to burn. I'm tired of living in a two-bedroom apartment with three room-mates. After everything I've done for you, I should be renting beach-front in Malibu."

"I've sunk everything I have into this show. And I didn't get where I am by letting idiots like you blackmail me," Peter Dixon snaps. Then his voice takes on a more menacing tone. "You'd better drop this line of thinking if you know what's good for you."

"Look, I'm just saying that this is escalating way beyond anything you've told me to do before. It's going to be nearly impossible," Anton says.

"All you have to do is make sure the fireworks are in place by the time Dawn Taylor announces the season winner, and Bryan will make sure it goes kaboom, got it?" Peter says. "If we pull this off, the ratings will be off the charts, and maybe there'll be something extra in it for you."

"Sure, fine," Anton says. He cuts a look at the camera, and this time, Peter Dixon follows his gaze. But Peter Dixon doesn't show any sign that he's noticed something's amiss. He's smiling the same affable smile I've seen him wear when dealing with Dawn Taylor.

He slaps Anton's shoulder. "Come on. Play your cards right, and we'll have an *explosive* finale."

I hit pause. Daniel and I exchange a look.

And then we run.

RAW FOOTAGE: "DAWN TAY'S INFERNO: LOVE IS HELL," SEASON 1, FINALE (UNEDITED)

[Footage: Dawn Taylor and contestants Chase and Alice are at the volcano's edge.]

DAWN TAYLOR: The first person to throw their partner into the volcano wins . . . and gets one million dollars!

CHASE DE LANCEY: Alice, I love you. I really screwed up with you, and I told myself that I'd make it up to you someday. It looks like that day has come. The money's all yours, babe.

[Footage: Alice dives into the volcano.]

CHASE DE LANCEY: Alice? Alice!

DAWN TAYLOR: What the hell was that? Why did she jump in?

CHASE: Uh . . . does this mean I win?

LEAH GLEESON [OFF-CAMERA]: Peter's saying that it doesn't count. It was a test. You're both supposed to jump in together, or not jump in at all.

CHASE DE LANCEY: Oh. Should I jump now?

LEAH GLEESON [OFF-CAMERA]: If you want to. Wait, actually, hang on—

[Footage: Ava pulls herself to the top of the volcano and hoists Noah up behind her.]

AVA DAWSON: Hey, is there going to be a consolation prize? That's standard for finalists, and I think it's only fair—

AVA DAWSON: Wait, where's Alice?

DAWN TAYLOR: Should I just—? The whole thing? Again?

LEAH GLEESON [OFF-CAMERA]: Yeah, I think so. Anyone got eyes on Lex? Lava's messing with our sound—

[Footage: Dawn Taylor turns around to greet Ava and Noah.]

DAWN TAYLOR: Congratulations, Ava and Noah. You made it to the summit first. Now I know the two of you have been through hell to get here. But I'm afraid your trials aren't over yet. The theme of this week is, as you know, treachery. And I have decided that there can only be one winner in my inferno. The first person to toss their partner into the volcano wins . . . and gets one million dollars!

AVA DAWSON: And if we don't, we get nothing?

DAWN TAYLOR: That's right, babes. Nothing. Zilch. Nada.

[Footage: Close-up of Ava and Noah whispering to each other.]

NOAH WATSON: Ava, we worked so hard for this. Just do it. Throw me in. Take the money.

AVA DAWSON: No, you dork. It's clearly a test. We're supposed to say we don't want the money, or whatever.

[Footage: Pan of the volcano as Ava takes Noah's hand.]

AVA DAWSON: Noah, we did this together. I don't want the money if it means I have to betray you. All the riches in the world aren't worth anything without you.

NOAH WATSON: I . . . I love you, Ava. You're my whole world. If it means having to betray you, then I don't want the money either.

AVA DAWSON: Is that it? Do we win?

DAWN TAYLOR: You won! Congrats.

DAWN TAYLOR: Bryan, where the fuck have you been, and why do you look like roadkill? Hurry up and set me up for the season finale!

Chapter Twenty-Eight
Hell Is an Explosive Finale

We sprint back through the tunnel until we get to the trapdoor Daniel found. But when we get to the base of the volcano, it's deserted.

Ava, Noah, and Chase are still at the top of volcano with Dawn and the camera crew. Loud victory music is blaring.

"Chase! *CHASE!*" I scream at the top of my lungs. But it's no good. There's no way they can hear us from up there, especially with the music playing.

"We have to get to the top," I tell Daniel. He's eyeing the volcano.

Will we even have enough time? Chase and I just finished scaling the volcano, and I don't know if I can do it again.

"There has to be some way to get up there without going through the challenge course," I say, studying the area. "The crew's up there, and there's no way they climbed up with their cameras."

"This way," Daniel says. He takes my hand like it's the most natural thing in the world, and we're running around the perimeter of the volcano. We find a portable staircase, like the kind that gets set up for airplanes, and then we're going up. It's better than climbing the course all over again, but not by much. My knees burn and my thighs ache as we make our ascent.

Daniel swings himself over to the top, then reaches back to help me up.

At the summit, it's chaos. Confetti cannons are going off one by one.

White smoke is billowing from a smoke machine somewhere. Ava and Noah are getting down to the music, while Chase cheers. And at one end of the platform, Dawn Taylor is descending from the sky, cables connecting her to a giant crane. She's covered head to toe in a shimmery white dress. Large silver wings unfurl from her shoulders, and in her hands is a giant golden trophy. She looks like a model in a Victoria's Secret fashion show, but with slightly more clothes on.

Daniel and I push through the crew, ducking under the cameras to burst out into the open.

"Dawn!" I scream. "You have to get down from there!"

But Dawn Taylor continues to smile beatifically as she holds up the trophy.

"Alice," Daniel says urgently, "Peter Dixon's here."

I follow Daniel's gaze, and yep, there's Peter Dixon making his way over to us. His usual genial smile is gone, and he looks *pissed*.

I look around frantically, scanning the scene. Peter Dixon said in the video that they would use fireworks to cover for the explosion, but that doesn't tell me much.

My gaze falls on the trophy that Dawn is holding. A spray of sparklers is just barely visible over the top.

"It's the trophy!" I shout to Daniel. "We have to get it away from her."

"I don't think so." Peter Dixon shoves a cameraperson aside, and in an instant, he's upon us. "You're not going anywhere."

Daniel steps in front me. "Go! I'll handle Peter."

"Drop the trophy!" I yell up at Dawn desperately. She looks down at me, her nose wrinkling in confusion, and shakes her head.

I want to scream in frustration, but there's no time. I'm already casting about for another solution. If Dawn Taylor won't drop the trophy, I have to get up there somehow. I look at the rock formation acting as a backdrop wall. It must've been part of the labyrinth set or something, because there are handholds on it. The top of the wall is just high enough for me to jump over to Dawn Taylor and grab the trophy. It's risky, incredibly so, but it's possible. And right now, it's my only choice.

I take a running leap at the wall. I manage to scrabble up several feet, but then someone roughly drags me down. My arms scrape against the rock face painfully as my feet hit the platform, and I scream when I'm jerked around to face Bryan.

"You know, I really don't know what Chase saw in you," he sneers, grabbing my arm and wrenching it behind my back.

"Fuck you, Bryan," I spit. I throw my weight forward, trying to get him off me, but he wrenches my arm again, sending pain shooting through me. He forces me forward and I catch sight of his shoes with their narrow, distinct pointy tip. They match the shoeprints near Anton's body.

"Ohmygod, *you* killed Anton," I blurt out. "Peter Dixon told you to do it, didn't he?"

Bryan just shoves me again, harder. "You know, I never thought I'd regret asking Chase to come on the show. He's dumb as a rock and easy to manipulate. He should've brought a trophy girlfriend, not someone who's such a pain the ass. But don't worry, I know exactly what to do with your type."

I'm breaking out in a cold sweat now. I don't want to find out what Bryan means by that.

"Hey, man, what is this?" Chase's voice cuts through my panic. He comes up to us, looking from me to Bryan, like he can't quite believe what he's seeing.

"She just went psycho," Bryan said. "Started screaming and going crazy. You really dodged a bullet with this one."

"Peter Dixon is trying to kill Dawn Taylor!" I tell Chase. "And Bryan's helping him!"

"You're not going to believe this bitch, are you?" Bryan laughs.

"Oh, shut up," Chase says and punches him. Bryan stumbles back, cursing, and I break free. Bryan tries to block me, but Chase gets in the way.

"Chase, keep him occupied," I yell as I start to climb again.

"You got it," Chase says, inexplicably rolling up the sleeves on his short-sleeved Hawaiian shirt.

At this point, my arms feel like they're about to fall apart from Bryan's manhandling and having to go rock climbing for the second time today. I never want to do this again. As I push myself upward, muscles screaming in protest, I vow to unsubscribe from all those Rock World Gym emails I've been keeping in my inbox because of some delusional idea that I'll magically become the kind of person who rock climbs.

Hilariously enough, it's the thought of things going back to normal that allows me to push forward. I can't wait to go back to my regular life. I can't wait to clear out my marketing emails, and play board games with Cindy and Tara, and craft the perfect lesson plan, and make dinner with my mom.

I make it to the top of the wall and gauge the distance between me and Dawn. It's daunting, to say the least.

"I can do this," I mutter to myself. I inhale for several seconds, then exhale. I can feel my world narrow to a point, to this one moment and what I have to do. Calm washes over me, with an undercurrent of adrenaline. I summon the feeling of complete concentration and focus that I used to take my team to victory time and time again back in high school.

I pivot, carefully hanging onto my handhold while angling myself at Dawn Taylor.

Finally, she notices me. Her eyes widen in surprise, and it's at that moment that I leap. I grab onto Dawn, wrapping my arms and legs around her. The weight of my body causes us to careen sideways.

"Hey! Get off me!" Dawn shrieks in rage. She attempts to bat at me, but her dress is limiting her movements. The trophy is crushed between us.

I make the mistake of looking down. The ground feels very, very far away, the trees minuscule dots of green. Below us on the platform, Chase has gotten into a shoving match with Bryan, while Daniel is wrestling Peter Dixon to the ground. The crew, along with Ava and

Noah, don't seem to know what to do with this turn of events.

I close my eyes against the height and compose a to-do list:

• Get the trophy.
• Get down somehow.
• Stop the explosive.

Easy.

Three steps.

I open my eyes again, snake my hand between me and Dawn, and yank the trophy out from between us. Step one, done. But how am I going to get down? I'm just high up enough that I'd break something if I jumped onto the platform, and I can't catch myself with a front roll, considering I'm holding this heavy trophy. And with the way we're swinging back and forth, if I drop at the wrong time—I don't even want to think about it.

"Alice!"

I look down, and there, right in the middle of the platform, is Daniel. His arms are open wide.

"When I tell you to jump, just jump!" Daniel shouts. "I'll catch you!"

"I don't know if I can!" I shout back.

In the middle of all the chaos, he actually has the gall to smile up at me. "Yes, you can. I *know* you, and you don't let anything get in your way. You're Alice fucking Chen!"

When he says it like that, I find myself believing him. I grip the trophy harder and take a deep breath, summoning that same focus and concentration from before. I imagine myself the way Daniel sees me. Smart, sharp, brave. Capable of doing anything. Capable of jumping down. Capable of trusting Daniel to catch me.

Because when it comes down to it, I do trust him.

"Jump!"

I let go.

I fall away from Dawn Taylor, and all I can see is her figure wreathed in light, her wings brilliant in the sun. Then Daniel's arms close around me, strong and solid, and he lowers me to the ground. I'm safe.

"I got it," I say weakly. I hold out the trophy, and Daniel takes it. Together, we peer inside. Below the sparklers, there's a mess of wires.

And then it starts beeping.

"Oh shit, oh fuck," Bryan moans from where he's sprawled out on the ground. Chase is sitting on him like he's a chair. "We're all gonna die!"

Nestled among the wires is a little timer with glowing red digits.

Ten.

Nine.

Eight.

I dart a look at Daniel. He's studying the wires, brow knit in concentration.

Seven.

Six.

I grab the trophy. I chuck it into the volcano.

Five.

Four.

The trophy sinks into the lava in a burst of red bubbles.

There's exactly three seconds before bomb goes off. Those three seconds seem to slow and expand. Daniel looks at me, and I can see the desperation in his eyes. I know what he's thinking because I'm thinking the same thing myself. If this doesn't work, these are the last three seconds of our lives.

And I know how I want to spend them.

I reach for Daniel, and suddenly his arms are around me, his lips on mine.

Three.

Two.

One.

Boom. Lava explodes upward in a huge geyser, then showers down on all of us. It's raining slimy red goop, but we're all alive, and that's the only thing that matters.

We don't stop kissing until Dawn Taylor yanks us apart.

"Babes, someone seriously owes me one *hell* of an explanation."

TRANSCRIPT OF INTERVIEW:
CHEN, ALICE AND CHO, DANIEL (CONT.)
Conducted by detectives from Pedazo de Paraiso, Islas Marias

ALICE: So after the trophy exploded, Daniel and I made sure everyone was okay. Chase, Ava, and Noah kept an eye on Bryan.

DETECTIVE: And Mr. Dixon?

ALICE: Daniel knocked him out, but it turned out that he'd been playing dead. He actually tried to escape.

DANIEL: But Dawn was on the platform with us by then, and when she noticed that Peter was trying to get away, she grabbed a tiki torch—

ALICE: Oh, yeah, this part is good.

DANIEL: —and yelled, "Your flame in hell is about to be extinguished!"

ALICE: And then she whacked him really hard. He stayed down after that. Then it was just a matter of having Leah and the PAs drag him and Bryan off and put them in the pantry, which we've been using as our makeshift brig.

DETECTIVE: . . . Okay.

ALICE: I know. I feel like I've lived a lifetime in these last two weeks.

DETECTIVE: Ms. Chen, during your retelling of the moments leading up to the finale, you mentioned several other accidents that had happened before Mr. Brophy's death. Can you tell us more about that?

ALICE: I can do you one better. I've prepared a couple visual aids to help me explain and account for everything. I gave them to your partner before we came in here?

DETECTIVE: Oh yes. They're right here. You really didn't have to make this for us.

ALICE: Actually, I made this before we knew we'd be talking to you.

DANIEL: She was really excited to get her hands on a paper and pen. It was like seeing a raccoon eat a hot dog.

[Detective glances at diagram, 10 seconds]

DETECTIVE: Why don't you sum up your findings for us?

ALICE: Yes. Great. I'd love to. Basically, Peter Dixon wanted to take over *Dawn Tay's Inferno* and replace Dawn Taylor in season two with Selena Rivera as host.

DANIEL: To be clear, Selena had no idea Peter Dixon had this role in mind for her.

ALICE: Yes, thank you. Selena had nothing to do with any of this. I think Peter Dixon saw a beautiful, accomplished woman and decided he could use her for his own designs. But clearly, he underestimated her and us. Anyway, Dawn felt threatened by all of this and tried to bully Selena into leaving the show by giving her food poisoning, exploiting her fear of the dark, and who knows what else.

DANIEL: At the same time, Peter Dixon was trying to force Dawn Taylor off the show by intimidating and manipulating her. He made her think her stalker was on the island and placed her dangerously close to a fireworks blast, among several other incidents, all orchestrated with the help of production assistants Anton and Freya, as well as Bryan, a producer.

ALICE: But Dawn Taylor wasn't having it. Then Anton decided to blackmail the wrong person—

DANIEL: That person being Peter Dixon.

ALICE: And Peter Dixon had Bryan kill him. Then, when it became clear that I was investigating Anton's murder, Peter Dixon tried to scare me off with a snake in my helmet.

DANIEL: Don't forget that he had Freya push you off the balcony.

ALICE: Oh yeah! I almost died!

DANIEL: Twice. The bungee cord, remember?

ALICE: Ohmygod. I think I was blocking that out. Note to self: Email admin and ask if my insurance will cover therapy for near-death experiences.

DANIEL: Did you just say your note to self out loud?

ALICE: It's been a very long week, Daniel.

ALICE: Anyway, after all that, Peter Dixon tried to murder Dawn Taylor by rigging the winner's trophy to explode. And here we are.

DETECTIVE: That was . . . thorough.

ALICE: Do you have any more questions for us?

DETECTIVE: No. It sounds like you've all been through quite an ordeal. We may want to reach out to you later, so please stay available via phone. I'd like to extend my thanks to you, Mr. Cho, and Mx. Wex for your cooperation and—

ALICE: Wait. I'm sorry, Lex's last name is *Wex*?

DETECTIVE: Yes. It is.

ALICE: Wow. Thank you for this key piece of information.

DETECTIVE: Please leave.

Chapter Twenty-Nine
Hell Is Saying Goodbye

Eleven minutes is how long it takes to explain everything to Dawn Taylor and the rest of the crew. Dawn, with the world-weariness of someone with a long and storied career in Hollywood, merely takes it in stride.

Eleven hours is how long it takes for the local authorities and paramedic teams to get clearance and make it to the island after Leah calls them. It turns out they'd been trying to come here ever since the eliminated contestants alerted them a couple days before. Once she'd left the villa, Selena had led the other contestants and some of the injured crew in staging a coup. They'd managed to get their phones back and get in contact with the mainland. Unfortunately, their calls had coincided with the last wave of the storm, so no one could get to us until now.

In short order, many things happen at once, and after eleven days of having the island all to ourselves, insulated from the outside world, suddenly the pristine white beach we'd landed on is crawling with people.

Daniel and I give our statements separately and then together. I immediately track down Lex after I find out their last name. They tell me that it's "a bit" that they have "fully committed to."

Afterward, a team of very apologetic and stressed-out representatives from FlixCast arrives. We're reminded of our NDAs and our contractual obligations, then given our phones and our updated travel itineraries to go home.

The real icing on the cake is getting to see Peter Dixon hauled out. He'd spent the last day or so locked in the villa's makeshift hold—the pantry—with a bunch of granola bars and H2Whoa for sustenance. I manage to catch a glimpse of him as the authorities lead him away to be officially taken into custody. His hair is frazzled, his linen shirt is rumpled, and he's glaring mutinously at everyone around him. Freya and Bryan are being escorted just behind him, Freya sobbing into her hands and Bryan cursing out everyone who gets within three feet of him.

"Fuck you, and fuck you, and especially fuck *you*," Bryan spits out when he sees me, Daniel, and Chase watching.

"Which one of us do you think gets the special 'fuck you'?" Daniel asks us.

"Probably Alice," Chase says. "She figured the whole thing out."

Peter Dixon looks back at Bryan. "Knock it off," Peter Dixon says. "There's no need to be rude."

"Oh, really? Most of all, fuck you!" Bryan says. "If it weren't for you and your big ideas, we wouldn't be in this mess."

"Shut your mouth," Peter Dixon snarls, finally losing his cool. His face is turning lobster red. "That was all you. I didn't do a damn thing."

"No, you didn't *do* anything. You just planned and funded it all," Bryan says.

"Shut up, Bryan," Freya hisses.

"No, no, please keep talking," says the detective dryly as Peter and Bryan continue to bicker over Freya's protests. He directs them to a boat waiting at the dock. "I'm *very* interested in what all of you have to say."

Finally, as the sun sets, the boat sails out of sight, and it's over.

....

Afterward, Daniel and I wordlessly head back to the villa, where we stumble into our suite, exhausted beyond belief.

At the very top of the volcano, when I didn't know if we'd make it out alive, it had been so easy to hold on to Daniel, the boy I'd wanted so badly to beat in high school becoming the man I'd come to care about so much.

Surviving this show feels like a gift, but one I'm not sure what to do with.

Could Daniel and I work?

I technically still live with Chase. We share an apartment and a bank account, among many other things. And of course, my mom needs me. I can't just get up and leave her to visit Daniel. Plus, Daniel doesn't live in our hometown anymore, and while the flight to see him might be short, realistically, I don't have the money, time, or vacation hours to visit him all that often.

Daniel and I would be looking at a long-distance relationship borne out of a short and intense eight-day partnership on a reality show. I don't know how any of this would fit into my regular, everyday life. My brain, usually so good at logistics, is spinning up all the ways it's impossible for us to be together.

And most importantly, I don't know what Daniel wants.

"Alice?" Daniel asks.

I realize he's said my name a couple times already. I focus in on the present moment. I may not have all the answers, but that's okay. Whatever happens next, this is our last night together in the villa. After tonight, everything will change.

So when Daniel holds out a hand to me, looking so lovely and hopeful, I don't hesitate to let him steer us into the shower. All my thoughts and doubts are pushed aside as we shed our clothes and step into the hot spray.

After a day like this, being together and alive is a balm. We lather each other up, not because it's sexy but because we need to check on each other, to know we're both in one piece, to know we survived.

And then—because it *is* sexy—I pull him close, our bodies sliding together. The scent of him wafts around us, keying me up as I tug his mouth down to mine. He mirrors me, the kiss deepening from warm and tender to intense and heated as his tongue nudges my mouth open. Electric desire surges down my body and up again like a live current. My hands start moving on their own, my fingers tangling in his hair, relishing how soft it is, as he groans into my mouth.

He pushes me up against the shower wall and kneels before me, his mouth tracing a dizzying path down my body and straight to my center. I arch into the mind-melting pleasure of his tongue. I don't know what sounds I'm making, but when Daniel hums his approval, I feel like I'm going to fall apart.

"Wait," I gasp right before I lose my mind. Daniel immediately lifts his head, his face concerned. I groan and stroke his cheek. "It's just, I want you so much."

He kisses my fingers. "Alice, I don't know how I'll get through the day without touching you."

In answer, I drag him up and kiss him deeply. I'm about to ask about condoms when he grabs one from behind the shampoo.

"Clever," I say, kissing his cheeks with a laugh.

"I heard organization was sexy," he says, grinning, and pushes the condom into my hand.

His hands wander while I tear it open, and I take immense satisfaction in how his fingers tighten on my hips as I slide the condom on and run my own fingers up and down the length of him.

His breathing goes ragged, and the noise and the sensation of stroking him is like throwing gas on an open flame. In the next heartbeat, I need him desperately. He must feel it too. He braces me at the same time as I wrap my legs around him, using the leverage to take his face in my hands and kiss him messily, ardently.

When he sinks into me, it feels like everything and not enough all at once. I beg him to move, and he obeys, every drag of my hips wrenching a moan from him. His hands trace a circuit on my bare skin, at first whisper-light, then more demanding with every thrust. My world narrows down to the solid grip of Daniel's hands on my thighs and the building fire between us until finally, *finally* I can feel myself unravel into bliss.

Later, we wash each other off again. Once we've toweled off, we fall into bed together. I rest my head on his chest.

I still can't find it in myself to ask the hard questions, but I also don't want to go to sleep.

"If you could do anything, what would it be?" I ask him softly. There's no need to whisper, but it feels right in this small, precious moment between us.

"I'm not sure. I'm not sure. It's been a while since I dreamed about the future like that." He looks thoughtful for a moment, then he grins, a dimple popping up in his cheek. His eyes light up, and I'm over-whelmed with the need to kiss him.

"There! What were you just thinking about?"

Daniel looks a little embarrassed. "Your face when you ate the tteok."

Even though we literally just had sex in the shower, I find myself blushing, too. "Weird. What about it?"

"It just made me so happy to share that with you. I wish I could share that with other people. It's not like I want to be a chef, though."

"Well, you have lots of time to figure it out."

"And you, Slayer?" he asks, turning my question back on me. "Anything you want to change about your life? Anything you dream of doing?"

"Well, I like my life. I like my friends. I'm happy that I live near my mom. And I love teaching."

"That's what I admire about you," Daniel says, his fingers tracing circles on my arm. "You knew what you wanted, and you went for it. You wanted to win Quiz Bowl, so you worked until you won. You wanted to be a math teacher, so you became a math teacher."

"But it's not everything I want." I sigh. "I wish I could help other kids struggling with their studies, not just my own students. I don't think it's fair that only students who can afford tutors get that extra help. And of course, I wish I had more time and energy to take care of my mom."

"And yourself," he prompts me.

"Yeah, yeah." I snuggle into Daniel, tangling my legs with his.

He presses a kiss to my head. "I mean it," he says warningly. "If you don't take care of yourself, then I will."

"You know, if you'd asked me just a month ago, I never would've believed that the great Daniel Midas Cho would be talking about taking care of me, rather than, oh, crushing me into dust."

"Hey, you were the one who was always trying to crush me, if I recall correctly. And can we drop the Midas name now that we're no longer mortal enemies?"

"You don't like it?" I ask.

"King Midas turns everything he touches to gold. He's doomed to live a lonely and unfulfilling life, even though it seems like he's surrounded by so much that should make him happy," Daniel says.

"When you put it like *that*," I say, "it does sound pretty dismal."

"Please, tell me what I ever did to you to make you wish that on me, so I can apologize," Daniel says. "I know it was because of the Quiz Bowl Regional Finals, but believe me when I say that I wish you hadn't been at a disadvantage that day. I hate that our last match together wasn't a fair one."

I roll on top of him. "Daniel. Midas. Cho. That's not why I call you Midas at all."

He peers up at me. "Oh?"

"I called you Midas that day because you were the golden boy." I search for the right words. "It's like . . . everything you did came so easily to you. Everything you touched turned to gold."

Daniel laughs, low and deep, as he reaches up to brush a stray strand of hair away from my face. "That does make me feel better. But you know, I didn't have everything I wanted. Because even then, what I wanted was you. And that hasn't changed."

"What do you mean?" I ask, but I already know the answer. I can see it his eyes, feel it in the way he touches me.

"I love you," Daniel says simply. I can feel the heat simmering under those words. I want to bask in it, the way you'd bask in sunlight. "But I don't want to mess this up. You're too important to me. I think we should take things slow."

I nod, feeling relieved and nervous all at once. I'm still mourning my old life with Chase, still processing the near-death experiences I had on the island, and I still have my mother to think about. She has to be my focus—not this blossoming romance, no matter how exciting and wonderful I know it'll be.

Take it slow. I can do that.

There's still more conversations we need to have. But as we lie beneath a sliver of moonlight, bathed in the sounds of the ocean, with my head on his chest and his arms around me, it feels like this moment exists separate from all of that—a weightless point in time, unattached to reality. It feels right not to say anything at all and to just soak up this last night together, before reality can force its way in.

....

The next day, the crew and the cast members who were at the finale take a boat from the island to the mainland, then from there, a shuttle to the airport.

At the airport, it finally hits me that this is it. This odd adventure I shared with everyone is coming to an end, and after this, we're all stepping back into our regular, everyday lives.

Before she goes, Ava actually stops me to shake my hand. I'm so shocked that I stare down at our linked hands for a moment before remembering how to be a normal human and returning the handshake.

"I wasn't expecting much out of you and Chase, or you and Daniel for that matter," Ava says.

"Okay?" I'm wondering if there's a way to get a refund on handshakes.

"But I'm very impressed with your initiative in stopping Peter Dixon and saving Dawn Taylor's life," she finishes.

"You certainly made us work for our win. Thanks for being such great competition," Noah says, clapping me and Daniel on the back. "You were real value-adds."

Before their flight, Lex comes over and lightly punches my shoulder. "Take care of yourself, kid."

"I'll miss you too," I say, wrapping Lex in a hug.

"Yeah, yeah, get off me," Lex says, brushing me off with a laugh. They ruffle my hair. "Stay in touch, okay?"

When she sees me, Leah tries to unruffle my hair. "Of all my contestants, you were—" She pauses, searching for the right word.

"Your favorite?"

"The most trouble," she concludes. "But you did stop our executive producer from literally blowing my boss up, so I guess that also makes you my favorite."

"I'll take it," I say.

Dawn Taylor has already left on a private jet, but one of the PAs does give Daniel and me a handwritten note card from her, which reads:

> *Thanks, Alice & Daniel.*
> *xoxo Dawn*

Chase finds me later as I'm waiting to board the plane back to the States. I hadn't gone out of my way to talk to him these last couple days. I knew we'd end up at the same gate.

We are going to the same place, after all.

Chase and I are together again, a mirror of the day we arrived less than two weeks ago—but our relationship has irreparably changed. When Chase approaches me, his hands are in his pockets, and he looks sheepish, like he wants to ask me a question but hasn't decided how he's going to do it. He starts with, "Can we talk?"

We should. But I don't want to.

But, as I thumb the engagement ring in my pocket, I know we have to be on the same page. Plus, we're going to be both flying and driving home together, so there's no point in making things awkward. I pat the seat next to me on the bench, and Chase sits down at an appropriate distance for formerly engaged exes.

It's a far cry from the first day of filming, when I was cozied up to Chase on a yacht, desperate to say the right thing on camera. Everything has changed so much since then, in ways I couldn't ever have predicted.

"I still can't believe that asshole did it," Chase begins.

"There's a unique and very specific body of evidence that indicates that he did, indeed, do it," I say, and Chase laughs.

"Yeah, I get it, Detective Pikachu," Chase says. He clears his throat. "So we're not getting back together, are we?"

"No," I say. "We're not."

"I really love you, Alice. I'm sorry about everything," Chase says earnestly.

"I love you too, Chase, but—" I stop because tears are welling up, and for once I don't do anything to hold them back.

There are no cameras around. No one cares what I look like—and the truth is that Chase has seen worse. He's seen me at my lowest—when I had to retake all my second-semester midterms because I'd burned out in my senior year of college, when I couldn't land a job and I didn't know where I was going to teach post-credential, when my mom had been diagnosed, and the nightmarish days following the news.

And while we'd loved each other through all of it, I'd always been looking for something more. Someone I felt I could truly count on. Someone who could challenge me and push me to be better. And someone who would always surprise and delight me.

I take a deep, steadying breath and face Chase. "We can't be together. I think this hasn't been working for a while, for either of us. Even if we still care about each other, that's not enough, you know?"

Chase nods. "Yeah. Okay."

"Maybe you and Selena should give it a go if that's still on the table." I take the engagement ring from my pocket and hand it over to him. "Here."

Chase shakes his head and pushes the ring back. "Keep it. It's yours. You can return it or do whatever you want. Buy your mom the best bedsheets there are at Macy's or replace her wok."

"Are you kidding? You know she loves that thing."

"True, she did tell me once that it's her second child," Chase says. "Alice, if there's anything I can do to help with your mom, just let me know, okay?"

"Thank you," I say, and I mean it. I reach over and hold his hand until it's time for us to depart.

....

It's much too late when I finally let myself into my apartment. Chase is crashing with a friend to give me space. It's strange, coming home alone.

I'm so tired, I practically faceplant into my bed, only stopping long enough to pull off my clothes and pull on an oversized tee. But instead of going to sleep, I take out my phone and tap out a text.

ALICE

hi

DANIEL

Hi

ALICE

oh no are you the type that uses caps and punc and stuff when they text

DANIEL

I might be one of those. Aren't you a teacher? I feel like you should approve.

ALICE

a math teacher

DANIEL

Why are you texting so late, Slayer?
Shouldn't you be asleep?

ALICE

i was thinking about you. when
you say we're taking things
slow, what does that mean?

DANIEL

Slow enough to not screw it up,
but not so slow that we (I) go crazy

If it'll make you feel better,
I'll draft you up a rubric

ALICE

that would be THE most romantic
thing anyone has ever done for me. ♥

DANIEL

😊 Go to sleep, Alice. I'll send you my
thoughts tomorrow.

ALICE

i'm counting on it

STORY NOTES FOR EDITORS:
"DAWN TAY'S INFERNO HELL-ALL:
JOURNEY BACK TO HELL"

[Image: All-black screen with words in italicized white,
"In memory of Anton Brophy."]

[Footage: In front of a studio audience, twenty tulip chairs circle a raised
platform that holds two armchairs and a tufted loveseat. The show host
for the evening, Tony Warren, dressed in a gold-trimmed suit, walks on-
stage to applause from the audience. He turns to face the camera.]

TONY WARREN: Welcome to the highly anticipated tell-all reunion special for hit reality TV show *Dawn Tay's Inferno*!

TONY WARREN: This show became the center of attention last year when it took a left turn from a sexy, up-and-coming reality TV show to a show plagued with scandal and a death on set.

TONY WARREN: Tonight, we're bringing everyone back together for a tell-all segment where no topic is off-limits. We'll be revisiting the iconic moments, hearing untold perspectives, and getting exclusive, behind-the-scenes insights from the cast themselves!

[Footage: The couples from Dawn Tay's Inferno walk
onstage and each take a chair. The final three couples are
not present. Their chairs remain empty.]

TONY WARREN: Get ready for an evening of heartfelt confessions, dramatic revelations, and maybe even a few twists!

Chapter Thirty
Purgatory Is a Reunion Episode

Three months later, I'm behind the set of the *Dawn Tay's Inferno Hell-All* special. Not because I want to be here, but because I'm contractually obligated to show up for any and all post-show promotional reunions. I listen to the introductions and initial commentary of all the other contestants who didn't make it into the final three, and nervously await my cue to walk onstage.

Cindy screamed when I told her that, despite several ongoing court and legal proceedings involving nearly everyone who'd been on *Dawn Tay's Inferno*, the network was going to be allowed to run the Dawn Taylor tell-all—I'm sorry, *hell-all*—and that none other than Tony Warren of *Cats with Hats* fame would be the host interviewing all of us on the events at the villa. Well, okay, Cindy's scream was mostly because I was going to be seeing Tara's favorite (in her words) "Canadian cat lover, reality TV host dad," and less about my anxiety over the legal ramifications of the show, but still.

I wanted to scream for entirely different reasons:

1. Chase is going to be there.
2. Daniel is going to be there.
3. The special is going to be filmed live.

I haven't seen either Chase or Daniel face-to-face since we parted ways so many weeks ago, but it's the third item that's particularly terrifying to me. If I cross my legs wrong and everyone sees up my skirt, or if I lean over too far and the camera has a view down my shirt, anyone watching will see it, and the moment will live on the internet forever, and oh god, what if one of my students sees it? And of course, there are no retakes if I flub my lines, and no handy coaching from the sidelines from Leah.

Backstage, I can feel anxiety lodge itself like a hard knot just underneath my rib cage. In my head, I start to make a list:

- Do not say anything your lawyers told you not to say outside in regard to Peter Dixon, Dawn Taylor, or the show
- Take a deep breath in between major ideas when you talk
- In fact, take a deep breath now
- Figure out what you were instructed to do with your hands when sitting because you forgot—

My internal list-making is put on pause when Selena walks in, and now I'm nervous for a different reason. I haven't seen her in person since she was knocked off the bridge during the Heresy Challenge. In fact, my last memory of her was the look of betrayal on her face when it was revealed that Chase was still in love with me.

But now she looks completely different. She's in a slinky, champagne-colored dress that falls around her like shimmering water. Her hair is in long tousled waves, and she looks poised and confident. And to my surprise, Chase follows her in, looking smart in a matching champagne blazer. They're holding hands, and when they catch me looking, Chase grins sheepishly.

"Hey, Alice," he says, waving.

"Alice, it's so great to see you," Selena says.

"Is it?" I ask. I wrinkle my nose at her to show that I'm teasing.

"Of course," she says, pulling me into one of those careful hugs where no one wants to mess up their clothes or makeup. I'm sure to anyone watching, it looks like two Barbies trying to embrace. "Are you glad to see me?"

"I am," I say, and I'm a little surprised at how much I mean it. "It was incredibly messed up what we all went through, but I'm glad we came out of it as friends."

Selena gives my hand a squeeze. "I'm glad, too."

STORY NOTES FOR EDITORS:
"DAWN TAY'S INFERNO HELL-ALL: JOURNEY BACK TO HELL" (CONT.)

DAWN TAYLOR: Honestly, babe, I wish I could say I was surprised by Peter's actions, but I should've seen it coming. Not everyone can handle the pressure of Hollywood. Some of us bloom, and some of us self-combust.

TONY WARREN: Now, Dawn, from what we've heard about what went down on the island, it sounds like some of the events that happened were intentional and at your direction. I think we all want to hear what you have to say about that.

DAWN TAYLOR: Of course. I'm so glad you brought that up, because I want to take this moment to deeply, truly apologize to every single contestant and especially Selena Rivera. There were things that Peter Dixon did on the set that I incorrectly assumed were coming from Selena, too. And because of that, I got carried away trying to hold on to my role as host. I lost sight of what was important. I let Peter get in my head.

TONY WARREN: What do you mean by "things he did on the set"?

DAWN TAYLOR: Peter knew that I had a stalker years ago, and that's part of why I quit acting for a while. He took advantage of that history—leaving madeleines outside my door. Slipping me threatening notes. I assumed Peter and Selena were in on it together, trying to bully me out of my own show. But later I realized that Selena was an innocent victim in all of this. That instead of letting Peter turn me against her, I should've been working *with* her in this male-dominated industry. So, inspired by what happened on the island, I'm starting *Dawn Taylor's Internship Inferno*, a YouTube miniseries where I select five young women in the industry to mentor and, of course, put through hell. The one who wins will get to be my personal assistant!

TONY WARREN: What a great way to turn a negative experience into something constructive.

DAWN TAYLOR: Yes. From now on, I'm here to lift up my fellow women. And on a personal note, tonight I'd like to officially invite Selena to be my cohost of the next season of *Dawn Tay's Inferno!*

[Audience applause and cheers.]

DAWN TAYLOR: Thank you! Thank you. Yes, it just feels like the right thing to do. After all, being a woman in this industry is its own kind of hell.

I don't feel any less nervous by the time Dawn gets through her segment and Chase and Selena are called onstage.

I'm wandering around backstage trying to distract myself when I spot Lex. They're rummaging around the craft services table.

"Lex!" I shout, running up to them.

"Keep it down!" Lex says. "You probably just ruined their take."

"Lex!" I stage-whisper with the same enthusiasm. "You're off-duty here, right? Giving an interview instead of recording one." They brought some of the crew in to give their side of the story. "Why are you stressing about the sound?"

Lex gives me a wry smile. "Old habits die hard."

"You must be slipping if you're late getting to the snacks," I tell them.

Lex shakes their head. "Tell me about it. And there isn't anything to drink here. What's up with that?"

"I got you!" I reach into my bag and pull out a bottle of H2Whoa.

"Thanks. I better go get my mic on now. Weird to be wearing one instead of listening in."

"Yeah, sorry about that. I guess since Daniel and I were talking about how the three of us solved this thing together, they decided to rope you into talking about it, too."

"It's cool. I just got a new haircut, so I might as well show it off," Lex says. They turn their head to show off their fresh new undercut, and I *ooh* and *ah* appreciatively. Then Lex gets called onstage.

I'm surveying the craft services spread when Leah walks by, notices me, and stops short. Her eye-catching red jumpsuit emphasizes the red in her curls, and for once, she's not messing with them upon seeing me.

"Alice, so nice to see you," Leah says, raising a hand when she gets close to me, and I instinctively look down at myself, wondering if my hair's out of place or if I've gotten something on my dress. Leah laughs at my reaction and says, "You look wonderful, I promise. I'm not going to adjust you. If there's anything I learned from *Inferno*, it's that you can take care of yourself."

"Sorry. Reflex." I lean into the hug that I now realize she was trying to give me from the start. "I wasn't sure if you would be here."

Leah makes a face. "I wish I weren't. But it's in the fine print of my contract to do this, which means I've got to actually go on camera and talk about what happened."

"You don't sound thrilled," I say.

Now Leah does tug at her curls. "I'm not used to being the one on screen." Leah takes a deep breath. "Wish me luck."

"Wait," I say. "Uh, where's your purse?"

"I left it backstage. Why?"

I pull a lip gloss out of my own bag and wave it at her. Leah bursts out laughing and then obediently purses her lips for me. I lightly touch up her gloss.

"There, perfect," I say. "You're going to do great."

"Thank you," Leah says, smiling at me.

"Any last-minute advice for me?"

Leah squeezes my hand. "I can't believe I'm saying this, but just be yourself." She starts to walk off, but then pauses and calls back to me, "And don't slouch!" She is almost out of sight when she can't resist turning back one last time to shout, "And don't fiddle with your hands!"

Then she hurries off to her interview.

"She's right, you know," says someone new.

That voice.

I recognize it instantly. I know without turning around that Daniel Cho will be standing behind me, looking unfairly devastating in a black tuxedo or whatever the hell wardrobe decided to put him into. And I know that he'll be giving me that trademark half smile of his that I know and love so well, and my heart keens.

We haven't seen each other in person since we left the island. That had been part of the agreement to take it slow: stay apart while we sort out our lives, be methodical and logical, and make sure whatever this is between us isn't some trick of the lighting on set.

For me, going slow meant making a spreadsheet of everything in my life I had to disentangle from Chase and everything I wanted to do for my mom, and a checklist of signs that I'd be emotionally ready to take the plunge into a new relationship.

I've just completed "get Chase off of my Netflix account," and a part of me is wondering if I'm ready to move forward.

But hearing Daniel's voice in person, and not on FaceTime or one of those extended phone calls where we'd talk late into the night and accidentally fall asleep on the line, I think that maybe it's time to let go and, yes, forget the spreadsheet.

When I do finally turn around, Daniel's just as I imagined. He smiles at me, fixing the cuff on his suit. His tie matches the color of my dress. He must've chosen it after I'd texted him a photo of the look I was going to wear to this.

Seeing him physically here, it's almost impossible not to reach out to him. I step forward to close the distance between us, and every one of my senses is attuned to him—the way he tilts his head toward mine, the timbre of his voice, the scent of the cologne he's wearing.

And my mind goes back to what he said before I turned around: "She's right, you know."

So of course the first thing out of my mouth is "If you're talking about what Leah said, I already know not to slouch."

He smiles, shaking his head. "I meant the other thing."

"About folding my hands?"

"Ha. No, I'm talking about you being yourself. That's why people are watching tonight."

"Is it? I thought people were mostly here to see Tony Warren live and in person," I say.

"No, *you're* what the people want," he says. "I watched the show. Did you?"

I nod. I cringed through so much of it, reliving some of my worst moments. But there were also some of my best, too.

"You stole the show. The crowd wants you. Or maybe I'm biased in this particular instance, because I'm very certain you're what *I* want," he adds softly, folding my hands in his, bringing them up to brush his lips against my knuckles.

My heart stutters in my chest, and I close my eyes.

"Daniel, what are you saying?" I ask.

"Remember what we talked about last time?" he asks, knowing damn well how excellent I am at remembering discrete pieces of information. "I'm ready when you are."

Damn him. He's going to make me tear up.

"You have the worst timing," I say. "We're about to go on live TV. And I'm only eighty percent done with my relationship readiness checklist."

He laughs. "Only eighty? You've been slacking, Slayer. I'm starting to worry you're not properly motivated." He raises a hand to my cheek, and I all but melt at his touch. "But knowing you, the last twenty percent is likely overkill."

"Overkill is the best kind of kill," I mutter. But he looks so damn good right now, I'm ready to throw out the whole checklist. I don't need a spreadsheet or a balanced equation to tell me that I want him. I can feel it in every part of me that this is right. This is what I need.

He laughs. "At least I know you'll never let me get complacent."

"How gracious of you to give me a lifetime to keep your ego in check," I reply, and now I laugh too, because at last, finally, we're here. "But seriously, Daniel? Right before we go onstage?"

"I had to say something now," he says, earnest. "I don't ever want you in front of a camera again without knowing how I really feel. Whatever they ask us up there, you need to know that when I talk about what I want for us, for both of us, it's not just for show. It's the truth."

"I do know," I say. "And there's something I've been meaning to say to you." This is it. Daniel watches me intently, and I know he's waiting to hear the words that I've been wanting to say since the last time I was in his arms.

"I love you." It's easier than I thought it'd be. This feels like a dam bursting, all of the feelings I've kept pent up finally being set free.

Daniel grabs my hand as someone on set signals us to watch for our cue, and I squeeze his hand back in return, feeling more sure than ever.

"Ready?" he asks as a crew member in all black signals to us.

"Not really. Let's get this over with."

Then we're beckoned forward.

"Please welcome Alice Chen and Daniel Cho!" says Tony Warren from the stage.

The music cue comes on, and I wave at the audience in what I'm sure is the perfect impression of a robot homecoming queen as Daniel and I enter stage left. The bright glare of spotlights follows me, and with the applause, it's hard to perceive anything except the pounding of my heart and the weight of Daniel's hand in mine as I step onto the platform.

In a way, it feels the same as jumping into the ocean on day one, except that instead of being left on the platform while Chase leaps headfirst without me, I have Daniel right here with me.

Tony Warren smiles encouragingly at me as I sink into my designated love seat. The audience continues to applaud, the noise overwhelming me. As Tony introduces us, I sneak a look at Daniel, who smiles softly at me, and suddenly I feel a lot calmer.

"Now, Alice," Tony says, earnestly staring at me from his chair, the paragon of active listening, "we all know you've been through so much. Can you paint a picture for us about your experience?"

I nod. "Well, Tony, for me, it all started when my ex-fiancé Chase learned about this new reality show from his friend Bryan."

Dawn Tay's Inferno: Where Are They Now?

If you're wondering what ended up happening to all of those couples on the pop culture phenomenon _Dawn Tay's Inferno_, we've got you covered!

Brittany and Jaxon have used their fifteen minutes of fame to put their bed-and-breakfast on the map. Fans of _Dawn Tay's Inferno_ have been flocking to this B&B, and they recently announced they've saved up enough to buy their own farm.

After a failed attempt at launching Alpha Up, a paid lifestyle coaching service, **Dominic and Zya** had a very public and very messy breakup. Zya is campaigning to get on _Dancing with the Stars_, though rumor has it that casting is already complete. Dominic is attempting to launch his own podcast, _The Dominic Republic_.

Naiah and Sage are using their platform to promote rainforest conservation projects—namely by camping out in the rainforest and posting about it on Instagram.

After their separation, **Firefly** is busy preparing for her next visit to Burning Man in the fall, while **Barry (aka Bacon)** is steadily moving up the corporate ladder of the tech start-up Cheerm. But all hope is not lost for this star-crossed couple! The two were seen getting smoothies together as recently as last week.

Kendall and Tarun are currently on a whirlwind tour of culinary hot spots throughout Asia. Only follow along if you're prepared to be very hungry.

Bella and Blake, not the most popular couple on the show, have since broken up. Blake has found his niche doing appearances at nightclubs, while it seems like Bella has joined a commune for former influencers.

Ava and Noah are using the prize money to retire early and travel together. Who knew these workaholics could unplug?

Mikayla and Trevor, formerly #Trekayla, have split up. Trevor can now be found under the account @TrevOnMyOwn. Mikayla has decided to take a break from social media and is currently on a meditation retreat sponsored by Lotus Meditation known as "Meditation Unplugged."

Selena and Chase can be found together on their next adventure, *Race to the Top*, coming next spring! And don't forget, in the fall you can catch Selena cohosting the second season of *Dawn Tay's Inferno* with Dawn Taylor.

Alice is still teaching. **Daniel** quit his lawyer job and is cooking up a culinary adventure shipping Korean snack boxes worldwide.

ALICE'S DAY PLANNER

Priority items

- ~~Pay Hospital Bills~~ — DONE DONE DONE
- ROMANTIC SURPRISE #1 and #2
- Finalize "Our Future" presentation

Can't wait for tonight! –D.C.

Friday

6:15 a.m. Leave for School

7:35 a.m. 7th Grade Math

8:35 a.m. 8th Grade Math

9:35 a.m. 7th Grade Math Honors

10:35 a.m. Remedial Math

11:35 p.m. Lunch break → CALL CINDY TO GET ONIONS FOR DINNER

12:10 p.m. Team Planning

1:10 p.m. FREE PERIOD → Finish up grading before weekend

2:10 p.m. 8th Grade Math Honors

3:05 p.m. Wrap up and pack for Mom's house

4:00 p.m. Block for INTENSE COOKING HERE

6:00 p.m. Dinnertime!

7:00 p.m. Romantic Surprise #1

8:00 p.m. Romantic Surprise #2

9:00 p.m. Netflix and Chill 😘

10:00 p.m. Literally chill, probably

Chapter Thirty-One

Paradise Is Coming Home

"Toss it to me!" I shout.

"It's too late," Daniel says woefully.

"It's never too late for salt!" I tell him as he lobs the canister of salt at me. I sprinkle it on the chicken, never mind that the first twenty dumplings went into the pot unseasoned.

From the couch, my mother shakes her head at us.

"Don't listen to us," I tell her.

Cindy gives me a thumbs-up and elbows Tara to turn up the volume on the K-drama that the three of them are watching while my mom tries to ignore the mess we're making in the kitchen.

"Perhaps we were overambitious," Daniel speculates, eyeing the battlefield around us. In addition to the dumplings, we're trying to sauté two different types of mushrooms and roast a chicken.

"It's a special occasion," I remind him.

He leans over to kiss the flour off my nose. "I know. But I wouldn't have minded spending our one-year anniversary pampering you and your loved ones at a five-star restaurant instead of seeing you stress over forgetting the salt."

"This isn't the time for what-ifs," I tell him, waving my spoon. "This is the time for making the rest of these dumplings so we can get them into the soup."

"Understood," Daniel says, getting back to quickly folding the dumpling skin around a little spoonful of the chicken filling.

"Besides, you're basically a five-star cook yourself now."

He snorts. "I'm more on the business side of that."

After Daniel left his job at the law firm, he cofounded a start-up with a famous South Korean chef to bring high-quality Korean snack foods to people all over the world. It's still in the early stages, but the nicest thing about it is that there's plenty of flexibility, so even though Daniel is working long hours, he always makes time for me.

Case in point, we come over twice a week to cook for my mom. Cindy and Tara have started coming around to eat and hang out with my mom, too. They're halfway through the latest hot K-drama on Netflix, and they seem to really enjoy each other's company.

Mom has even admitted that our attempts at cooking are getting better—though in this particular case, Daniel is perhaps correct that we got cocky. It's our one-year anniversary, and it feels like we've hit our stride both as a couple and in the kitchen, so I really wanted to go for it. But perhaps the third dish was overreaching.

Not that I would ever tell Daniel that. Even if I've gotten used to accepting that Daniel is often right, I try not to tell him too frequently. Wouldn't want it going to his head.

"Whatcha thinking about?" Cindy says, and I jump as I realize she's right next to me, grabbing a sparkling water from the fridge and cracking it open. "Share with the class."

"Daniel's indefatigable ego," I say honestly.

"No way! You wouldn't be smiling like that. You can say it. It's his abs, isn't it? Me and Tara were wondering if it was the oil the stylist used on him that gave him that six-pack or if it was a special camera filter."

"I'm right here," Daniel points out, not even looking up from his dumpling assembly station.

Cindy waves him off while I sputter, a hysterical giggle bubbling out of me. "Cindy! My mom's in the other room!"

"I hate to break it to you," Cindy says, reaching around me to snag a nub of carrot that I'd left on the cutting board, "but she ogled the same chiseled abs, just like Tara and everyone else in America."

"It was the oil," I murmur, and Daniel responds by throwing an entire green onion stalk at me.

"I knew it!" Cindy crows, putting her arm around me. "I'm proud of you, by the way," she adds, her voice going soft.

"For what? Giving you TMI about my boyfriend?" I ask, and even after so many months, the word "boyfriend" settles pleasantly in my chest like the first sip of hot cocoa on a cold day.

"No, for going on TV. It was a brave thing to do, to try something so far out of your comfort zone. I didn't realize how unhappy you were with Chase—with everything, really—until I saw you and Daniel together on the show."

"You know Daniel and I were just acting in most of the interviews."

"It wasn't just the interviews," Cindy insists. "It was the way he looked at you. You just seemed to get each other."

I glance up from the soup to Daniel, and his gaze meets mine, a soft smile crossing his lips.

"Thanks, Cindy," I say, and she rubs my arm. "But that still doesn't make up for the fact that you killed my plants while I was gone."

"If you recall, I was watering them right when I got your phone call."

"And you knocked them all over."

"My best friend jumped into a volcano! I was in a state of distress!" Cindy ruffles my hair. "I promise I'll get you some new plant babies."

"I'm holding you to that. Now get out of the kitchen. Some of us need to actually cook." I swat at Cindy with a kitchen towel, and she scampers back to the couch.

With a minimal amount of swearing and burned fingers, we manage to put the three-course meal on the table by the time my mom's show is wrapping up.

"Beautiful. Delicious. Amazing," Cindy raves.

"Mmfm mm," Tara agrees, already digging in. "Guys, this is incredible."

Daniel and I exchange a nervous glance as my mom takes her first bite.

"Well, Mrs. Chen? Does it pass muster?" Daniel asks.

My mother gives the dumpling a shrewd look, and I pray she got one that had salt.

"Not bad," she says finally.

Daniel and I high-five each other across the table.

"High praise from Mrs. Chen," Daniel says.

"I think I've reached my finest moment as a daughter. Lightning should just strike me now before I mess anything up," I murmur. I spoon more mushrooms onto my mother's plate.

Daniel and I might not have won any money, but after the show aired, H2Whoa reached out to me. Apparently because I was drinking their product in almost every shot, they wanted me to become their official brand representative. For ten thousand dollars each month, I post three silly videos of me drinking H2Whoa—drinking upside down on the floor, drinking next to a weird cat statue, drinking in the park while beet red from attempting to improve my cardio fitness. They don't care how I do it, which has made it fun. Ten thousand dollars a month is enough to pay off the medical bills and buy my mom all the best mushrooms that we can cook.

I also managed to convince the company to sponsor a weekend tutoring program to help students struggling with math. They call it H2+2=Whoa, which is so wrong that I can't even begin to explain it to their brand rep, but I still take the money they pay me to run the program and make them look good.

Thinking of H2Whoa, I take a little video of a can of it next to my prized mushroom dish. "Perfect pairing?" I caption it. When I post it, Selena is actually the first one to reply, with a bunch of heart-eye cat emojis and the comment "ur killing it, girl!"

Selena and I have stayed in touch. Selena actually started a group chat with me, Daniel, and Chase which is of course called Secret Alliance. Mostly it's just cute animal videos and recipe links, but it's been nice keeping in touch. We're not quite at the point where we're all going on double dates or anything, but I can tell that in the future we'll all be friends. Especially now that I don't have to be the one worrying about Chase's taxes.

As everyone is eating, Daniel clears his throat. "As you all know, this is the one-year anniversary of when Alice and I got together."

Tara and Cindy cheer together.

"And I wanted to take a moment to mark this occasion, now that we've successfully avoided burning down the kitchen." From under the table, Daniel produces a huge bouquet of flowers—the tropical kind that the production crew would have out for filming, filled with hibiscus and orchids set against palm fronds.

"Ooh!" Tara says. "Stunning."

"Did you get those from Costco?" Cindy asks, admiring the flowers.

Even my mom looks impressed.

"Yeah, tell her where you got them. I haven't gotten flowers in a minute," Tara teases. Cindy laughs, leaning over to kiss her.

I take the flowers and breathe deeply—and I'm transported back to the island and those early days of our time together.

"It's gorgeous," I say, as Cindy and Tara snap pictures. "But if you thought I was going to let you win this round so easily, you're dead wrong."

Everyone chuckles as I run to the freezer and pull out my secret weapon. "Smoothie popsicles for dessert!" I announce. "Based on the famous slash infamous smoothies the production crew made for us."

Daniel and I clink pops and take our first licks together. They taste just like the smoothies Leah would bring us. The sharp sweetness of pineapple contrasts with the mellow coconut. And yes, there's just a little rum.

Cindy airdrops me the pictures and I text a photo of the popsicles to Lex.

ALICE

thinking of old times on the island! ♟

LEX

Stop texting this number.

ALICE

come on i know you love me!!! 😶

LEX

LOL You two look good.

ALICE

and you?? what are you up to?

Lex shoots back a selfie. They're underwater in a shark cage, with a great white shark swimming by. After everything that happened on the set, Lex decided to do something safer than reality TV—a documentary about great white sharks.

After we finish eating, my mom gives each of us a hug before she turns in for the night.

"Leave the dishes. You two better be getting about your night," she says to Daniel.

My mom is nearing the end of her cancer treatments, and all signs point toward remission, but I don't want to take any chances with her health when it seems so fragile. And I have time now, and money—enough to take care of us both.

"Go to sleep, Mom," I say, shooing her to her room.

My mom tsks at me, but between Cindy, Tara, Daniel, and me, it's only ten minutes of work, and then we lock up my mom's place.

"You kids be good," Cindy sings as she and Tara hop in her car.

We wave as they drive off, and then I turn to Daniel.

"Race you home," Daniel challenges me.

"You're faster than I am," I protest.

"Why would I challenge you if I didn't know I could win?" He smirks. "I'll give you a prize if you beat me."

He *is* faster than I am, but I know the streets better. And I can't resist

KARA LOO AND JENNIFER YOUNG

trying. Without giving him any warning, I break into a sprint.

"Hey!" he shouts, racing to catch up.

My laughter floats behind me as I duck around corners and cut through an alley. I leap over the uneven steps where I skinned my knee as a kid. I hop over a half fence that guards a coffee shop's back patio.

He follows my path, but he doesn't know exactly where I'm going, so he can't get ahead of me.

"Some people would call that cheating!"

"It's not cheating if there are no established rules," I call over my shoulder.

We reach the apartment at the same time, but I get my hand on the door first.

"I won," I tell him triumphantly, but when I turn to gloat, he's on his knees. No, he's on one knee.

"I did promise you a prize," he says, holding out a little gray box with a diamond ring inside.

I make a little squeaking sound.

"Alice Chen, you are my greatest rival and most infuriating adversary. You're also the cleverest, funniest, and most determined person I've ever met. You're the one who pushes me to be the best version of myself, beyond what I thought I was capable of. There is no one that I admire more, trust more, or adore more in the world."

This is the second time that I've been proposed to, but the two experiences couldn't be more different. Chase's proposal felt rushed and half-hearted, like it was the step we both felt we should be taking in that moment, so we did it.

Daniel's proposal is the opposite. It's a surprise, although now it makes me suspicious about my mom's comments as we left. Did she know? Of course she knew. Daniel probably asked for her permission first.

I used to think that love was a problem to be solved, an equation that I could balance if I just worked at it hard enough.

But my love for Daniel isn't like that. It's unpredictable and fun. It's racing through your hometown, laughing as the streetlights flick on, one by one. It's listening to each other and caring for each other. Daniel challenges me and understands me. He's a true match for me in every way, and a problem I never want to be done solving.

Daniel takes my hand in his. "You, Alice, are the love of my life. We've been through hell together, and it only made us stronger. Alice Chen, will you marry me?"

"Yes," I manage to get out between the tears streaming down my face. I pull Daniel to his feet and into a long, deep kiss.

When we pull apart, I look down at the ring. It's a gorgeous solitaire diamond set on a platinum band. I've never been a jewelry girl, but suddenly I know I'll never take this off. There's just one thing.

"What's wrong? You don't like the style?" Daniel asks. "I know that look."

"The ring is perfect. The proposal was wonderful, but . . ." I say, giving him the sharpest glare I can manage, given the circumstances. "I can't believe you beat me to it. I've been working for months on a romantic PowerPoint proposal recapping all of your finest traits and our best moments, and researching the most comfortable and responsibly sourced men's rings!"

He visibly relaxes and kisses me again, this time taking my breath away. "I've always told you you're too thorough for your own good."

"Do you want to hear the very flattering things I'd planned to say or not?" I demand.

"I do," he says, leaning in eagerly.

"Daniel Cho," I begin, "you've been my nemesis from high school, and the person I least expected to ever have any sort of romantic feelings for—"

"I thought you said this was flattering!"

"All of that to say, it's a tribute to your disarming and charming nature that I not only found myself able to tolerate being in a fake relationship with you, but soon started having genuine feelings for you. I am so delighted to have found someone who I can count on to have my back, someone I can always trust, even when things get hard."

Daniel puts his hand to his heart like he might faint from the praise.

"I love you, Daniel Cho," I conclude. "And if anyone asks, I'm going to say that we proposed at the same time." I take a titanium ring out of my pocket and hand it to him. "I've been carrying this around all month."

"You know, even if you tell people that we proposed at the same time, I'll know the truth. I won this round."

"Fine," I concede. "But just wait for the wedding. I'll plan a surprise so thoughtful, it'll blow yours out of the water—"

Daniel stops me with another kiss. "I wouldn't have you any other way, Slayer."

"Good," I say in between kisses. "Because I don't know any other way to be."

When I dreamed of romance when I was younger, I used to imagine something a lot like Villa Paradiso: luxury, drama, a beach at sunset. But being with Daniel is so much more than that. Our relationship is about the push and pull, the spark of passion and the warmth of love, the heat of debate and the lightness of delighting in each other. When I'm with Daniel, it's my own slice of paradise.

I hold my hand out to Daniel, trusting him to meet me halfway. He slides the ring onto my finger, and it's a perfect fit. We link hands, and together, we step into the house.